THE
Queen's
Spy

CLARE MARCHANT

avon.

Published by AVON
A division of HarperCollins*Publishers*
1 London Bridge Street
London SE1 9GF

www.harpercollins.co.uk

HarperCollins*Publishers*
1st Floor, Watermarque Building, Ringsend Road
Dublin 4, Ireland

A Paperback Original 2021
1
First published in Great Britain by HarperCollins*Publishers* 2021

A catalogue copy of this book is available from the British Library.

ISBN: 978-0-00-845435-7

Typeset in Bembo by Palimpsest Book Production Limited, Falkirk, Stirlingshire
Printed and bound in UK by CPI Group (UK) Ltd, Croydon CR0 4YY

MIX
Paper from
responsible sources
FSC™ C007454

This book is produced from independently certified FSC™ paper
to ensure responsible forest management.

For more information visit: www.harpercollins.co.uk/green

Dominic, Tobias, Laura, Bethany, Imogen, Gregor
— you are my world

Chapter One

June 2021

The loud noise as she exhaled sharply, a violent 'psssw' of air and spittle, echoed around the almost empty, cavernous border control area. A cathedral for a modern age, welcoming all to its hallowed halls. *Or possibly not all*, Mathilde thought as she stood before the sour faced man in front of her. Incongruously, behind him a dusty sign announced: 'Welcome to England'. Most of her fellow travellers were now in their cars and continuing their journeys, whilst the final few foot passengers disembarked from the ferry, dusty backpacks on tired shoulders. Here she was though, waiting in this enormous, cold, echoing space while an officious old man in an ill-fitting uniform kept firing the same questions at her.

'Do you have dual nationality?' he repeated slowly, waving her passport at her, held open with his thumb, 'are you French, or Lebanese?'

'*Oui*, French,' she spoke slowly to give the impression she couldn't understand, hoping he'd give up with his questioning and let her continue her journey, 'I am French.'

'But here,' he showed her a page of her passport, 'it says born in Lebanon.' He enunciated each word slowly. She looked at him blankly, slowly unfurling her fingers from the clenched fist they were gripped in and stretching, before curling them back up again. Usually her vacant expression worked, but this old man was tenacious and she found herself being marched to a small interview room where they gave her a plastic cup of tepid water, while they waited for someone to find a French interpreter. They were twenty-seven miles from France, how hard could it be?

Opening her bag, she pulled out the letter which had brought her here. It was on thick, cream coloured vellum, the sort of correspondence which immediately convinced the recipient to open it. A frightening, bureaucratic piece of mail. The solicitor sending it had embarked on a long expla-nation about how he'd seen a photograph she'd taken in *Amelia* magazine whilst visiting Stockholm and had subse-quently tracked her down. Given how she'd spent her whole life moving about to avoid being noticed, he'd been lucky. If the publication had used her pseudonym rather than accidentally printing her real name, she'd still be living her anonymous life. But the letter insisted she made urgent contact regarding a property called Lutton Hall in England. Norfolk, to be exact. She'd changed her mind about coming to England three times before eventually booking her ferry. She might not understand what they wanted, but it seemed these solicitors were extremely keen to meet her.

And now here she was, as directed by the letter she was holding, en route to the village in Norfolk where she

2

was hoping to find some answers. Or at least she would be, if these time-wasting idiots let her go. It was the same old story, someone with too much time on their hands and a uniform on their back who took one look at her slightly less than salubrious converted ambulance and immediately became suspicious. Especially when they asked to see her passport, the numerous visas and her place of birth showing she was always on the move. What else did they expect from a photojournalist? She wasn't going to get many gritty, political or war zone photos sat in a one bed apartment in Paris, was she?

Her thoughts were interrupted by another man coming into the room.

'May I have the keys to your van please?' he asked. She looked out of the window to where she could see two police officers, both holding on to the leads of bouncing, energetic, springer spaniels, barking manically. She smirked slightly. They wouldn't find any drugs in there; she knew exactly what those dogs were trained to sniff out. Reaching into her pocket she held out the keys.

'I have plants in the front,' her eyes narrowed, 'herbs, not marijuana,' she added. 'Please make sure your dogs do not damage them.' His face remained blank as he took the keys and disappeared. She watched as the police carefully sniffed at the myriad of herbs and spices she was growing, but eventually together with the disappointed looking dogs they locked the van up again.

Finally, at the point where she'd begun to wonder if she'd ever get further than Dover, someone on the end of a phone was able to confirm that although originally from Beirut, Mathilde now held French citizenship and therefore had every right to be entering the UK. With a snarl she snatched up her bag together with the returned keys and stalked out of the room, her passport in her hand. She'd already had enough of this godforsaken country and she'd barely stepped onto the soil. The sooner she could accomplish what she'd been called upon to do, the sooner she could return to her roaming existence, far from rules, the authorities and a society she neither liked, nor understood. Somewhere she felt safer.

Chapter Two

All around him crowds of people, men, women and children pushed each other as they disembarked, standing on the quayside looking around in confusion, as if shocked they were finally back on dry land. The air was full of the smell of the sea, now so familiar to him he could taste it lodged in the back of his throat; sharp salt together with the harsh tang of the fish he was so sick of eating, mingling with the reek of sweaty unwashed bodies he barely noticed now. After two days on the boat his legs felt shaky, and although he was on dry land, he could feel himself still swaying slightly. A small boy beside him clutched a cage containing two small yellow birds flitting back and forth. He smiled and winked at the child who grinned back. Everyone seemed delighted to have arrived, even though thankfully it had been a smooth and easy crossing. Above him huge white cliffs soared away to a pale, cold unwelcoming sky. Tom questioned his belief that this journey would help him finally find everything he'd been searching for.

A large hand slapped him on his back, and turning he was pleased to see his shipmate William. They'd become friends on the crossing when both men realised they were carrying similar luggage containing plants and bulbs. Despite Tom having been both deaf and mute since birth, the two men managed to communicate with rudimentary hand signals combined with Tom's lip reading and writing some words on a wax tablet Tom had brought with him. A piece of smooth ivory overlaid with many layers of wax meant that he could scratch words in it then rub them over afterwards to use again. It was easier than forever searching for scraps of parchment. He'd needed to learn how to convey and share information from a young age, and his adoptive mother had taught him as they worked together in the stillroom where they created potions and medications from herbs and other plants. Now he understood most words and was never taken for a fool. William enjoyed the fact Tom couldn't engage him in idle mindless chatter, and they'd sat together on the deck for hours watching the wheeling, ever-present gulls in companionable silence. He indicated to Tom to pick up his baggage and follow, and together on unsteady legs they made their way off the quay.

They'd barely walked a few yards when Tom felt a pull on his arm and turning, he was face to face with one of the port guards. The man was speaking to him and Tom watched his lips in silence hoping to catch an occasional word he understood, to guess the gist of what was being said, but he was at a loss. His English was poor despite it being his mother tongue; he hadn't used it for many years and this, combined with the fact that the man was talking rapidly, resulted in him being very confused. The wafts of foul, sour breath together with the man's blackened teeth made him wince and take a step back. The hand on his arm gripped tighter so it was pinching his skin. Tom had no way of hearing him although he could tell from the man's red face and the way the drool was flying from his mouth that he wasn't happy with the lack of response. Tom was used to it. He attempted to start his normal hand signals to indicate his deaf and mute status, but it wasn't easy with one arm held fast.

Suddenly the man's head whipped around behind him as over his shoulder Tom could see a fight break out beside the ship they'd just disembarked from, and then the guard was gone, running towards the affray. Tom wasn't going to miss the opportunity to make himself scarce and hefting his sack of belongings higher onto his back he turned and hurried after William towards the road to London. His lack of hearing and speech made him more noticeable despite his desire to blend into the background and he was used to being apprehended everywhere he went. Suspicion and mistrust were the same in every language.

The sack containing his belongings was heavy and his precious triptych, a painting in three separate parts crudely hinged together to appear as one when it was opened out, dug into his shoulder with its sharp corners, but Tom didn't mind. He was pleased to be back in England, the place where he'd been born over forty years previously. His recollections of living here were hazy now, having been taken by his adoptive mother to France when he was still a young boy, just hours before they were hounded from their home by

His Majesty's men. After his father – the only father he could remember – had been murdered by the King. Killed for no reason other than having worked alongside a secretary by the name of Francis Dereham who'd been convicted of committing adultery with Queen Catherine, the King's fifth wife. Dereham had been executed and his innocent father had died whilst being tortured for information he didn't have. His adoptive mother had kept their memories alive though, in her drawings, her sign language and the saffron she grew. Nevertheless, he hoped to find a home here once more, somewhere he could feel safe and accepted. People didn't like you if you were different, and he was certainly that.

Chapter Three

June 2021

Mathilde stood for a moment in the gathering dusk, gazing up at the ancient hall in front of her. It resembled every old English building she'd ever seen in a book, and was much larger than she'd expected. Squat and broad, like a solid British bulldog dozing in the evening warmth. Washed with the soft pink of the setting sun behind her, the worn wooden beams crossing the façade in dark relief to the pale panels between, it reflected off the windows which mostly appeared to be made up of tiny panes of glass, shining and flashing at her.

She looked again at the address on the letter she'd been sent. Lutton Hall. This was definitely it; she'd seen a tired, faded board as she turned off the country road. The drive was so long, she'd thought at one point it was simply yet another ridiculously narrow lane. Overgrown hedges and dusty nettles brushed against her van, until finally it opened out into this wide drive with a large courtyard in front of the building, the gravel patchy and almost invisible beneath a thick covering of weeds. The whole exterior gave off an air of being unloved and uncared for. Shabby. Mathilde immediately felt an affiliation with the place and suspected that nobody was going to be offended with her being parked here. She swung the van around so it faced back towards the drive. Always make sure you were ready to leave at a moment's notice: the number one rule her mother had taught her.

Going over to the broad, dark wood front door studded with black bolts, crouching beneath a smooth stone lintel, she realised there was no knocker or bell. She banged hard on it with her fist, before stepping to one side to cup her hand against a window and try to peer in. The room beyond was dark and apart from a few angular white shapes looming up, she couldn't see anything.

'Yes, can I help you?' Turning towards the voice, Mathilde felt her heart give an uncomfortable jolt. In the doorway stood a woman who appeared to be a similar age to herself, and although shorter she had exactly the same dark, deep set eyes under thick straight brows. Mathilde's hair was much darker and lay in a heavy curtain down her back, whereas this woman had mousy hair cut in a bob. There was something familiar about her.

'I have a letter about this house,' Mathilde scrabbled in her bag for the envelope, which after having been removed and put back so many times was now looking decidedly creased and scruffy, a far cry from its original state. She handed it over, thankful it was in English so she didn't need to explain. She watched the blood drain from the woman's face as she read it.

'You'd better come in,' her voice was croaky as she cleared her throat, but she managed a shaky smile as she stood to one side, waving her arm to usher Mathilde into the house. She did as she was bid.

The entrance hall was huge and every bit as intimidating as she would have expected from the exterior. The walls, panelled in dark wood and dotted with oil paintings of people with dour expressions, soared up to a vaulted ceiling like a church, decorated with colourful bosses high above her. With a large stone fireplace and a substantial wooden staircase winding away to one side it looked like a stage set. It was also extremely cold following the warmth outside. She gave a small shudder as she turned slowly round. The space felt odd, edgy, and the hairs along the back of her arms stood up. It wasn't the first time a building had made her feel strange. Over the years she'd become used to her ability to gauge the emotions of a room, the memories of all that had gone before seeping back out, reaching to her. The silent pulse of a heart beating, soft breath on the back of her neck from someone who'd been there once but was long forgotten. She'd never felt it as strongly as with this building though. Something here had been expecting her. Watching and waiting.

'This way, we're in the kitchen,' the woman said over her shoulder, disappearing down a corridor that looked as gloomy as the rest of the hall, and Mathilde followed quickly. The uneasy feeling of being accompanied drifted beside her.

They stepped into a large, light, open kitchen dominated at one end by an ancient cream coloured range. It looked familiar, similar to one she remembered from her own child-hood which belched out smoke and heat in equal measure.

11

The woman was busy filling a kettle and talking as she did so, unfortunately far too quickly even for Mathilde's reasonable knowledge of English, so when she turned around with her eyebrows raised and awaiting a response, Mathilde just shrugged.

'Sorry, my English, can you talk a bit slower please?' She'd recognised the word 'sister' as the woman was talking and was now even more confused.

'No, no, it's my fault,' she apologised, pulling a chair out and indicating for Mathilde to sit, before taking cups out of the cupboard and holding them up. 'Tea?'

'Yes, thank you,' Mathilde nodded. Opposite her a little girl perched on the edge of a chair watching her intently. Who were these people, and why had she been summoned here? It was obvious the woman was shocked to see her but this was the address she'd been directed to. And there was no denying the look of astonishment after Mathilde's letter had been read. She wished someone would explain why she was here, in this ancient house, in a country she had no desire to be in. Finally, they sat down with mugs of dark brown tea and a plate of thick cheese sandwiches on the table. Pushing the plate towards Mathilde the woman asked, 'Hungry?'

It had been a long time since she'd last eaten, and with a brief nod of thanks Mathilde snatched up a sandwich and ate quickly, adding two spoons of sugar to her tea and gulping it down. The other two watched in silence.

Eventually she'd eaten everything in front of her and the time had come to find out what was going on and if this was some wild goose chase: *une fausse piste*. Holding up the letter, she flattened it out on the table.

12

'I do not understand why I am here,' she stated, waving her hand at the piece of paper. 'This letter says I must meet this man, this,' she paused as her eyes skimmed the letter, 'Mr Murray, and it has something to do with this house. So why have I been brought here?' She flapped the paper at the woman.

'I don't know why he was so secretive in his letter but it's about your father. And his death.'

'My father died almost thirty years ago, why does someone need to talk to me about him now?' Mathilde's voice began to rise in confusion.

'No. Wait. Why do you think he died years ago? He passed away in February. In all honesty, I didn't think they'd find you. Did you hear what I told you? I'm your sister. He was my father too.' Jumping to her feet she snatched a small framed photograph from the dresser behind her, pushing it across the table. The man was standing in a neat, well-tended garden, his foot resting on the edge of a spade as he grinned into the camera lens. Her own eyes stared out from the picture and despite her not wanting to admit it, she knew immediately this man was related to her.

'This cannot be true,' Mathilde blustered, 'my mother was told at the hospital that he was too badly injured in the bomb blast, that he had hours at most. He'd been coming to collect us and then he was gone.' She drained the rest of her tea and glared across the table, waiting for an explanation. The little girl had obviously become bored with their visitor, and sliding off her chair she disappeared through a door across the room. Within seconds the sound of a cartoon on a television could be heard. Smiling and rolling her eyes, the woman went and pushed the door to, reducing the level of noise. She sat back down on the chair closest to Mathilde, taking one of her hands. Mathilde could see that her own fingers were much longer and thinner than those clasping it.

'Your hands,' the woman smiled as she stroked them, 'just like his.' Mathilde pulled them away.

'So, tell me why I'm really here,' she said.

'Honestly, I'm telling you the truth, I'm your sister. Rachel.' For a moment Mathilde couldn't take it in. It was nothing to do with the language barrier.

'*Non*. I do not have a sister,' she replied, 'why are you saying this?'

'Your father was Peter Lutton – see, it says it here on your letter that his solicitor sent. Lutton Hall is the family home. Well, he was my father too. We're sisters. Half-sisters. I've always known about you; he'd often talk about my older sister. He met your mother in Beirut when he was a journalist and as you just said he was on his way to collect you both and bring you back to England when the cab he was travelling in was crushed by masonry. A nearby building had been hit by a bomb. He knew nothing else until he came out of a coma months later, in a hospital in London. With a brain injury and broken spine, it was a miracle he survived so I'm not surprised your mother was told he didn't stand a chance. His heart stopped more than once, his injuries were so severe. It was eighteen months before he could return to find you and by then you'd both disappeared. He never got over the shock and he *never* stopped looking for you. Whenever possible he'd be on a plane to Lebanon and later France, adverts in papers, everything. We spent many summer holidays there while he continued his search. To be honest I didn't think the solicitors would find you but they obviously did. You look so much like him. He ended up working in London on Fleet Street and then married my mum. We've always known about you though; you were certainly not a secret. How on earth did old Mr Murray at the solicitor's find you?'

Mathilde could feel her whole body shaking. She'd been on her own for years. Ever since her mother's death she'd been travelling in her van, taking photos and selling them when she could, often putting herself in dangerous situations for a good shot and becoming renowned in her field. And now it seemed her journalistic genes came from her father, a man she couldn't remember. The dead father that her mother couldn't bear to discuss.

'My name was in a magazine with a photograph I took.' Her voice came out in a stutter.

'In Beirut? Did you return after the war? Is that where you're living now?'

'*Non*. No. We escaped when the bombing became too bad. My mother told me it was just months after my father died, or thought he had. We moved to France as refugees and settled there when I was small. I don't remember Lebanon at all, and I've never been back. There's nothing there for me. My mother wouldn't tell me of our journey to France and how we ended up living as we did. The bombs, the death, it never left her. She was . . .' she looked around the room as if searching for the word she wanted, hidden behind the shadows in a corner, '. . . *traumatise*. Now you would say she had PTSD. She kept everything deep inside. She died when I was sixteen.' She felt her eyes well up as she remembered the scared, mentally scarred woman her mother had been, always trying to hide from the world. Scenes of her childhood, the whispering behind hands and pointing fingers at the *'femme folle'*, the 'mad woman' who wasn't mad but mutilated inside. It was hard to imagine a young woman happy and in love, as she must have once been. And now it was too late, and she'd never know the truth of what happened the day he didn't arrive to collect them.

'Look,' Rachel briskly rubbed the back of Mathilde's hands, 'I can see you're in shock. I hadn't realised you didn't know about us. I thought old Murray might have at least given some explanation, although his letter does say he'll enlighten you when you meet. I don't think he imagined you'd come straight to the house and not visit his office first. I've rather taken the wind out of his sails there, I always did have a big mouth,' she laughed. 'Perhaps I shouldn't say anything else, we can ring him tomorrow morning and make an appointment for you. And in the meantime, you must stay here tonight. The bedrooms are a bit musty and damp, but some are better than others.' Her voice slowed down and came to a stop.

'What else is there for me to know?' Mathilde asked, 'you just told me that you shouldn't say anything more. Are there other members of the family? more brothers or sisters?'

'No more siblings, just me. Dad had a sister, Alice, and she and our uncle Jack live close by in the old farmhouse. And there's my daughter, Fleur,' Rachel nodded her head towards the door through which they could still hear the television blaring, 'she's five. My husband Andrew and I live in Peterborough which is about ninety minutes in the car. I'm a primary school teacher and it's the summer holidays now so I've been staying here during the week since Dad died, trying to sort out his stuff and clean the place. Alice has been helping too; this is a big house and there's still a lot to go through. Although now that you're here, really, we should go home. I think Andrew will be happy about that, he's sick of microwave dinners.' She laughed again and Mathilde caught a slight hysterical rise at the end. She realised Rachel was talking continuously, barely drawing breath. It seemed clear nobody expected her to be found and she still hadn't been told why she'd been summoned to this ramshackle old hall.

'So, what else is it you're not supposed to tell me?' she demanded, her chin jutting out. 'You can tell me now. I will act . . .' She held her hand over her mouth and opened her eyes wide, '. . . like this, when I meet,' she consulted the letter again, 'Mr Murray.'

Rachel sighed. 'I don't suppose it really matters if I tell you or he does, you'll know soon enough. Our father left you this house – well, the whole estate – in his will.'

Mathilde opened her mouth and closed it again. Finally, she said, 'This is a mistake, no? It has to be. He didn't know me, why would he leave me his house? You're his real daughter, it should be yours.' She wanted to add that as far as she was concerned, he'd been dead for many years, even though she'd just been told it wasn't true. Her whole life shaped by the false information that he hadn't survived the blast. The reality was too much to grasp.

'Oh, don't worry, I wasn't forgotten in the will. Our father made some very shrewd investments during his lifetime and had a nice pot of cash and bonds which he left to me. He knew I wouldn't want to live here; my life and career are in Peterborough. And anyway, he insisted that as his eldest child this house would be yours: your birthright. It's been

17

in the family for a very long time. Look,' she changed the subject, 'let's go and find you a bedroom for tonight and wait until you've seen Mr Murray tomorrow, he'll explain everything.' Rachel called through to Fleur who after much cajoling eventually reappeared and followed her mother upstairs where she was presented with a pair of pyjamas and ushered into a bathroom. Mathilde caught sight of an enormous, dull, white enamel bath that looked at least fifty years old and was almost the size of a hot tub. Only not as inviting.

'The bedding isn't anything special but it's okay.' Rachel pulled worn flannelette bedlinen in pastel shades from a huge walk-in airing cupboard. The hot water tank gurgled ominously as Fleur ran taps in the bathroom. They walked down a long dark corridor that seemed to disappear into a black hole, the end somewhere in the distance. Along the walls which were lined with yet more dark panelling, faces in ornate frames glared down as if furious their slumbers had been interrupted. Mathilde would need to wait until daylight to investigate them further. Rachel opened a door that she hadn't even noticed and ushered her into a room.

The two windows opposite had the same tiny glass panels between a lead lattice frame as downstairs, and threw in just enough light to display a huge bedroom. Hastily Rachel switched on lamps sitting on bedside tables either side of an enormous dark wood four poster bed, casting a more inviting glow into the room.

'There are no main room lights upstairs,' she explained, 'so we've always had to make do with lamps. Apart from in the bathrooms, although there are only two of those and they're pretty ancient. This was Dad's room; I think he'd have been pleased for you to use it.' As she spoke, she quickly started making the bed, throwing old blankets and a shiny satin eiderdown covered with a paisley print onto the floor. Mathilde was wandering around the room in a daze, picking up ornaments and putting them down, looking at pictures on the wall. She felt like a tourist, as if there should be a thick red rope cordoning off the bed to stop stray children from climbing on it and a volunteer sitting beside the door eagerly waiting to answer any questions. She didn't think about offering to help, missing the scowl on Rachel's face as she scooted around the bed numerous times, tucking in the sheet and wrestling with the heavy covers.

'You saw the bathroom as we got to the top of the stairs,' Rachel wiped her hair from her now sweaty forehead, 'and I've dug you out some towels. Do you have toothpaste and shower gel? You can use ours if you want but I don't have a spare toothbrush.'

'No, no, I have these. In my van, I'll go and fetch them.' Mathilde hurried back outside before Rachel locked the house up. The night air was still, wavering between twilight and darkness, minutes that belonged nowhere in the day. The only movement were the bats swooping and diving overhead and moths gathered around the open door attracted by the light pouring out. There was no breeze, the trees surrounding the courtyard poised, waiting for her next move. As she walked around to the back of her van, she had the uncomfortable feeling someone was watching her but a quick glance up at the windows and around her proved otherwise; she was quite alone. Collecting her bags, she hurried back inside.

Despite her long drive and a feeling of exhaustion that had crept into her bones making her limbs feel heavy, Mathilde couldn't sleep. The thin curtains which appeared to be held together by a festoon of cobwebs which she'd noticed as she'd pulled them close, did nothing to prevent the bright moonlight from shining into the room. She lay with her eyes open, picking out the edges of the dark furniture. Her body may be tired but her mind was still running in overdrive as she tried to make sense of all that had happened over the past few days.

It had taken several weeks for the letter from Mr Murray to reach her, the moment she'd submitted the photos to *Amelia* magazine she'd been on the move again. There was a protest scheduled in Croatia with some corrupt politicians potentially attending and she'd heard a rumour of trouble. It was always worth going along to such events. The letter had reached her whilst she was there, but she'd stayed until after the demonstration which had, satisfactorily for her, resulted in a huge riot with numerous arrests. Exactly the sort of outcome she liked. After emailing the photographs to several agencies, she'd packed up the van and spent a week driving across the continent until finally arriving at this strange old house, only to discover that not only did she have a sibling she knew nothing about but also her lifelong belief that her father passed away when she was a baby, was untrue. And now it seemed she'd inherited this old place from him. Very generous considering he'd never found her. If he had, all her mother had gone through, her mental health shattered, could have been avoided. Her shoulders felt heavy, just as they had so many times in her childhood, weighed down by a stuffed backpack, containing everything she possessed. Both their lives spun into a shadowed web of how they might have played out if he'd found them; it hardly seemed possible.

Outside the ugly shriek of a vixen made her jump. She was used to the noises of the night; her van certainly didn't muffle any of those. But here they seemed to echo around the walls inside and felt menacing, intimidating. The whole house had sunk into darkness as if she'd fallen into the past. A splintering of time, a savage edge rubbing against her tortured thoughts. The feeling had been there from the moment she walked in and now in the hollow hours of the night it was deeper, more oppressive. She didn't like it. Was it her father, devastated that she'd finally turned up when it was too late to find each other? Either way, she decided she wasn't going to lie awake worrying about it any longer. Jumping out of bed and pushing her feet into her Converse, she crept back downstairs to the front door. She'd seen the shelf where Rachel had left the key and a minute later she was curled up on the mattress in the back of her van with her familiar duvet and old crochet blanket pulled up to her chin. Her head was spinning with all she'd just discovered but as her breath slowly slid out and her lungs emptied, she closed her eyes and finally gave in to sleep.

Chapter Four

January 1584

It took ten days to walk to London, stopping off to rest for two days in Canterbury where they were able to exchange some of the medications they were carrying for food and ale. Each time Tom delved into his pannier containing his precious herbs and medicines, his fingers would curl around a crumpled piece of parchment he'd been given in Calais, containing long black, stick-like pods. On the paper, the word 'vanilla' had been written.

Whilst waiting for a passage to England, he'd used some of his comfrey, known to most people as knitbone, to save a ship captain's leg from rotting away. It had been precarious, his stomach turned as he remembered the smell of the festering flesh, the worry etched in the wife's face. His apothecary skills were beneficial wherever he went, despite his lack of communication. He'd learnt at a young age, not even tall enough to see over the top of the workbench, by tasting, inhaling scents and sketching and labelling as he absorbed everything his mother had shown him. Her skills, learnt from the monks of long ago, were now his. A universal language. In exchange for his help in Calais, he'd been given the twist of paper containing the strange black sticks, together with a letter of introduction to the captain's brother, an apothecary living on Cheapside, one of the main thoroughfares through London. Tom was sure it would prove invaluable.

After days of walking in the fresh open air and drinking from streams when they couldn't find a farmhouse to sell them ale, London was a shock. The crowded streets bustling with every shade of life, the smell of effluence from the drains running beside the Thames and the buildings hanging overhead, which were crammed closely together. Towering up towards the sky with floor upon floor jettied out further than the one below, sometimes as many as five storeys high. If they were inclined, Tom thought, a person could lean out and touch the wall of the house opposite. Even the windows were built out onto the street like glass boxes trying to steal every piece of space possible. Lifting the sunlight away and reducing the streets to gloomy darkness, whilst tall brick chimneys soared up into the smoky air. Sometimes with his keen eyesight, Tom would spot people lurking in alleyways watching the world go past, waiting for a chance to enter it momentarily. He could see people here were furtive and he held on to his belongings even tighter. His triptych, his paints, his plants and his medicines were all he had. That, and now his precious letter of introduction.

Cheapside was easy to find, although Tom would have had trouble making himself understood with just his wax tablet to assist him whilst asking directions from the busy and seemingly irritable city traders. Such a simple thing to do, yet without his friend Tom may have wandered for hours until he chanced upon his destination. Here, there was more sunlight and fresh air, despite the street being full of people, horses, hawkers and traders. The smell of hot pies from a stall close to the tall stone conduit gushing water out for the city good-wives, made Tom's stomach gurgle with hunger.

Eventually, after much striding up and down, William paused outside a shop and opening the door, ushered Tom inside. Tom handed over the ship captain's note and waited while the other two men talked together. At one point the shopkeeper looked across at him, his eyes screwed up as if he was expecting some sort of monster. Tom was used to the sweeping looks, the silent scrutiny of others. Finally, the man nodded and after holding his hand up in a universal sign to wait where they were, he gave them both a beaker of ale and disappeared through a door at the rear of the shop. Grateful, Tom drank it down in one, his throat dry and rough from the dusty streets they'd walked down.

The shopkeeper reappeared several minutes later, ushering Tom into a back room. He had no idea what was happening but picking up his bag he waved goodbye to William and followed.

Instantly, he found himself somewhere he felt at home, a dusty and dim stillroom, the walls lined with shelves and stacked with rough pottery flagons and jars containing powders and ointments. The ceiling was hung with bunches of dried herbs, the air filled with the familiar scents of juniper, rosemary and burnt sorrel. Spotting a stool in the corner, he sank down on it, glad to be able to rest his weary legs. He and William had been walking since the early hours and he was exhausted.

After what felt like hours waiting in the stillroom, the warmth from the fire consuming him as his eyes closed and his head dropped to his chest, he was shaken awake again by the shopkeeper. Behind him stood a middle-aged man with a neatly clipped beard and kindly dark eyes. He was smiling encouragingly at Tom, whose heart started to slow down after his sudden awakening, and he stood up slowly, his legs stiff and sore.

The shopkeeper had produced a rough scrap of parchment and a quill and the new visitor began to write. A mug of ale appeared on the bench beside Tom and he downed it in one. Eventually, the paper was passed to Tom and he read it, pausing frequently on the English words. It had been decades since he'd needed to read his native language and he was rusty. Having reached the end, he went back and read it again. His eyes widening, Tom looked at the two men stood in front of him. Had he understood correctly? Misunderstandings were a permanent feature of his life: nuances missed because he couldn't hear the inflection in people's voices, relying on facial expressions to help him understand. This man was Hugh Morgan, the Queen's apothecary, and Tom now had a position as Hugh's assistant at Greenwich Palace, or wherever else Her Majesty might decree they were to attend her. He was to be a part, even a small part, of court life. His work in Calais had paid dividends.

Chapter Five

February 1584

Tom's room at the palace was, despite its lowly position behind the stillroom, the height of luxury compared to anywhere he'd slept for a very long time. A space to himself with a truckle bed, a small three-legged stool and a chest for his belongings. There was a small window, its glass thick and opaque, although with no fireplace it would doubtless be freezing in winter. However, the stillroom next door had a fire burning all day so he could always sneak in there to sleep. The thought of it made him smile, remembering how his adoptive mother would often draw him a story of how she'd found him the first time, in exactly that position, asleep in front of the stillroom fire. Nobody ever discovered how he'd got there but he'd stayed with the family until he was an adult. Perhaps that was why he was always searching for a place that finally felt like home.

His belongings were stowed in a plain oak chest at the end of his bed and his fingers were itching to open the triptych and start adding scenes of all that had happened to him since landing on English soil, but he had no time at present. At the bottom of the hessian sack he carried was the small twist of vanilla pods he'd been given, and walking back through to the stillroom where Hugh was mixing up a stomach remedy for one of the Queen's ladies, Tom held it out to show him.

Having realised on their boat trip to the palace how to talk to Tom so his lips could be read, Hugh turned his face full on, raising his eyebrows in question, *'what is this?'* he questioned.

Unwrapping the pods, Tom showed the piece of paper where the ship's captain had written the word 'vanilla'. He pointed to the plants he'd brought and separated two of them, holding them up. The captain had assured him these plants could produce the same black pods and he was keen to find out if it were true.

Hugh was waiting for another explanation. Tom ran the pod under his nose and inhaled the sweet scent, then held it out for Hugh to do the same. He raised one eyebrow before smiling slowly and nodding. Tom mimed pouring a hot drink and Hugh took him through to one of the smaller kitchens, the two girls working in there ignoring them. Wandering around looking for something, finally he found the cold larder where a jug of milk stood with a piece of linen over the top. Pouring some into a pan he placed it on the fire until it began to simmer. Then pouring it into a cup with some honey, he carried it back into the stillroom and taking one of the pods he sliced a piece off and crushed it slightly in the pestle and mortar before adding it to the cup and stirring briskly. He wasn't sure if he'd made the drink correctly, but the captain had made him something with a piece of the vanilla added and he hoped he'd got the flavours correct. With two of his senses missing, the others were flint sharp in compensation.

Blowing on the hot drink, he sipped it and grinned. It was just the same sweet, custardy flavour. He passed it to Hugh who also took a sip, followed by a larger mouthful. He was also smiling now, alternately blowing on the milk and trying to take larger sips, the milk leaving a thick white line on his moustache. Hugh picked up the piece of paper again and going to a ledger on a trestle at one end of the room, he carefully copied the letters down. Then he picked up the plants Tom had indicated and examined the leaves, smelling them and pulling a tiny piece off to chew it. He looked across and grimaced, and Tom nodded in agreement. He'd also done exactly the same thing when he'd first been given the plants but it neither smelled nor tasted the same as the seeds from the pods.

Collecting up all the plants, Hugh beckoned Tom to follow. He disappeared out of a door which, Tom discovered, led to a long corridor leading to various storerooms and at the far end, a door to the kitchen gardens.

In the corner was a physic garden, filled with the herbs and plants needed by the apothecaries for their medications, laid out in traditional flower design, each 'petal' dedicated to plants to cure a separate part of the body. To one side was a bed which seemed to be a mixture of many different shrubs, and it was here that Hugh crouched down. Kneeling beside him, Tom helped bed in his herbs together with the vanilla seedlings. He could see Hugh's lips moving and he wondered if he was saying a prayer to encourage them to give forth more of the strange black pods which gave such an amazing sweet flavour. The captain had been sailing for over a year before he'd arrived in Calais, he could have collected them from any port in the world.

Smiling, Tom leant over and ran his fingers through some long grasses at the back of the bed. It was something he recognised immediately, a plant his mother had grown his whole life. Saffron. So much hard work to acquire but such a precious spice. One that had increased his father's wealth significantly, to such a large extent he climbed the court from his position as a well-established merchant and minor courtier, to an extremely rich man and eventually in a position working for the Queen at that time. An ascendance that eventually cost him his life.

Chapter Six

March 1584

Life in the palace was very different from anything Tom had ever experienced before. It was just as hard work but now he didn't see any of his patients. Instead, Hugh would attend the Queen, her ladies and courtiers, then return to explain their ailments. The two men, with a combination of writing on the wax tablet, pointing at jars and Tom reading Hugh's lips – which became easier after Hugh trimmed his bushy moustache – would decide on a suitable remedy. They also provided medications for the palace staff, who would either appear at the open door to the stillroom looking morose or send a message requesting Hugh to go and investigate. Tom realised that despite his new luxurious surroundings, his silent world had just got a lot smaller and he escaped to nurture the plants outside as often as he could.

One evening, as he tidied up before retiring to bed, he saw a movement and realised a servant was standing in the doorway, talking to him. Hugh had already gone to bed with a headache and Tom was on his own. He watched the man's lips, trying to decipher the words he could understand. *Queen, sleep, tisane.* Picking up his tablet, he pointed to his ears and mouth and shook his head, a quick explanation of his disability. He then wrote what he thought the man was asking for. Did the Queen require a nightcap to help her sleep? The servant nodded gratefully.

Tom thought for a moment. Hugh hadn't yet let anyone else try the vanilla and he was unsure about giving it to the Queen, but what was the worst that could happen? If she didn't like it Tom may lose his job, but he was confident he could find another in the city. And he knew it wouldn't poison her or have an adverse effect because neither he nor Hugh had suffered after drinking it. The servant began to tap his foot, jigging his body up and down, no doubt keen to get the demand undertaken in all haste.

As quickly as he could, Tom prepared a warm milk and honey drink with an added spoonful of crushed vanilla, identical to the one he'd concocted days previously. The tiny black seeds floated to the top as he fished the piece of pod back out. He and Hugh had already discovered that the outer casing was not edible. Would the Queen drink something so unfamiliar? Certainly, the servant wasn't looking very happy as he stared at it. Tom took the beaker and sipped a little, then passed it to the other man to do the same. Maybe once he realised that neither of them had dropped down dead, he'd be content to take it.

The servant's reaction to the new flavour was every bit

as gratifying as Tom had hoped, and as he blew out the candle and went through to his bedroom, he hoped the Queen was equally delighted with it.

A violent shaking of his shoulder woke Tom up with a start. The early glow of morning light was crawling in through the window, and in the murky gloom he could see Hugh's face close to his own. It was too dark to see what he was saying and getting out of bed he followed his boss back to the stillroom, lit by candles. The flagstone floor was freezing beneath Tom's bare feet and in just his linen smock he began to shiver, hopping from foot to foot and edging closer to the fire which was sparking and spitting where kindling and two large logs had been thrown on.

Hugh held up the wax tablet with Tom's words on from the night before. What was he so het up about? Tom felt his skin crawl as he began to wonder if he'd accidentally killed their sovereign. Instinctively his hands rubbed around his neck as he mentally questioned if it was about to be encased in thick, coarse rope. He nodded slowly.

'What did you make?' Hugh asked. Tom pointed to the small kitchen and then to the pestle and mortar which still bore the residue of the vanilla he had crushed. 'Milk, honey?' Hugh mouthed, and Tom nodded.

Quickly snatching the tablet from Hugh's hand, Tom rubbed his words away and wrote 'Queen ill?' on it. He was wondering how long he had to make his escape but to his astonishment and relief, Hugh shook his head before doing a demonstration of the Queen drinking it and then pulled the sides of his mouth into a wide grin. Tom immediately

32

understood that it had been very popular and his racing heart slowly returned to its normal pace. It seemed his vanilla was a success and his place at the palace, at least for the time being, was secure.

Chapter Seven

June 2021

A constant banging reached Mathilde aggressively through her sleep and dragged her back into wakefulness. Bright, harsh sunshine streamed in through the front windscreen of the van which was already warming up inside. She kicked off the covers and rubbing her eyes, leaned over and opened the back door. Fleur stood outside, dressed in short, pink dungarees and a matching T-shirt. Her face was serious.

'Mummy says,' she whispered, 'it's time for breakfast.'

'Okay, *oui,* yes, thank you.' Mathilde nodded, yawning widely. She was used to waking up in her own time and she didn't appreciate an alarm call. Was this what families did? If so, it was going to take some getting used to.

'And,' Fleur continued in a small voice, 'Mummy said "*what's wrong with the bloody bed?*" Was there something wrong with the bed? I wanted to sleep in it but Mummy said no.'

Mathilde chuckled. She guessed this wasn't part of the message the little girl had been sent outside with.

'I'm used to sleeping in here,' she explained, 'see? I have a bed built-in so it's all comfortable.' Fleur's eyes grew round as she observed the small but neat interior, every inch fitted with wooden storage, before she skipped back inside with Mathilde following.

They found Rachel in the kitchen from where an enticing scent of breakfast cooking drifted, making Mathilde's mouth water. It was a long while since she'd had something hot to eat.

'Sandwich?' Rachel smiled and pointed to a plate on the table piled up with rolls, crispy bacon hanging out of the edges. She poured two cups of tea from the biggest pot Mathilde had ever seen. She hadn't believed the English actually made tea in a pot and really, she wanted coffee, thick and bitter. She'd have to bring her cafetiere indoors, however long she was staying.

'So, you decided to sleep in your van then?' Rachel raised her eyebrows as she passed the tea and Mathilde's eyes shifted to Fleur who was busy eating her breakfast, a line of ketchup rolling down her chin.

'I'm more used to being in there,' she explained, 'it's small,' she wrapped her arms around her as if trying to explain how it made her feel, 'I couldn't sleep in such a big bed.' And there was no point getting comfortable; as soon as she'd visited the solicitors and discussed her options, she'd be on her way again. The house could be sold and the money would certainly be useful. Even sitting in the bright kitchen, she could feel the dark atmosphere pressing down once again, trying to get under her skin. The doormat beside the back door said 'Welcome', but there was nothing welcoming here. The air reverberated with the whisper of previous lives, grazing against her.

The moment her watch said nine o'clock, Rachel was on the phone. Offering her mobile as she waited to be put through to Mr Murray, Mathilde shook her head. She could understand English if it was straightforward and she could see someone's face as they talked, picking up the emotions they displayed, but there was no chance of comprehending legal talk over a telephone. Rachel must have got through to him, because she could hear exclamations and a lot of 'I know, amazing!' being bounced back and forth. Finally, Rachel ended the call and announced, 'Three o'clock this afternoon at his practice in Fakenham. I can take you, if you like? I need to go to the supermarket anyway so I could drop you off and go shopping.'

'Thank you, that would be kind,' Mathilde replied. After helping Rachel to clear away the breakfast dishes, she disappeared upstairs to the bathroom to get washed and dressed. However much she loved living in the van, having hot running water was a welcome novelty.

When she arrived downstairs, Rachel was also dressed and drinking yet another cup of tea.

'Shall we do a tour of the grounds?' she asked, 'there's quite a lot of it so we can't do it all today but we could make a start?'

Mathilde shrugged. She hadn't told Rachel of her plans to disappear the moment she'd signed any relevant paperwork that afternoon but she had nothing else to do so a walk around outside would be pleasant. She may even find some varieties of herbs to add to her collection. Remembering them, she quickly found a jug in one of the kitchen cupboards and filled it with water before going out to her van and laying her plants in their ceramic pots on the ground.

'These are pretty,' Rachel exclaimed having followed her, 'what are you growing?' She bent close to examine them and Mathilde was certain that what she actually wanted to say was 'which one of these is marijuana?' She was way behind the border police.

'They're herbs — *basilic*, thyme, *safran*, feverfew. And these plants, they're vanilla. They need a greenhouse but the front of the van is very warm in summer and I stand them along the *tableau de bord* when I'm parked up.' She waved her hand across the dashboard which was littered with empty crisp packets and crumbs, 'I use a lot of herbs for medications; it's useful when you're always on the road. It's what my mother used to do and she taught me which plants to use for different illnesses.'

Fleur had already skipped away down a path that led through a gap in the tall hedge bordering two sides of the courtyard, and snatching up her camera Mathilde followed. Opposite the house the view was open: old metal railings guarded against the flat exposed fields that stretched towards a patch of rushes in the distance, the silver underside of the leaves catching the sunlight as they rippled in the breeze, the brown cigar tops swaying. The wide, pale blue sky was occasionally streaked with soft brushstrokes of white clouds, symmetrical and straight as they dissipated in the morning heat. She was used to the uniform, never-ending fields of France, tall metallic pylons marching imperially across the vista, but Mathilde could see this was very different. Here the landscape was dotted with trees and small woods, thick ancient hedgerows crouching between pastures, watching the changes over the years as their roots dug ever deeper into the ground. This landscape was more subtle, carved out over hundreds of years. Rooted, like the hedges, in eternity.

They arrived in an overgrown garden which Mathilde suspected at some point must have been cared for, and much loved. A lawn stretched away, the grasses tall and dotted with poppies, ragwort and willowherb. Between them she could see raised beds and rose bushes, now straggly and unkempt. Crouching down so the feathery tops of the foliage were at eye level, she took a couple of photographs before following the others as they disappeared behind a rhododendron. Letting her hand trail through the grass tops, she curled her fingers into a fist, pulling at the seeds and allowing them to flow through her fingertips onto the ground to be crushed beneath her feet.

The path spread out a little as it wound behind some ramshackle brick stables and then on to another patch of garden. This was even more overgrown, brambles and thistles jostling for place amongst fruit trees and plants Mathilde didn't recognise.

'That other part used to be the formal lawns,' Rachel explained, 'when my grandparents lived here. Dad wasn't interested in anything other than his vegetables though and eventually he got too poorly to do much. Just here was the orchard and vegetable garden. A mess now, as you can see. Nothing a strong man with a petrol strimmer couldn't sort out.' She grinned at Mathilde, who nodded, thinking, *whoever bought the place could have fun doing that, then*.

'But this is exciting, come and look,' Rachel turned and led her through a small coppice of beech and silver birch trees until they reached a clearing. In the centre was a tiny stone chapel. Still intact, ivy grew up one wall, winding its way into the eaves and poking out from between the roof tiles.

'Wow,' Mathilde breathed, slowly and instinctively bringing her camera up to her face and firing off a volley of shots. Creeping to one side she continued to take photographs. '*Incroyable*,' she whispered. Behind her a crashing of wings shattered the silence as a flock of pigeons unused to human interruption flew up out of the trees, calling to each other as they disappeared. The spell was broken.

Standing in front of the doors, pale, gnarled and roughened by centuries of weather, Mathilde ran her hand down the wood, the grain sharp and uneven beneath her fingertips. All around her the air trembled, waiting for her to do something. An expectation, as if the world had gasped, holding its breath. She shuddered. It was the same feeling she had in the house but far stronger: anticipation and longing. Turning the heavy metal looped handle, she pushed, but the door didn't move.

'It's locked,' Rachel stated the obvious, 'but I think I might know where the key is if you want to look inside? There's a load of random keys in the cabinet in the hall; I'll show you when we go back. I need to give you a tour of the house anyway.'

'Yes, I'd like to,' Mathilde confirmed. She was surprised her sister hadn't wanted to look herself.

Slowly they made their way along a path that looped back towards the house. Rachel pointed out a low, red brick thatched roofed farmhouse across the fields.

'That's part of the estate as well. It's where our aunt and uncle, Alice and Jack, live. Dad allowed them to live there rent free but it'll be up to you if you let them stay. It's all part of what you've inherited. If the solicitor couldn't find you after twelve months then she'd have got the lot.'

As they'd circumnavigated the garden Mathilde felt a pull towards one corner, a tug on her consciousness. She didn't mention it to Rachel, she was fully aware of how others saw her: strange and a little otherworldly. Mysterious, unexplained feelings were always best kept to herself. She strode through the foliage alone and as she approached the area she felt the feeling becoming stronger; an electric singing in the air and vibrations that threaded through the hairs along her arms as it drew her closer.

The space looked no different to the rest of the garden, grasses competing for space with tall Jerusalem artichoke plants running amok and overgrown soft fruit bushes still managing to produce tiny sprays of green, underripe currants at the tips of their branches. And yet this was where she wanted to be, unmistakably it was pulling her in.

Once back inside the house, Mathilde soon became disoriented as Rachel continued her tour. The sitting room just off the kitchen had old battered sofas sagging in the middle, together with a modern television which Fleur immediately switched on. A small pink pig with a squeaky voice seemed to be bossing various other animals around and the little girl was transfixed.

Mathilde could understand why they were using the small living room as she surveyed the huge formal reception rooms. Tall ceilings with decorative, elaborate plasterwork soared above their heads. A large oriel window threw light into the drawing room which was part of the original medieval hall, and the dust covers thrown over furniture gave the effect of ghostly galleons sailing through.

Upstairs on the floor they were sleeping on were a further four bedrooms.

'And up here are the old servants' rooms,' Rachel opened a door in the corridor and pointed up a flight of dark stairs, 'and the attics too. But also, lots of spiders, so I've avoided going up there. If you want to see them, you're on your own.' Having sneezed several times because of all the dust, Mathilde declined the offer to go and investigate; the estate agent could do that at a later date.

'There are still lots of our father's belongings to go through, so I'd appreciate your help,' Rachel explained as they made their way back downstairs, 'and maybe it'll help you feel closer to him, to know him a little bit.' Mathilde wasn't sure she'd be around long enough for that but she kept her mouth shut. It was always safer to not divulge what was in her head.

After showing her the drawer containing a selection of old keys, Rachel went to make some lunch before they left for Fakenham. She asked pointedly if there was anything that needed ironing before the appointment with Mr Murray but Mathilde just shrugged and said 'no'. She was happy in her jeans and plaid shirt so he'd have to be as well.

Rummaging through the keys of every size and description, she'd put money on most of them now not fitting any lock in the house. Some were huge and old, decorated with patches of rust and she decided one of those was most likely to be the one she needed. She'd just have time to try them out before lunch. Collecting them up she slipped quietly out of the front door. She needed to do this on her own.

Now knowing where she was going, it only took five

minutes to hurry along to the chapel. Two pigeons had reappeared, wandering around pecking at things and watching her in silence. She began trying the keys in the enormous metal keyhole until with the fourth there was a dry, grating sound of metal on metal and with a small wiggle it slowly rotated. Mathilde held her breath as she turned the handle on the door, giving it a hefty shove with her shoulder. It opened about twelve inches before the warped wood caught on the floor but it was enough and twisting sideways she crept inside.

The interior was murky, the stained-glass windows mottled and dull, one of which was obscured by the ivy growing up the outside. She could see where it had made its way between broken panes of glass crawling down the wall inside as well, trying to take over. Beneath her feet the stone slabs were rough with dust and grit and she noticed the tiny skeleton of a bird on one of the wooden pews. The altar was nothing more than a plain oak table and around the walls were a couple of memorial slabs. It smelled musty, of ancient hymn books, the air still and heavy with dead prayers. Had her father sat in here and thought of her and her mother? Knowing that he'd been alive and living in this corner of England all these years made the hollow space in her chest that ached for a family echo with emptiness. It had been here all along, if only she'd known. So many years wasted that she couldn't get back.

The strange feeling she'd had when stood outside earlier had followed her in, as if there was someone stood in silence next to her. Who was it? she held her breath and closed her eyes but nothing happened. *'Qu'est-ce?'* She whispered, her voice dissipating into the stagnant space.

Back outside, she locked the door again; she would come back when she had more time. There was something here, someone trying to talk to her and her interest was piqued. Behind her the trees rustled, the leaves grazing against each other as she hurried back to the house.

Chapter Eight

June 2021

'I'll pick you up here in about an hour then,' Rachel shouted through the open car window, adding: 'don't wander off please!' Behind her, Fleur's solemn face watched from the back window as they drove away and Mathilde turned around to face the smart double fronted Victorian villa. It looked to her as if it was simply someone's house, but the discreet brass plaque beside the dark blue front door confirmed it to be Murray and Browne, Solicitors.

The receptionist made a big play of not being able to understand what she was saying as Mathilde explained who she was and that she had an appointment. She may not be dressed very smartly but she'd put on her cleaner canvas shoes, a pair which weren't frayed around the edges, and plaited her long dark hair into a thick rope which hung down her back. She knew her accent wasn't so strong that she couldn't be understood but the woman's abrasive attitude was nothing new; it slid off her shoulders like water. People took one look at her and made their own minds up; it had always been that way. Probably just as well she hadn't pulled up to the car park in her van or she may not have been let in through the door. She kept her steady gaze on the woman and repeated who she'd come to see.

Thankfully Mr Murray, who was old enough to be her grandfather, was far more accommodating and despatched the receptionist to bring coffee and biscuits. Mathilde warmed to him immediately. She rarely met another human she felt instantly comfortable with, someone who wasn't judging and finding her wanting; he was as polite and welcoming to her as she was sure he would be to any of his clients. When the refreshments arrived, Mathilde pointedly took a handful of biscuits, her eyes never leaving the receptionist's face.

'Merci,' she sang in a sing-song voice before taking a bite.

Mr Murray explained he'd known her father for many years. He also knew how much time and effort her father had expended looking for her and she felt again the stab of raw pain that she'd missed out on that relationship, so many years lost. She explained in halting English how her mother thought he'd perished in the bomb blast, so it was a huge shock to find out he hadn't died then and had in fact spent years searching for them.

'Your father was adamant we carried on looking in order that you may inherit Lutton Hall,' he assured her, 'with you being the eldest child. It's been in your family for centuries, but I'm afraid there's no money for work to be done, all his liquid assets went to Rachel. There is however some rent from pasture let to local farmers; there's over a hundred acres of estate. Your Aunt Alice and Uncle Jack live at Home Farm and although they don't pay for the privilege there's no reason why you shouldn't start charging them. Your father was very soft with his sister, the whole family spoiled her really. And there are bound to be ways of diversifying to keep the place going. Now, I just need you to sign some documents and then it's all yours. I'll have the land registry send their paperwork straight to the hall.' He began to shuffle through the file laid in front of him. Mathilde knew this was the perfect moment for her to explain she was going to sell up and ask him to take care of it but she couldn't open her mouth and say the words. She decided to wait a couple of days and email him, rather than say it out loud, and taking the pen proffered, she signed on the various lines he'd pencilled with a cross.

With a copy of the paperwork he'd given her in an A4 envelope, she was waiting on the side of the road when Rachel appeared thirty minutes later.

'All done? You weren't very long,' Rachel said, waiting while Mathilde clicked her seatbelt into place, 'what did he say?'

'Not a lot,' Mathilde replied, 'he told me the hall has been in the family for hundreds of years and our *papa* wanted me to have it. One day I have no family and now I have a hundred . . .' she paused as she tried to think of a word, '*fantômes* who are a part of me.'

'Do you mean ghosts?' Rachel suggested. 'Well yes, it's true that the hall has been our ancestral home for a long time, although there aren't any ghosts; I wouldn't have hung around if there were.'

Mathilde slid her eyes sideways and watched her sister as she drove. She might not have encountered any but there was definitely something, or someone, hiding in the dark corners behind the shadows waiting there for her to appear, and she had a strong suspicion it wasn't their father.

As they carried the shopping from the car Rachel pointed to the pile of abandoned keys Mathilde had left on the top of the cabinet in the hall.

'Did you find the one for the chapel earlier?' she asked, dropping the bags of food onto the kitchen table. Mathilde was unloading a bag into the ancient fridge which was so iced up there was little room for any food. Rachel had already kicked it twice when it stopped working.

'Yes. I went and looked quickly, before we went out.'

'Oh, you should've said, I'd like to see inside too. Can we go together and investigate later? When I was a kid we were always told not to go in there as it was for "praying not playing",' she made quote marks with her fingers in the air, 'although I'm sure Dad had been in when he was a young-ster and I believe my grandfather used to use it for its proper purpose, although I don't recall him saying they had services in it. I'll organise for you to meet Aunt Alice and Uncle Jack as well; they've been asking about you but I told them to give you a day to settle in. She'll probably know more about the chapel as she's always lived here.'

'Yes, we can go,' Mathilde agreed reluctantly. Despite the plain disappointing interior there was something special, different about the chapel and she felt as though she didn't want to share it. She was being stupid, she told herself. Rachel had spent years of her life in this house so she had as much right – maybe more so – to look around any part of the estate.

After dinner, they walked back to the chapel. Fleur was kicking a new ball purchased earlier in the supermarket and she was happy to be left outside playing while the two women went in. Rachel hadn't forgotten the warnings she'd had to stay out and she wasn't going to allow her daughter inside until she'd looked herself.

'So, after your meeting with Mr Murray, do you know what you're going to do with the hall? Will you stay? I'd really like to get to know you properly, you're the sister I thought I'd never meet.'

'Stay? *Non*. No. Of course not. Why would I?' Mathilde realised her answer had been harsh; she could see it immediately in the way her sister's face creased with disappointment. 'I have to travel for my work, I told you that.' Inside her chest though, her heart was churning. She'd yearned for a family, a blood connection her whole life and yet now she had found it she was too frightened to remain. The look on Rachel's face filled her with remorse; an uncomfortable emotion she was unfamiliar with.

'Maybe I'll stay for a week or two,' she relented, 'then I'll decide what to do.'

Rachel's smile was shaky. 'Thank you,' she replied.

Inside, it smelled the same as before, the stale air heavy and damp, a sharp contrast with the fresh summer evening outside. The strange feeling she'd had before of not being on her own wasn't apparent this time. Now, it was just an old dilapidated building in need of some acrow props and urgent restoration.

'Well, it's a bit of a disappointment, isn't it?' Rachel stood in the middle and turned around slowly. 'There's nothing in here apart from the pews and a table which I'm guessing was an altar? And why has the wall on this side been covered with plaster but it's bare stone opposite?' She walked over to the wall on their left and banged it with the flat of her hand to show Mathilde what she meant. A shower of dust fell to the floor. 'Actually,' she raised her eyebrows, 'that isn't plaster, it's boarded up, it sounds hollow. That's a bit odd.'

'Maybe the wall was starting to come down? Or bits fell off?' Mathilde waved her hands as she tried to think of the word she needed.

'Disintegrate?' Rachel supplied. 'I suppose it may have, that would explain all the warnings about not coming in here, but it was a bit of a botched job if all they did was stick some panels over it.'

'What's this?' Mathilde rubbed her fingers over the board where the paint was flaking away, revealing a pale design in soft grey, travelling diagonally away from the corner towards the centre of the panel. 'It looks like a snake,' she added.

'It does rather,' Rachel peered at it, 'I wonder why they'd have that in a church? Unless it's something to do with Adam and Eve.' She looked at her watch. 'Look at the time, I'd better find Fleur and head back. I told Aunt Alice to come over for seven-thirty, we can ask her.'

Locking the door, they fought their way through the brambles and nettles at the side of the chapel to look at the exterior wall where the panelling was, but it seemed exactly the same as the rest. The mortar was dry and crumbling as Mathilde pushed her finger in and watched it scatter on the leaves below.

She paused for a moment letting the other two go on ahead; she wanted a few minutes to herself. She was used to living a solitary life and since she'd arrived the previous day she'd been required to be sociable non-stop; she needed a break, a chance to breathe more easily. Perhaps that was why she kept having this odd feeling she was being watched. As if someone had been waiting for her to walk onto the stage in a play she didn't know she was starring in. She gave herself a shake. It was probably just everything that had happened recently making her feel this way. After all her years of wishing, yearning, suddenly she had a family, other people she was related to, and her mother wasn't alive to see it. No wonder she was feeling crowded. So much so that she was imagining people who weren't even there, when she had plenty of new relatives who were physically present.

Following slowly behind the others she detoured across the garden, pushing through the undergrowth until she reached a fence, broken in places where the wood was rotten. Beyond her a field of ripening wheat was starting to turn from pale green to gold.

'*Papa*,' she whispered, 'how did I not know you were here? Suddenly I don't know who I am anymore and you aren't here to show me. Our lives should have been so different; another path we would have walked but now I don't know which route to take.' She rubbed the back of her hands against her eyes as the view in front of her blurred and wobbled.

Behind her she heard the sound of tyres on gravel. Plucking some yellow ragwort flowers from their woody stalks, she dropped them on the ground before turning to follow her sister back to the house, ready to meet the rest of the family.

Chapter Nine

March 1584

If Tom thought the sleeping draught was the last of his dealings with the Queen, he was mistaken. Expecting Hugh to take all the praise for the drink she'd started requesting every night, that suited him well. He preferred to stay in the shadows where he remained invisible and didn't need to go through the endless rigmarole of trying to explain he could neither hear nor speak. It was tiresome, to say the least. Although Hugh took all the praise for the velvety sweet spice, it seemed the servant who had arrived downstairs that night told one of the Queen's ladies it was Hugh's assistant who'd made the drink and suddenly Tom's presence was demanded in the Queen's chamber.

At first, he tried to avoid going but Hugh soon made him realise that saying 'no' to the Queen wasn't an option. Taking a deep breath, he changed into some cleaner clothes, although they still bore the residue scent of the dried prunella flowers he'd been grinding up. Washing his face, he combed his hair and quickly trimmed his beard, before following Hugh.

Walking across the courtyard and up the back stairs to the state apartments, Tom's face reflected his incredulity. Never in his life had he seen a world such as this. They were standing at the end of a long corridor, one side lined with windows made of tiny diamond shaped leaded panes of glass, flooding it with light. Opposite, the dark walls were hung with thick tapestries, rich with a myriad of colours that made his heart sing. Such a contrast with the dreary tones and hues of his own world. He moved towards them to touch the lustrous shining threads but Hugh pulled on his arm and shook his head. There were strict rules up here and Tom realised he needed to understand them. Putting his hands behind his back and keeping his eyes lowered he watched Hugh's feet, following him to the end of the corridor which opened out onto a magnificent gallery.

This arena was also lit by glorious floor to ceiling windows, the glass clear and fine, unlike the dull mottled ones in the stillroom. Around the tops of the windows tiny panes of stained glass shone beacons of coloured lights into the room. Banks of beeswax candles burned despite the early hour of the day, lending a blue, slightly smoky atmosphere which caught in Tom's throat, making him want to cough. Thick, finely stitched drapes and tapestries decorated the walls, the glossy strands flickering in the candlelight. The courtiers' attire dazzled in a myriad of peacock colours, gowns and doublets in brilliant hues. At one end of the space a large, ornately carved throne stood on a dais, whilst around it several women chatted quietly as they attended to their sewing. Perched on the throne was a slender woman in a sumptuous, heavily embroidered gold dress threaded with hundreds of tiny pearls glowing in the candlelight. It almost looked too large for her tiny frame. She had red hair, reminding Tom of his mother and he knew immediately, even without the numerous guards and the richly dressed gentlemen stood around, this was his Queen. The urge to cough grew stronger.

Hugh began to walk slowly towards her, his eyes on the floor. A luxurious carpet with an intricate design in blues, golds and reds lay thick and soft beneath Tom's feet, entrancing him; he'd only heard of such things. He followed, watching Hugh's feet until they stopped in front of the Queen and Hugh bowed down on one knee, Tom copying a second afterwards.

As they stood up Tom could see a terrible incident being played out before the court. The key player, a man who unlike the courtiers was wearing plain garb in dark fustian and worsted fabrics, had been thrown face down on the floor. Whatever was being said to him was lost on Tom but he could tell by the Queen's wild gestures, her hands balled into fists and her eyes flashing whilst she spoke through gritted teeth, that she was terrifyingly angry. The man had his head in his hands, congealed blood where his fingernails used to be and Tom could see his swollen face was bloodied and bruised. One of the guards hauled him to his feet and held him there as the man wobbled about as if his legs would give way. Tom felt his gut quiver in fright and for once he was relieved he couldn't hear the screaming he imagined was happening, if the wincing from the other people around the room was anything to go by.

Finally, the Queen pointed to a door hidden in one corner of the room where the panelling had opened up to reveal a stone staircase beyond and the man was hauled off by his feet, his head dragging across the floor as if he were already a corpse. Tom caught a glimpse of the man being pulled away and down the stairs, the back of his head bouncing off every step as he disappeared from view. Hot acid bile clawed at the back of Tom's throat. What on earth was he doing here? As he and Hugh were ushered forward it took everything he had not to vomit. As he knelt again, he could see specks of blood in front of him on the floor.

He turned his attention to the Queen. She was talking to Hugh but he caught the gist of what she was saying from the occasional word. Her mood seemed to have switched in an instant – all thoughts of the poor wretch dragged away just seconds earlier gone – as she exclaimed her delight for the vanilla flavouring which she'd never tasted before and insisted the two apothecaries sought out more.

She got to her feet and turned towards Tom, her small dark eyes burning into his as if she could read everything tumbling through his mind; his thoughts and his fears laid bare before this diminutive woman who was the most powerful female in the world. His legs began to shake, her supremacy and confidence rolling from her in waves. Now they were closer he could see the pale face paint she wore was disguising a harsh pockmarked complexion and together with her hooked nose she was less attractive than the portrait he'd admired as he followed Hugh along the corridor a few minutes previously.

'I am told by my apothecary that you are responsible for bringing this new spice, vanilla, to my court.' Tom had to watch her thin-lipped mouth carefully as she spoke. Thankfully she seemed to consider each word for a moment before she said it and he had little trouble understanding her. He bowed again from his waist, before standing up so he could watch her face once again. *'And you can neither hear nor speak and yet understand what those around you say?'* Tom nodded, wondering what she was thinking and if his time at the palace was about to come to an end. He watched as she made her way back to her throne behind her, the weight of her gown almost swamping her tiny frame and preventing her from moving.

Once she was perched on her throne and her skirts carefully arranged around her by a young girl with blond hair, dressed in a lovat green dress with simple ribbon decoration who'd spent the entire time stood silently to one side, the Queen addressed him once more.

'You intrigue me, Tom Lutton. You cannot hear and yet you are able to understand everything that I say. I have never come across someone like you before and I wonder if you may be of use to others at my court. And not just because you make a delicious bedtime drink.' She looked over to Hugh. *'You are both dismissed,'* she told him, before turning her attention to Tom and adding, *'for the present.'*

Tom followed Hugh as they backed out of the room, their eyes firmly downcast until they reached the doors which as before were opened by the guards to usher them back to the corridor outside. The cool air rushed into Tom's lungs as he breathed in as deeply as he could. He was certain he'd held his breath the whole time they'd been in front of the Queen; she was small in size and yet her presence was enormous.

'I do not need to explain to you why we do not want to upset the Queen,' Hugh spoke slowly as they made their way back

to the stillroom, *'did you understand what was happening when we arrived?'* Tom shook his head. *'That man is in the employ of the Spanish ambassador, Bernardino Mendoza.'* Tom didn't understand the man's name despite Hugh repeating it twice and he waved his hand to make Hugh continue. *'He was taking information from here at court to the ambassador and they had devised a plot to remove the Queen from her throne and replace her with her Catholic cousin, Mary. The feud between them goes back many years. The Spanish are desperate for our Protestant Queen Elizabeth to be gone, because the Catholic church did not recognise the marriage of her mother Anne Boleyn to her father King Henry; they consider her a bastard and not heir to the throne. Instead, they say her cousin Queen Mary is the rightful successor. The plot all centred on a man called Throckmorton who's now spilling all his secrets, helped no doubt by Walsingham's men at the Tower. The rumours are that Mendoza is to be expelled from England. Throckmorton will be executed of course, as will everyone else involved, including that poor wretch we just saw. He had no say in whether he was to become embroiled and now he's got hours left to live.'*

Tom shuddered as what Hugh had explained, sank in. Being at court had felt like an honour but the memory of fleeing to France when his adopted father fell foul of the monarch reminded him of exactly how precarious it could be. If a mere servant was instructed to carry a message they couldn't refuse and then suddenly they were caught up in a situation from which there was no escape, he wondered if this was a place he'd rather not be.

Chapter Ten

June 2021

'You don't look a bit like your father,' Aunt Alice's voice trembled a little as she looked Mathilde up and down. They were all assembled in the small living room beside the kitchen and she had the distinct feeling she was on trial. Although it contradicted her usual attitude, she had prepared herself to be pleasant to this new aunt, yet immediately she was on the defensive. Rachel offered hot drinks whilst exclaiming brightly how delighted she was Mathilde had finally been found and how pleased their father would have been. Aunt Alice, it seemed, did not agree.

'Are the solicitors doing a DNA test, just to make sure?' She turned to Rachel, ignoring Mathilde. 'She could be a fraud,' she added, *sotto voce*.

'Of course not!' Rachel exclaimed, 'you can see she looks like me. And actually, rather like you too; we don't need a test. I've already explained Dad was searching in the wrong place, that's why he couldn't find her in France. But now she's here and I have a new sister and you have a new niece; which is wonderful.' This last sentence was said more as an accusation, daring her aunt to disagree. Alice swallowed hard, her thin lips disappearing into her doughy face and she said nothing, her fingers constantly twisting her wedding ring around on her finger.

'So, what happens now?' Alice's voice was strained and high pitched, 'everything will change. We're too old for all this.'

'For goodness' sake, she's only been here twenty-four hours, give her a chance to settle in before she decides what she wants to do. Then you'll know if you've got anything to worry about. Anyway,' hastily Rachel changed the subject, 'we had a look round the chapel this afternoon, Mathilde wanted to look inside.'

Alice let out a long sigh. 'You were always told not to go in there,' she said quietly, her eyes welling up. She dabbed at them with a tiny lace edged handkerchief she'd pulled from her sleeve. 'She hasn't been here five minutes and already everything is changing. That place is dangerous; Peter told you not to go in.'

'Well, we couldn't see anything hazardous and we were very careful. There's ivy getting in through a broken pane but none of the walls seemed dodgy. In fact, one of them had been covered over with wooden panels, did our father do that?'

'No, I'm sure it was always like that, certainly since before my time. Your grandfather took us in once or twice when we were children, I remember the wall you're talking about. We were told the place was holy, sacred, and we were never to go in there unless to pray. And we didn't, although I'm not sure if your father did more recently. The wall is probably panelled to stop it falling down.'

'It would need more than some pieces of wood nailed to the wall to stop it then,' Rachel pointed out. She glanced at Mathilde whose interest in the conversation had perked up as they discussed the chapel, trying to follow what they were saying. It had been a long day and her head was beginning to ache.

'Well, it's getting late and it's Fleur's bedtime,' Rachel announced as she got to her feet and with a false looking wide yawn and stretch Mathilde followed. Thankfully their guests took the hint and picked up their coats to leave.

'I'm sure we'll see you again soon,' Alice lifted her chin and smiled at Mathilde, her mouth moving but the gesture not reaching her eyes, 'then we can discuss what you intend to do with this lovely house. I know your father wouldn't want it sold off, he'd be turning in his grave.' She kept eye contact for a moment longer than necessary before hurrying out, struggling to pull her anorak on as she went. Jack, who had barely said two words the whole visit, just held a hand up in a half salute and nodded his head once before scuttling after his wife. Mathilde frowned at their departing backs, her mouth moving silently as she tried to work out what Alice's departing words had meant.

As soon as a very tired and protesting Fleur was tucked up in bed, Rachel came back down and made hot chocolate for them both. Mathilde sat at the kitchen table watching her.

'Alice, she does not like me,' she stated the obvious.

'I'm sure she will in time, it's just a shock. We all knew about you but never thought we'd get the chance to meet you. And if you hadn't been found then Alice would have inherited the hall, so she's bound to be pretty miffed about that. There was no need for her rudeness though, that was unacceptable.'

'Miffed?'

'Cross. Actually, at the moment she's more than cross, she's probably scared of what the future may hold but it still doesn't excuse her. Maybe once she realises that you're staying, even if just for a week or two to start with, then she'll calm down.'

'It's fine,' Mathilde shrugged, 'most people don't like me. I don't fit in with what people expect. It doesn't matter, I'm used to it. Anyway, I don't know if I will stay,' she added. 'Being in a house day after day, the same place, it isn't easy. It makes me hurt inside. I need to keep on the move. Changing views. It's what I've always done.'

'But you said you would.' Rachel's voice rose slightly as she put the cups of hot chocolate on the table too sharply, the contents slopping over the edge and making milky, pale brown puddles. She grabbed a threadbare old tea towel and rubbed at the mess. 'How can you have changed your mind already? I get that you aren't used to being in a house, and yes this is a pretty big place, but you've turned up after all these years to claim your inheritance. We didn't even know if you were alive for God's sake, our poor father imagining the worst and then you can't even make up your mind whether to hang around? We've waited so many years for you, I think you owe us that much, don't you? We're family, surely that means something?' Her voice tailed off into a plea.

Mathilde was shocked at the outburst. As ever, she'd only considered her own feelings, without thinking how her arrival would affect her sister. But they hadn't ever met her, so why was she so upset? All the years she'd wished for a family, this wasn't how she'd imagined it would be.

'Yes, yes, that's easy for you to say,' she muttered. If she'd thought Rachel wouldn't hear her, she was wrong.

'Of course you're family.' She laid her hands across the table as if reaching out to take hold of Mathilde's, 'it took a while to find you but now you're here where you belong. It's not too late for us.'

'Not "a while",' Mathilde corrected, 'a whole lifetime. And too late to meet my father.' Her voice came out more forcefully than she'd intended. Her heart had been torn for so long, a permanent rupture in the fabric of her life and from that fissure everything she'd suppressed began to pour out. Wretchedness that had been bottled up inside. 'And too late for a proper childhood. You grew up here with everyone all around you, all this. Your aunt and uncle down the road, stability and belonging. You were so lucky. I never had that. My childhood was spent moving all the time, place to place, sometimes with no roof over our heads at night. Winter when it was cold, summer when the mistral came and blew the dust in our eyes and made our hair . . . *rigide,*' she pulled her hair out to demonstrate, 'nobody would accept us. Nowhere to call home, no security. Always people avoided us, my poor *maman* constantly fighting the demons in her head. At first others would be kind . . . almost welcoming. But it never lasted, once they saw how she was, they wanted us gone. We were refugees, outsiders. *Émigrées*; it's the loneliest word in the world.' She got to her feet and walked to the back door before turning back. 'I'll stay then, I'll stay for the summer. But no longer. In September I'm gone.'

Chapter Eleven

June 2021

Striding over to her special corner of the garden, Mathilde filled her watering can from the butt. She needed time to mull over what had just happened with Alice and Jack, and what Rachel had said. All her life she'd longed for family, roots, somewhere to anchor her, stop the constant need to be on the road, and for one moment she'd started to wonder if she'd found it; blood relatives. But how long would it be before they too decided she was a bad person, rejected her and told her to be on her way? There was no reason why they'd be any different, people were all the same; her childhood had taught her that. And her newly acquired aunt and uncle had made it very clear she wasn't welcome here. And if this wasn't a place to call home, a place to rest, then she had nowhere. She'd wasted years of her life yearning for something that didn't exist.

Arriving where she'd laid out her herb pots, she gave them another good watering before sinking onto the ground and lying back, her hands behind her head. Somewhere nearby in the grass, she could hear the slight rustling of a tiny creature disturbed by her movements, trying to make its escape. The twilight air was warm and she closed her eyes for a moment, enjoying the cool beneath her as the grass started to chill, the smell of the summer foliage making her breathe out gently as her heart slowed to its normal pace. Sharp pieces of dried cowslip dug into her shoulder but she couldn't summon up the effort to move. Gripping the grasses beside her she tugged at them, her hand slipping slightly before they gave way and tore off in her hand. She dropped them and started again with another handful.

Eventually the dusk thickened and she turned her head to one side to listen to the high-pitched squeak of bats as they swooped to snatch small moths from the air. Suddenly conscious she wasn't alone, Mathilde looked across to the small coppice beside her. She hadn't heard anything; whoever or whatever was there, was stealthily quiet.

Keeping perfectly still, she held her breath and waited for whatever it was to make a move, which surely it must sooner or later. Then as her eyes adjusted, she thought she saw a dark shape in the shadows. Was it a deer? It was now dark under the thick shaded canopy of summer leaves and she could just make out the indistinct outline of someone standing with their head bowed. Black on black. She screwed her eyes up; whoever it was blended into the velvet darkness so well she could barely see him. What were they doing there?

''ello? Who is there?' she called. There was no response and as she spoke the person turned away from her and was gone.

Thinking the visitor had walked away through the woods towards the stables, she jumped to her feet and hurried around the exterior of the trees to surprise them at the other side. It was now too dark and far too overgrown to be able to catch up as she crashed through the undergrowth. When she got to the other side, the person was nowhere to be seen. And, she told herself, in truth she hadn't expected to find anyone there. It wasn't the first time she'd seen something that couldn't be explained: a guest from another time. She was certain that was who'd been visiting her. Although what he was doing in the middle of the woods, she had no idea.

From somewhere close to the house she heard Rachel calling to her, but hunching her shoulders and pushing her hands in her pockets Mathilde slipped around the side of the house and opening her van she crept inside and lay down beneath her blanket. There was so much racing around her head she simply couldn't take any more. She couldn't adjust to the present, while she was still trying to understand her past.

The following morning after a surprisingly good night's sleep in her van, Mathilde appeared in the kitchen early. The others were already there, Fleur slowly eating a bowl of cereal, dripping milk from the bottom of her spoon into her lap.

'Coffee?' she smiled hesitantly at Rachel, unsure of her reception after her outburst the previous evening. Any frostiness she may encounter would be her own fault and after a night's sleep she could see that.

Ruffling Fleur's hair as she walked past she took a piece of toast from the plate on the table, wedging it in her mouth before dropping three large spoons of coffee granules into her cafetiere. She held it up and raised her eyebrows but Rachel smiled and shook her head pouring herself more tea. Sisters they may be but their upbringing firmly dictated their early morning drinking habits.

'I'm sorry,' Mathilde said, turning to face her sister, 'I was too sharp last night, it wasn't fair of me.'

'No,' Rachel held her hand up to stop Mathilde saying anything else, 'you don't need to apologise. I can't begin to imagine what this must be like for you, it's all been a huge shock. It's fine honestly. Look, we've had a letter,' Rachel showed her an envelope, 'it was pushed through the door when I came downstairs this morning. It's addressed to both of us so I opened it but really it concerns you.'

Mathilde paused, her coffee cup halfway to her mouth.

'It's from Aunt Alice. She must have gone home and really wound herself up because it says that she's taking legal advice to contest the will. But don't worry she won't be able to. I was with Dad when it was drawn up and Mr Murray knows it's all sound. It could get messy if it goes to court though.'

'Contest? There is a contest?' Mathilde's face creased in confusion.

'No,' Rachel laughed, 'in English that means she's going to try and change the will, by going to court and asking a judge to give her the house instead of you. But it won't happen so don't worry.'

Mathilde shrugged. She had enough to think about without their hysterical aunt to contend with as well. Hopefully the woman would keep her distance.

'So,' Rachel changed the subject, 'what are your plans for

today? Did Mr Murray give you the deeds and a map of the estate?'

'No, he said they come from . . . land people?'

'Land Registry I expect,' Rachel nodded, 'they have to register you as the new owner and they'll probably send you a copy of the deeds. Then you may be able to see who owned the hall over the years, depending on how old the paperwork is. I was intending to go through some more of our father's belongings today, would you like to help?'

'Yes, thank you, I'd like that.' Mathilde nodded, her mouth widening into a smile. She wanted to discover more about her father, this man who'd been lost to her almost her entire life. If the cab he'd been travelling in had just been a minute earlier, everything would have been different. She'd have been living here with her *maman*; Rachel wouldn't have been born but perhaps she'd have had other siblings. It was like a mirror, looking in on a life she'd almost lived.

'I've already sorted out Dad's clothes.' Rachel walked towards the hall, talking over her shoulder, as Mathilde followed. 'There was nothing even worth donating to charity; he liked to wear his old gardening clothes morning, noon and night. He was a right scruff!' she laughed to herself remembering, 'he used to say he'd had enough of wearing a suit to work for years and he was going to spend retirement feeling comfortable.' Mathilde tried to imagine him in khaki shirts with the sleeves rolled up and baggy trousers tucked into wellington boots. She'd spotted the boots still stood beside the back door, as if waiting for him to slip his feet in, one last time.

Rachel led her down a short, narrow passageway behind the stairs and into a room at the back of the house. It wasn't large but it was flooded with light from a window that looked out over the sprawling vegetable garden close to where Mathilde had laid her pots of herbs.

'This was his office,' Rachel explained, holding her arms out to the side. Her voice cracked slightly and Mathilde looked across to her, feeling an unexpected scratchiness behind her eyes. They smiled at each other and Rachel rubbed Mathilde's back for a moment as if soothing a child. There was a brief pinprick of empathy, both of them washed with the same brushstroke of sadness for their father, a sharing of emotions. A sensation Mathilde had never experienced before.

The walls were lined with shelves haphazardly stacked with books together with the dusty remains of the detritus of his life; a mug proclaiming the delights of Southwold filled with pens, document storage boxes, frames filled with photographs. Mathilde gazed round the room trying to drink it all in. Everything in here was a part of him. She closed her eyes trying to feel blindly for his spirit, his essence, some tangible evidence he was still in there with them. She wondered if he'd been the shadowy figure beneath the trees the previous night.

'As you can see, he wasn't a very tidy person. Thankfully he only lived at the back of the house for the last ten years, all those formal rooms I showed you have been covered in dust sheets and closed for ages.'

'This desk is lovely,' Mathilde ran her fingers across the tooled leather inlaid into its dark mahogany top. It was solid, appearing to have grown up out of the floor, its roots buried beneath the ancient frame of the house and now pitted and scarred by centuries of use.

'Dad kept everything important in here,' Rachel explained dropping to her knees and pulling out a deep drawer at the bottom of the pedestal. 'I've seen this before of course,' she took out a sturdy cardboard box and laid it on the desk, removing the lid and tipping it up slightly so Mathilde could see the contents. 'It's everything he collected and kept about you, your life.'

On top was a faded photograph of a young couple with a baby held between them, in front of a backdrop of mountains. Mathilde lifted it out and for a moment she pressed it against her chest and squeezed her eyes tight, determined not to let the tears out, before looking again.

'It's us, my parents and me,' she whispered, 'I've never seen a photo of us before but I recognise this dress, my *maman* wore it for years and years. Maybe she remembered when this photo was taken. Mourning him.' Laying it reverently on the desk she began to sort through the rest of the contents, spreading out everything carefully until they created a patchwork of her first twelve months, a prelude to the life she should have had.

'See here, these are clippings of articles our father wrote for the paper, when he was in Beirut,' Rachel began to point, 'and these are adverts he placed in newspapers, trying to find you. Both in Lebanon and later in France. He eventually managed to find a government official who confirmed your mother had left with other refugees. And look,' she picked up a tatty, folded map, 'he ringed everywhere on this map of France he went looking for you.'

'He was so close to us, if only we'd known,' Mathilde murmured gazing at the areas marked.

'Where exactly were you living?' Rachel stood beside her.

'All over this *département*,' Mathilde waved her hand over the area around Toulouse, 'we moved about constantly. Always. My mother insisted it was the only way to stay safe. She was so traumatised from the war, the constant bombing, she had nightmares her whole life, couldn't hold down a proper job; she was forever broken. She'd lost my father, our home, her whole life, and she never recovered. When she didn't feel too bad she'd work in bars or pick fruit in summer. We had to find places to live and they were always temporary. Sometimes we'd squat in barns or derelict houses and occasionally we'd find a holiday cottage to break into. I didn't always go to school; if my mother was in a dark place, I needed to stay with her. We dressed differently, we didn't blend in. We were often suspected of stealing so we kept moving on, we had no option. And then, when I was sixteen, she died in a fire. A curtain caught on a candle flame. I was out and when I returned the cottage was ablaze. Since then, I've been on my own.'

'How awful, I'm so sorry, it's incredibly sad you had to live like that. I'm glad you're here now and that we finally found you. This is your home from now on. Please always remember how much our father loved you.' Rachel wrapped her arms around her and for a moment Mathilde relaxed into the warmth of another human body. It was alien to her but she admitted to herself, it felt good.

'It's not that easy,' she said in a quiet voice, 'I can't just change into someone I'm not. Travelling, living day to day, that's who I am. It's all I've ever known. All this,' she waved her hands around the room, 'it's too late. I don't deserve it. I don't even remember my father so why would I stay here?'

'Because you *do* deserve it.' Rachel hugged her closer, 'just because you had a hard start in life doesn't mean you have to carry on that way, it's not a sentence to be served in perpetuity.' Mathilde frowned and Rachel paused for a moment before saying: 'Forever. You don't have to carry on leading that nomadic lifestyle, now you have the chance for a fresh start. Although your beginnings were traumatic they don't have to colour your whole life. Don't you want to be a part of a family?'

'I wanted it yes,' Mathilde nodded, 'it was everything I dreamed about growing up. We'd walk past big houses with toys in the garden and I'd wonder what it was like to grow up with *maman* and *papa* and a proper house to go back to every day, year after year. Always there in the same place. A secure place to anchor in the storm when people came after you, shouting at you to move on. Except nobody would do that, would they, if you lived in a house all the time, if you'd put down roots?'

'Then let me in and I can help you,' Rachel whispered.

A shout from the living room interrupted them, and with an apologetic grimace Rachel left the room leaving Mathilde standing in the same spot, paused in time. The smallest speck of her angst against the world dissipated into the air as her shoulders dropped, just a fraction. Her enduring belief her father had abandoned them by dying that day had been based on a misunderstanding and yet it had coloured everything, her whole life. Was it really possible to change now? If she opened her arms to this new family could she really trust them?

Her lower lip was caught between her teeth as she carefully packed everything away in the box again, placing it back into the drawer from which Rachel had taken it. As she did so, she heard a knock against the wood and sliding her fingers in they touched something cold and metallic. She grabbed and pulled hard, drawing out a smooth round object attached to a long, fine chain. It was tarnished and dull but it appeared to be gold, and as she turned it over in her hand, it sparked a memory. She remembered the painting in the chapel, the one she and Rachel had thought was a snake. It wasn't though she realised, they were mistaken; it was a chain with a locket on the end. She wondered what the connection between this item and the chapel was as she went to share her discovery with her sister.

Chapter Twelve

April 1584

In the murky gloom of twilight as the day began drifting towards night, Tom went as he did every evening to ensure the plants in the physic garden were all well-watered, and to put the top on the small frame he'd made for the vanilla. He was nurturing it as carefully as if it were his own child.

He loved being outside and always took as long as he dared, ambling around the gardens, the scent of the individual plants as familiar as friends. The gardeners and cooks knew not to touch anything, especially as some plants may be poisonous if used incorrectly. Out here the air was fresh, he could smell the river even though he couldn't see it, and through a gate at one end of the kitchen garden he could see the flowers laid out in beds in the formal gardens where the Queen and her retinue often walked on fine days. The comparison with the stuffy, dark interior of the palace was great.

Standing up from plucking off the tops of some thyme,

Tom watched as two men strode across the garden from the direction of the gate. Despite the thickening night and their dark clothes, with his sharp eyesight he could see they were dressed impeccably and were heading straight for him. He felt a shudder of trepidation twist in his gut. Whoever these men were, their sombre countenance and the supreme confidence they exuded, scared him. As they approached, he removed his cap and bowed politely, before standing up again and waiting for one of them to address him.

The slighter of the men dressed all in black, with dark, swarthy skin began to speak, his white teeth shining in the dusk. He spoke quickly and Tom had to catch some words to decipher what he was saying.

'It is said at court that you are both deaf and mute, is this true?' the man asked. Tom nodded. *'But you can tell what I am saying?'* Tom nodded again. Wasn't that obvious, given his previous answer?

'I'm informed you understand what people say, just by watching their mouths?' Tom paused, unsure how to answer. If people were speaking very fast or their mouths were obscured, or they weren't English or French then no, he couldn't. But he wasn't able to explain all that so instead he relied on his hand signals and holding out his hand, palm down, he rocked it from side to side, hoping they realised he meant both yes and no.

'Hugh tells us you travelled here from France?' Tom wondered where this questioning was going, given that the French and English were not remotely friendly. He nodded a little more hesitantly.

'So, you speak French? This is good. Did you meet any Frenchmen on the boat over that you have since seen at court?'

This time Tom wasn't certain he'd understood correctly, and shook his head.

'*Excellent. My name is Sir Francis Walsingham and this gentleman is my Lord Burghley.*' The man held out a piece of parchment with the two names written on it. '*We work for the Queen. Sometimes she requires people to collect information for her without divulging it to anyone and pass it on to me. Do you understand?*' Tom was becoming fed up with all the questions and wished he was in a position to ask a few of his own. He wasn't remotely sure he wanted to work for these two gentlemen. He was happy in the peaceful garden and in the stillroom where he only needed to communicate with Hugh and where he knew what he was doing. At least, it *had* been peaceful. Before he could try and explain that he'd rather decline their suggestion, the man called Walsingham continued.

'*I see that you are hesitating but I think you misunderstand me. We will assume that you are confused because you could not hear what I said. I am not a man to say "no" to, unless you wish to end your stay in London far quicker than you had intended. The Thames washes up bodies in the swirling waters beneath London Bridge almost every day. Miscreants — and people who do not do as others wish — find themselves unsteady on their feet as they walk along the riverbank where it is easy to slip on the mud and be pulled under the water by the strong current. I'd hate for that to happen to you, Tom Lutton.*' Tom had understood everything that Walsingham had said that time and the way both men were standing, upright and foreboding, shoulder to shoulder, told him even more than the speech that had just been delivered. He looked them both in the eye and nodded his acquiescence, despite the intense rush of foreboding that washed over him.

'Good.' Walsingham's smile didn't reach his eyes. *'As I say, you could be very useful to us. Sometimes I may ask you to watch people and see what they disclose, then write it down and bring it to me. Hide in the shadows, nay, hide in plain sight. Nobody will suspect you, as you seemingly cannot hear what anyone is saying nor whisper it in others' ears. You could make an exceptional spy. Do not tell of what we have said and we will call for you when we have need of your skills.'*

Tom nodded for the final time and bowing low, he waited for them to disappear in the direction from which they'd come. Breathing in the cool night air he held it in his lungs as long as possible, before slowly letting it out again. This was not what he had come to England for but it had been made very obvious to him that he had no choice, not if he wanted to stay alive. But as he walked slowly back to the kitchen to see what scraps were left from upstairs for his dinner, he kept coming back to Sir Francis Walsingham's final sentence. That his lack of hearing and speech was a skill. Not a hindrance nor weakness, but a talent. Something worthwhile. Slowly he began to smile a little as he pulled his shoulders back, and walked a little taller.

Chapter Thirteen

April 1584

The plants Tom had brought with him continued to thrive, although his precious vanilla plants were not growing as well as the others, despite the frame he had built. One of them was coming into flower and every morning he lifted the piece of glass off, before replacing it at night. He was hopeful it would produce some pods and more importantly seeds with which he could continue to propagate more. He'd been despatched to the warehouses along the river front again to try and procure more of the vanilla but with limited success. They were having to eke out the supplies they did have, only using it for the Queen. If they could grow their own they wouldn't be dependent on it being brought from overseas.

One afternoon as he worked in the stillroom, Tom had a visitor. Adding anise and pepper to a honey tisane for one of the courtiers' children who had suspected putrid throat, a movement at the door made him look up. Standing in the doorway was a lady. She was slender, little more than a child in size although he could tell from her features that she was older, perhaps in her thirties. Her gown was a pale yellow and her hair caught up in a net at the nape of her neck was as dark as the ravens at the tower Hugh had shown him as they came down the river to the palace on that first day. Immediately, he stopped what he was doing, bowing low.

When he looked up again her face was alight with the sweetest smile he'd ever seen, dimples creasing the sides of her mouth. Her eyes were the soft lilac colour of saffron flowers. He realised she was speaking to him so he concentrated on her face to try and read what she was saying. He'd been so busy admiring her figure he'd missed the first part of what she'd said. As she finished and stopped he grabbed the tablet he and Hugh used to communicate with and asked her to repeat herself. He was cross and embarrassed that unlike a normal man, he couldn't always understand what someone was saying.

Thankfully she didn't seem to mind and nodding she repeated the words slowly, giving him the opportunity to watch her mouth, the pink lips glossy where she had licked them nervously before she started speaking again. She introduced herself as Lady Isabel Downes, and this time he understood perfectly as she described a headache she kept getting across her forehead. He indicated a chair beside the door before abandoning the tisane he was working on and starting to prepare one for her. He wanted to explain that her head probably hurt because of the tight hoods the ladies wore but he knew drawing attention to any part of her attire was not gentlemanly, so instead he dropped a pinch of sage with the coriander and feverfew he was grinding together and poured the powder into a twist of paper. He demonstrated how she should add it to hot water and indicated that there was enough for two cups, if required.

Then, before she could get up to leave, he quickly wrote 'Tom Lutton' on the tablet and pointed to himself. She smiled and nodded and his heart melted, just a little. He watched her lips as she mouthed *'goodbye Tom Lutton'* and with a quick grin and the briefest of curtseys, she was gone. He hadn't even had time to bow in return.

Sitting down in the chair she'd just vacated, the warmth her body had left seeped up through his hose. He couldn't suppress the huge smile spreading across his face. She was the most beautiful woman he'd ever seen and his mind raced as he tried to think of a reason to see her again. But he knew in all sense, it was impossible. With a dress of the finest wool and matching silk slippers she had to be one of the Queen's ladies; the highest-ranking people in the kingdom. Whereas he was an assistant apothecary who slept in a tiny closet-like room at the back of the palace: he had no place in her world. There had been a time when his adoptive father was a courtier and he stood a good chance of following in his footsteps even with his lack of hearing, but all that was lost decades ago when his father was tortured to death and they escaped to France.

Tom carried a candle through to his room. Despite being no more than an enlarged cupboard he was nevertheless very pleased to have it, a tiny piece of privacy which he found to be invaluable. He lit the other two beeswax stumps on the chest. He'd become adept at swiftly removing any that were discarded from sconces upstairs and that could be used by the servants. These were far superior to the tallow candles he otherwise had access to and didn't produce the harsh acrid smoke which made his eyes sting and water.

From the chest at the end of his bed he retrieved the triptych he'd carried with him whilst travelling across Europe. It was bulky and quite heavy, and he'd lived in dread of someone deciding they wanted it for themselves, but thankfully his broad muscular frame prevented people from trying to start a fight with him. As long as nobody detected his deafness, he was mostly left to his own devices but as soon as his disability came to light it was a different story. Everyone was wary of someone who was different; suspicions and fear rose to the surface all too easily. That was always the point at which he moved on. Here at the palace though, he hoped to make a home.

Laying the triptych out across his bed he knelt on the floor holding a candle close in order to see it better. Every scene on the now completed left-hand panel showed his life before he returned to England. His early memories of warm days and fields of lilac coloured saffron flowers shimmering in the early morning sunlight. Of the night when he'd helped his mother with the heart-breaking task of hiding her tiny stillborn baby in a priest hole beneath the floor, before they fled their home, travelling through the freezing winter weather to France where they could be safe. The small house in a village close to Lyon where, finding shelter, once again his mother had grown and sold her saffron, helped by her ever-present companion Joan. Building a comfortable life and living in a community close to the monks, as she had done as a child. Now, the smell of it, its honey warmth and sharp spice always made him think of her. She too was an accomplished apothecary and he'd learned so much working with her as she painstakingly drew pictures of every plant and spice they used, writing its name in Latin beneath.

If it weren't for her he'd be nowhere. Her exemplary skills had ensured she'd led a long life. He knew she'd forever miss his father, but as always, she'd accepted what life threw at her and had learned to be happy. Content with her quiet routine and the love of those around her. She'd told him he always needed to keep breathing and to have hope that things would turn out all right.

Eventually he'd made his way across Europe, painting little scenes to remind him of all he'd seen and done. Especially when he'd had the chance to view the incredible triptych in the palace in Brussels which inspired him to start painting his own. And now having finished painting his journey to England – a small boat and view of the magnificent white cliffs as they arrived in Dover – it was time to start on the centre panel, to record his life at court. The sights, the smells, and the people: all that this new life may bring.

Chapter Fourteen

June 2021

Finding Rachel in the living room, Mathilde showed her the locket and chain, explaining how she'd found it wedged at the back of the drawer.

'How odd,' Rachel took it and held it up watching it slowly spinning round on the end of its chain, 'I've never seen this before. I wonder where it came from?'

'Do you think it's what we saw painted on the wall in the chapel?' Mathilde reminded her, 'we thought it was a snake but maybe it's a necklace? I'd like to take a closer look at those wooden panels and maybe try and take one off to see what's behind?' Her interest was piqued. She'd be careful to ensure she didn't do anything to upset any souls lodging there: people who'd never moved on. She had a strong suspicion that was who – or what – she'd seen in the garden.

'I don't think you should remove them,' Rachel said sharply, her voice revealing her concern, 'supposing they really were put up to stop the wall coming down?'

'I'll be careful,' she promised, 'I won't do anything dangerous.'

'Well I'm not having Fleur anywhere near it just in case, so you're on your own.'

Mathilde was unprepared for the disappointment she felt that her sister didn't want to accompany her. She wanted to share the investigation; they were both invested in this. As Rachel handed the locket back to her she pressed it against her palm and felt a warm, soft pulse. She couldn't decide if it was her own heart beating or the object she was clutching.

She quickly filled a watering can from the butt on her way to the chapel, pouring the contents over her herbs. The vanilla plants were fragile and really needed to be in a greenhouse; the summer warmth wasn't reliable enough in England. There was only one greenhouse in the garden and it had more broken panes than complete ones, the floor inside covered in vicious shards of glass. Rachel had already fixed a chain and padlock around the door to prevent Fleur wandering in. Mathilde promised herself she'd drive back into Fakenham to the DIY store and see about something temporary, or some glass to make a propagator. Now she was staying for the summer it was worth constructing something more permanent.

Taking her tools from the back of her van she walked across to the chapel, the key in her pocket digging into her thigh.

The pigeons were in the trees again calling to each other, their soft cooing carrying on the wind, but she ignored them as she opened the door and stepped inside. Now the space was a little more familiar it didn't feel quite so eerie but it was intensely cold and the awful dead smell still hung in the air. Rubbing her fingers over the painting it now seemed obvious that it was a locket and chain twisting across the board, and now she was certain she was supposed to find the pendant; it was a sign that she needed to carry on investigating. Something was encouraging her, waiting for her. Placing her bag on a pew she removed the claw hammer. Its wooden handle was worn smooth but it was the only one she possessed and had belonged to her mother before her.

Going to the wall and examining it closely she could see there were two separate panels, each of them in a frame. She gave a tentative push to see if either would conveniently give way but they were both stuck fast. Carefully she slipped the claws of the hammer between the frame and panel, levering it back as far as it would go, wincing as the sound of splintering wood echoed around the empty space.

Her first attempt only lifted it an inch but it was enough space to give some leverage and the rest came away more easily. At one point she had to drag a pew over so she could stand on it to pull at the top of the board but finally with a loud crack she pulled it from the wall.

She wasn't sure what she'd been expecting, just more of the stonework similar to the opposite wall but possibly crumbling down. She drew her breath in sharply as she gazed at what the panel had revealed. On the wall in front of her was a wide, heavy, gilt edged frame and set within was a triptych – three narrow paintings, the centre one wider than the two either side. It was covered in dust and she could just about make out dozens of tiny people dotted about it. It was astonishing; why on earth had someone boarded over it?

Excited to see if there was another work of art behind the second panel, she picked up her hammer and, standing on tiptoe, started on that one. Smaller than the first it came away easily but to her disappointment there was no picture, just a memorial stone plaque which she couldn't read. She realised with a jolt that the locket chain snaking across the larger panel appeared to have been pointing to this one.

Taking her mobile from her back pocket she snapped several photos of each. Stepping backwards she stood with her head on one side, staring silently at the strange painting in its flamboyant frame. Her heart was thumping in her chest and she could hear the blood pulsing through her ears. Something – or someone – had led her here, if only she could understand what they were trying to tell her. She had no idea.

Rachel and Fleur were in the kitchen finishing lunch when Mathilde burst in through the back door insisting her sister come immediately to see the discovery. Rachel quickly pushed the rest of her sandwich into her mouth whilst Mathilde flitted around the kitchen tidying items on the worktop, unable to stand still.

It felt like hours but was less than five minutes before they were back at the chapel, the door left ajar where Mathilde had run out. Fleur waited on the grass outside with a bag of crisps as Rachel followed Mathilde in.

'It's amazing,' Rachel murmured the moment she saw what Mathilde had been so excited about. 'What on earth is it doing here hidden behind that piece of wood? Why would anyone want to conceal something so beautiful? It looks old. I mean *really* old. We need to brush the dust off the front to see it more clearly but it's probably better if we don't. It needs to be professionally cleaned to avoid any damage. But look at all these little people all over it involved in tiny scenes, they're incredible. I've never seen anything like it. And look, on this panel there're flames.'

'Yes, *les feux de l'enfer*. Fires of . . .' Mathilde searched for the right word.

'Hell?' Rachel suggested.

'Yes, that is it, hell. On religious triptychs the third panel shows people going to hell. To frighten *les pécheurs*,' she paused again, 'bad people?'

'Sinners? Blimey, you know a lot, have you been researching?'

'No, but I grew up in France. A Catholic country. I've seen these in churches many times. How can we find someone to tell us more?'

'I'm not sure but I'll make some enquiries; I can start with a museum or the art department of a university and go from there. There's bound to be someone on the end of a phoneline or video call. I think we need to take it off this wall if we can and then bring it inside the house where it'll be safer. We don't want it to be damaged by any falling masonry that might have been disturbed taking the panels off. It's going to take both of us to carry it; I don't mind going backwards.'

Mathilde took several more photos of the picture in situ before they began to ease it from the wall. It required the use of her hammer again but they managed to remove it without inflicting any damage.

Walking very gingerly they stopped several times to lay it on the ground and rub their fingers where the ornate frame dug in. Back at the house, at Rachel's suggestion, they took a dust cover from a sofa in the formal drawing room and leaned it up against the back.

'It's out of the way of inquisitive hands in here,' she said, nodding towards Fleur waiting at the door as instructed as she said 'inquisitive'. Mathilde took a few steps backwards as she tilted her head to one side, before moving closer again and investigating the top of the frame.

'There is a shield here,' she pointed, 'like a family . . . badge? Do you recognise it?'

Rachel shook her head. 'It's a coat of arms. Dad never said we had one,' she said, 'and he certainly didn't use it. Another thing we'll have to wait to ask the experts. Let's go and make a coffee and see if we can find anyone locally. Otherwise, I suspect we'll be dragging it to London and I don't fancy trying to manhandle this on the tube.'

As Rachel went to start her search for the specialist they needed, Mathilde held back for a moment screwing up her eyes to scrutinise the left-hand panel. Despite the dust on it she could clearly make out several small scenes of people in what appeared to be extremely old-fashioned clothing. The very first image in the top corner attracted her attention as she leant forward. What initially just looked like a swirl of black showed itself to be a tunnel – or perhaps a hole – with a tiny face at the other end. It looked so bleak, so sorrowful. A cold aura wrapped her in a cloak of desolation and with a shudder she pulled her eyes away and followed Rachel out of the room. The painting disturbed her; she could feel it trying to tell her something, and she wasn't sure she wanted to hear it.

Chapter Fifteen

June 2021

'It may well take us weeks to find someone who can help,' Rachel warned as she typed and clicked her way through numerous websites. 'It would probably save time to actually speak to someone but I've no idea where to start.' Mathilde shrugged in response. She was depending on her sister to discover someone who could explain why a triptych that was making the hairs on her arms stand up was hidden away in a tiny family chapel in the middle of Norfolk. She was sure it was connected to the strange atmosphere in the house and garden, and the dark shadows that shifted just out of her field of vision when she was alone.

'Remember I'm only here for a couple of months, then I'll be on my way again,' she reminded her sister, although it was as much for herself as for Rachel. Already there were threads from the past threatening to bind her to the hall. She felt them tighten the moment she pulled the panel from the chapel wall.

'I know,' Rachel replied in a small voice, 'I'm trying not to think about you going again so soon.' Mathilde felt a pang of discomfort.

'I was thinking though, as I'm going to be here a couple of months, maybe I'll move back into my bedroom if that's okay with you?' she suggested.

'Yes, of course. I'd like that, to have you closer,' she was rewarded with a shaky smile, 'and I think Dad would have liked that too.'

It took several days of internet searching and phone calls before Rachel eventually tracked down an art historian, Oliver Bathurst, who specialised in religious art. Luckily for them he lived in neighbouring Suffolk, about twenty miles away. She called the number she'd been given and with a quick grin and a nod of her head as the phone was answered, she went into her now well-practised spiel of how they'd found an old triptych in the family chapel. She smiled as the man offered to drive over the following day to take a look. In the meantime, he suggested she send him some photographs so he had an idea of what he was coming to see.

The two women punched the air in excitement as Rachel jotted down his email address and ended the call.

'I didn't think we'd find an expert in the next county; I hope when I've sent him the photos he still wants to see it and doesn't decide it's some old fake of little interest,' she said as they went back to the drawing room. Mathilde ran upstairs to collect her camera and the best lens she had for the artificial lighting indoors and she soon had pictures of all three panels, the frame and the crest, in case they were also of interest to him. She sent the shots over to Oliver including the ones inside the chapel whilst Rachel was busy searching for him online to confirm his credentials.

'He's a professor at the local university,' she read from the screen, 'and an expert in Medieval and Restoration art. I think we may have struck lucky.'

An enthusiastic reply arrived from Oliver saying he was very intrigued and he looked forward to seeing them both the next day.

Chapter Sixteen

June 2021

With Oliver due at nine the following morning, both women went to bed early the night before. Mathilde realised she was looking forward to sleeping inside and the novelty of a double bed.

She was asleep within minutes, falling into a deep, shadowy dream. Surrounded by darkness a small pool of dim light hung above her like the sun trying to push through the clouds on a foggy day. There were walls around her, damp and close. Desolation clutched at her, enveloped in a desperate air of misery, sadness. A dank smell crawled up her nose and settled in her pores. The worst place in the world, an oubliette, a cramped dungeon deep beneath the floor. A movement above her in the light caught her attention. Someone passed something to her and she reached up to take it. Looking at what she held in her arms it looked like a small alabaster doll, almost weightless, wrapped in a ragged scrap of linen. Carefully she laid it on the floor beside her, so precious, so small. Then she held her arms in the air and someone reached in and pulled her up towards the flickering glow above her.

And then she awoke, sitting bolt upright, her heart racing. The dream had been so real she was relieved to find herself in her own bed and she gave a shudder as she slowly lay back down again. It was nothing – just a dream – she told herself. But not one she ever wanted to revisit. The feeling of grief and sorrow the dream had initiated was still lodged in her chest, like a hideous memory twisting her heart. As she drifted off again she was being rocked from side to side, a cool breeze on her face and the splashing of waves against the boat she was standing in. Ahead of her she saw the Dover cliffs rearing up, huge and brilliantly white reflecting the sun shining from behind her and throwing her shadow across the deck.

The following morning, Mathilde was up and out early watering her plants. Having spent the remainder of the night continually waking up, unable to shake off the despondent feeling, she was now pleased to be outside in the open again. Perhaps she shouldn't have abandoned her van. There was no doubt her bed in there wasn't as comfortable as the one in the house but in the van she could relax. Nobody was trying to reach out to her. It was almost as good as sleeping outside with just the inky black sky and stars to blanket her. And she'd done that often enough as a child.

Oliver Bathurst arrived promptly at nine o'clock, his black Mini pulling up beside Mathilde's van with a small spray of gravel. As he unfolded himself from the seat, Mathilde, who was watching from the drawing room, wondered how on earth he squeezed his tall body into such a small car. He paused for a moment and looked up at the house, as if taking it all in. Even though she knew nothing of English architecture Mathilde knew it was an impressive building, the weathered wood frame and the tall decorative twisted chimney stacks reaching up to the sky. For the first time, she felt a tiny frisson of pleasure it was now hers. There was a bang on the front door and she and Rachel walked through the house to open it, with Fleur scampering behind.

'Hello, pleased to meet you,' Oliver shook hands with the two women and then with a grave look on his face he bent down to shake hands with Fleur, who stared up at him silently. Close up, Mathilde could see he was not only well over six foot but also his shirt was straining at the seams over his broad shoulders. Not remotely similar to the ancient, scruffy old professor she and Rachel had both agreed he'd undoubtedly look like. No sign of the tweed jacket, waistcoat and carpet slippers that Mathilde had drawn to make her sister laugh. She wondered again about the logistics of him fitting into that small car. Leading the way, Mathilde returned to the drawing room where the triptych was still propped up against the sofa. Oliver's eyes roved around the walls, taking in the antiquity of the building's interior.

'Amazing,' he breathed as he gazed at the painting. He'd removed an eye glass from his pocket and leaning as close as he could without disturbing it, he slowly looked over every inch. 'Where did you say you found this?'

'In the chapel; it's a private one for the occupants of the house. The painting was hidden behind a wooden panel,' Rachel replied, 'we can show you later if you want.'

Mathilde was standing to one side, her arms wrapped

around her body as she watched Oliver scrutinising the picture. She noticed he was humming to himself under his breath and it made her smile. She was content to wait until he'd seen everything he needed to but Rachel was more impatient.

'So, what do you make of it? Is it as old as it looks?' she asked, 'and what's this coat of arms on the frame? Would that belong to whoever had originally owned the painting?'

'From first look, I'd guess it's possibly sixteenth century, or earlier, maybe fifteenth. If I can collect some shards of both the paint and frame to have them carbon dated then we'll know for sure. It's in the style of Hieronymus Bosch; all these little people in scenes remind me of his *Garden of Earthly Delights*. But although the style is similar, this is far cruder. Of course, it may be a facsimile. The testing will confirm either way, although, given how you found it, it seems unlikely.' He examined the crest on top of the frame. 'This crest has the crowned English lion rampant of the Tudor royal family, just here, can you see? Together with a crown on the top. It was treason to include that on a coat of arms unless it belonged to the monarch, or they decreed it. In fact, this appears to be the royal crest which might mean this once belonged to the sovereign. That may explain why it was boarded up, if it was stolen. You wouldn't be able to show it off if you valued your head staying on your shoulders.' He roared with laughter at his own joke but his amusement was infectious and both the women joined in.

'How about a coffee while we show you where we found it and then we can discuss what needs to happen next?' Rachel suggested. Oliver looked reluctant to leave the triptych but after taking several photos on his phone he was finally ready.

'If it's okay with you, I'll take some samples as we discussed? I can do some very basic cleaning of it here but obviously a full restoration can be done at a later date at the university art department or a gallery or museum if you prefer, once we know what we're dealing with. But it's very exciting; you may have unearthed a masterpiece.'

Taking their coffee with them they all walked over to the chapel. As it came into view Oliver whistled through his teeth in a low hiss.

'How amazing to have this on your property,' he said, 'made of local stone, so it's been here at least as long as the house and quite possibly longer. Has it been in use as a place of worship?'

'Not for several years,' Rachel admitted, 'I asked my aunt, who lived here as a child, but she said nobody has been in it recently. She wasn't very happy that we had either. She lives in the farmhouse on the estate now, if you want to ask her any questions.'

'How long has the house been in the family?'

'Goodness knows, but a long time. Our father said it was generations.'

Listening to the conversation, Mathilde felt a stab of sadness that she hadn't had the same opportunities as her sister to ask their father any questions. There were so many things she wanted to know and now she'd never get the chance.

Inside, the sunlight streamed in through the grubby windows, the caked-on dirt filtering the light into soft shafts catching the dust particles hanging in the air, disturbed by the draught they'd caused. Oliver wandered around the tiny room gazing around him, his eyes wide, before coming to a stop beside them in front of the wall where they'd discovered the painting.

'What a fabulous place,' he said, 'just imagine having this on your doorstep. It must have looked amazing when it was in use. And this is where you found it?' he pointed at the wall, 'did you say it was behind a panel?'

'Yes, this,' Mathilde showed him the piece of wood, still leant together with the smaller piece against a pew. 'There's a picture here of a locket and chain which we have in the house. This was also covered up,' she added, indicating the memorial stone on the wall. Oliver took a step closer to look at it.

'I wonder why they were both hidden,' he mused, 'I can't read this but I expect a colleague could take a look; it might give us a clue. There's definitely someone's name which you'd expect on a memorial plaque.'

'So, what's next?' Mathilde asked as they walked back out into the open.

'I'll take some fragments for testing as I suggested and then would you mind if I came back with some cleaning brushes to remove the worst of the grime so we can have a better look?' He was smiling at both of them and Mathilde, who at five foot ten inches was not used to having to look up at people, realised she needed to tilt her head back in order to see his face. She liked his open smile, his white, even teeth and the way his blue eyes crinkled at the sides.

'Yes, come back again,' she told him. As he drove away down the drive, she realised with a shock, she was still smiling.

Chapter Seventeen

July 1584

Tom had almost forgotten about Walsingham, his days busy with work, tending his plants and trying to catch the occasional glimpse of Isabel who sometimes walked in the gardens whilst he was outside in the physic garden. In fact, she often appeared to be there at the same time as him when the weather was fine. After her visit to the stillroom he frequently thought about the way she had smiled at him and his heart beat faster. He cherished the moments he saw her from a distance but his heart sank knowing that was all he'd ever have.

The low supplies of vanilla continued to worry Hugh and Tom. The Queen was requesting more and more custards and tarts to be flavoured with the sweetness she loved and the two men went out one morning to search the warehouses at both Wheatsheaf and Baynard Castle to try and buy more. The sooner they could grow their own, the better.

As the wherry, the small, two-person boat slowly made

its way up the Thames towards the city, Tom looked around him taking everything in. The river was full of boats, from small ones similar to the one they sat in to huge ships berthed as they waited for their turn to dock at Customs House and have their freight unloaded. On the far bank the village of Rotherhithe crouched amongst the marshy fields dotted with grazing sheep. Small, wood framed houses with spirals of smoke climbing into the sky huddled around a lone church. The murky, pewter grey water slapped against the side of the boat splashing up droplets making his knitted hose damp.

Only one merchant could provide some vanilla; having no idea what it was used for he hadn't been able to sell it on. Hugh and Tom were delighted to take the large bundle of pods from him. It would keep them going at the palace for a while and they explained to him that he could charge a handsome price if he brought more to the palace.

With their valuable prize tucked under Tom's jerkin, Hugh encouraged Tom to follow him with a wave of his hand; there was something he wanted to see. Happy to be away from work for a few hours, Tom did as he was bid and they hurried along the city streets. He realised that the crowd surrounding them were all heading in the same direction and it was starting to increase. Amongst all the jostling it was difficult to keep up with Hugh and Tom wondered where they were all going.

Eventually the throng stopped in front of a wide, open space surrounded by tall elm trees, their densely packed leaves dancing in the breeze as a fine rain draped over the waiting crowd like a morose blanket. Tom recognised they were at Tyburn and before him a wooden scaffold with gallows on top swayed slightly in the wind. He wriggled through the crowd until he was stood next to Hugh and nudging him with his elbows, he raised his eyebrows.

'There's going to be a hanging,' Hugh demonstrated a rope around his neck. Tom nodded, even he could work that out, but he wondered why there was such an enormous crowd gathered. He pointed to the people all around and pulled his questioning face again. *'He's a traitor,'* Hugh explained, *'It's Throckmorton.'* He repeated the word slowly. *'Remember I told you he was plotting to kill our Queen? Well now he is about to receive his punishment.'* Tom didn't understand most of what he'd just been told; it would have to wait until they were back at the palace with the wax tablet.

He stood with the rest of the onlookers, their faces alight with expectation and he could tell from their jeering faces just how much they were enjoying the spectacle as the prisoner was dragged up onto the scaffold. A priest was praying for his soul but Tom was certain that even if he'd been able to hear the man his words would have been lost in the noise from the crowd who were pushing and shoving as their enthusiasm swelled. Within minutes, the man was thrust up onto a tall step and the rope placed over his head. With a heavy boot the executioner kicked the stool away from underneath the prisoner, his body jerking and dancing as the rope tightened and squeezed the life from him. Tom's stomach heaved and although the others around him – men, women and even young children – continued to watch on enthralled, he looked down at the grass beneath his feet. The fragrant scent from the vanilla still inside his jerkin caught in his throat.

Pushing his way out of the mob around him he stood at the back where he could breathe more easily and waited for the nauseous feeling to subside. Slowly the people were beginning to drift away and after a couple of minutes he felt Hugh touch him on the arm and they began to make their way towards the river to find a wherry to take them back to work. For once Tom was pleased he couldn't talk, he didn't want to discuss what he'd just witnessed. Why people found watching another man killed entertaining, he had no idea.

Back in the stillroom, Hugh found the wax tablet and wrote out a brief explanation for Tom about why the hanging had been so important. How this man had been in collaboration with both the Spanish and the English Catholics to remove Queen Elizabeth from the throne and the Queen's spies had found evidence damning him. Tom began to realise the extent of the work Walsingham carried out and exactly why he shouldn't displease the spymaster. He was certain it wouldn't take much to make him angry and Tom didn't want to find himself swinging on the end of a rope. The sick feeling from earlier washed over him once more.

Chapter Eighteen

August 1584

Kneeling at the edge of a newly turned patch of earth Tom carefully plucked the top shoots of mint from the bush, the smell of rich, fertile promises making him nod to himself in appreciation. A movement to one side made him turn and he saw Lady Isabel bending and picking stalks of the abundant lavender which grew around the borders in both the physic and kitchen gardens. Noticing him watching she inclined her head and scrambling to his feet he bowed to her whilst rubbing his muddy hands against his jerkin. Expecting her to turn away and continue with what she was doing to his surprise she walked across smiling as if she'd come to the garden hoping to see him.

'*Good morrow, Tom Lutton,*' she spoke slowly, her eyes vibrant as if she was lit up from within. He bowed again and waited for her to continue. '*As you can see, I am selecting some lavender flowers to dry and use for pomanders, could you please assist me?*' He knew how cherished the silver or gold perforated case filled with sweet smelling flowers and spices was for disguising bad smells that often accumulated inside.

Nothing could please him more than accompanying her as they strolled around the gardens and he selected the finest scented blooms for her. He was convinced she'd sought him out and as their eyes caught and held for a moment, he hoped she felt the same attraction that he did. Albeit one that was doomed; the chasm of their positions in society a vast gulf between them.

He could have walked with her all day but as they strolled together she suddenly tapped him on the arm and pointed behind them. Turning around he spotted a small page boy who came to a halt in front of him. His inability to notice if someone walked slowly towards him from behind was a constant concern to him. If someone strode on dry, hard ground or indoor floorboards he could feel the vibrations beneath him but soft wet grass absorbed all indications and warnings. He looked down at the impish face of a young page, his dark hair a shining cap on his head. Tom smiled at him and after a moment's hesitation the boy gave a quick smile in return. He could just imagine what had been said to the page, given his worried face; probably that he was a monster. The child bowed to Isabel and then beckoned to Tom to follow. With a wry smile of apology Tom bowed his head to the woman he'd rather have stayed with and followed the page.

Inside the palace they walked through numerous corridors and then upstairs before reaching what appeared to be Walsingham's apartment. He gazed in admiration at the magnificence around him; the vaulted ceilings decorated with stencilled designs in pink and grey. When he entered the apartment, he discovered Walsingham sitting at a large desk and he indicated for Tom to sit in an adjacent chair. Tom lowered himself down slowly, running his palms along the smooth fabric. It was as soft as the mole pelts caught by the groundsmen outside. Walsingham tapped his knee to gain Tom's attention; he stopped looking around, tearing his gaze away and watching as the man explained why he had been summoned.

'*I have a job for you,*' he enunciated the words slowly and carefully as Tom nodded, wondering if he'd been practising as this was far easier than before. He couldn't help noticing how white the man's teeth looked compared to the darkness of his skin. He'd come across Moors occasionally during his travels on the continent but never one who held such a high office as this one. '*I need you to attend the banquet planned for this evening. You'll have to stand in the shadows behind the guests so you aren't noticed. Understand?*' Tom nodded slowly. He knew what Walsingham was saying but not what was expected of him. Frowning he swept the back of his hand down his body and raised his eyebrows in question. Walsingham looked at him quizzically and then nodded slowly.

'*You're right, you cannot be at court, even in the shadows, dressed like that. We'll disguise you as a servant and give you ale to serve. Then you'll merge in with the crowds trying to see the Queen.*' There was a pause while Tom tried to understand what he meant by 'disguise' but with some miming from Walsingham he eventually smiled weakly. He hoped he'd be able to keep the new clothing as his own were now quite worn and shabby.

'*I want you to watch,*' a piece of paper was handed to Tom

on which was written 'Earl of Leicester'. Tom nodded and the scrap was taken from him and flung into the fire, which despite the warmth outside was still burning in the grate. The paper caught and in a bright orange flash it had disappeared forever. *'I will be sitting next to him so I'll hear almost everything he says, unless he whispers in Her Majesty's ear, but I'll be able to assess how well you can hear people by watching what they say. Do you understand?'*

Tom had caught enough to get the gist of what was expected of him – this was a test of his abilities – and he nodded once as Walsingham waved him away, jumping to his feet and bowing before leaving the room. He would have liked to stay and explore the apartment and the paintings in greater detail; the huge images depicting illustrious mythical battles in heavy ornate frames bearing the royal crest embedded in the top of each one, but he knew a dismissal when he saw one.

The corridor beyond Walsingham's rooms was darker than the one he'd arrived through, the only light trickling in from a window halfway along. The walls were covered in a mix of wood panelling and tapestries which all contributed to the dark and foreboding atmosphere. He gave a shiver. He could feel the ghosts of those who had displeased the monarch – and her advisers – drifting past him in a cloud of melancholy regrets. Not having any desire to join their unhappy throng, he had no option but to do as he was bid.

Later that same day, as he began to detect the sharp scent of roasting meat drifting in from the kitchens, Tom knew dinner would soon be served upstairs and he needed to be mingling with the other servants. He managed to explain to Hugh that he was needed elsewhere and his friend just nodded and waved him away. Walsingham's men had already informed him Tom was now in their master's employ whenever his particular skill set was needed.

Before heading outside to sluice off the day's sweat and grime under the water pump Tom found a new uniform laid out on his bed, the rich red of the Queen's servants complete with a Tudor rose decoration. It was the smartest and most elaborate outfit he'd ever owned and certainly the most colourful. All his clothes were the practical and hard-wearing type, rough and brown. Racing outside with a piece of lye soap he scrubbed himself as best he could, washing his hair in the cold water which made him catch his breath as it poured from the pump and over his head.

Despite the fact that it was supposed to be worn loose, the uniform was a tiny bit on the tight side across his torso; hard work his whole life had resulted in a muscular physique and broad shoulders, whilst the average royal servant, unless they were a guard, wasn't as well built. If he didn't breathe in too deeply he should be fine. It took several attempts to wiggle his feet into the leather boots which pinched his toes but hopefully he'd find a good vantage point and stand in one place to avoid walking. Smoothing his hands across his hair to keep it as flat and tidy as possible he walked across to the banqueting hall. Grabbing a jug of ale from the many lined up on a trestle table he followed the other servants inside.

For several minutes, Tom completely forgot why he was in this strange environment as he stared around in amazement. If he'd been impressed with Walsingham's apartment it was nothing compared to the grandeur of where he now found himself. The room was ablaze with light from hundreds of candles throwing shadows dancing up the walls and reaching into the rafters as if trying to escape. The bodies packed in all around him of those hoping to see the Queen or gain the attention of those close to her meant the atmosphere was stifling. The heat from other people together with the huge fire blazing in a fireplace that looked as large as Tom's bedroom was oppressive. He was thankful he couldn't hear any of the babble of noise as he watched people's mouths moving constantly; the overload on his senses would have been too much. As it was, the smell of the food, the over-whelming scent of rancid body odour and the heat was almost enough for him to push his way through the throng and back down to the darker and cooler confines of the stillroom.

He had a job to do though and needed to get on with it. He'd worked out that saying 'no' to Walsingham would be the same as saying it to the Queen herself and he'd seen what the punishment for that would be. Holding on to the jug of ale he began to weave his way through the crowds until he got to the front. The tables groaned with the food laid out: glistening, fatty carcasses of geese, a shield of brawn and small song birds heaped up together with dishes piled with vegetables shining with thick pungent sauces. All around the tables people sat eating, stabbing knives into thick slices of meat, juices dripping onto their clothes. From his vantage point he could see the Queen and her entourage at a long table placed on a platform. In front of her sat a decorated swan, its feathers and head reattached to the tight, burnished roasted skin. Surrounding it were dishes of fruit, jellies, pies and custards. He'd never seen so much food and his stomach rolled as he sniffed the fragrances wafting from the tables, tormenting him.

Thankfully where he'd positioned himself was exactly the right place to watch the important dignitaries sat with Her Majesty. He recognised Walsingham and Leicester and as he cast his eyes along the row his face broke into an involuntary smile as he spotted Isabel. She hadn't seen him – of course, why would she? She wasn't expecting him to be in the banqueting hall. Carrying the jug of ale which he'd twice slopped onto his boots he gazed at her and for a moment forgot the task in hand.

She was dressed in pale blue damask, her stiff white ruff around her throat, her elegant white neck rising from it. He could see the stomacher narrow into her waist, the full sleeves decorated with tiny seed pearls and threaded with ribbons of deep green matching her French hood. She was chatting with another lady sitting beside her and he saw her throw her head back and laugh. As she closed her eyes in merriment he felt a lurch in his chest. He'd barely met her and yet he'd never felt like this about anyone. What he wouldn't give to hold her in his arms and experience that laughter rippling through him.

Tearing his eyes away he turned to where the Earl of Leicester was sitting. At present he was eating, tearing meat off a bone with large, strong teeth. He looked like an animal and Tom wondered why the Queen was so enamoured of him. Hugh had explained there were rumours flying around court that one day the Queen would marry Leicester. Tom frowned as the earl wiped his mouth with a cloth; he had no chance of lip reading if people covered their mouths. But then Leicester dropped the napkin on the table and turned to the Queen.

'*I hear we have excellent entertainment this evening, Your Majesty,*' he said, '*a group of travelling mummers has arrived, word tells they have a very funny play which you won't want to miss.*'

'*No indeed, I shall look forward to that. Have you tried this cake?*'

Tom tapped his foot in frustration. This was hardly riveting stuff to report to Walsingham. Although this was only a test to ensure he could accurately translate what was being said he could still have made this up and laid in his bed all night. Just then Walsingham himself leant his head close to Leicester, turning away a little but not far enough so that his face was obscured.

'*Word comes that Paget has been seen in Rheims,*' he said.

'*I have heard this,*' Leicester nodded, '*but do we know who he is meeting there?*'

'*Not yet,*' Walsingham replied, '*I expect to know shortly, however. My spies are watching him.*' With this Walsingham got to his feet and bowing towards the throne he stepped away from the table. Tom saw his eyes scan the outskirts of the room and guessed it was possibly himself who was being sought out and he stood perfectly still not moving a muscle. Nevertheless he felt the Moor's dark eyes lock onto his, the burning sensation of recognition. Walsingham gave the merest twitch of his head in acknowledgement and he was gone. Tom put down the jug he was holding on a side table behind him ready to return to his room and divest himself of the tight tunic and uncomfortable boots. He wasn't sure of all of the words used but he was confident he could write them down in a way Walsingham would understand. His eyes alighted one last time on Isabel. As if she was aware of him her gaze caught his and for a moment there was nobody else in the room; he could feel the blood roaring through his veins. One of her eyebrows quirked just a little and he tried but failed to stop a shy smile edge across his face hoping Walsingham was no longer watching him. Her exquisiteness outshone the brilliance of the candles in the room and he wondered why the Queen would choose to have a lady within her close retinue who far eclipsed her own beauty.

The summons he was expecting came from Walsingham the following morning and now back in his work clothes Tom followed the secretary who'd been sent to take him upstairs to the same room as before. Once they were on their own Walsingham beckoned him forwards and asked, *'well?'*

Tom mimed Leicester and the Queen and their discussion about the evening's entertainment and then pointing at Walsingham he mimed and used hand signals to explain what he understood had been said. He had to write down *'Rhiems'* and *'Paget'* and he knew the spelling of the words could be wrong but his translation pleased Walsingham who smiled and nodded in agreement. Tom had repeated almost exactly what had been said but with no hearing or speech he'd never be suspected of passing on information.

'You, my friend,' Walsingham mouthed, *'will make the perfect spy. An intelligencer. The Scots and the Spanish will be thwarted in every plot they have for we have a silent apothecary working for us.'* He smiled broadly, his mouth wide but Tom caught a gleam of malevolence in his eyes. The situation he was now in made his skin crawl, icy splinters growing along his skin.

Chapter Nineteen

June 2021

The sun was already warm despite the early hour as Mathilde left the house, the familiar weight of her camera slung around her neck: a comfort. She didn't have any plans as to where she wanted to walk but she'd had enough of other humans, both dead and alive, and the confusing vibrations they all created. The air shivered with them, prickling against the hairs on her skin.

Walking to the end of the drive she spotted a footpath sign on the opposite side of the road and remembered Rachel saying it led to the village a mile down the road. Climbing over the stile she began to walk.

After little rain for several weeks the ground was dry and dusty. She was beside the marshy area she'd seen from the house, tall reeds brushing against her arm. Somewhere beyond them was a river which fed these marshes but Mathilde knew better than to try walking through them to look for it. Although the footpath was dry it wouldn't be underfoot if she ventured off it and she hadn't needed a warning from Rachel to know that the mud, with its sulphurous stench, could suck you down to your death. Nobody could live in the wilds as she had with her mother for all those years without having a great deal of respect for the quirks of nature; it was always one step away from killing you. If it wasn't marshy ground, then it could be poisonous plants and berries or violent weather; she'd seen cattle struck by lightning and it wasn't a pretty sight. Mother nature could be your friend or a powerful enemy and it was best to always keep a watchful eye.

Kneeling down she aimed her camera lens through the reeds, taking a couple of photographs of the tall sturdy stems leading into the distance before continuing her walk. The path led from the marshes into a small wood where she met an old couple out walking their West Highland Terrier. The dog came running across barking and wagging its tail at the same time and Mathilde bent down to make a fuss of it until the owners called it back. They waved a hand in salutation to her and although surprised Mathilde responded in kind. She wasn't used to people being friendly and she'd heard that English people were the least welcoming of all. She continued on, her step a little lighter. Cooler in the shade the sunlight filtered through leaves to dance on the ground like fireflies and Mathilde looked for plants useful in her herbal medicines. Snatching the tops off some mallow covered in delicate purple flowers, she pushed them into her jacket pocket.

The village green was almost empty apart from a young woman with a pushchair beside the pond. The woman appeared to be passing bread to the child to throw to the ducks which were squawking furiously, flapping their wings in anticipation. She then snatched the bread back with a prolonged 'noooo, not you, it's for the ducks!' before throwing it into the pond herself. This happened several times as Mathilde watched them but still the mother persevered with encouraging the child to feed the birds.

Crossing over she headed towards the village church. Small and squat and made from the same pale stone as the chapel at Lutton Hall, it had a short, round Norman tower and was set back slightly from the houses. She took a couple of photos looking through the lychgate towards the heavy wooden door. Would there be any clues as to the owners of the hall here in the graveyard? It may help if Oliver or one of his colleagues could decipher the name on the plaque in the chapel. But what did it matter to her? She'd be gone in a couple of months.

Wandering around the churchyard she snapped a few more pictures; ancient headstones furred by grey-green lichen tilted at precarious angles as the passing of time slowly eroded the ground beneath them. Tall grass that had long since been tended to, no ancestors left to care about them. Gone *and* forgotten. A blackbird disturbed by her movements flew up into an overhanging beech tree, pinking loudly in alarm. She didn't know what she was looking for but the calm and peace of the dead made her shoulders slowly lower a few degrees from their usual stiff, hunched position. There was no judgement from anyone here.

She eventually arrived at the more recent burial plots, their granite headstones still shiny, many with vases lovingly filled with flowers. These weren't as interesting as the lives lived centuries ago and she just glanced at the names as she wandered past until something caught her eye and she stopped to look again. A newer plot had a simple wooden cross carved along the horizontal patibulum: 'Peter Lutton. 14 March 1949 – 8 February 2021. A loving father and grandfather, sadly missed'. Her father. It was her father's grave. Stupidly she hadn't even imagined she may find him here and she hadn't thought to ask Rachel where he was buried. Well, now she knew. Kneeling down on the grass she stared at it. She had nothing to say and yet she had everything to say. So much so that she didn't know where to begin. Wrenching small tufts of grass out from around the edge of the mound, Mathilde let them drop to the ground to dry out and crumble like the body beneath.

Before she could even open her mouth, her thoughts were interrupted.

'I don't know what you think you're doing but you can leave him alone.' Standing the other side of the churchyard wall as if she had appeared from nowhere was Aunt Alice. How long had she been watching her? 'Isn't it enough you've turned up to take everything that isn't rightfully yours without laying claim to my brother's resting place as well? We've taken legal advice and you won't win you know; I shall make sure the estate comes to me, the family who were here for him.'

'It's my father's grave,' Mathilde retorted, 'and I have every right to be here and to visit him. I'll come and talk to him whenever I want to.'

'Rachel told me you were only staying a week so I'd say that you've outstayed your welcome now and you should be on your way before anyone else is upset.' Alice's face was slowly turning a pale puce colour.

'I haven't noticed that anybody other than you is upset by my arrival. And my plans have changed, I'm staying until September. I have things I need to organise while I'm here.' Mathilde's dark eyes met with Alice's almost identical ones and held them.

There was a pause as Alice's mouth moved, as if reciting an incantation, and then gripping her handbag with both hands in front of her she turned and hurried away across the green, her short body encased in a flowered cotton dress wobbling slightly from side to side as she moved. Mathilde sat back on her heels and watched her.

Getting to her feet she walked slowly back to the lychgate, disturbed by the altercation. By this point, Alice was the other side of the village green, disappearing into the distance. Mathilde stalked across the green and down the road back towards the hall. In her pocket her fingers jangled the keys to her van, every fibre in her body pulsating with the urge to drive away and never come back. With her other hand she snatched angrily at the tops of the willowherb growing at the side of the road. The animosity from her aunt made her feel sick. All these years, her whole life she'd been desperate for family, somewhere to call home, stability and love, and now her own blood relative was turning against her as everyone else had ever done. *Plus ça change.*

113

Chapter Twenty

September 1584

As Tom approached Walsingham's apartment he could see something was different. Usually the corridor was empty save for an occasional courtier or servant scuttling past. There were so many dark and shadowy corners where people could be arranging clandestine meetings, exchanging private information before slipping away. Plotting and treason. He hadn't even begun any assignments and yet he was already beginning to think like a spy.

As he approached the pair of guards stood sentry outside the door crossed their staffs in front of him and prevented him from entering. Tom wished he could dress like a courtier and not always look like the servant he was.

One of the guards lifted his hand and rapped on the door with the back of his knuckles. It was opened from the inside and Tom could see yet more guards. After a moment, his passage was no longer barred and he was allowed to enter. Immediately he understood the reason for the extra security as he dropped to one knee in front of the Queen who was sitting on the chair beside the fire where he himself had previously perched when instructed to wait. Her enormous gown, white velvet embellished with hundreds of tiny blue jewels, was spread out so far he wondered how the heat of the fire didn't cause it to melt or combust.

With a frown Walsingham waved him back to the corner of the room as he continued his conversation with the Queen. Tom, from where he was now standing partially hidden behind the guards, was in the perfect place to watch them as they talked. Or rather, as the Queen talked whilst Walsingham with his grave countenance nodded in agreement.

'This situation is becoming intolerable,' she said, her features drawn into an unattractive scowl, her thin lips almost invisible, 'from what your spies are telling us the Spanish are increasing their campaign to put Queen Mary with her heretic Catholic faith on the throne and return England to the arms of Rome. We have to stop them. Even now you tell me they are yet again plotting a Spanish invasion and to have me killed.' There was a pause as she appeared to be listening to Walsingham speaking. 'I just cannot have her executed,' the Queen remonstrated, 'remember she is my cousin – that is why I have held her captive for these past sixteen years. Otherwise we would be fighting both the Spanish and the French, the Catholics so committed to seize our fair country. You need to find these plotters with all speed.'

As she uttered her final words she rose to her feet and everyone in the room sank to the floor. Tom felt the draught from the heavy door as it opened and saw the edge of her dress, the hem richly embroidered with blue and red flowers, sweep around in an arc, and disappear from view. The floor vibrated with the boots of her guards as they marched out behind her. Tom remained where he was until he felt someone tap him on the shoulder and looked up into the face of Walsingham who was wearing a wry – and very rare – smile.

'As you have no doubt realised Her Majesty grows increasingly concerned about the enemies amassing at her gates.' Tom wasn't sure he'd understood everything that had just been said but he was fairly certain he'd got a good idea and this was confirmed as Walsingham continued. *'The only way to truly keep the Crown secure is to eliminate the threat of Mary Queen of Scots and have her killed. But Her Majesty will not countenance it. So, until Burghley and I can persuade her, we will have to carry on battling and exposing the plots that put her in peril.'*

Walsingham quickly explained with a combination of speaking and the occasional word written on a piece of parchment that he wanted Tom to follow a man suspected of being involved in one such plot and to report back on who he met up with and what was said. The recording of what was said was easy enough, so long as his subject didn't realise he was being watched, but the trouble was Tom had no idea who anyone was. He could only explain in terms of physical appearance but his new boss seemed content with that, telling him to be outside the gatehouse at seven o'clock that evening; he'd be taken to a tavern where they anticipated their target to be drinking. Tom nodded, it all seemed simple enough.

Before leaving Walsingham stared into Tom's eyes. *'Do not make any mistakes,'* Walsingham mouthed slowly, *'or it will be the last thing you do.'* Tom wasn't sure if he meant as a spy, as an employee of the court, or before he was disposed of in the river. He suspected, from the dark look on Walsingham's face, he meant the latter. He was passed a small pouch with some coins in for beer and dismissed.

Hurrying towards the door through which he'd emerged from the back stairs into the state apartments, he spotted a small group of ladies coming towards him. They were chatting amongst themselves and didn't appear to have noticed him in the shadows. He knew that he couldn't reach the door he wanted before their paths crossed and instead stood with his back against the wall so that they could pass by him.

As they drew closer, he realised one of the three was the lady Isabel and his mouth involuntarily quirked into a smile before he quickly bowed low until they passed. She'd obviously abandoned her foraging for flower buds. He saw the fluid movement of their skirts brushing against the herringbone design of the wooden floor before standing up again and casting a quick glance at them. Even seeing the back of her head with its glossy dark hair made him happy. Then, as if he had willed it, she turned her head just enough for him to see her beautiful smile, her pink lips directed towards him. Her eyes were downcast as if she were listening intently to her companion but he knew it was directed to him and his body flushed with pleasure. There was no chance of anything more between them than an occasional meeting; she was one of the Queen of England's confidantes and he was merely the assistant to her apothecary, hidden away in a dark and dusty stillroom on the other side of the palace. Any association between them could not be countenanced whatsoever. There was a distance between them as wide as the sea he'd travelled over but even these glimpses of an occasional smile lit up his whole life.

That evening, dressed in his normal attire so as to blend in with the other drinkers, Tom was met at the gatehouse by a man dressed in a similar way to himself although Tom, who noticed every nuance of people's movements and characteristics, could immediately see he was a gentleman dressed as a commoner. His deportment, his clean fingernails and soft white hands all gave him away. No wonder Walsingham needed someone who could genuinely blend in with other servants and the lower classes.

They travelled by wherry upriver to put ashore at Blackfriars. There was a heavy drizzle in the air as the clouds slumped low to graze the white tops of the choppy water. The lamp beside the boatman rocked from side to side and Tom clutched on to the side of the boat, its wooden hull rough against his fingers. He was sure he'd never get used to the frequent boat journeys Londoners took in their stride. After alighting he walked up the dark narrow lanes, careful not to lose his footing on the slippery flint cobbles. Behind several windows came the faint flicker of candlelight. They arrived at The Magpie public house and entered, swallowed into the hot, crowded interior. The floor was covered in a thick compacted layer of rushes, the innkeeper obviously just throwing fresh onto the layer below until it was as solid and rigid as the boards beneath. Tom could almost see it moving with the tiny creatures inhabiting the space beneath his feet, living off the ale which slopped through. The stale, rancid smell which permeated upwards mixed with the sweaty bodies, yeasty beer and pipe smoke. Tom kept his eyes on his accomplice until he felt a nudge in his ribs and with the merest twitch of his head he indicated a rotund young man with thick unruly dark hair and beard, wearing a black velvet cap. So, this was the man called William Parry.

Walsingham hadn't given Tom a lot of details; he suspected

the spymaster was getting frustrated with the extra effort required to communicate with him. All he knew was that he needed to watch his quarry and report back as to who he met with, and more importantly, what was said. For a man so finely dressed, Tom was surprised to see Parry in a tavern as rough as this one. He realised the gentleman who'd guided him to The Magpie had gone, slipping away silently without even disturbing the air around him: like witchcraft. Tom knew he too would need to be able to perform the same disappearing act if anyone became suspicious of him.

After buying a jug of ale he stood close to the fire, a good vantage point from where he could watch his prey. A foul smelling drinker who'd already imbibed more beer than was good for him jostled against his arm, causing his own drink to almost slop out of his cup. But without having the ability to remonstrate Tom stepped further back into the hollow shadows at the edges of the room where it was emptier and he could still watch.

Parry was making merry with a whole host of people at his table but then slowly each person drifted away. Tom could read his lips well enough to gauge that he was merely greeting everyone as a man with a belly full of beer after a long day. Despite having a beaker in his hand, it barely moved to his mouth. He may be behaving as though he were the worse for wear but in fact it was a pretence and he was as sober as Tom was and by the way his eyes continuously flickered towards the door from the street, it seemed as though he was waiting for someone. Tom realised that reading people's lips wasn't enough in this game. He also needed to be reading people's body language and the surrounding scene. A quick check around the room confirmed to him that he, at least, wasn't being watched by anyone. He was invisible.

The door to the street swung open again admitting two men, their hair sparkling with rain as they brushed off their coats, spraying water over the people standing close by. One of them was tall with flaxen hair, smooth against his head from where he'd been wearing a close-fitting cap he'd removed to shake off the droplets. His wild beard had streaks of auburn in it and down one side of his face a jagged scar ran from his nose up into his hairline. His accomplice was much shorter and looked young, his face almost completely smooth of lines, his beard patchy and short. From his position Tom scrutinised the other men's mouths opening and closing, recognising some of the swear words spilling out. He smiled to himself. These two new drinkers were the people Parry – and therefore he – had been waiting for, he was certain. Although they were dressed in rough working men's clothing and wouldn't stand out to anyone else, Tom could see they were simply costumes. They weren't comfortable in the coarse hemp and one of the men kept running his finger around the collar of his shirt, probably unused to something that wasn't the finest cambric. Or perhaps he was doing it out of nerves. Or both.

They stood beside the fire for a few minutes not acknowsledging Parry, even though they were adjacent to him. Tom was beginning to wonder if he was wrong in his supposition but then he saw one of the men say 'let's go out to the yard, it may be quieter out there.' From the way his lips hardly moved Tom could tell he was trying not to alert anyone who might be listening in but he couldn't fool a deaf man who'd spent his life reading other people's lips, faces and body language.

The two newcomers slipped round past Parry and out through a back door Tom hadn't noticed, berating himself for not having paid more attention to his surroundings. Within seconds his prey followed and Tom quickly wove his way between his fellow drinkers holding his ale steady to ensure he didn't spill it on anyone as he moved carefully towards the door. He wanted to see where they were going and what was being said but he needed to ensure he wasn't noticed himself.

As another drinker pushed past him and out through the door Tom took the opportunity to slip out behind him as if they were together. Outside the yard was dark and the rain had intensified. The man he'd followed out immediately stood up against the pub wall and began to urinate and Tom stepped sharply to the left to avoid being splashed. He wrinkled up his nose; sometimes his heightened sense of smell did him no favours. Pretending to follow suit he looked around the yard for the men hoping they too wouldn't be relieving themselves. In the bright moonlight he watched as one of them passed Parry a small package which he slipped into a pocket inside his cloak. It was too murky for Tom to watch their lips and catch what they were saying and after a minute Parry disappeared back into the alehouse, his two accomplices disappearing out of the back gate into a passageway leading away down behind the buildings.

Tom stepped around the widening pool at the other man's feet and stole back inside. Parry was already leaving and by the time Tom squeezed his way between a heaving group of heavy-set revellers and out of the door his quarry had gone. The empty street gleamed with the rain that continued to bounce off its surface, dripping from the upper floors protruding out above his head. Hunching his shoulders up and pulling his cap down to cover his ears Tom headed back towards the river hoping he could find a boatman willing to set out on this gloomy night and take him back upriver. This was not the life he'd imagined when he'd set off for London but there was no way of evading it. He was caught up in Walsingham's web and leaving the palace would mean never again catching sight of the most beautiful woman he'd ever seen. He wasn't yet prepared to forsake that pleasure.

Chapter Twenty-One

June 2021

When she returned to the hall Mathilde found Rachel and Fleur cooking pancakes, the kitchen filled with a haze of blue smoke from the frying pan.

'I wondered where you were,' Rachel said brightly, 'I assumed you went for a walk as your van was still here. Pancakes?'

'No,' Mathilde shook her head, 'thank you,' she added as an afterthought. She opened a cupboard and took out the coffee making equipment without another word.

'Are you okay?' Rachel flipped another pancake onto Fleur's plate and passed her the chocolate spread and a knife before walking over to Mathilde and placing a hand on her arm to stop her for a moment. 'I can tell there's something wrong,' she added.

With a sigh, Mathilde briefly explained as best she could what had happened at the church. 'I didn't know our father was there,' she said, 'it was a surprise. And I wasn't doing any harm.'

'Of course you weren't,' Rachel exclaimed, 'and you have as much right to be there paying your respects as she does. I expect it was just a shock seeing you there; she's still getting her head around you turning up. I don't know what's come over her, I really don't. She's always been feisty but never as hostile as this. Give her time though and hopefully she'll calm down.'

She was distracted by Fleur's attempts to apply the chocolate spread to her pancake, ending up with it all over herself and the table. Mathilde was about to take her coffee back upstairs when Rachel stopped her.

'Oh, I almost forgot,' she said, 'Oliver called me to say he'll be over mid-morning, he's got some results about the date of the triptych and he wants to get it cleaned up a bit so he can take a closer look. I said that's okay with us.'

'Yes, of course,' Mathilde agreed before carrying on through the house and upstairs, a ghost of a smile playing at the corners of her mouth. Her day may have started badly but at least it was improving.

She was out in the garden with her camera when Oliver arrived. Watching the world from down the end of a lens felt safer that morning, one step removed from reality. She'd been checking her plants and was pleased to see fresh shoots appearing on them. They seemed to be happy in the warm English summer. There were even new buds on the vanilla plants but she needed to keep an eye on those, ready for the moment she'd be required to intervene in the germination process.

A movement to her right attracted her attention and she spotted Fleur in the opposite corner of the garden, her blond hair just visible above the weeds, like a new shoot herself, starting life and blooming amongst the foliage. Out of everyone she'd met since arriving in England Fleur was the person she empathised with the most. It was nice that others were friendly, welcoming – or not, in the case of Aunt Alice – but Fleur, she suspected, was most like her. Not prepared to give any of herself freely until she was completely certain it was safe to do so. Her face was guarded, shut down, a façade Mathilde recognised and understood.

Walking over to the little girl, deliberately making a lot of noise by crashing through the undergrowth so as not to startle her, she arrived where Fleur was now bent over watching something on the ground, looking up as Mathilde approached before returning her gaze to the path.

'Caterpillar,' she announced as Mathilde arrived behind her, pointing to a hairy caterpillar making its way slowly across the old brown bricks.

'He probably wants to eat all these plants,' Mathilde waved her hand over the beds which in places still bore the occasional hardy vegetable amongst the nettles.

Fleur nodded. 'Grandad grew these,' she informed her aunt, 'he liked plants.'

'Here?' she asked, 'he grew these? They're vegetables,' she explained, 'for dinner,' she added, unsure of whether her accent would prevent the child from understanding. Mathilde was happy to think of her father out here and it made her warm to the little girl even more. Fleur nodded again, keeping her eyes firmly on the caterpillar. Slowly lifting her camera to her face, Mathilde gently depressed the shutter and took several shots of Fleur's face deep in concentration. The background of feathery overgrown asparagus plants, their leaves a sharp green foil to the crown of yellow hair framing her small, solemn face. *What must it be like to have so few cares in the world?* Mathilde wondered. She couldn't remember a time when she wasn't always looking over her shoulder, waiting for the next indication of danger to appear brazenly on the horizon.

'Mathilde, Oliver is here,' her thoughts were interrupted by Rachel calling from the back door behind them and she followed Fleur who skipped back to tell her mother about the caterpillar.

Their guest was already in the drawing room with the triptych and Rachel carried through cups of coffee and a packet of Jaffa Cakes. He got to his feet as they entered and gave Mathilde a warm smile that made her stomach flip in a way completely alien to her. She couldn't help a shy grin as she turned away, sitting down in an armchair and deliberately avoiding the seat next to him on the sofa. Thankfully Oliver didn't seem to notice her reticence and immediately began to explain his findings.

'I have an excellent update,' he announced, 'as I suspected the triptych itself is mid to late sixteenth century. The paint has been analysed but it's thrown up some anomalies because some of it has a different chemical compound to other samples, indicating it was made in different places. Possibly different countries. I showed the photos I took to some colleagues who specialise in ecclesiastical art from the Middle Ages but they didn't immediately recognise the style. It's similar to Bosch and yet more naïve; it's possibly a copy or facsimile. However, the exciting thing is this.' He stood up and pointed to the crest at the top centre of the frame. 'This crest doesn't belong to your ancestors or whoever painted this because it's the coat of arms of the monarch. Or, to be more precise, Queen Elizabeth I. Isn't that incredible?'

'Wait, what? Are you saying this belonged to her? Was it stolen and brought here?' Rachel held up her hand to stop him talking for a moment, her mouth open in surprise.

'Who knows? If it is and it could be proven it would be reclaimed by the government for sure. But they would have to establish that, otherwise it's yours. It adds to the provenance of the period though. If it's okay with you I'll give it a rudimentary clean and then we can see what we've got here more easily. I've still got some feelers out with experts across the world, so we may yet get more answers.' He looked to the two women for agreement.

'Yes, of course,' Rachel answered, 'what about the plaque that was also hidden, have you got any answers about that?'

'Not yet but maybe we can take a closer look another day?'

'Good idea. So, what do you need for your cleaning?' Rachel got to her feet as if to start collecting items but Oliver held up his hand to stop her.

'I have everything I need,' he explained, indicating the canvas bag at his feet, 'but it's quite dark in here. Do any of the other rooms have better daylight? Could we move it? And if you have some old towels that would be helpful. I don't want to spoil anything, although I'll be very gentle so unlikely to do any harm.' Again, there was that smile making Mathilde feel a warmth creep down inside her. After the disastrous start to her day, her tiny break-through with Fleur followed by Oliver's open friendship had gone some way to mend her mood.

'Of course.' Rachel nodded. 'Let's put it on the table in

the dining room.' She and Oliver lifted it and began to carry it through, while Mathilde went on ahead opening doors.

As Rachel took Fleur through to start making lunch Mathilde settled back down in her chair, crossing her long legs and tucking her feet underneath to watch what was about to be revealed by the cleaning process. Pulling her phone out of her pocket she typed 'Queen Elizabeth I' into Wikipedia and started to read about this queen who'd possibly had a connection to her new home. She felt a ripple spin through the air in the room and turning around she looked for an open window but there was none. Something had disturbed the atmosphere and she rubbed her arms briskly as a chill crept along them.

The triptych was now propped up on the dining table which was still covered by a dust sheet. Rachel had insisted on a proper cover, explaining the walnut veneered table was an antique, and she'd protected it further with a thick wadding of felt on which Oliver assembled an easel.

'This is only preliminary cleaning,' he explained, 'it can have a professional restoration at a later date; either an auction house or a museum can organise that. And in the meantime please don't touch any of it. The oils and sweat from your fingertips could do untold damage. Where it's been hidden for so long it's helped preserve the pigments in the paints but this will soon start to degrade. It's also better if you keep the curtains closed in here when I'm not working so the sun doesn't do any harm either.'

From time to time Mathilde darted glances towards Oliver as he worked, the pair of them in silence. She noticed how he caught his tongue between his teeth as he concentrated and it made her smile, such a simple quirk and yet it made him more human. As if he could tell she was observing him he suddenly looked up and their eyes met. Her heart thumped hard in her chest.

'Come and watch,' he suggested, his eyes creasing at the edges as he smiled. They were the clearest blue colour she'd ever seen, the sort that appeared in children's picture book illustrations but were never found in real life.

'Are you sure I won't disturb you?' She was embarrassed he'd caught her watching and although she wanted to run from the room she was too interested in what he was doing.

'No of course not. But stand well behind me so that if you make any movements it won't cause a draught. I don't want any of the debris I am trying to remove getting blown back across a section I've already cleaned.'

Getting to her feet she skirted around the edge of the room, sliding between the pieces of furniture still hidden by dust sheets until she was leant against a window jamb. She watched over his broad shoulder as he delicately swept the surface with a fine brush until eventually he stood up and beckoned her over.

'I've made a good start,' he pointed to the left-hand panel which was now considerably lighter than the other two, 'but it needs proper restoration to show the colours in their true intensity. All these scenes are connected, I think, as if it is one person's journey.'

Mathilde moved closer so she could see, conscious of the heat from Oliver's body beside her and the musky scent he gave off mixed with a warm spicy aftershave.

'So have you lived here your whole life?' Oliver spoke as he continued to work, stooping over the triptych. 'It really is the most incredible house.'

129

'*Non,* no.' She explained briefly about what had happened over the past few weeks, the letter that had led her to the house and the discovery her father hadn't died in Beirut as her mother had been told. That he'd spent years looking for them, if only they'd known.

'Wow, that's a lot to take in. Your head must be all over the place.' He turned slightly to look at her so their eyes met. She smiled and nodded.

'A whole new family, and the knowledge that right here was my proper childhood, the one I didn't get the chance to live.'

'So what will you do, are you going to live here now?' Oliver had turned back to his cleaning as he talked.

'No, although Rachel really wants me to . . . but no, I need to keep on the move. I'm just staying for the summer.' She paused for a moment before continuing, trying to both change the subject and distract herself from the attraction she was feeling standing so close to him. 'So, what else can you tell me about the painting? Have you any idea who the artist was or how it got here?' All around her the air quivered and she wondered if he could feel it too.

'Not yet and to be honest we may never do so. But once it's properly clean, hopefully we'll know more. I need to do some more research, see if any of my colleagues in universities on the continent have seen anything similar. Now, let me cover it up then I can give you a hand to close the curtains again and I must be on my way.' Mathilde felt a stab of disappointment that he was leaving before reminding herself he was only there because of the triptych.

The curtains proved to be difficult to close and they were both soon laughing at their own efforts. As the final pair came together and the room was plunged into a semi darkness, Mathilde almost tripped in her efforts, stopped from falling forwards by Oliver's hands on her arms as he helped her upright. She could feel the heat of them burning through to her skin, his chest only inches from hers. She looked up at him in the half light, for a moment his pale eyes holding hers before he let go and laughed a little, brushing his hands against his trousers.

'It's a good thing you don't have to open and close these every day,' his voice sounded thick as he quickly stepped back. There had been a flash of magnetism and she was certain he'd felt it too.

Long after she'd closed the front door and the sound of his car had disappeared, the heat in her body continued to curl its way further down inside.

Chapter Twenty-Two

September 1584

Tom wasn't surprised to receive a summons from Walsingham the morning following his visit to The Magpie. A page arrived with a note telling him to go not to the usual apartment but to the Walsingham family home on Seething Lane. Clutching a map drawn for him by one of the secretaries, he set off. He also carried a full purse of coins to try and purchase some vanilla at the merchant warehouses at Queenshithe quay. They'd almost run out again and although he'd nurtured the plants he'd brought with him he had not been able to encourage any flowers to grow. He had no idea how or when the plant would produce blooms but he was certain that unless it happened, there was no chance of cultivating the black pods filled with seeds which produced the sweet creamy flavour now loved by the courtiers and of course, Her Majesty. Whatever the Queen wanted, she got. It hadn't taken him long to realise that.

The weather hadn't improved overnight and Tom tried

to skirt along close to the buildings to shelter under the overhanging upper floors but after narrowly avoiding a bucket of slops left out for the night-soil man to collect, he moved out into the street. This was not without its dangers and he was knocked sideways as a water carrier's horse, spooked at a noise he hadn't heard, danced across the cobbles and barrelled into him, almost sending him flying and soaking him in the process. People around him looked askance and he realised they'd probably been shouting at him to get out of the way. It wasn't the first time his lack of hearing had resulted in an injury; he still had a deep scar under his hair where a raft of roof tiles had cascaded down upon him. Often, he could tell in advance something was about to happen because of the reactions of people around but not if they were behind him. Rubbing his shoulder, he looked down at his map and walked past St Olave's Church, cutting through the churchyard. He paused for a moment to take a drink from the lead conduit on the church wall, from which locals could collect their water, and then proceeded on to the leafy wide Seething Lane. Opposite him stood Knollys Inn, here there were less people and the houses were considerably larger, their huge oak frames infilled with majestic red bricks instead of the pale wattle and daub panels of the small and cramped together city houses. As with every city there was a huge gap between the rich and the poor.

It didn't take long to find Walsingham's stately looking manor house; exactly what Tom expected from a man who had the ear of the Crown.

The rooms were airy and despite the small windows still appeared reasonably light. The boards beneath his feet were covered in rush mats, the walls hung with thick, luxurious tapestries and colourful paintings of what appeared to be heroes from Greek myths. He followed the steward into a room dominated by a huge, ornately carved wooden desk. Two walls were covered in shelving mostly stacked with documents and bound files, with an occasional book bound by thick ribbed leather laid on its side as if placed there momentarily and never returned to; by someone busy with fingers in numerous pies. A man who devoted his life to protecting his Queen.

'*Well?*' Walsingham was sitting in a big wooden chair behind the desk. Tom noticed there was nowhere for him to sit down. He'd written down everything he'd seen and he handed it over. He'd wanted to give a full account of what he'd seen but the previous evening sitting beside a paltry fire in the stillroom with a stinking tallow candle and his still damp clothes freezing into ice prickling against his skin had made him desperate to write it all as quickly as possible. Over the years his writing had become similar to his sign language where one word could communicate a whole sentence; it was far more condensed than talking. He'd remembered to get up early and simplify it where necessary into a document that could be understood by anyone, before he arrived before his new master.

'*You have done well,*' Walsingham said slowly, '*this way of writing is very interesting and I am pleased with your work. I will have more jobs for you in the future. For the present though you are dismissed.*' He rummaged in a small wooden coffer on the desk and tossed a coin over to Tom who caught it before he waved his hand in dismissal. Turning to leave the room Tom quickly glanced at what he held. A quarter-angel: now that made a stinking night in a tavern and having to walk the dangerous streets in icy rain worth it. Smiling to himself he set off for the warehouses where Hugh had suggested he try to purchase more vanilla.

There had only been a small amount of the spice available and Tom spent hours walking from merchant to merchant around the warehouses at the foul smelling docks where the effluence from London's streets flowed into the river. As he approached London Bridge, its wide arches marching across the wide river, the wooden buildings on top so tall they looked as if they would topple over and into the fast-flowing, churning current beneath, he saw some guards pulling a bloated body from the water. He averted his eyes from the gruesome heads on spikes as he passed underneath, their eyes pecked out from hollow dark sockets, skin pulled back from the teeth in a rictus grin. After seeing Throckmorton's execution and Hugh explaining the constant dangers faced by the Queen he now understood why Walsingham wanted the gruesome body parts of conspirators displayed at city gates or here on the bridge to deter others. It was not far to Traitors' Gate at the Tower, the entrance that nobody wanted to cross. There was rarely a return journey and passing by these heads was sure to remind those prisoners of their fate.

A pale watery sun was finally trying to break through the clouds making the wet limestone beneath his feet shine and Tom screwed his eyes up, temporarily blinded. He could tell from where it hung above him together with the growling deep in his belly that it was already past lunchtime and he still had an errand of his own to run. One that would be made more pleasant thanks to the coin in his pocket. Turning westwards he headed towards the burnt spire of St Paul's, no longer standing high above the buildings that surrounded it after a bolt of lightning had all but destroyed it.

The streets surrounding the great cathedral were busy. The repulsive stench from Fish Street market turned his stomach and he decided against sating his hunger with a pie, instead pushing on to the enormous churchyard full of bustling bookbinders, goodwives shopping and preachers reading from religious tracts. Tom could see the zeal they felt without needing to be able to hear them as he tried to edge his way through the throng. He kept his eyes alert at all times for the numerous street urchins who darted through the crowds on skinny legs and bare feet looking for an opportunity to snatch anything which could contribute to their next meal. The shops in the vicinity of St Paul's were mostly book shops and printers but Tom was certain he could find what he was looking for. Away from the smell of fish his empty stomach refused to be ignored and after buying himself a hot pasty from a street trader he set off down Paternoster Row where he soon spied a shop selling inks, quills . . . and paints.

When Tom returned to the stillroom it was mid-afternoon and Hugh had a scowl on his face; no doubt displeased with how long he'd been without his assistant. Hugh's muscles were taut as he ground something into powder in the mortar, the still with its candles burning beneath the glass flasks bubbling with a pale yellow liquid giving off a noxious gas, and instantly Tom identified the smell of crushed prunella flowers and juniper oil. He showed how little vanilla he'd been able to purchase and Hugh pulled a face at the paltry amount. They really needed to be able to cultivate their own, Tom thought. Removing his jerkin he left it in his room with the paints he'd just purchased still in the pocket.

He helped Hugh pour the liquid he'd created into a small earthenware jar. Snatching up the table book, a small memo pad they used to communicate when Tom's tablet wasn't handy and simple lip reading or signing wasn't enough, he wrote that one of the Queen's ladies, Cordelia Annesley, was complaining of a bad cough and Tom was to take the remedy up to the withdrawing room. He'd noticed that Hugh, who often had trouble with his lungs, had all but given up walking upstairs when he could send agile Tom to run the errands. He didn't mind, enjoying the opportunity to gaze at the luxurious opulence of the royal chambers where everything shone. No wonder when the Queen was so much closer to God than her subjects.

He'd been sent previously to the withdrawing chamber so knew where he was going, passing through each set of guards as he made his way towards the Queen's inner sanctum. He was never sure if she'd also be in situ but just in case he pulled a rag from his pocket and rubbed it over his face in case he was still grubby after the soot and grime from the streets he'd walked that morning.

Outside the chamber stood two further guards. He held up the jar and knowing he couldn't speak they just nodded and opened the door. Stepping inside behind one of the guards Tom watched him say *'the apothecary'* which made him smile and wonder what Hugh would say to that. Maybe as he never ventured upstairs now people didn't realise he was still working for the Queen.

To his surprise, instead of a group of ladies sewing, playing the lute or enjoying a game of cards, there were only two women present. One of whom he suspected was his patient. Sure enough she took the proffered medicine and hurried through a door to the rear, leaving Tom and the guard together with the other lady in the room who remained seated. The most beautiful woman in the palace, indeed the whole of England. He gazed at Isabel, a small smile spreading across his face making his eyes crease up in delight. He wanted to stand there for hours just looking at her but having delivered the medication he knew the guard was waiting for him to leave. He bowed low and Isabel, whose face had remained completely straight despite the sparkle in her eyes, inclined her head in dismissal. He turned and left the room, his heart beating hard in his chest.

The corridor outside, which had been still and empty as he'd approached the chamber, was now a hive of activity. Numerous courtiers had appeared and were milling around. The bright colours of their damask and silk doublets, the puffed-up sleeves slashed to display the contrasting lining and fresh white stiffened ruffs around their necks made them appear like a flock of peacocks. Tom was wondering what had brought this flurry of gentlemen to a place which had been empty not five minutes previously when the reason became obvious as the throng parted ways and sank to the floor, the Queen making her way along the corridor.

She was walking slowly, sedately, as if God were watching her every move. Being scrutinised and not to be found wanting by her subjects, nor her God. She was with the Earl of Leicester and her hand, adorned with several rings, each of them set with a large stone, was laid on his outstretched arm. Her gold, heavily embroidered gown was encrusted with so many tiny sparkling jewels it looked like the royal lawns on the mornings when a heavy hoar frost decorated every leaf and winter flower, sparkling in the dawn sunshine: almost blinding. As she swept past, Tom bowed low with everyone else. He could feel the collective drawing of breath from those around him, wanting to be noticed and yet totally in awe. Lifting his eyes a little he watched her silk slippers, decorated with pearls and embroidered with gold threads, move past.

After dinner that evening, Tom quickly tidied away the remains of some clary sage with which he'd been making an eye ointment for one of the kitchen boys who could barely see out of one side of his swollen face. It was still light outside and he was intending on adding a new scene to his triptych. He knew exactly what he wanted to paint, to capture the beauty of a certain lady who had stolen his heart.

Sweeping the bench clean with a coarse horsehair brush he didn't realise he was no longer alone in the room until a small, pale hand caught hold of his sleeve and stilled his arm. Startled he dropped the brush and turned to see, as if materialised from his own thoughts, Lady Isabel. Her clear violet eyes shone forth from the surrounding thick dark lashes.

'It is very difficult for me to speak when others are present,' she told him, 'and it is rare that our paths cross in the royal apartments.' Tom nodded although he didn't understand why she had come to seek him out to explain what he already knew. The disappointment in their situation was constantly lodged like a hard stone in his chest making it difficult to

139

breathe. The space between the lives they each inhabited was vast, even though he was becoming more confident that the attraction he felt was mutual. What she said next confirmed his suspicion and fuelled the tiny filament of hope in his heart.

'Meet me in the knot garden tomorrow evening at nine. Can you do that?' His eyes widening in surprise, Tom nodded. 'It will be dark enough that we won't be spotted by any of the night guards. Then we can be alone.' She'd been gripping his hands with both of hers and after giving them one last squeeze she was gone with just the lingering scent of her rosewater to suggest she'd ever been there.

Bemused, Tom leant against the bench looking at the empty doorway. They both knew that any inappropriate connection between them was impossible and yet she had thought of a way for them to meet. He could see no future in it but at that moment he didn't care. He knew he'd be in the knot garden waiting for her.

Tom still had time to start the new addition on his trip-tych with the paints he'd bought and lighting several candles as the sun outside started its descent towards the horizon, he began.

He wanted to record so much of what had happened since he arrived at court, the new role he now had, and what he was expected to do; although it needed to be vague in case his painting was ever discovered. The Queen had enemies and as a consequence of him spying for her they had become his foes as well. But this was a pictorial history of his life and it was important he included everything. He'd never be able to tell anyone what he'd been through so this was the best way.

Then he thought of a certain young woman he'd been with only minutes earlier and a smile spread across his face. Opening his paint box he selected some colours and began to paint.

Chapter Twenty-Three

June 2021

Unsure of the emotions Oliver stirred up in her Mathilde found it difficult to settle into anything for the remainder of the day. She'd had short-term flings with men before, her transient lifestyle lending itself to brief relationships which she could end before anyone thought of doing it first. Nobody was allowed to get close. But this felt different, this wasn't just an immediate physical attraction – lust which could easily be satisfied – she felt as though she wanted to get inside his skin and understand what made him tick.

After a late dinner accompanied by a bottle of wine, she and Rachel stayed up to watch a film. As the credits rolled Rachel complained about the entirely implausible ending as she headed up to bed while Mathilde made herself a hot drink.

Pouring the hot milk from the pan just before it boiled over she scraped the inside of one of her vanilla pods from a jar on the windowsill and added the seeds to her drink with a squeeze of honey she'd found in the larder. It was the mass-produced supermarket kind, not the thick, gluti-nous pale gold nectar she bought in France from tables left at the end of a drive. This didn't have the scent of warm sweet hay and flax flowers redolent of fat, contented bees sated with pollen.

Walking through the house to climb the stairs carrying her drink she paused for a moment at the entrance to the small vestibule off the main hall through which they reached the formal rooms of the house. On a whim she opened the dining room door, leaving it wide to illuminate the room from the hallway without needing the overhead light on. The shrouded furniture in the room cast ghostly shadows across the floor and walls as they rose up in the half light.

Crossing to the triptych she stood back a little to see it more clearly in the small glow she'd allowed herself, bathed in pale shafts of yellow light from the old-fashioned bulb. Having already examined the left-hand panel with Oliver earlier she turned her attention to the larger central one, all the time keeping her eyes averted from the third piece. If she could help it she had no intention of ever examining it, however interested Oliver was. Just standing in front of the painted flames made her tremble with fear, her lungs burning and her eyes smarting as her breath came rapidly, churning up memories buried deep within her.

Instead, she concentrated on a cluster of scenes in the top right-hand corner. There was a pale sandstone palace with towers and many windows looking similar to a chateau she'd seen as a child. Had this originated in France as she had? It would explain the pictures of a sea crossing. Beside the palace was a painting of a young woman, just the head and shoul-ders, and Mathilde was instantly attracted to it. The artist had caught her turning towards him so only half her face was showing but she was smiling, her eyes an unusual and vibrant violet colour. Oliver was correct when he said the colours had been preserved incredibly well, hidden behind the panel in the church. They were still no further in knowing why it was there. She couldn't help smiling back at the young woman, a look of love in her eyes flooded out from the painting, captivating the viewer.

She took a sip of her drink, already beginning to cool, and turned to go upstairs. As her eyes scanned the rest of the room behind her in the dark of the corner she noticed a shape; blacker, more solid than the shadows it inhabited. She blinked and looked again but whatever she had seen – or thought she'd seen – was gone. Not waiting to see what or who else may be occupying the room with her she hurried as fast as she could without spilling her drink, running upstairs taking the stairs two at a time.

The hot milk had the desired effect and despite her adrenaline she managed to convince herself she'd imagined what she'd seen after a long day. Was her father trying to let her know that everything was all right? Trying to reassure her? Her mother had a great deal of respect for what she called *les esprits*, the thin veil between the living and the dead. She lay on her back and gazed up at the ceiling, waiting for sleep to take her.

As she drifted off, she was standing in the shadows of a large room lit by hundreds of candles and full of people. She felt afraid, her heart beating a tattoo which made her whole being vibrate. There was a smell of smoke and it felt oppressive, made worse by the now familiar total silence. She could feel her chest moving as she breathed deeply in and out but she wasn't making a sound. In her hand she was holding a jug of ale. Her eyes were trained on two men on a dais in front of her. There was a slight, dark skinned man wearing a black cap and doublet, the only relief the white ruff around his neck. He was talking with a tall, well-built, attractive man with dark hair who was sitting next to him. They were across the cavernous space full of people sat at trestle tables, eating. She couldn't hear them or anything else and yet she knew everything they were saying. Her eyes strayed to the woman beside the dark haired man. Sitting upright she was thin with red hair and pale skin, dressed in what appeared to be a thousand shimmering gems sparkling in the candlelight. She turned her head as momentarily their eyes met and with a shock Mathilde woke up and sat up, all in the same movement.

Swinging her feet round she sat on the edge of her bed letting the cold of the floor work its way up her legs, a cool reminder she was awake. The moment her eyes had made contact with the woman, Mathilde had realised she was looking at Queen Elizabeth I. *It was just a dream* she reminded herself, but it all felt so real. And how could she understand what those two men were saying when she was nowhere near them and couldn't hear a thing? *Dreams were simply the brain assimilating what had happened during the day*, she told herself, *that was all*. The people on the triptych were dressed in clothes similar to those worn by people in her dream so it made sense.

Lying back down again she put her hands over her face. She wanted another drink but her experience in the dining room put her off wandering about the house in the dark.

Waking early after a few more hours of fitful sleep Mathilde dressed and made herself toast before quietly slipping out of the back door and walking around the side of the house to her van. There was no sign of Rachel or Fleur, the television standing quiet and reproachful at the lack of lurid cartoons and strange crime fighting animals Fleur was often glued to.

A layer of mist hung eerily above the marshes in the distance, the reeds poking out of the top as if suspended in the air; there was the promise of a hot day once it had burnt off. Turning on the engine of her van with her eyes closed wondering if it would start after two weeks of idleness, she was relieved when with a small bang the engine turned over and fired up. She needed to be away from the house.

Remembering her decision to buy some sort of glasshouse she headed to a garden centre she'd noticed on the outskirts of Fakenham when she'd visited Mr Murray. She arrived just as it opened and found a whole myriad of greenhouses on display. She stopped for a moment, unable to choose. As she surveyed them all stood in front of her, the sun shining off the glass roofs and making her squint, she heard a voice behind her.

'Don't you have enough space already in that enormous house?' Turning, she saw Oliver stood behind her with a broad grin on his face and his eyes crinkled up in amusement at his own joke. She felt her heart begin to beat faster at the sight of him and her mouth widened to return his smile. She couldn't think of another time, certainly since the death of her mother, she'd ever felt such a wave of pleasure wash over her on seeing another human. It was a shock but she couldn't deny how it made her feel as her face flushed with pleasure. She hoped she didn't look as pink as she felt.

'Lots of space inside, yes,' she nodded, 'but outside I have plants that won't survive an English summer.'

'But the weather is glorious,' he held his arms out as if to catch the early morning sunshine and show her, 'we don't always get summers this good.'

'Yes, this is lovely but you've just admitted it may not last long so I need to protect some of my plants. I just want something small to last until autumn.' There, she'd said it. She'd made sure Oliver hadn't forgotten she was only here on a temporary sabbatical, and she needed to remind herself, as much as him. As soon as the leaves on the trees began to turn and fall to the ground she'd be back across the water and resuming her itinerant lifestyle where she wasn't beholden to anyone and she only needed to trust herself, her instincts. Where she could be self-reliant and safe.

'So, which one are you going for?' He'd paused before continuing as if he hadn't taken in what she'd said, although she was certain he had.

'This is fine,' she indicated a plastic covered half greenhouse that could be erected against a wall, 'I can weigh the bottom down with bricks or stones; there are plenty lying around the place. Then I can just leave it behind when I go.' She'd managed another subtle hint. Actually, not so subtle at all.

Oliver picked up the bundle containing the flat packed greenhouse and carried it through to the checkout for her. As she paid she suddenly realised that he didn't have any purchases with him.

'You haven't bought anything,' she pointed out.

'Oh dammit, I forgot,' he smacked the heel of his hand against his forehead, 'I'll carry this to your van and then go back. I wanted a plant for my gran, I'm visiting her later. She's in a nursing home and she loves pelargoniums. This garden centre grows especially nice ones, which is why I

147

came out here. Do you want a hand putting this up? I could swing by after I've bought the plant and help?'

'Thank you, that would be kind.' Mathilde had no idea what 'swing by' meant but she'd guessed the gist of what he'd suggested. And however much her internal monologue warned her, reminded her she wasn't staying, she couldn't prevent herself wanting to see him again.

Stowing her purchase in the back of her van, he looked around in amazement.

'I had no idea this was kitted out so well,' he exclaimed pointing to the fitted bed and the wooden cupboards and shelves where she stored everything while she was on the move. Mathilde breathed a sigh of relief that she'd taken out some of the soft furnishings and her bed wasn't the usual mess of sheet and duvet in a crumpled pile. Right now, it was looking considerably tidier than usual.

'Well, I live in here,' she shrugged as if that was explanation enough before slamming the doors shut.

They agreed to meet up back at her house and she drove home realising when she was halfway there that she'd had a silly grin plastered on her face the whole time. Not only would she now have some help erecting the greenhouse – which would be useful as the instructions would be in English – but she could also tell him about the dreams she'd been having. And the uncomfortable feeling that someone was with her sometimes. Watching her? Or trying to tell her something? She wasn't sure but it unnerved her.

She found Rachel and Fleur playing with a cricket bat and ball in the garden.

'Where did you get to?' Rachel asked.

'I went to buy a little greenhouse for my plants,' she

explained. Behind her, she heard the sound of tyres on gravel. 'I met Oliver at the garden centre,' she added, 'he offered to come and help me.'

'I must show you later where Dad's garden tools are kept, he'd have loved for you to use them,' Rachel suggested and Mathilde felt her eyes prickle with tears.

'Thank you,' she said smiling, 'I'd love that.'

It took barely an hour to put the pieces together and fit the clear plastic covering before they placed it against the back of the stable wall weighing it down with pieces of flint and stone. Mathilde collected her vanilla plants and placed them inside.

'So, these are the flowers that are too precious for our English sun then?' Oliver asked, bending close and running his fingertips along their glossy leaves.

'Yes, these are vanilla orchids. They're native to Mexico originally so they need extreme heat. These are flowering late, it hasn't been warm enough for them. See here?' she pointed, 'tiny buds. When they open I have to push the flowers together to germinate them and then the pods grow. European bees don't like them so it has to be done by hand.'

'How weird,' he remarked peering closer at them, 'the plant world can be amazing sometimes, can't it?'

Mathilde nodded. 'I love being out here in my father's garden,' she swept her arm around indicating the overgrown vegetable patch laid out in front of them, 'to think that all these plants began as seeds he nurtured so they grew tall and strong.'

'Like he would have done for you, if he'd found you?' Oliver suggested softly. 'I spent hours gardening with my grandfather when I was a kid. They lived on the Norfolk coast and we'd spend the summers there, my brothers and me. Our parents

149

would leave us there when we got older and just come up and visit at the weekends. We used to run wild, disappearing for the whole day sometimes.' He chuckled to himself at the memory. 'We could walk to the beach, go and watch the seals. Carefree times. I'd often hang around to work outside with Grandad, helping with whatever needed doing. There's nothing quite like the scent of freshly dug earth, is there?'

'That sounds a wonderful childhood,' Mathilde's voice faltered a little, 'I've never had a garden where I could cultivate plants and know that I would be able to hang around long enough to see them grown. Pick the flowers or eat the vegetables.'

'And now you do. If you stay longer than just the summer you can nurture your own plants and help them grow. Why don't you think about it? You know how much Rachel wants you here.' She held his gaze and her breath as his arm came across her shoulder and pulled her to him, holding her there for a moment against his chest where she could feel his heart beating, strong and steady: secure. She thought she felt the brush of his lips against her hair and then, as if he considered he'd overstepped the line, he moved away, rubbing the tops of her arms briskly as he did so.

'Umm, do you want a cup of coffee or some water?' Mathilde swiftly changed the subject, brushing her hands down her trousers and looking at her feet. She could feel her ears burning although at the same time she felt strangely cold and empty without his arms around her.

'Yes please, I'd love a cold drink.' He was displaying none of the awkwardness that she was feeling. 'Any chance of having another closer look at your triptych? I've got my eye glass in the car.'

'*Oui,* sure, of course,' she agreed. A perfect excuse to keep him at the hall a while longer. She hadn't yet explained to him about her dream and she wanted to prevent him from rushing off to visit his grandmother.

Once inside Mathilde took their drinks through to the dining room where she'd covered the painting with a cloth to keep any dirt off. Pulling the curtains open a little the dust rose into the air in the shaft of light, flooding the room like champagne from a shaken bottle, and she was pleased she'd protected everything.

'It really is amazing,' Oliver bent close over the left-hand panel examining the myriad of scenes.

'I had a strange dream about it,' Mathilde blurted out hardly knowing how to explain to Oliver without sounding like an idiot. 'Several dreams in fact. Each time I was living in the scenes on the triptych. These here,' she pointed to the boat scene, 'it was just like when I came over on the ferry from France but I was in an old boat like this one and last night I was here in a palace watching people. Everything was silent and I saw your queen, Elizabeth I, and she looked at me.' Even to her ears it sounded ridiculous and she wasn't going to mention the first dream she'd had in the black, soulless hole depicted at the top corner of the first panel. She shuddered. 'And I thought I saw a ghost in here the other night, while I was looking at the painting.' Oliver straightened up and looked at her.

'Everyone has strange dreams from time to time,' he said slowly, 'but most people don't see ghosts. Tell me more.'

She relayed what had happened the previous night realising as she told him how unlikely it all sounded. He must think she was some hysterical foreigner who imagines things. Why

151

was she trying to tell him how scared she'd been about a dream for goodness' sake? She didn't have the English words to describe how it had made her feel. Terrified, sucked into a world that felt as real as the one she was living in. Perhaps it was just as well she couldn't explain or she might never see him again.

'There's probably a simple explanation for what you saw,' he reassured her, 'although there are plenty of people who believe in ghosts. Maybe the dreams are a backlash from all the emotional turmoil recently? Discovering a family you didn't know existed, that your father didn't pass away all those years ago and suddenly inheriting this house. All of this is light years away from what you're used to so it's bound to have an effect.'

Mathilde nodded slowly keeping her eyes on the painting in front of her. She knew what she'd seen and it wasn't her imagination. And she was certain the dreams she'd had were connected to the eerie feelings she was getting around the house. Someone or something was trying to talk to her, to explain something. And it was connected to the triptych.

They both moved at the same time to lift the dust cloth back over the painting, their hands brushing together momentarily. Mathilde snatched hers away as if she'd been burned, pushing them into her pockets and letting him finish off. He unnerved her and yet she couldn't stop gravitating towards him: she was a moth dancing towards his shining light.

Chapter Twenty-Four

October 1584

As directed, Tom was waiting at the knot garden. The air was still, the darkness closing in around him like a cloak. He stood with his back against the palace wall and watched for any movement, his head twisting back and forth as his eyes swept across the grounds laid out in front. He wasn't certain if this was some sort of trap, especially after his spying mission, and he wanted to see anyone approaching.

After a couple of minutes he spotted a shadowy form move slowly across the garden. The moon was behind the building and he could see the movements the person was taking: short, light strides, creeping along. A gentle night breeze wafted across the scent of apple blossom and roses and instantly he knew it was her. He stepped out from where he was hiding, deliberately kicking at the stones to alert her.

Within seconds she was standing in front of him. He could just make out the silhouette of her features etched in the half-light as he saw her smile and her lips move as she spoke. She clasped his fingertips in hers and her soft warm skin felt like velvet. He couldn't see well enough to understand what she was saying. Even if he'd had a candle it would have been too dangerous to light it and alert anyone to their clandestine meeting. He shook his head; he still couldn't grasp the words and although she was also now moving her hands he was lost. She pointed to herself and him and he nodded in understanding but the next part seemed to just be random arm waving together with whatever she was saying. Frustrated he shrugged and held his arms out shaking his head and pointing up to the dark skies above them, now pinpricked with the first of the night's stars where on the horizon a thin strip of faded orange clung on to the remains of the day. Maybe meeting outside as twilight claimed the day hadn't been such a good idea. And he had no indication if she understood as he couldn't see her mouth.

She hung her head down, shaking it slowly before reaching forward and giving him a hug, after which she was gone. He waited for over half an hour wondering if she was coming back before realising she wasn't. Walking back to the side door from where he'd crept out to the garden, he continued into his room and sat on the bed, his head in his hands. Once again his deafness had robbed him of something special. It was doubtful she'd be throwing him any smiles or meaningful glances next time their paths crossed. Nothing changed. His good looks may win him a smile from a pretty girl but as soon as she realised what hard work it was trying to communicate with someone who could neither hear nor speak, she'd disappear like the mists at dawn. He was destined to be alone forever.

Tom awoke the following morning with his head hurting,

a frown etched into his forehead from where he'd slept in a bad mood. Staggering through to the stillroom he stoked up the embers of the fire and proceeded to make himself a tisane of feverfew and camomile to stop the ache. When Hugh came through carrying some bread and slices of cheese together with a platter of fruit and a jug of ale, Tom watched him take one look at his morose expression and put the breakfast on the floor beside him.

Knowing he couldn't spend all day brooding over the catastrophe of the previous evening's meeting he quickly ate the food Hugh had given him before getting to his feet and helping in the preparation of an ointment needed to soothe the bed sores of one of Elizabeth's former ladies who was now too frail to move from her bed.

He was so busy working, pounding the herbs into the grease to make a smooth paste, that he didn't notice Isabel standing in the doorway. With the sleeves of his shirt rolled up his muscular forearms were taut with the effort he was exuding and suddenly she was there, close to the bench and bent down so her face appeared in his field of vision. Startled and a little horrified he stepped back and automatically bowed to her. After the embarrassment of the previous evening had she come to gloat or to tell him never to come near her again?

She was smiling at him and his heartbeat began to slow down a little.

'*I do not think,*' she spoke slowly and he watched her perfect pink lips, '*that meeting up at night is very beneficial to us.*' He frowned as she said '*beneficial*' and she thought for a moment before supplying '*helpful*'. He nodded slowly and waited for her to tell him they needed to stay away from

155

each other and go back to leading their separate lives as dictated by their stations.

'*Perhaps we could try meeting at dawn?*' she suggested. '*The same place tomorrow?*'

Tom was so astonished at this turn of events he could only nod his head in delight, trying not to look too over enthusiastic. But he hoped she saw his eyes shining with appreciation that she was prepared to risk another meeting with him.

'*Tomorrow then,*' she mouthed before turning, her heavily embroidered gown in rich burgundy sweeping behind her as she left the room. He watched her as she hurried down the corridor, her head high and her back straight. She had the walk of a woman who was confident and strong, sure of everything in life.

He returned to his work, this time with a wide smile lighting up his face. Hugh had left the room as soon as Isabel entered, as if by a secret signal Tom had missed, so as he stepped back in and raised his eyebrows in question Tom would only waggle his head slowly from side to side, his sign to Hugh that he wouldn't – or couldn't – explain.

Chapter Twenty-Five

July 2021

Enjoying the cool of the early morning air, Mathilde walked across the field towards the marshes and the river lying beyond. The ground was already beginning to dip, the grass becoming increasingly coarser. Away to her left stood Alice and Jack's farmhouse, rising up from the meadows, a custodian of all that had happened in the past. Beneath its coarse thatched roof, the dormer windows looked out like dark, suspicious eyes watching the world pass by. Lifting her ever-present camera to her face, Mathilde took shot after shot, the pale blue sky beyond a perfect washed out backdrop. She thought she saw a movement behind one of the windows but decided it was just the reflection of the oak tree opposite the house as it danced in the wind.

Pausing at the edge of the reeds, she quietly lowered herself to her haunches. The grass was still wet and she didn't want to kneel on it; these were her last pair of clean jeans and she hadn't yet asked Rachel how to operate the ancient washing machine that lurked in the boot room off the kitchen. It made a loud screaming noise when it got to the spin cycle; the sort of sharp wheeling thumps that would have made her mother cower, hands clasped over her head. Thank goodness Mathilde had still been young when they left Beirut and couldn't remember the sounds of war.

Her memories were interrupted by the warbling of a bird somewhere in the tall rushes in front of her. Without moving them it was impossible to see the water beyond although she heard an occasional splash and wondered if it was a bird or a mammal enjoying its secluded, safe life. Isolated, hidden from predators who would take what they wanted. She'd been dragged into a life exactly like that and thinking about her mother had brought it all back. Always running away, moving on. Now as an adult she understood her mother had been too frightened to stay anywhere for long, her mental state too precarious after living with the bombs falling night and day. She'd learned to hide, secrete them away from danger and then run. Flee to France where life would be quieter. Except she wasn't able to stop the tortured memories that haunted her and every time they seemed to be settled somewhere, a villager would start a rumour or make an accusation about their unconventional lifestyle and they were off again, moving on. It had broken them both.

She took several photographs through the tall reeds at the sunlight filtering through, a wavering dapple of dusky hues. There was a sudden flash of electric blue as something hit the water and it sparkled like a diamond winking at her, then it was gone as the ripples stilled once more. Getting to her feet she stretched her legs where they'd cramped up. Reminiscing wouldn't do her any good. All she'd missed out on, everything she had wanted in life had been here across the water and she hadn't known. But perhaps the chasm that had always been gaping in her life could finally be completed by this new-found family. Maybe, just maybe, they would close the exposed wound she carried inside. Pulling at the tops of the grasses and throwing the seeds to the ground she walked back up to the house, a frown etched on her face, her eyes dark.

After much pressure Mathilde had promised Fleur she could take some photographs with her camera, so after lunch the two of them went out for a walk. It was the first time the little girl had properly connected with her and Mathilde didn't want to mess it up.

'Stay around the grounds, won't you?' Rachel called as they pulled their shoes on, 'it's not always easy to see where the boggy land begins.'

'Yes, yes, we'll be careful,' Mathilde reassured her. She knew the dangers of the flat land around them, understood the way the water beneath their feet seeped up through the earth and laid in thick muddy crevices ready to pull an unsuspecting person down beneath its depths. She caught hold of Fleur's hand and smiled down at the little girl. A child who carried her blood, whose grandfather was her father. *Parentes,* kin. She'd looked the word up in her dictionary.

Out in the vegetable garden Fleur immediately found a butterfly, its white wings tipped with soft, pale green and dotted with velvety black smudges. Mathilde kept the strap to the heavy camera around her own neck and silently crouched down, pulling Fleur into the circle behind the camera, the little girl's warm back pressed against her torso as she looked down the lens and squeezed on the red button as Mathilde had shown her. The clunk of the shutter disturbed the butterfly who took flight and in its haphazard way wavered away across the potato flowers.

'*Papillon*,' Mathilde told her. 'In French, *papillon*.' She showed Fleur the photo she'd just taken on the screen on the back of the camera and the little girl sighed in delight before squeezing out from under the strap and skipping away around the garden looking for more things to photograph. Lifting the camera Mathilde took several shots of her small face and blond plaits weaving between the overgrown plants. Her relationship with the little girl was growing and felt so natural but there was still a wall between herself and Rachel, as they danced around each other trying to carve out a bond that had been stalled for so many years. It was developing slowly but being a sister was new to both of them; at least they had that in common.

They ended up beside the chapel. Rachel had insisted locking the door again, saying someone might start squatting in it. They couldn't be too careful of travellers she'd added, and Mathilde felt her blood start to sing in her veins as Rachel realised what she'd said. She knew that was exactly how Mathilde and her mother had often found accommodation, when times were hard. An abandoned house or building could offer them protection when the weather was rough or cold. Thankfully in the south of France it rarely snowed but it certainly got cold at night. And when the mistral whipped up and threw hot wind and dust into people's eyes you needed somewhere to shelter. Mathilde had opened up to her sister and tried to explain what her life had been like but in that single throwaway comment she'd wondered if her sister could ever truly understand.

Fleur slumped against the wall, her legs braced out in front to stop herself sliding down. Mathilde took a few more photos, the sound of the shutter alerting the little girl. Instead of disappearing as the butterfly did, her niece turned her head towards the camera, the sun behind her making her hair shine like a pale gold halo around her head. She smiled shyly and in an instant Mathilde had caught her, digitally, forever.

'Time for tea?' she suggested and the little girl nodded pushing herself to her feet against the wall and trotting on ahead back to the house. Mathilde paused for a moment, looking up at the silent building. She was no further in finding out why the triptych seemed to have some sort of hold on her nor why the locket had drawn her to find it hidden in this tiny place of worship, but she was convinced it was trying to tell her something.

Back in the kitchen Mathilde felt her heart sink as she saw that they had company; the two people she least wanted to see. Alice and Jack were sitting nursing cups of coffee, their faces like a pair of matching gargoyles, stony and scowling.

'Ah, there you are,' Rachel's voice sounded falsely bright, 'we have some visitors.'

'Yes, I see.' Mathilde filled a glass with water and drank it down in one go, the condensation from the outside dripping onto her T-shirt. She laid her camera on the table. 'What do you want?' she asked, putting one hand on her hip.

'We know what you're up to and we're here to tell you to stop.' Alice's voice came out as if she was spitting shards of glass across the room. Mathilde raised her eyebrows and looked at Rachel in puzzlement. She had no idea what they were talking about. Jack, who rarely said a word, merely nodded, his hair bouncing up and down in agreement.

'What do you think Mathilde is up to?' Rachel kept her voice quiet and modulated. No wonder she was a primary school teacher, Mathilde thought, she had the ability to take the reaction out of a situation.

'I saw her taking photos of the estate this morning; of our house. Spying on us just like when I found her in the village. Ready to run round to the estate agents and get them measuring up. I bet old Danny Jones at Harbord and Jones is rubbing his hands together at the commission for this place. Well, I'm going to stop you in your tracks young lady. You know we've been to see our solicitor. The farm-house is our home and we'll stop you inheriting so don't bother with your "For Sale" signs; we're going nowhere.' They both held smug smiles on their faces, as if they were holding a royal flush in a game of poker and they no longer cared who knew it.

Mathilde looked at them in confusion, she had no idea what her aunt was talking about.

'Yes, I took photographs this morning,' she agreed, 'I take photos, that's what I do. I sell them to agencies, it's how I earn my money. But even though I wasn't taking photos of your home to sell this morning, somebody else will be in September when I leave here and the house is put up for sale.' Saying the words out loud felt wrong and her chest was tight even if it was the truth.

'And you're mistaken about the will,' Rachel turned to the couple on the other side of the table. 'You'll get nowhere.

I was with my father when he drew it up. There was a discussion about the farmhouse and Dad decided he didn't want to split up the estate. He was absolutely clear in his decision that Mathilde was to have it all to do with as she pleased. Yes, if she couldn't be found within twelve months then it would have reverted to you but I for one am very pleased we finally have my sister here, where she belongs.'

Mathilde turned to Rachel feeling tears prickle at the back of her eyes as what she'd said sank in. She couldn't disguise the smile creeping across her face and beneath the edge of the table she felt Rachel's fingers grip hold of her own. She had someone on her side.

Laying on her bed, the curtains open and the brilliant new moon shining in through the windows lit up the bedspread and painted a white line along the edge of her legs and over her flat stomach up to her breasts. Mathilde wished she had her camera but she'd left it on the kitchen table; it would make a great photograph.

On her laptop laid on the bed beside her, she continued her research into Queen Elizabeth I. She was becoming intrigued about the plotting between those who remained Catholic and those who followed the Queen's new Protestant faith. The old faith had been outlawed and a person could be killed because of their beliefs. But backed by the Spanish the 'heretics' risked everything to bring the Queen's cousin, the Catholic Mary Queen of Scots, to the English throne. To prevent being overthrown, Queen Elizabeth had Mary locked away in a castle for years. Many plots were concocted to free Mary and put her on the throne, even if that meant assassinating Queen Elizabeth.

So, a country torn apart because although they prayed to the same god they chose different ways of doing so. Just like in her homeland, the wars in Lebanon; nothing really ever changed. Switching the laptop off and closing her eyes, Mathilde felt the soft arms of sleep begin to gather her in.

All around people were jostling her and the room was dim, candles in sconces around the wall which guttered and danced as the door kept opening and closing. She was in a tavern and the silence around her was profound. A horrible smell – rank stale sweat and heavy, yeasty beer – made her feel nauseous. There was a fire burning in the grate, a couple of logs that were now just glowing red as they broke down to join the scattered grey ash which lay on the hearth. She looked all around until her eyes alighted on a man speaking with another, their heads close together and their eyes constantly darting around the room at their fellow drinkers. As she watched their mouths she realised that once again she could understand what they were saying even though she could hear nothing. They slipped out of a door behind them and without a second thought she followed them. Her heart was beating so hard in her chest she thought they'd be able to hear it as she stepped out into a damp, dark yard. It was drizzling, the wet instantly laying like a cloak on her skin, and someone pushed past her and began to urinate against the wall. She crinkled up her nose in disgust. The two men she'd been watching were exchanging a package, slipped from beneath one coat to the next, a subtle movement barely there. Then one of the men stole back in through the door they had exited from whilst the other disappeared through a gate at the back of the yard. She tried pushing through the throng inside but whoever it was had disappeared.

She awoke with a start. Her face was damp – was it sweat or the fine drizzle of her dream? – and her heart was still racing. The moonlight had moved around the room as it climbed into the sky and in the dark corner beside the door she thought she could see the outline of someone sitting in the chair where she usually threw her clothes. A silhouette of shadow against the night. A face, picked out by the moonlight, turned away from her as if deep in thought, finely carved as a statue and just as still. Cold as marble. She gasped and leaning across she fumbled as she switched on her bedside lamp. The room was empty. She knew it would be even though she was certain of what she'd seen; there had been something or someone there, she was sure of it. Just like the evening when she was out with her plants beside the woods. Rachel had assured her there had never been ghosts at Lutton Hall; nobody had ever mentioned seeing anything. Whatever was there had been waiting for her. Someone from the past. The veil between their two worlds had drifted apart and let him slip through, just for a moment.

Chapter Twenty-Six

July 2021

'We're driving over to Wisbech today to meet up with Andrew. It's a good halfway point and there's a nice café and play park there. Do you want to come with us?' Rachel was buttering toast and cutting it into fingers for Fleur who was dabbing her spoon into a boiled egg, the yolk already running down the outside of the shell and eggcup, pooling onto her plate.

'No, I don't think so. Thank you.' Mathilde was used to being on her own and she knew it would soothe her soul to have some solitude, just for a little while. 'You should have some time to yourselves,' she added, trying to soften the blow. She paused momentarily in her coffee preparation as she thought about what she'd just said. For the first time in her life, as far as she could remember she'd said something to make someone else feel better. Thought about someone else's feelings before her own. It was an odd feeling but a not unpleasant one. Just then, Fleur thrust her spoon into her egg and the cup and plate skittered off the table and onto the floor where it broke into several pieces, the egg splattering everywhere. The ensuing screaming broke the atmosphere and was enough to make any number of unpleasant expletives spill out of Mathilde's mouth so she quickly ran upstairs before she said them.

Outside the warm weather they'd enjoyed over the previous three days was threatening to break. The sky was still blue but its radiance had been replaced with a deeper cerulean, saturated with foreboding. On the horizon hanging above the marshes malevolent dark grey clouds piled one on top of each other, an atmospheric game of Jenga. The air was heavy and still, difficult to breathe in as it anticipated the inevitable. As she watered her plants, the vanilla just days away from fertilisation, Mathilde was constantly swatting away storm flies, so prevalent her lungs must have been full of them. Even Rachel had complained that the previous day she'd found one in her bra when she took it off to shower.

She was keen to capture the oncoming weather on her camera so dashing upstairs she grabbed her bag and pushed her feet into her Converse before heading off towards the marshes, taking shots of the clouds in the distance. A small whip of wind caught at the tops of the grasses as she walked through them then all was still again. As she reached the edge of the reed beds she noticed it was eerily quiet compared to when she had last visited, the birds cowed in silence. Waiting. The sun was now behind the clouds which were turning the dark purple of a fresh bruise and appeared so low that Mathilde reached her arm up as if to run her fingertips through them.

She turned to her left and began to walk along a narrow

path still skirting the edge of the marsh. It wasn't a direction she'd walked in before but if she'd gone to her right she'd have been close to the back of Alice and Jack's garden and she was keen to avoid another confrontation with them. This path eventually led to an old farm track, dusty and dry with deep grooves where vehicles' wheels had dug in, the centre a ridge of tall grass. It didn't seem to have been used for a long while. Maybe her father had driven down here heading for the river.

Beginning to walk along it she hoped to arrive at the road to take her in a circulatory route back towards the house. The buildings remained visible, an advantage of the flat land they stood on, and she took some more photographs. From a distance, her van hidden by trees and the top of the chapel just beyond, the house appeared timeless. She could have been stood on the path – which quite possibly had been there when the house was built – looking across at her home five hundred years before. It was solid, a statement, a moment captured in time forever. The pale, mellow walls were darkened by the gunmetal grey of the sky above but the house showed no fear. Storms and lives would come and go but Lutton Hall would weather all.

Another gust of warm wind blew across the top of the hedge beside her, rustling the leaves and scratching them together with more urgency. The air was sharp and hot reminding her of the mistral at home in the south of France, how it would blow up out of nowhere throwing dust into every crevice, keeping every sane person and animal sheltering inside. This wouldn't be the same though, she thought, as the wind began to increase and a low rumble somewhere behind her made the ground beneath her feet vibrate. England wasn't susceptible to the violent weather of home. Nevertheless she began to walk a bit faster, wondering if she'd mistimed her walk.

A brilliant flash of lightning lit up the clouds from behind followed by a crack of thunder making Mathilde hunch her shoulders up and flinch just seconds before fat droplets of rain began to land on the dirt at her feet and disturb the dust, making it dance on the ground. She quickly put her precious camera back in its bag and spotting an old dilapidated shed further along the track she tucked her bag under her arm to prevent it from banging against her hip and began to run towards the shelter, holding her cardigan over her head as it flapped uselessly in the wind.

The doors were closed but not locked and with the rain now gathering speed and ferocity Mathilde pushed her fingers into the small gap between the two doors and pulled one open, darting inside into the dry. The noise of the rain on the galvanised steel roof was deafening but at least it wasn't getting in.

Looking around behind her Mathilde could see a number of rusty farming implements with grass and weeds climbing around them as if they'd been there for centuries, untouched, slowly disintegrating into the earth. Peering out at the sky she wondered how long she'd be waiting for the storm to pass. Another flash was echoed by a crash of thunder almost immediately, indicating it was already overhead and hopefully on its way elsewhere.

Eventually, as she had suspected, the storm rolled on and the rain began to ease a little. As the noise on the roof abated Mathilde realised she could hear something else. A small, high-pitched squeaking as if something that required oiling

169

was swinging back and forth in the gusting wind. She cocked her head to one side listening for it.

Before long she heard it again, this time more clearly and she immediately knew what it was. This wasn't a rusty hinge. Getting down on her knees she laid her head flat against the ground and peered under the machinery at the back of the shed. Sure enough, just as she had guessed, a pair of china blue eyes stared back. The owner of the eyes squeaked again.

'Hey, *petit chat*,' Mathilde murmured, making clicking noises with her tongue and waggling her fingers at it. The kitten, a tiny black scrap as far as she could see, didn't move. She looked around the shed as if she'd suddenly spot its mother or some other obvious explanation as to why it was hiding in there. She needed a way to catch the kitten to take a closer look. Her usual *modus operandi* when attempting to photograph wildlife was to lure it with food but she had nothing in her bag other than a banana she'd picked up as she left. She gazed around spotting a long narrow twig and rummaging as quietly as she could in her pocket, she pulled out an old tissue. Attaching it to the end of the stick she began to flick the makeshift toy back and forth. Eventually, just as her arm began to ache, a tiny, furry, black paw swiped out at the dancing stick. Her ploy was beginning to work. Silently she stretched her arm out for her cardigan which she'd draped across an old wheelbarrow in an attempt to dry it and as the kitten became bolder and finally emerged from its hiding place, she threw her cardigan over and scooped it up.

Immediately the bundle began to squirm ferociously, small stiff limbs poking out in all directions, sharp claws sticking through the knitwear as a terrible high-pitched, pitiful wailing filled the shed. Inching the fabric back so its face was uncovered, Mathilde made a dash for home, holding her still wriggling captive close to her body as she ran.

Once inside the kitchen she placed the tiny fluffy prisoner on the floor and shook away her cardigan, mindful of its flailing claws. Her arms bore testament to how needle sharp they were, small beads of blood running along numerous scratches. Now freed it made a bolt for the closest dark space beneath the ancient fridge in the corner. Mathilde tutted and after running her arms under the cold tap and dabbing them dry with kitchen towel she put down a saucer of water and another containing some tuna she'd found in the cupboard. She had no idea if her visitor was old enough for proper food and she hoped she wouldn't find it regurgitated later but she kept her fingers crossed that the fish might lure the kitten back out from under the fridge. She probably also ought to take it to the vets but her command of English wasn't good enough to do that on her own so she'd need to wait until Rachel returned.

Her sister's reappearance didn't happen as soon as Mathilde had envisaged. A text arrived at four o'clock informing her a tree had come down in the storm at Swaffham and she'd decided to turn around and drive back to Peterborough to spend the night at home. She made a joke about leaving her in peace but Mathilde suddenly realised the day on her own hadn't been as enjoyable as she'd anticipated. Having spent her whole life seeking out the shadows to hide in, finding solace in solitude, suddenly a night by herself didn't sound so restful. Or as quiet as a small squeak from beneath the fridge reminded her of her new house guest. Running upstairs to have a shower and get out of her wet clothes she left the kitten where it was, the two saucers temptingly beside the fridge.

By bedtime her visitor still hadn't reappeared. Mathilde was loath to leave it hiding all night in case it escaped to another part of the house, and shutting all the doors other than the one to the small sitting room, she arranged a temporary bed on the sofa. She switched the light off and lay in the dark, her ears alert to any suggestion food or drink was being consumed in the kitchen.

All around her were the sounds of the house settling down for the night but they no longer unnerved her; she was now used to the creaks and rasps of the floorboards and water pipes. Soon after midnight, she heard the faint sound of china grating against flagstone flooring and creeping across the room on her hands and knees she peered around the corner. Sure enough the kitten, almost invisible in the darkness, was crouched over one of the saucers.

'Hello Shadow,' she whispered into the night before crawling back under her covers.

Chapter Twenty-Seven

October 1584

Tom could barely sleep that night, worried he'd sleep too late and miss their meeting. It was harder to creep out at dawn with plenty of servants already hard at work preparing the palace for another day and no darkness to use as cover. Nevertheless, he walked to the outer door he'd previously used when carrying the trug in which he collected the herbs for medicines and let himself out into the gardens. There were sweet scented herbs growing in the knot garden and sometimes if the plants in the physic garden were a bit sparse he and Hugh would take some from there. Outside the clouds were pale and wispy, still wearing their deep pink skirts of night as they scattered across the sky and dispersed. The tall, fortified stone walls of the palace towered over him and he couldn't help looking up at the windows, reflecting the sun as it climbed over the horizon, and wondering if there were eyes looking out, watching him. There were spies everywhere, nobody was safe.

As he approached the place where they'd met up before he could see, even though it wasn't yet completely light, that she was waiting, enrobed in a long dark cloak with a thick squirrel fur collar. He hurried over glancing back over his shoulder to ensure they were completely alone.

'*This is much better, is it not?*' she whispered, smiling at him and he nodded.

'Dangerous,' he signed to her, 'we mustn't be seen.'

'*Then we must find somewhere to meet that is more private.*' She raised her eyebrows in question. Tom wondered for a moment if this was some sort of trick, a cruel joke. It wouldn't be the first time someone had used his deafness as a way of poking fun and making entertainment for friends. But Isabel seemed so spirited and sure of herself, used to having whatever she wanted. And she was so exquisite it was worth the risk. He could hardly believe someone as beautiful and high born as she would be interested in a deaf and mute assistant apothecary but he wasn't about to turn the opportunity down.

He nodded and signed 'where?'

'*My home. I have a house on Cordwainer Street.*' Although she was talking slowly, his eyes kept flicking over her shoulder, constantly watching for guards walking past and he kept missing words. He frowned and shook his head. He'd understood house, but not where. He signed to her to write it down, and she nodded.

'*I'll somehow get a missive to you with one of the pages,*' she promised, patting his arm. She smiled up at him and he felt himself falling into the depths of her deep violet eyes. Then she was gone, skirting around the edge of the garden and keeping close to the wall until she disappeared around the corner of the building.

Tom walked back to the door, snatching up a few lavender flower heads as he went and dropping them into his basket. Did she say she had a house? He wondered if he had misread what she'd said. Because why was she at court if she had a house to live at, in the city? He hoped he'd soon get the chance to find out.

That evening, a page arrived in the stillroom. He was tiny, much smaller and appeared younger than the other boys stationed around the palace as they ran errands whilst learning the rules and regulations to become a courtier. He looked quite afraid to be in the servants' rooms, a long way from the apartments and galleries of the palace he usually inhabited. Tom smiled to put him at his ease, and the little boy looked across to Hugh who must have spoken to him. The boy held up a letter, sealed with a blob of wax and answered. His face was in profile so difficult to read his lips, but Tom saw the word *'Lutton'* and he stepped forward just as Hugh pointed to him.

The page bowed as he handed the letter over, and with an equally solemn face Tom bowed in return. The boy was quivering a little, as if afraid and Tom wondered what awful tales were already circulating about him. They'd lead to him being forced out; they always did. Someone would associate his disability with the devil, witchcraft, someone falling ill and he'd be deemed a bad omen and told to be on his way. A familiar story. The page turned and scampered away, not looking back.

Opening the letter, Tom quickly scanned it.

I have a house on Cordwainer Street. I can explain more when we are there. I shall go to visit it tonight; the Queen has given permission that I may be away from court for three days. Please come tomorrow night if you are able and we can talk more easily.

Tom tucked the letter into the pocket of his jerkin. He had no idea where the street was but Hugh had grown up in the city and Tom was sure he'd know. Although he didn't want his friend to know why he was asking; this assignation was just as dangerous as any asked of him by Walsingham.

Tom slapped his hand against his thigh in delight. Of course, that was how he could find out where he needed to go; he'd pretend to Hugh it was another spying job and then ask him quite openly to draw a map. Hugh would assume the letter was from Walsingham and would ask no questions. Tom approached Hugh with his wax tablet and explained his dilemma.

Hugh had known exactly where Tom needed to go and the following evening with a carefully drawn map in his pocket Tom left the palace and hurried down to the wharf where a number of small craft bobbed on the water waiting to take court officials to business in the city. The night air was warm and still, holding its breath in anticipation, a pause in time. It wasn't yet dark with the sun glowing orange low in the sky, lighting up the city buildings in the distance and picking out the church steeples that soared towards the night as if they were alight, lances of fire.

Tom held out a piece of paper with the address spelled out; he'd copied it from Isabel's letter so nobody could read what else she'd written. One of the waiting men nodded and climbed down the greasy steps to the dark water slapping against the side of the wharf. Tom followed turning at the last moment and hopping into the small wherry, making it rock from side to side. He sat down quickly and they began to move upstream following the tide, the oars slicing smoothly through the water as still and smooth as glass. The movement caused a slight breeze as they moved and Tom pulled his velvet cap further onto his head. The boatman was old and concentrating on his work so thankfully didn't try to engage Tom in conversation and he managed to avoid the inevitable arm waving and pointing to his ears and mouth to indicate he couldn't communicate.

Hugh had drawn a detailed map and it didn't take long for Tom to find the house he wanted. As he arrived, he considered finding the back entrance given the state of his clothes but he'd been invited by the lady of the house so instead he strode up to the front door, knocking on it sharply.

The steward who opened it looked less than impressed to see him standing there and waved him back down the drive. Tom waited where he was, wondering how to explain he was expected by Isabel but thankfully just then she appeared in the hallway and immediately the steward stood to one side to allow Tom admittance. Although the disdainful expression didn't leave his face.

The hall was large and dark, a long room almost the width of the ground floor. Linenfold panels reflected the many candles burning together with a fire that despite the warm evening was burning brightly in the wide, smooth stone fireplace. The ceiling was decorated with plaster ribs between the beams, red Tudor rose bosses at the cross sections were echoed in the swirling plaster frieze around the top of the wall. Several benches and a chest lined the walls with two chairs pulled up beside the fire where Isabel indicated for Tom to sit while she poured out cups of wine for them both. It tasted sweet and Tom sipped at it nervously. In the

177

far corner of the room another maid was sewing, her head close to the work she was bent over.

'*This is my house,*' Isabel spoke slowly her face lit up down one side by the firelight. It was so much easier to see her face in this light, her lips glossy and dark from the wine. '*I was married to a courtier but he died just six months after our wedding. He was older than I and became ill. This house is now mine although the Queen decrees I am to remain at court. I was one of her ladies before my late husband Sir Geoffrey Downes noticed me and asked her for my hand in marriage. My parents are both dead so there was nobody to object. Except me of course but I had no say in the matter. And then within months he had died but I now have some independence as a widow and thankfully he was quite rich. His son from his first marriage inherited the country estate and the title but he left me this house in his will. And now I have a place to run away to when the commotion and noise at court becomes too much which suits me well.*'

Tom could hardly take it all in. He knew she must be high born to be one of the Queen's ladies but she was independently wealthy with a large house in the city of London. And what was he? A poor apothecary who couldn't even hear what she was saying to him; who had no idea what the sound of her voice was like and never would. He couldn't imagine why she was attracted to him but he was in too deep now to stop it. His heart was caught.

'This house is magnificent,' he wrote on his tablet, 'I didn't realise you owned all this or that you had once been married.'

'*It isn't relevant now,*' she shrugged. '*But it's much easier for us to meet here instead of creeping around the palace worrying about being seen. I can't be here often or the Queen will suspect something but if I say I have business that needs attending to then she is usually content to allow me absence from court for a few days or a week or so. This time she agreed to just three days as we're leaving for Westminster for a few weeks on Friday.'*

Tom felt his heart sink. He and Hugh wouldn't be expected to travel with the entourage as the Queen would take her physician and use local apothecaries if required. It may be weeks before he saw Isabel again and the thought filled him with sadness. His emotions darted across his face and were instantly picked up by Isabel.

'Come again on Wednesday evening,' she suggested, *'before I return to court on Thursday to help prepare for the journey. We can get to know each other better then, and when I return from Westminster I will ask leave to return here again. I would like to learn more about you, Tom Lutton, I am sure you have a story yet to be told.'* She smiled at him so sweetly he felt his insides knot with desire. He'd never seen anyone as beautiful, her fine boned face with its pale pink skin like the rose petals he collected in the gardens. He couldn't think of anything he wanted more than to be here in this house with her and cared not about the potential consequences if their clandestine meetings were discovered. He was in heaven and he found himself praying for God to consider him worthy of her. It was all too good to be true and when that happened something always came along to spoil it. He shuddered as the hairs along the back of his neck prickled in foreboding. Something wicked was stirring, he was sure of it.

Chapter Twenty-Eight

July 2021

A knock at the front door woke Mathilde up and getting groggily to her feet she was about to walk through and see who it was when she heard a second knock at the more usual entrance, the back door.

'Yes, one minute,' she called out hastily pulling on her jogging trousers. Hopping across the cold kitchen tiles in her bare feet she looked around for the kitten but it was nowhere to be seen. However, the two saucers on the floor were empty.

Through the dirty window of the back door she instantly recognised Oliver's now familiar silhouette.

'What are you doing here?' Opening the door a little bit she grabbed his shirt and pulled him through the tiny space before slamming it behind him. Not before she'd noticed how soft his faded, much washed denim shirt was beneath her fingers.

'Well, that's a very pleasant welcome. Not.' His eyes

twinkled as he teased. Mathilde didn't understand the idiom and frowned at him in response as she ushered him into the kitchen and shut the inner door behind them. Oliver looked around the room with all the doors which were usually left open firmly closed.

'Is there something going on?' he asked, 'why are we shut in here? Have you got a man hiding upstairs?' the teasing tone now absent from his voice.

'Eh *stupide*.' She rolled her eyes. 'I have a kitten in here. I found it yesterday and I don't want it to escape.'

'What do you mean, you found it?'

'It's . . .' she paused as she searched for the word, '*sauvage*. Wild.'

'Oh, feral? Are you sure?'

'Yes, I'm sure,' she pushed up the sleeves of her long-sleeved T-shirt to reveal the myriad of scratches along her forearms.

'Ouch. You may be right. So where is it now?'

'I don't know but I kept the doors shut all night so it must be in here somewhere. And the food I left out is gone.' She indicated towards the empty saucers. 'It was under the fridge so maybe back underneath?'

Getting down onto her knees she peered into the darkness. Joining her Oliver got out his mobile phone and switched on the torch, shining it across the dust covered floor. At the back, crouching down, covered in clumps of fluff and its eyes shining in the torchlight was the kitten, watching them.

'Hey, Shadow, kitten cat, come here,' Mathilde cooed, waggling her fingers.

'Shadow?'

'Yes. He's black, so . . . Shadow.'

'Look he isn't going to come out of there while we're staring at him and waving a torch in his face. You need some proper kitten equipment; go and get dressed and we'll find a pet shop.' Oliver stood up and opening the door to the hall he ushered her upstairs. 'I'm just going to have a quick look at your triptych,' he added, shutting the door behind him and disappearing along the hall into the dining room.

Mathilde found him in there when she arrived back downstairs twenty minutes later, her damp hair twisted into a topknot bun, her sharp cheekbones exposed for once instead of hidden behind her curtain of hair. She didn't notice Oliver's look of appreciation, his eyes sliding sideways to look at her as she joined him in front of the painting.

'Have you got any more information about it?' she asked.

'Not yet,' he replied, 'but I came over because I was hoping to do some more cleaning. I'm sorry, I should have called first; I had an unexpected day off and I wanted to be here so jumped into my car without thinking. By the way, have you had any other strange dreams or visions?' he added. Mathilde nodded slowly.

'This,' she pointed to a dark room which appeared to be full of people, 'I was here. It was hot and crowded and smelt of beer. And humans,' she wrinkled her nose at the memory before explaining the rest of the scene and the exchange she'd witnessed.

'How odd. It does appear you're dreaming about each scene but I'm sure that a psychologist could offer a rational explanation. Some sort of suggestive thing that happens after you've looked at the painting.'

Mathilde agreed, trying in vain to stop her eyes from wandering to the fiery pit on the last panel. She didn't need to dream about that; her memories were all too real and if she let them escape from the closet in her brain where they were locked away she'd never get them back in. It's where they needed to stay or her world would splinter into a million pieces around her.

Oliver's Mini was immaculately clean inside and Mathilde breathed out silently, relieved they hadn't decided to go in her van, the front of which resembled a household bin. She gave it an occasional sweep out but only when the dirt that flaked off her boots together with crumbs from the sand-wiches and crisps she ate on the move became too much for even her derisory standards. She wasn't sure why but she didn't want him to see her at her worst.

Pulling into the car park of a large out of town pet super-store Oliver rested his strong tanned forearm, his sleeves now rolled up, along the back of her seat as he twisted round to reverse into a space. Mathilde caught a faint drift of musky aftershave as he turned his head and she felt her stomach twist, heat flooding her body. The moment he applied the handbrake she unclipped her seatbelt and jumped out of the car, the confining space suddenly feeling much too small. If Oliver thought there was something amiss he didn't mention it.

'Right, let's sort Shadow out,' He collected a trolley and headed towards the back of the shop where an enlarged photo of a kitten swung from the ceiling, Mathilde following in his wake.

They were soon filling the trolley with everything a kitten could need. Conscious of her budget Mathilde decided against a special bed but after grabbing food bowls and a box of pouches they stopped beside the toys and her face

183

broke into a grin surveying the colourful range in front of her. There was a pause while Oliver tried to explain what cat nip was but with the help of his phone translator she finally understood and added a mouse containing the herb alongside a fluffy snake at the end of a stick which she thought might entice the kitten from under the fridge.

Once their purchases were stowed in the back of the car, Oliver suggested they bought a makeshift picnic from the supermarket next door and have lunch together.

'Just quickly then,' Mathilde agreed, 'because we've left Shadow on his own.'

He drove them to a picnic area beside a shallow river where they sat at a table eating the food they'd bought. The previous day's storm hadn't eased the hot weather and the sun directly above them dappled through the beech trees dancing shadowed patterns on the ground. The air was filled with the drone of bees drifting between the nettle flowers behind them. On the other side of the river a heron stood, a silent statue set in stone watching the water.

'So, tell me more about your childhood,' Oliver said, 'what was it like?'

Mathilde was watching the heron and it was a long time before she answered. 'It was frightening a lot of the time. And tiring having to be the grown up when I was just a kid. Now it feels strange being in one place when I've been so used to moving around.'

'What about when you were a child? You must've stayed in a house for a while then, when you were school age?'

'Houses, caravans, sheds, any place we could find shelter really. We didn't stay anywhere for long so my education was very patchy.' She gave him a quick smile, her usual ploy to divert sympathy. She hated compassion and could sense it coming. Deep inside she could still feel the rising terror of spotting the signs when her mother's mental state began to wobble again and the locals started to notice how she'd run and hide, often in outbuildings that weren't theirs, any tiny space she could crawl into to escape the bombs that were no longer falling around her but that she could still hear. That was the point when people would start to point their fingers and when Mathilde knew it was time to move on.

'Was it just you and your mum? Any siblings?'

'Just us. I always wished I had a brother or sister, someone to share the load with. And now I discover I do have a sibling and I had a dad who was alive and looking for me. Who could have taken all the weight from my shoulders and my childhood would have been completely different. A world apart from how it was and my mother could have accessed the help she so desperately needed.' Mathilde began to scuff at the grass beside her feet with the side of her shoe, making a groove in the dirt as she explained. 'Anyway,' adeptly she steered the conversation away from herself, 'you mentioned before that you have brothers?'

'Yes, two brothers. Twins: Simon and Miles. They're both younger than me. My parents thought they couldn't have children and adopted me when I was a baby; they were already in their late thirties. Then no sooner had the ink dried on the adoption certificate my mum discovered she was pregnant. Who'd have thought it eh? So, then she had three boys running riot.' He chuckled to himself.

'Do you ever wonder about your birth parents?' Mathilde asked.

'Not these days. I went looking for them in my early twenties – I was curious – but they weren't very interested even after all those years. They were both troubled people and really, I had a lucky escape being adopted by Mum and Dad. Both of our lives seem to have started with an escape of sorts, don't they?' Mathilde hadn't really thought of it like that but she nodded slowly as she considered what he'd said.

Then, suddenly jumping to her feet she brushed off the back of her jeans. 'Shall we go now? I want to get back to Shadow.' She flashed him a quick smile to try and soften the abrupt end to their conversation.

Oliver got to his feet and began to collect up the remains of the picnic, his concerned eyes never leaving her face. She could feel him trying to probe the shutters she'd pulled down but her emotions were buried so deeply even she couldn't find them. If she'd wanted to.

Pulling onto the gravel in front of the house they saw Rachel and Fleur were already home and Mathilde hoped they hadn't disturbed the kitten. She left Oliver to bring the shopping in as she hurried through the house, the slapping of her feet on the wooden floor echoing across the emptiness of the hall.

The kitchen door was still closed and walking in she found Fleur on all fours crawling around the floor making mewing noises while Rachel was putting away food from several carrier bags on the kitchen table.

'Was that a joke about the cat?' Rachel smiled at her, 'because Fleur has spent the past fifteen minutes trying to find it but it hasn't shown its face or made a sound.' Mathilde shook her head, her heart beginning to thump. Had it died while she'd been out wasting time at a picnic? She looked at the saucer on the floor and saw the water she'd left had gone. Kneeling down beside the kitten's hiding place she shone her phone torch underneath. Her breath escaped in a long hiss of relief as she saw the now familiar blue eyes peering back. Feeling a movement beside her Fleur's little face squashed up next to hers to look. She could smell the strawberry shampoo and feel little wisps of soft curls brush against her face and she resisted the urge to wrap her arm around the little girl and pull her close. Never before had she felt as she did about these two people who shared her DNA. It stirred up a feeling of protectiveness and love that she couldn't recognise, alien as it was.

'See, here he is,' her voice sounded gruff and she cleared her throat. 'I called him Shadow because he's black and he likes hiding under here in the dark.'

The door swung open behind them and Oliver staggered in with the bags of kitten paraphernalia from the pet shop.

'Have you got enough stuff?' Rachel laughed as she took it from him, 'and where exactly did you find this kitten?'

'I was out for a walk yesterday,' Mathilde sat back on her haunches and explained about the storm and sheltering in the shed, 'he's very thin so I gave him some food and now I think he's mine. He can stay in my van with me.'

'Okay,' Rachel sounded dubious about this plan, 'but you won't be able to take him back across to mainland Europe unless you get lots of vaccinations and a pet passport.'

'Whatever,' Mathilde waved her hand as if shooing away Rachel's objections, 'he needs the injections yes, but he will be hidden so no one will know I have him.' She missed Rachel looking at Oliver and raising one eyebrow, before letting the matter drop.

'Is he going to come out of there so I can play with him?' Fleur asked, her face still pressed against the floor.

'Not if he's feral,' her mother warned, 'he'll scratch. Come and sit at the table and have your snack. If he comes out then you're to leave him alone, do you understand?' Fleur nodded, her mouth turned down at the corners.

'When he's more used to everyone then he might not mind you playing,' Oliver reassured her.

Mathilde emptied a pouch of food onto one of the saucers and Oliver poured some water into the other one, then they finished unloading their purchases and setting out the litter tray. She saw Rachel glance at it and wrinkle her nose up in displeasure and she turned her back.

Within minutes Shadow had crept out from his hiding place and as they all held their breath, he crouched down in front of the food and began to eat.

'Ooooh,' Fleur whispered, 'Mummy can I have a kitten?'

'No, you can't.' Rachel frowned at Mathilde but she was too busy watching the tiny scrap of black fur, pale grey in patches where years of under appliance dust had collected on his coat.

After he'd finished eating and drank some of the water, he carefully walked a little further from his hiding place, investigating his new surroundings. Mathilde slowly reached for one of the catnip toys they had just bought and pushed it towards him trying not to make any sudden movements. She didn't want to make him bolt back to the dark safety of the fridge. Seeing the toy shift slightly, Shadow immediately stood upright with straightened legs as he bounced on all fours towards the plaything before jumping on it. Fleur let out a little giggle of delight.

188

'I think we all need to ignore him,' Rachel said, 'and then he'll get more used to us. I'm doing pasta for dinner in a while; do either of you two want some?' She looked across at Mathilde and Oliver.

'Not for me thanks,' Oliver replied, 'I really need to get home. I'm expecting to hear from some colleagues in London about your triptych in the next couple of days and when I do, I'll give you a call.' Ruffling Fleur's hair and flashing Rachel a quick smile, he walked back through the house to the front door, Mathilde following him.

'Thank you for your help today,' she said, 'and for the picnic.'

'I enjoyed it,' he smiled at her, his eyes creased up, the lines that usually fanned away from them almost disappearing. He was so open. She couldn't imagine being able to behave in that way, allowing herself to show emotions so freely. 'And thank you for talking to me about your past. I know it couldn't have been easy.'

'It's nothing,' she shrugged, 'as you say, it's in the past.' She looked down, kicking at a weed growing out of the doorstep.

'So maybe now it's time to stop letting it cloud your future?' He tilted her chin up so she had to look at him. He raised his eyebrows waiting for her to say something. She smiled briefly, shaking her head, the corners of her mouth turned down. Dipping his head his lips brushed softly against her hair before he turned away to his car and climbed inside.

She stepped backwards into the hall and shut the door and a moment later she heard the sound of his engine starting up and driving away.

'Goodbye,' she said quietly. Too late.

Chapter Twenty-Nine

October 1584

With his visits to Isabel temporarily suspended, Tom took out his new paints and was soon using them to add some of the many sights he'd seen around London. He thought twice about adding Throckmorton's execution but knew that day had been an important episode in his introduction to the city and to his clandestine work for Walsingham. It showed the outcome of the work of spies. He painted the city houses tightly packed together, the dark shadows beneath in the twisting lanes, the washing hung up high out of windows to dry. He painted the people, so many Londoners living in those houses, their worlds entwined with each other's as they all tried to survive in the existence they'd been dealt. The apprentices who ran through the streets almost knocking others out of their way, the goodwives and their hungry children. What did they know of plots to kill their Queen when their lives were spent trying to keep their families alive? His thoughts were grim, dark, and he tried to lighten the images he was capturing by including vanilla flowers and foliage as decoration around the scenes.

He also replicated the many plants he and Hugh grew in their now expanded physic garden. Alongside the usual herbs they needed for their medications were the saffron crocuses he'd planted in the late spring and which would soon be coming into flower. He didn't need to paint any more of those, the left-hand panel of the triptych scattered with images of the tiny lilac flowers. One of his earliest memories were the fields of blossoms around his grand home in Norfolk, undulating in the soft breeze like waves upon the sea, and the autumn sun warm on his face. Although his adoptive mother had continued growing the spice after their desperate flight to France to escape from the King's soldiers, it hadn't been in such large quantities, and she was dependent solely on her children and friends to help harvest it. Back breaking work. But the sharp, metallic scent of the saffron they gave up would stay with him forever and he was looking forward to collecting his own.

Unfortunately, however, the vanilla plants he was attempting to grow hadn't borne any fruit. Despite their exquisite, fine flowers they produced no pods of seeds and he was once again walking around the warehouses on the river front trying to find merchants whose ships had brought some back from Venice or Calais.

It didn't take long before once again Tom was summoned to Walsingham's office at the palace. He couldn't help a small frisson of pride that he was able to serve the Queen in this way but he worried about where Walsingham may send him next and what danger he may end up entangled in. The missions he was now being sent on were risky and he had no doubt Walsingham considered him dispensable.

Entering the now familiar apartment he found the man alone writing at his desk. Tom bowed low before standing up again, awaiting his instructions. Walsingham didn't look up from his frantic scribbling, quill going from ink to parchment and back again at a surprising speed. He waved over his shoulder towards the cushioned settle beside the fire and Tom walked over, sitting down gingerly. Being in such opulent surroundings in his unkempt clothes and apothecary apron always made him feel uncomfortable.

The room was bright and warm whilst outside the grey, dour clouds threw occasional splatters of rain against the window as if demanding entry but the dark weather was no opposition to the numerous beeswax candles alight in the room. Who needed sunlight when you could have so much candlelight? There weren't as many pictures and tapestries as in other parts of the palace; he wasn't surprised the austere and plainly dressed Walsingham with his black clothes and cap kept his apartment as unfriendly as he was. There were few pieces of furniture but one wall was taken up with a long, dark ornately carved chest in thick oak, the front adorned with a frieze of carved animals. His house in Seething Lane had been more homely, perhaps his wife Ursula insisted upon it. Here though there was no need for anything more than the plain, polished panelling, shining in the light of the fire. He watched a small grey mouse with tiny pink claws and tail scuttle back and forth alongside the wall opposite, oblivious to the people in the room, intent on its mission.

Walsingham finished his letter, shaking sand from a silver shaker across the words to dry them before sealing it, the wax dripping across his desk as he took the block from the candle he was melting it in and trickled it on the folded parchment before pressing his seal in. A young page arrived in the room; it was the same small boy Tom had seen before and his eyes darted between the two men, his shoulders hunched and stiff as he approached to take the letter, nodding so fast it looked as if his head would fall off. He was probably afraid of what may happen if he didn't immediately do as his master bid and snatching up the letter, bowing and walking backwards as he went, he disappeared out of the door again. Tom wanted to give him a smile of comfort but the boy's face was turned towards the floor. Tom looked across at Walsingham who was now looking at him waiting to make eye contact.

'*Tom, why have you come here wearing those awful old rags?*' he spoke slowly, '*when you come up to the state apartments you should be more smartly dressed. Suppose you happened to meet the Queen as she moves along the corridor? She will think you are a beggar who has broken into the palace and evaded the guards.*'

Tom had no idea how to respond. The livery he'd originally been lent had disappeared from his room as mysteriously as it had arrived so he could only wear his mended and patched old clothes. That was why he made sure he wore his apron at all times. He supposed maybe he should have removed that but when he was summoned all he could think about was getting upstairs as quickly as he could and also because being in that part of the palace meant there was always a slim chance he may see Isabel. He suspected she was still at Westminster but he hoped every day that she'd soon be home.

'*Don't you have anything neater?*' Walsingham asked after a pause, as if he had been waiting for Tom to reply to his comment before realising he wouldn't be able to; not without a lot of signing that Walsingham was unlikely to understand. Tom shook his head. Yes and no questions were so much easier. Walsingham frowned and opened his mouth then closed it again. Walking to a door set in the panelling behind him he disappeared only to reappear a couple of minutes later with some pale coloured kersey hose and a smart blue broadcloth coat together with a cap which was in much better shape than the one he currently wore. A jaunty feather, the ends of the barbs sticking together as it drooped, was still attached to one side.

'These should fit you,' he said, 'I took them from someone who wasn't acting as he should towards his Queen. He didn't need them where he was going.'

Tom shuddered. He could well imagine where that was but he was grateful for the smart clothes that he would never have been able to afford on his apothecary's wages.

'I have someone I want you to meet,' Walsingham went on, reaching for a wax tablet he kept nearby when talking with Tom. He picked up a blunt quill and scratched a name and turned it round to show Tom: Kit Marlowe. Tom shrugged. Was he supposed to know this person? 'He's an undergraduate at Corpus Christi,' Walsingham continued, 'and he has some useful friends in the theatre. They are watching some of Queen Mary's spies and we need to know more. I hope to discover what secrets they hide but I want you to hear what they do not, by reading people's lips. The men who are in the shadows are the people to be aware of. That is where the truth lies.'

Tom nodded. He hadn't understood 'Corpus Christi', but other than that he had caught the gist of what he'd been told. He held his arms out sideways and raised his eyebrows

194

in question. He needed to know where he was meeting this Kit Marlowe. Walsingham picked up a scrap of paper and dipping his quill in the pot of ink he wrote 'Bell Inn' on it with a day and time and passed it to Tom who looked at it and nodded.

'Wear your new clothes.' Walsingham pointed to the bundle on Tom's lap and he realised that was his cue to leave. Getting to his feet he gave a low bow leaving the room in a similar way to the page, twenty minutes earlier. He glanced back just before he pulled the door to and saw Walsingham scribbling away on a document, Tom already forgotten.

Chapter Thirty

October 1584

The evening he was due to meet Kit Marlowe, Tom grabbed some bread, cheese and figs and ate quickly in his room. It would have to suffice as he didn't have time to eat supper with the other servants as he usually did. A stew bubbling in a huge black pot over one of the two enormous fires that burned in the kitchen smelled of rich appetising venison for once, and he was sorry to miss it, but he couldn't do anything to upset Walsingham's plans.

Dressing in his new clothes he ran his fingers over a pair of new boots, the leather burnished and shining, that had appeared on his bed together with two shirts decorated with simple blackwork embroidery around the neckline. They were substantially less darned than his own and were made of fine cambric, softer than the linen he was used to. Better quality than anything Tom had worn since he was a young child, cool and smooth against his skin.

Tom examined them carefully, especially for any tell-tale

blood stains. He suspected Walsingham was obtaining these additional wardrobe items from the same source as his new blue coat and he was concerned as to where they may have last been worn. They smelled fresh however, and there were no unpleasant stains.

Once he was fully dressed he felt smarter than he could ever remember, slipping out of a side door to make his way to the wharf and find a boat to take him upriver. He was amused when the guards not only didn't stop him but also inclined their heads thinking he was a gentleman of the court. What he wore turned him into a different man he realised, holding his head higher and striding down to where a collection of small craft bobbed about on the choppy Thames water.

Although he was only going half a mile it was against the tide and the water was rough out in the middle of the river. He could see the sculler swearing and sweating as he pulled as hard as he could on the oars and slowly, they made their way to Drinkwater Wharf where Tom carefully negotiated the slippery steps which were covered in dark green slimy algae. The last thing he wanted was to spoil his new outfit.

Once on the quay he nipped along the passageway that led to Pudding Lane and then on to East Cheap. Here the city's butchers and slaughterhouses were situated and the metallic iron rich tang assaulted his nostrils. Outside every house carcasses and joints were hung as if they were on the spits in front of the fire they were destined for, thick dark blood congealing in pools on the cobbles.

Eventually he found The Bell Inn Theatre and spotted a man outside rolling barrels along the floor. He held his hand up to gain attention and showed him the piece of paper on which Walsingham had written Marlowe's name. The man nodded and pointed to a small door almost hidden in the dark wall. He said something to Tom but it was lost as he turned away before he'd finished speaking, continuing to move the beer. Walking over to the door he lifted his hand, pausing for a moment. The old Tom – the real one – would knock and wait for someone to answer. But what would this new one do? He'd be more assertive; he didn't need to wait to be bade entry. For the first time in his life he felt the faint stirrings of being an equal and it felt good. Knocking on the door he pressed down on the latch and stepped into the murky interior.

The dark corridor in which he found himself had a door at the end lit by a single candle in a sconce on the wall beside it. As he approached it was flung open and a man leant in the doorframe staring at Tom, a look of surprise on his face at finding someone there. Tom could see his lips moving but in the gloomy interior it was impossible to read them. He reached into his pocket for the memo note Walsingham had given him. The man had turned to speak to someone behind him so Tom approached slowly, holding the letter out and hoping he wasn't about to be run through with a sword.

He waited while the seal was broken and the contents read. The man's demeanour changed immediately as a smile spread across his face making him look more welcoming and friendly. Standing to one side he ushered Tom into the room with a bow of his head, pointing to himself and mouthing *'Kit Marlowe'*; not being used to such treatment Tom wondered what Walsingham had said about him.

The room was thankfully lighter than the hallway he'd entered by, a tall ceiling and thick candles in sconces with tall twisted metal holders revealed a group of seated men, some of them with bundles of paper in their hand. A fire had burned down in the grate and Kit picked up a log and tossed it on, causing sparks to fly up the chimney and across the hearth, already covered in a thick layer of velvety grey ash.

Tom watched the man explain who he was. It was much easier to read his lips in the brightly lit room and he recognised his own name, Sir Francis Walsingham and the words *'can neither hear, nor speak'* something he was very used to reading, together with *'help us with our obligations to the Queen'*. He didn't need to wonder about these duties; if Walsingham had sent him here this was a spying assignment and the other men were obviously part of his network. A large one, Tom was beginning to realise.

The group turned to look at him. *'You cannot hear us at all?'* one of the men asked. Tom smiled and shook his head.

'What?' One of the men got slowly to his feet to face Tom. His face had the florid hue of a man who liked his drink. He was short and slight with long arms which swung back and forth as he moved and he was flexing his fingers ominously. *'If you cannot hear me, how were you able to understand my question?'* His breath stank, his brown rotting teeth visible in pale swollen gums as he pushed his face close to Tom's who had to take a step backwards and was now pressed up against a table behind him, the edge of it pushing into his thighs. Kit must have said something to the man as his head turned sideways before he took a step backwards and held his palms up in apology.

'You are able to read everything I say?' he asked, pointing to his mouth before slapping Tom on the back. It felt as if

he'd been hit with a shovel. Kit had moved to one side so Tom could read what he was saying as he explained to the man whom he called Richard how he was able to lip read.

He felt self-conscious as all eyes turned on him and he looked around at them all, gauging their reactions. Slowly one by one each man began to smile and nod their heads. They turned towards Kit as he began to explain why Walsingham had sent Tom to them and he watched carefully as the reason became clear. The men around him were the Queen's Men: a theatre group who played for the Queen and who also went on tour around the shires. Who better to go with them and watch certain gentlemen suspected of being in the employ of Mary Stuart, than a silent spy? The men turned to look at him in a new, appreciative light. They were smiling at him, realising he was one of them; someone with a double persona.

Kit went around the room introducing everyone. Tom was surprised to discover Richard was the troupe's star clown and he proved it by immediately doing a backwards tumble across the room until he crashed into a bench at the other side. Tom was good at remembering names and faces and before long he knew exactly who everyone was. Kit passed him a beaker of ale and indicated for him to sit with them all as they moved their chairs to include him in the circle they'd been sitting in when he arrived.

'We're going away,' Kit explained to him indicating a map laid out on a trestle table in front of him, *'we need to visit certain establishments as directed by Walsingham.'* He pointed to various villages across Staffordshire and Shropshire, close to where Tom knew Queen Mary was incarcerated. *'Some of these houses used to be Catholic and it is suspected they may still be.*

Whilst we are performing, you, Tom, can be watching and reading that which people say, to discover what treason may be going on.'

Tom wondered how long he'd be away. Hugh would be displeased; he needed Tom's assistance in the stillroom and his constant disappearing to see Walsingham had already garnered complaints and scowls despite neither of them having any say in the matter. And what about Isabel? He'd possibly be gone for weeks, months even and his heart hurt to think he wouldn't see her during that time. She was due back from Westminster very soon. Supposing she forgot about him? He was hopeful she felt about him the same way he did about her, even though they'd only managed to meet in privacy a very few times. But could he really hope a lowly assistant apothecary who could neither hear, nor speak, would be able to get closer to – nay, marry – one of the Queen's ladies? As a widow she had more freedom to marry whomever she pleased, but surely she'd choose from the courtiers who surrounded the Queen? There were certainly plenty of single noblemen from which to choose. Rich well-educated gentlemen with money and status.

Once the meeting broke up and a route to the north had been decided, Kit told Tom to return to the theatre the following week. He explained he'd organise a horse for which Tom was very thankful, having walked all across France and Belgium, he had no desire to do a similar journey again. His feet had softened now and he didn't want to ruin his new boots.

Leaving the premises after waving goodbye to his new acquaintances, Tom wandered slowly back to the wharf. He wasn't in a hurry as Hugh had no idea when to expect him and with a flash of inspiration he detoured along Cheapside until he reached the Royal Exchange. Built by Flemish workers in pale grey stone, slate and glass it stood out amongst the other buildings with its magnificent gold grasshopper shining on top. He'd seen it on his way through London when he first arrived and knew it was where he needed to visit. It was a risky strategy but he had nothing to lose and everything to gain. Absolutely everything.

Inside the building he stopped for a moment amongst the bustle to take everything in. An arcaded courtyard housed many merchants and he could see bolts of brightly coloured silks and velvets as the mercers went about their business, gold and goods exchanging hands. Upstairs a gallery housed shops selling books, birdcages and armour whilst apothecaries prepared remedies for life's ills. The scent of sweet crushed pennyroyal wafted across. Arriving at a small goldsmith's shop he stepped inside. He didn't like to deal with shopkeepers, the usual banter and discussion being too confusing, but this time he had no choice. The man spoke to him as he entered, Tom missing what he'd said as he gazed around the small interior filled with every kind of bauble and jewel he could ever imagine. A glowing gold and ruby carcanet lay on a velvet pillow. It looked so heavy Tom wondered how any lady could wear it around her neck and keep her back straight. Then his eye caught on a small locket on a long chain. It was gold and cut in a filigree design. Would he be able to afford it? He carried his drawstring purse hidden beneath his clothing and strapped to his body so it sat under his arm, flush with his skin. It wasn't visible underneath his shirt so in theory wouldn't be found if he were set upon by cut throats. He also didn't trust his fellow servants at the palace, keeping it on his person at all times.

Tom pointed to the locket and the shopkeeper took it from the wooden display stand and laid it on the counter top in front of him. He knew that wearing the blue coat and smarter clothes Walsingham had given him resulted in being served far more politely than if he were wearing his usual attire. He picked it up and examined it carefully, running his fingertips around the intricate carved gold. Laying it back down, he raised his eyebrows hoping the man would understand that he wanted to know the price. As he did so he made a motion with his hand as if writing and pointed to his ears, shaking his head. It usually worked as a signal he wouldn't be able to hear a reply and sure enough the shopkeeper rummaged under the bench for a scrap of paper and a quill and wrote 'five gold angels' on it. The price was double the amount Tom had expected to pay but even in the much-exalted Royal Exchange he knew there would be some room for negotiation. How easily he could achieve that when he couldn't speak, he wasn't sure.

Shaking his head, he crossed out the figure and wrote down what he wanted to pay. The shopkeeper frowned and wrote down another figure. This to and fro of the paper and quill went on for a further two minutes until they reached a figure they were both happy with. Tom handed over the money he'd been saving and pocketed the locket. He could feel it cool against his skin, knocking gently as he walked along the street and jogged down the alley to where boats waited to take passengers up or down the river. He had a plan forming in his head. A way to know whether Isabel felt the same as he did and if there was a future for them as he so fervently hoped. It was reckless and could ruin everything between them but he had to try. Or he'd die always wondering.

Chapter Thirty-One

July 2021

Mathilde stood in front of the triptych; her brows furrowed. The pull it had on her was getting stronger, weaving its threads around her, and yet she was no closer to understanding what it wanted of her. The style was similar to Bosch and yet far cruder; surely not even one of his students would have produced something like this. But the little scenes across it were definitely related to each other as the same people appeared in different scenes. This had to be someone's life story.

She walked slowly around it until she was stood at the back of the frame. Typically, this was much rougher than the ornate decoration seen at the front. Plain, pale wood still with its rough surface and Elizabethan splinters. Oliver had drawn her a quick Tudor family tree so she could understand exactly how old the painting was. She knew which era it was in France and had touched briefly on the Tudors when she'd read about Catherine Medici and the St Bartholomew

Day massacre. They were bloody times, both sides of the channel.

One corner of the frame backing had come away slightly and Mathilde berated herself for being rough with it when she removed it from the chapel wall. Perhaps she'd caught the corner with her claw hammer. She gave it a small push with the heel of her palm to try and force it back into place but it sprang back out further than before and she cursed under her breath.

Leaning in closer she peered into the tiny opening, wondering if she could see what the rear of the actual panels was like. As soon as Oliver saw the opening at the back he'd want to arrange to have it closed again professionally in order to protect the integrity of the triptych. This may be her only chance as he was due to arrive later that day.

Screwing up one eye she pressed her face as close as she dared without actually knocking into it and sending it tumbling to the floor. The shadow from her head darkened the opening making it impossible to see and sliding her phone out of the back pocket of her jeans she switched on the torch and shone it inside. The back of the painting was rough, the wood it had been painted on was, as Oliver suggested, not of the finest quality. Her eye paused as she spotted something a little bit further down from the opening. It looked like a piece of cloth or paper, pale in colour.

She squeezed her fingers through the opening moving her first two fingers in a pincer movement to try and reach it but it was too far down as if it had slid down when the triptych was moved. She was going to need some sort of tweezers and she took her hand out while she wondered where she could find something to use. Then she remembered the pair of narrow, long nosed pliers in her van and running out she rummaged through her tool box until she found them.

Back inside she slid the end of the pliers in, easily removing the item. It was indeed a piece of paper, so incredibly thin that Mathilde held her breath worried in case just exhaling would make it drift away. Whisking the dust sheet off the other end of the table she laid it down carefully on the glossy French polished surface.

The paper appeared to have been folded, a brown line now ingrained across the middle. Mathilde didn't want to touch it without a pair of cotton gloves – Oliver always put some on before touching the painting – and this item was far more fragile. She peered closely but couldn't make out what it said, whatever was there had faded over the years. Across the room the curtains fluttered a little despite there being no draught. Picking up her mobile phone, still with its torch on where she'd dropped it on a chair, she called Oliver to tell him of her discovery.

She was disappointed when his phone went to voicemail and in her excitement she couldn't remember the English words she needed and her message ended up being mixed with French as she blurted out what she'd found. She hoped he could understand her use of *'cache'*. Walking through to the kitchen she went in search of Rachel to tell her the news.

He returned her call an hour later. Rachel was as excited as Mathilde, although she had joked it was probably a sixteenth-century shopping list. They were both delighted when Oliver promised he'd be over as soon as he could.

'This may be the clue we've been looking for,' he told Mathilde as they arranged for him to come after lunch, 'it might tell us why a work of art such as this was hidden away in the chapel.'

Mathilde was grateful his interest matched her own and realising she still had two hours at least to wait before he was likely to arrive she decided to go to the garden and do some more digging. She intended to make the patch she'd set aside for her herbs larger and wanted to start clearing the space around where she'd planted. It was the one space which seemed immune from the subtle edge of suppressed expectation that crept insidiously through the hall.

When she popped her head around the living room door to tell Rachel where she'd be when Oliver arrived, her sister jumped to her feet.

'Hang on, I said I'd show you where Dad's tools are,' she reminded her and delighted, Mathilde followed her around the end of the house to a ramshackle wooden shed she'd noticed previously. Pulling open the door, Mathilde stepped inside, breathing in deeply the scent of warm creosote and dried earth still stuck on the implements in front of her. She reached out and ran her fingers across the handle of a spade now worn smooth with age. A warm breeze crept in beside her, brushing her face.

'They're so special,' she whispered, certain that if she turned her head it wouldn't be Rachel stood behind her but their father.

'Use them,' Rachel urged as she wrapped her arm around Mathilde and gave her a squeeze, 'he'd have loved to know you were enjoying them.' With a smile she leant momentarily against Rachel's shoulder before taking the spade and making her way across the garden to the spot in the corner. Now was the time to transplant her herbs from their pots to the ground, a fragment of permanence.

Surrounded by the undergrowth and shrubs her father had tended, it was a link to her past which she felt most keenly there. He'd dug this ground, turned over the soil that had been here forever; and his father before him and however many ancestors before them. Feeling the rich earth run through their fingers, smell the potential in its damp power. Rachel was a blood tie and she could talk about their now deceased relatives, but it was all merely facts about dead people, dust beneath the ground in the tiny churchyard she'd visited. She wanted to know about their habits and peculiarities, the quirks that really made them who they were. Those were the pieces missing from the jigsaw of her father. What did he watch on the television? Did he read a newspaper? Did he insist on eating every meal sitting at the table? She needed to start asking more questions. These were the details she craved but Rachel wouldn't realise that unless she was more open.

Pushing the spade into the wet soil she began to dig, whilst wondering what she might plant next. A robin flew down in front of where she was working, its head on one side as it watched for any bugs she might turn over, and she smiled at it. A sense of calm settled like a mantle on her shoulders and for a moment she felt as if she'd been here before even though she knew that was impossible. The ghosts of her ancestors crowded in behind her, their long dead breath prickling the hairs on the back of her neck.

After washing her hands to remove the dirt ingrained under her fingernails, she ate a hasty lunch and waited for Oliver to arrive. She'd left the piece of paper on the table which she'd suddenly realised was a stupid thing to do in a house with a five-year-old running around and hurried through to the dining room to check it was where she'd left it. Thankfully it was, laid thin and delicate as a dead leaf, almost transparent. Perching on the arm of a chair positioned beside the window she watched for Oliver to arrive whilst also keeping an eye on the potentially valuable document at the same time.

At ten past two she spotted his car moving slowly along the drive. There were a number of potholes and she'd seen Rachel wince every time a wheel went down into one, making her car lurch to the side. She didn't notice them in her van which was built for rough terrain if required. Oliver was only ten minutes late but she had been feeling jittery he wasn't going to arrive, drumming her fingers on the arm of the chair in frustration as each minute passed. Fleur loved Oliver and was excited about him visiting, especially as he often had sweets in his pocket, and she had been hopping from foot to foot, running along the front of the house looking out of the windows in the drawing room in anticipation.

As he knocked on the door and before Mathilde could get to it, Fleur was standing on tip toe and reaching up for the lock. She opened it, a broad grin on her face.

'We were watching for you,' she said, standing aside to let him in. Mathilde felt her face flush with embarrassment. It might be true but she didn't want Oliver knowing. *Sometimes five-year-olds should keep their mouths shut*, she thought to herself.

After Oliver produced a bag of jelly beans from his pocket and told Fleur she must take them to Rachel he followed

Mathilde into the dining room. Taking two pairs of new, fresh gloves from his other pocket and passing a pair to her they both pulled them on. Standing in front of the triptych, he asked, 'So what did you find? I couldn't understand your message very well. It would help if you could just speak one language at a time.' His eyes were sparkling as he spoke and she knew he was teasing not criticising.

'At the back, here,' she showed him the space between frame and backboard, 'see that gap? I think I did it when I took it from the chapel wall. But then I was wondering how I could nail it back,' she paused as Oliver's hand shot out and held on to her arm.

'Please tell me you haven't been banging any nails into this?' He looked horrified. Before she could answer they were interrupted by Rachel bringing in a tray with three steaming cups of coffee on it.

'Oliver, you really should stop buying her sweets,' she admonished as she carefully placed the tray on a delicate side table, the legs of which looked so fragile it was a wonder it could bear the weight of the cups. 'But thank you, she's happy with a handful of jelly beans and playing with her toy zoo, so I've escaped to see what you're both up to in here. Where is this paper you found, Mathilde?'

Mathilde moved to the end of the table and indicated. 'I don't want to touch it,' she explained, 'because it looks so fragile and old. The writing is tiny and faded but it looks like it may be a letter?'

Oliver took out his eye loupe and bent down close to it. 'I'm not sure it's in English,' he said. Even his breath close up caused the paper to move slightly and he stood up before continuing. 'It almost looks like shorthand.' Rachel nodded but Mathilde looked blank and shrugged at him. He needed to remember that although her English was improving there were still some words she didn't understand. She looked between the two of them, her eyebrows raised and waited for a translation.

'Look,' Rachel held out her phone, on which she had brought up a picture of a section of shorthand, the squiggles and lines.

'That looks like an insect has walked in some ink and danced across the paper,' Mathilde exclaimed, 'how can anyone understand it?'

'You can if you are trained to,' Oliver explained, 'and it's a lot quicker to write than using full words so in times gone by secretaries used it to take notes and type them up later. It was like a sort of code I suppose.' As he said this last sentence his voice tailed away, his thoughts elsewhere. 'A code, of course. Of course,' he repeated while Rachel and Mathilde looked at each other in confusion, 'I think this might be written in a cipher. We just need to work out what it says: crack the code.'

'And will it tell us where the family jewels and gold are?' Rachel tilted her head on one side.

'Are they missing then?' Oliver replied, unsure whether she was joking or not.

'Not that I know of,' her face broke into a smile, 'but it would be nice to find some anyway. Why would someone write something in code and hide it behind here? Supposing we hadn't found the picture? The note would never have been discovered. Even now we can't decipher it. It seems like a waste of time to me.'

'Perhaps nobody was supposed to find it?' Oliver

suggested. 'If it's as old as this painting, sixteenth century, then it may be impossible to crack. They used to pass information in coded letters, that was how they plotted to kill royalty like Queen Elizabeth or organised other treason like the gunpowder plot.'

Once again Mathilde was lost as Oliver and Rachel started chanting about the fifth of November and fireworks and she blanked them from her thoughts as she studied the paper. Oliver had placed his loupe on the table beside it and she put it to her face to study the note or letter more carefully. The metal of the loupe was still warm from where it had been wedged in Oliver's eye socket and Mathilde liked the feel of it now settling on her own skin.

'There's something else on here, look.' She stood up passing the loupe back to Oliver and stepping back so he could get closer to the piece of paper. 'Between the lines of "shorthand" I can see very pale brown letters as if there's a second document on the same piece of paper.'

'Oh my God,' Oliver bent closer to the paper both hands either side of the document, his head bowed for a moment.

'What's wrong?' Rachel asked. Mathilde felt panic rising in her chest as he continued to be silent.

'Oliver?' she asked.

'The reason we can see two separate lines of writing, is because this is a palimpsest. A narrative has been added and it's in a crude sort of invisible ink between the lines of the original cipher which is why it's much paler; over the years the ink has slowly become more visible. I need to take this to someone who can properly investigate it for us. I know of someone in Oxford who may be able to help; I'll give him a call right away.'

'Do we have to?' Mathilde asked. 'I'm not sure if I want others getting involved. It was hidden here so it's linked to this house and to someone who once lived here. I think whoever that was wants us – me – to discover what they were trying to say.' It was the first time she'd admitted to the other two that she could feel forces from the past trying to reach out to her. 'Can't we investigate it? I'll need your help though,' she admitted to Oliver, unaware just how much her face changed when she turned to him, her enthusiasm lighting up her expression, smoothing away the lingering sadness he often saw there.

'I'm sorry,' he said, taking her hand in his, 'this is far more complicated than I can deal with, you need an expert in this field. I'm just an ordinary art historian and you need a specialist.'

They placed the letter into a dark velvet folder Oliver had brought with him and walked back through to the kitchen to discuss their next steps. Mathilde was only half listening as she felt the threads that tethered her to the triptych, and Lutton Hall, tighten further, fine silk cords that gripped and twisted every sinew in her body.

Chapter Thirty-Two

October 1584

Tom was wondering how to get a message to Isabel to tell her that he needed to see her. He'd always been reliant on her suggesting a meeting and since he knew that the Queen and her retinue had returned from Westminster he resorted to visiting the knot garden every day at dawn hoping that when she was able to get away, she'd come there too.

The day before he was due to leave to travel north, Tom slipped out of the side door as he usually did, skirting along beside the wall. There to his surprise and delight he could see the green travelling cloak he recognised and the face he now knew he loved. The cool morning air with its sharp spike of autumn prickled around him as he hurried over. Her face split into a wide smile and her eyes sparkled in pleasure as she saw him. Without a thought his arms went round her and he pulled her against him. If she rebuffed his affection then he'd know his ambitions were not to be. It was a risk he was prepared to take.

To his relief he felt her arms wind their way around his waist as she settled her body against his. The warmth from her trickled into him, through her cloak and gown, down into his body, his heart, the centre of his being. Her chest rose and fell slowly as she exhaled. She looked up at him, the dimple beside her mouth enticing him to kiss it.

'I've missed you,' she told him. He nodded and pointed to himself, pulling a sad face. She giggled and he could feel it reverberate through them both. And now he had to relate bad news to her. With much signing and waving of his arms he managed to explain he was required to go away with the Queen's Men and travel around the northern shires. She mouthed 'Walsingham?' at him, and he nodded. He knew she understood he had no option but to go. However, a small part of him was pleased at the look of disappointment on her face. This was the moment he needed to declare how he felt.

Tipping her chin up so her eyes met his, he pointed to his heart and then to her. Her eyes widened and he knew she'd understood the sentiment. She nodded slowly and pointed to herself and he felt his heart begin to thump so hard he wondered if she could hear it. Dropping his arms he took a half step backwards and reached into his pocket, taking out the locket he'd bought. He was certain she'd realise it was intended as a betrothal gift, but would she accept it? He held his breath. She may like him, even love him, but that held no sway as to who she'd choose as a husband.

Her hand flew to her mouth as she looked at the locket and taking it from his hand she carefully lifted it over the linen coif she wore and over her gown. The long chain meant it reached her waist and as she quickly tucked it as best she could beneath her clothes, pulling the stiff snowy white linen ruff away from her neck to coil the chain inside, he smiled at the thought of his betrothal gift being close to her skin. And hidden from prying eyes, he was sure that was the reason she'd hastily concealed it. He hoped she understood the meaning behind why he'd given it and as she put her hand over her heart, he was certain she had.

A movement at the far end of the garden as it sloped down towards the river alerted Tom to the fact they may not be alone for much longer. They could easily be seen now the sun was beginning to climb, fingers of sunlight reaching out to them from between the clouds. It caught the leaves on the bushes and edged them with molten gold, reflected in the still, calm waters of the river.

'I will write,' Isabel promised. Tom nodded and pointed to himself, indicating that he would try to keep in touch as well. Although he wasn't sure what he would have to tell her given that his spying was a deadly secret. Literally. He was risking his life, one that until that moment had not been important to anyone and yet now, maybe it was.

He watched her turn and hurry away to the door she always crept out of, keeping his eyes on her and memorising every inch of her body until she slipped out of sight. Even when she was gone he continued to stare at the place where she'd been, as if the outline of her body remained, embossed on the framework of time. Would she wait for him? He would in all likelihood be gone for months and every day she was surrounded by gallant, handsome courtiers who could offer her so much more than he could. Someone who could whisper words of romance in her ears, not just wave their arms about to communicate. He thought his heart would break if that happened. Slowly, thoughtfully, he turned and walked back to his room to finish packing for the long journey ahead, wondering where his nomadic life would take him next and whether he'd ever return to the palace and to Isabel.

Chapter Thirty-Three

October 1584

As directed Tom was at the theatre the following day with his belongings stuffed into a pair of leather panniers. Along with the smarter clothes he'd been given he also carried many twists of paper containing the most frequently used of his herbs. He'd stored pots of ointment for sores he was certain would be required after many long days in the saddle.

Kit was waiting for him together with two of the troupe; they were meeting the others on the road beyond Holborn. Looking Tom up and down, the look on Kit's face showed he wasn't impressed with his usual attire. Taking his bags from him Kit opened them and passed Tom his blue coat, indicating to him to put it on.

Tom couldn't deny that once wearing the more fashionable and stylish coat he could feel himself stand up straighter with a strike of confidence slice through him. It made him stand out which was something he'd always actively avoided and yet now he liked how it made him feel.

'That is better,' Kit told him, before doing a mime of Tom in his old jerkin and his shoulders slumped, a man hiding behind his own shadow, then in his blue coat with his shoulders back. He even included a small swagger and Tom smiled although he was certain he hadn't ever walked like that. 'What you wear makes you who you are,' Kit told him, 'clothes make a man.' He smiled and before he turned back to the horses waiting patiently Tom saw Kit repeat the phrase about clothes making a man a couple of times to himself, nodding slowly.

Once they were mounted, they rode down towards Newgate. It was a long time since Tom had ridden but after a childhood of riding bareback around the meadows of France he was soon in the rhythm of the movement beneath him. As they broke into a canter he could feel the thumping of the horse's hooves reverberate through his body as they struck the ground and he lifted his face to the wind rushing past, cold and exhilarating, whipping his hair against his skin. He could smell the fresh scent of wet vegetation crushed beneath the horse's hooves where it had rained overnight and he remembered just how much he loved being a part of nature and the countryside. He knew he'd been extremely lucky in getting such a prestigious job at the palace but with only the physic garden to tend to he missed the wide-open spaces he now found himself in.

The journey to their first engagement in Oxford didn't continue in the same happy mood they'd started in. After meeting with the rest of the troupe, dark clouds began to gather on the horizon and it wasn't long before the rain began to fall, heavy and persistent. It dripped off the trees and down the back of Tom's neck running in rivulets from his soaked hair onto his face to drip off his chin. The horses were walking and even they looked desolate as they picked their way around puddles and through mud. Tom kept giving his steed a pat on the neck in encouragement but he wasn't sure it was helping. John Singer's horse had stepped in a deep ridge and was now lame so he was riding pillion behind Kit, leading his despondent horse behind him. They rode through small villages dotted along the road, the cottages topped with dripping thatch, clustered around commons scattered with grazing animals. Smoke from chimneys was tugged away on the breeze. Tom was very relieved when after many days, broken up only with stops at inns that were both rough and uncomfortable, they arrived at their first venue.

Kit had already explained that their host was suspected of papist ways and being a supporter of the Queen of Scots and Tom was to keep alert to all that was said. The other men would cause the distraction and hopefully Tom could discover if anything was amiss. Nobody would suspect him and as a cover story he was supposedly their servant. Tom gloomily swapped his good coat for his old jerkin again, back to the position in life he was accustomed to. Just as Kit had pointed out, he felt his shoulders drop.

The players' entertainment went down well and the family and their assembled guests who'd come to see the performance became drunker and more verbal as the evening wore on. Tom stood at the side of the stage supposedly helping with props and costumes, in a perfect position to watch the audience. He'd already been introduced to, and dismissed by, their host. As soon as he'd realised Tom was simply a servant who was also deaf he became all but invisible, just as Walsingham had predicted.

In a particularly raucous and lewd moment in the play, as all the crowd including the ladies present were laughing and jeering, Tom saw their host turn to his neighbour and say quite distinctly, '*We have a Jesuit priest here who will take mass in the morning. You and your good wife are welcome to join us.*' His companion raised his eyebrows.

'*You should be careful,*' he replied, '*there are strangers amongst us.*' His eyes flicked towards the players as Tom quickly began folding up a cloak that had been thrown off stage. He felt his cheeks begin to burn as the two men looked over at him. They both looked away again and Tom resumed his observation.

'*It's fine,*' their host said, '*the men can't hear us with all the noise they are making, it is enough to raise the dead! And their servant is deaf so he cannot hear us either. What we say is perfectly safe.*'

'*Does the priest live here?*' The man was shredding a chunk of bread left from dinner into crumbs which scattered across the table. '*You will be hanged if anyone discovers him.*'

'*I could be executed for a lot more,*' came the reply, '*but yes, Brother John lives in the west tower; there is a priest hole beneath the stairs leading up to the top room. We had to hide him in there six months ago when the Earl of Leicester decided to visit.*'

'*And do you have word of the Spanish? Is there yet any information about how we get our right and proper Queen onto the throne and remove that usurper, the late King's illegitimate daughter?*'

'*Not yet but I believe it will not be long now. And nobody will suspect a thing.*'

221

Yes, they will, Tom thought to himself as he placed the folded cloak into the props bag. He wondered what else the household had been up to but he was sure that Walsingham had his ways to find out the truth. Tom had been on his way to a warehouse at the docks when he'd had the misfortune of seeing another man being hanged, despite his endeavours to avoid any executions after watching Throckmorton die. He'd been on the rack more than once and couldn't even stand up, so many of his bones had been broken, like a sack being dragged along the ground behind a horse. It had turned Tom's stomach and for a moment he doubted whether he should report what he'd just gleaned before reminding himself that his first allegiance had to be to the Queen. After all, his love Isabel was in her entourage and ultimately it was Her Majesty whose safety was paramount.

It was much later in the evening when Tom was finally in the barn sitting on the pallet he'd been given to sleep on; the players were lodging in the attics at the top of the house. It didn't afford him the comfort he'd become used to and with very little light coming in through the window he pulled out a book he'd been given by Walsingham. Sliding two fingers between the spine and the pages, he drew out a thin sheet of paper he'd hidden there for just this purpose. In the dark with just the stump of a candle that was left guttering in the draught blowing under the door he started to write out a letter, in code, to Walsingham. The message hidden back where he'd been told to secrete it, he'd make sure it was taken to London when they stopped at the next inn on their journey. After he'd finished his official business, he quickly wrote a few lines to Isabel hoping it would reach her safely. If it got caught up with the other letter there was every chance Walsingham would intercept it and quite possibly not pass it on, and for this reason Tom was careful to not mention anything of the locket, the betrothal gift she'd accepted from him.

The journey around the shires took ten weeks in total and it was almost Christmas before they returned to London. The weather had turned much colder over the time they'd been travelling and as they rode the final couple of miles Tom could feel tiny shards of ice collecting on his beard and crackling against his dry lips. He'd run out of soothing ointment for them two weeks previously along with most of the other medications. Once the others had discovered he had them they were constantly presenting themselves with various aches and pains. Ill health following a night of heavy drinking being the most common complaint.

The trip had been fairly unproductive after the initial information gathering apart from one of the final houses they'd visited where a visitor had been staying. Tom knew immediately who it was and from Kit's body language he could tell that he did too. Sure enough he caught Tom's eye and gave a slight jerk of his head towards the man. Tom gave a tiny nod in return, no more than a twitch to indicate he'd understood. He'd watched this person before and he fervently hoped that he wouldn't be recognised, because this was William Parry. Parry's visit to a prominent Catholic family would not please Walsingham. Tom decided to wait until he could pass on this vital information in person.

As the troupe made their journey back to London Tom was concerned that he hadn't received a single letter from Isabel during the time he'd been away. With them travelling all the time it was difficult for post to follow on and more than one of the players had complained about the lack of letters from home. But it was with a feeling of trepidation of what may be waiting for him, that Tom finally climbed from the boat at the palace gatehouse. He walked slowly back with his panniers to the side door that led to the still-room and his home.

Chapter Thirty-Four

July 2021

Mathilde sat up in bed with a jolt, gasping out loud. Fumbling to her left she quickly switched on her lamp and looked around the room expecting something to be different but everything was exactly the same as when she'd gone to bed. Her clothes slung carelessly across a chair, the jeans on the floor where she had stepped out of them, and the magazine she'd been reading before she dozed off still laid on the bed beside her.

She'd had another disturbing dream and gripping the bedcovers in her clammy hands she waited for a moment while her heart returned to a more normal speed. Slowly she lay back down again, keeping the lamp on. The clarity of the dreams seemed to be intensifying but she still couldn't understand what they were about. Only that they were connected to the triptych and were increasing the aura of anticipation, intrigue. And underlying horror. She wondered if they were also connected to the letter she'd found. The first part of her dream was the most vivid.

Standing in a garden she could smell the lavender and roses around her and she shivered. It was barely light, the night clouds relinquishing their hold on the day that was unfolding as the morning sun, erupting through the clouds began to light the sky with streaks of gold. She leant against the wall she was stood against, the pale stones damp and rough against her hands. They were cold and she pushed her hands up under her armpits in an attempt to warm them up.

She was keeping watch on the corner of the building ahead of her and eventually her surveillance was rewarded as a young woman appeared in her view and began to skirt along the wall until she arrived in front of her. The smile she gave was beautiful, radiating from her face as if the sun had competition, lighting her eyes up with warmth. She began to speak but as usual Mathilde couldn't hear anything yet somehow still understood what was being said as the woman spoke of having to go away.

Reaching into her pocket Mathilde's hand closed around something there. It was cold and metallic and drawing it out she held it out towards the woman whose hand flew to her mouth as her eyes widened. She smiled and asked *'for me?'* and Mathilde's head nodded before lifting the long chain with a gold locket attached over the woman's head where she hastily tucked it beneath the fine lawn caught around her delicate throat and it disappeared from view. She pushed and pulled at the outside of her stomacher close against her torso until she had wriggled it down her body, patting her stomach where it appeared to now be wedged, a slight bump beneath the stiff thickly embroidered velvet of her gown. She grabbed hold of Mathilde's hands and said something she couldn't catch but she felt the brush of cold soft lips against her own and then she was awake and in her bed with her heart racing and the feeling of cool skin against her own.

Looking down at her soft hands with long slim fingers Mathilde knew she'd been holding the locket, the one she'd found in her father's desk, the image painted across the board that hid the triptych. Whoever haunted her dreams was trying to tell her something, explain the mystery; if only she could understand. Who was this man she kept dreaming about?

Her eyes still wide open she kept wondering what it was about the dream that felt familiar. The setting certainly wasn't nor the woman.

She'd just seen the painter of the triptych give a locket – her locket – to the young woman. Now she knew for sure the person she'd been dreaming about, the man she became in the night, was the artist responsible for the triptych in the room below. Which had, for some reason she had yet to discover, been hidden in the chapel. She could feel him emanating from the painting in waves as if he'd been expecting her so he could tell his story. He'd used the locket to lead her to the painting and now the hidden note. Why her? What was he trying to say and why had he waited so long?

Chapter Thirty-Five

December 1584

The preparations for Christmas were in full flow and the moment he returned to the stillroom Tom was immediately hard at work. As he suspected Hugh hadn't been happy about being left to work solo for so many weeks and Tom found himself doing most of the heavy manual tasks whilst Hugh bestowed upon himself the jobs which could be done beside the fire. He also sent Tom to collect firewood several times a day so the room remained warm at all times. Tom was in no position to complain and hoping to catch sight of Isabel he didn't really mind that he was often outside harvesting herbs, now rimed with a harsh white frost, the ground harsh and unforgiving. He examined the vanilla plants that had been left outside in the winter temperatures; they appeared almost dead and he brought them into the stillroom and prayed they could be saved.

Eventually, after the abstinence of Advent and the relent-less menu of pottage with some occasional fish if they were lucky, Tom awoke on Christmas morning to a room that was, as ever, dark and gloomy. Climbing off his truckle bed and pulling his blankets around his shoulders as the breath from his body froze into tiny clouds in front of his face, he went to the window and looked out. As he had suspected a thick layer of snow now lay on the ground and window-sill. It was still too dark to see the sullen grey clouds tinged with yellow which he knew would be hanging in the sky over the shining white landscape as small white flakes scurried down, the wind blowing them into whirls before throwing them into drifts already piling up into banks against walls and hedges. Judging by the depth already banked against his window Tom guessed it wouldn't be stopping any time soon and he shivered. There would be no meeting up with Isabel whilst this weather continued, their footprints would give them away immediately.

Thankful for his winter jerkin lined with a thick layer of warm flannel he pulled it on over the rest of his clothes, having already slept in his shirt and hose. He went through and picked up the bellows to breathe some life into the barely glowing embers of the fire, throwing some kindling on top as he did. He soon had a blaze going and he tidied a couple of jars on the bench as he wandered around unsure of how to occupy himself. He and Hugh had worked hard – well he had mostly – to ensure there were plenty of supplies of medicines for the Christmas and New Year festivities. Especially ones for gastric disorders and toothache; experience told him there would in all likelihood be many requests for those. Hopefully he'd have little or no work over the next twelve days as the festivities grew rowdier and there would finally be plenty of appetising food. His mouth watered at the thought of it. He'd been able to smell warm, pungent spices and roasting meat for days, the hot fat catching on the fire and sending a delicious burning aroma through the servants' rooms.

He was joined by Hugh still pulling his clothes on and blowing on his hands before holding them out to the fire. Tom raised his eyebrows and moved towards the jar of ginger and rosemary ointment they kept for chilblains, making Hugh's shoulders shake with laughter. It appeared the festivities had finally thawed his boss's resentment after his extended break from the stillroom. The two men followed the other servants who wouldn't need to work over the holiday across the courtyard to where they'd eat at the long communal trestle tables, long table tops sitting on wooden hurdle-like legs in the great hall. Tom could feel his heart pounding in his chest. Now would be his best chance of seeing Isabel, even from a distance. After no correspondence for many weeks he had no idea if she still held any feelings for him and he was almost too afraid to find out.

He didn't have to wait long however, as mid-morning the revelry around the hall was interrupted as everyone suddenly rose to their feet before sinking to the floor in bows and curtseys, heralding the entrance of the Queen. Tom could feel the vibrations of her trumpeters but not so quickly as others had heard them so had to scramble from the bench he was sitting on, hoping he hadn't been spotted.

After five minutes crouched on the floor, finally everyone began to rise and take their seats again and Tom followed. Immediately his eyes scanned the group now sitting at the top table with Leicester in his usual place beside the Queen on one side and Burghley on the other. Tom then spotted Walsingham as he continued to scrutinise the entourage.

Eventually his eyes rested on what he sought. He could see she was also scanning the crowds but there were so many people and he couldn't draw attention to himself and risk someone else noticing. He kept his eyes firmly trained on her, drinking in her beauty as if he were a man in the desert dying of thirst. Her face was flushed, the thick gown she was wearing appeared to be made from a dark green broad-cloth, the sleeves in a contrasting white with matching green ribbons. The dancing orange light from the fireplace, decorated with garlands of ivy with sprigs of glossy dark green holly dotted with red berries and a huge yule log blazing close to where she was sitting, etched the outline of her face and enhanced her beauty. Her hair was visible around her face under a small hood perched on the back of her head.

Just as Tom despaired of ever making eye contact with her, he felt the heat of her gaze burning his skin as their eyes met across the crowded room. It was as if nobody else was there. The bodies pressed in close to Tom along the bench and there was an underlying unpleasant smell that was inevitable with so many people pressed together. Jugglers danced around the room, teasing people as they watched entranced. The sweet taste of the candied plums he'd been eating from the bowl on the table, the sticky feeling of syrup on his fingertips; it all blended into the background.

He didn't want to be noticed by anyone who happened to be watching him but he couldn't stop a wide smile from spreading across his face as their eyes met. Isabel glanced quickly around her, checking whether anyone was watching before she smiled back. It was as if the sun was radiating its

231

brilliance in the room and the still falling snow and grey clouds outside had dissipated. She then reached up to the ruff around the neckline of her dress and ran her fingers around it. Tom caught a momentary glint of a gold chain before it disappeared and he felt his heart soar as relief flooded through him. She was still his, he was sure of it; she was wearing her betrothal necklace. Whatever had happened to any correspondence over the past few months, it didn't matter now.

He was desperate to rush up to the top table and sweep her up into his arms but he knew that was the quickest way to find himself evicted from the Christmas festivities and probably from his job and home. He couldn't risk anything so stupid. How, he wondered, was he going to arrange a meeting when the snow was so thick outside? He suspected he'd need to wait until Isabel made contact and he hoped it wouldn't be too long until she did.

The rest of Christmas Day continued in the same vein as the morning. The yule log burned in the grate and there was more music and dancing. Tom could feel the vibrations of the music although he couldn't join in with the dancing, having no idea of the rhythm. He was happy though to sit and eat the marchpane and honeyed nuts that appeared with regularity on platters and drink the strong ale being passed around the table. By the time people were beginning to falter he could hardly keep his eyes open and after all the drink he'd consumed he was unsteady on his feet staggering back to his room.

The stillroom was almost in darkness, the fire just producing a small glow as he entered, holding on to pieces of furniture to guide his trembling legs. Immediately, he knew the room was occupied. The soft smell of lavender caught his senses and he felt its warmth weaving its way through the fibres in the air, teasing him. There was another person in there with him. He saw the shadows shift as she stepped out from where she'd been waiting in the dark corner. Winding her arms, still encased in smooth wool, around his neck she pressed her body against his own as he inhaled her fragrance, holding her head with one strong hand against his chest and his other arm across her back. He never wanted to let her go. He could feel her heart beating against his and her chest rising and falling as she breathed and bending his head he kissed her. He was drowning in her and he never wanted to move again.

Eventually she stepped back and taking a fine wooden spill from a pot beside the now barely lit fire, she found a flame and lit a candle she must have brought with her to find her way. Lighting her face from below it danced off the edges of her delicate features, her eyes still shadowed in darkness. But the glow against her lower face meant he could see her lips now a deep rose, bruised from kissing him.

'*I missed you,*' she told him, '*I couldn't find where you were to write to you without alerting anyone to our friendship.*' Relieved, Tom knew that at least she'd tried to keep in contact.

'I missed you too.' His mime was clumsy and he wished he'd exercised more constraint with the ale earlier but she seemed to understand him anyway.

'*I'm still wearing your locket,*' she pulled it out from around her neck, '*it stays beside my heart always.*' He smiled and nodded, putting his palm against his own heart then onto hers. She laid her small hand over his.

'*I know that our lives have not followed the same path and that*

233

for someone of my rank it is considered inconceivable that we may be together but I will risk everything for this to be so. I cannot think of anything I wish more than to be with you always. And, God willing, to have a family with you.'

Tom stared down at her sure he'd misread what she'd said. That she desired everything that he did too was more than he could have hoped for. Taking her hands he kissed them gently, holding them in his against his heart.

'I cannot leave court during Christmas,' she explained, *'but can you come to my home after twelfth night? We cannot go on in this way, we must do something.'* Tom couldn't understand what she intended but he'd caught the gist of what she was saying and he wondered if he'd got it right. Surely she wasn't speaking of marriage? It was more, so much more, than he had ever imagined.

'I will send a note to let you know when,' she explained and he nodded before bending down and kissing her once more and then she was gone, the candle she carried disappearing down the corridor until the darkness swallowed her up.

However much he was enjoying it all the twelve days of Christmas and the extravaganza of a royal palace at the turn of the new year dragged for Tom. The food and ale began to taste bitter in his mouth as he waited impatiently for life to return to normal so he could meet properly with Isabel. He had, as predicted, handed out multiple powders for upset stomachs to soothe the disagreement of so much rich food. The Queen was well known for eating very little but she was once again requesting powders for toothache after partaking of too much marchpane, together with sleeping draughts as her throbbing teeth kept her awake long into the night. The stocks of vanilla were running low and now they only used it in medicines for the Queen. It would be a long time before spring when the weather would be good enough for the boats to start to return from Venice and Antwerp again with more supplies. He wished he could produce the precious pods with his own vanilla plants but he'd had no luck and would have to hope the warmer weather would encourage the plant to bear fruit. At least he'd been able to save them by bringing them into the warmth of the stillroom.

The message he was waiting for finally arrived in mid-January, coinciding with a partial thaw of the snow. Isabel had been given leave to return to her home and she delivered a note to the stillroom before she went, asking Tom to be at her house that day or as soon as he could get away.

Tom was worried about the urgency intimated in her words. He was certain Hugh wouldn't agree to his disappearing from work whilst they were busy replacing the medications used over the festive season but Tom was determined to be at Cordwainer Street as soon as he was able.

He knew Hugh had seen him quickly read the note and slide it in his pocket and during the afternoon Tom disappeared into his room arriving back wearing his blue coat and with a silent shrug of his shoulders in apology did a mime of being summoned to Walsingham again. Hugh barely responded and Tom felt a stab of guilt that he was lying to his friend. But he couldn't help himself, he'd risk everything to see Isabel.

There were few boats waiting at the jetty, the scullers standing in a small group smoking their clay pipes and stamping their feet trying to keep warm. Tom held out a piece of paper conveying which wharf he needed to be taken to and hopped into a boat. Most of the boatmen knew him and someone peeled off from the group and climbed in, picking up his oars and pulling them out into the centre of the river.

Although the weather was fine there was no warmth in the sun which shone from a sky so washed out it was almost white. It was preferable to the ugly yellow clouds that dropped the unrelenting snow but the air that he breathed was still freezing, catching in his throat and burning the tops of his ears as they moved slowly through the water which was smooth and still like slippery silk, reflecting the pale sky above them. In his haste to see Isabel he'd forgotten his cap.

Arriving at Isabel's home the door was flung open as he arrived on the doorstep to show her waiting there, a huge smile on her face. Leaning forwards she pulled him into the warm hall and pressed her lips to his before springing backwards and exclaiming *'you're so cold!'* Tom nodded, taking her with him to the fire where he sat down and pulled her onto his lap. It was heaven, he never wanted to move again. Isabel however had other ideas.

'We need to talk,' she informed him. He raised his eyebrows and waited for her to continue. *'I want to be married and hopefully one day have a family. It is my greatest wish; children running through the house and a husband by my side.'* Tom pulled her against him and kissed the top of her head before taking her face between his hands. He pointed to himself and nodded in agreement. It was everything he desired too.

'We cannot carry on in this way.' Tom's heart plummeted. Had she brought him here, seemingly pleased to see him, just to tell him their strange, hidden relationship was at an

end? Surely, she could have put that in a letter. He went to stand up, trying to lift her back onto her feet but she resisted holding her hand up to stay him. *'Wait,'* she said, *'until I have finished what I need to say. I love you Tom Lutton and I want to spend the rest of my life with you. We can only do that if we get married. It will enrage the Queen when she finds out we have wed without her permission but I am prepared to risk that, are you?'*

Tom was astonished at what he was reading on her lips and wondered if he'd misinterpreted it. He nodded slowly, then still holding her he got to his feet and spun around the room with Isabel's feet flying out from their bodies. He could feel her shrieks of laughter against his chest.

Eventually, he placed her back on the floor where they both stood for a moment, waiting while the room stopped spinning on its own. Going to a desk in one corner she pulled out a sheaf of paperwork.

'I asked the priest at St Mary Aldermary to read the banns for us. We can get married tomorrow. Can you meet at the church at ten in the morning?'

Delighted, Tom nodded, of course he'd be back. He just needed to avoid Hugh for twenty-four hours so he wouldn't have to make up another lie about where he was. Isabel took his hand and led him into the small parlour beside the front door where a meal and sweet hippocras wine had been laid out. Sitting down either side of the fire, they started to plan their future.

In the end, it was easier to slip away from the palace the following morning than Tom had feared. He rose early and stoked up the fire before finishing a couple of jobs Hugh had started the previous night, straining medication and leaving other cures to continue their solidifying. As there was no sign of his boss, Tom took his chance and left an ambiguous note on the wax tablet saying he'd been called away before pulling on his coat and this time remembering his cap as he hurried down to the jetty.

He was waiting outside the church on the doorstep with the minister when Isabel arrived at exactly ten o'clock. He watched her as she swept along, always walking as if she meant business. In the dark shining locks tumbling down her back he could see pearls threaded through the braids that were tucked away from the side of her face. She was wearing a dress he hadn't seen before, made of fine damask in the palest green, and in her girdle she'd tucked a posy of dried lavender. As she walked up the path to the church door where the ceremony would take place, her lady's maid walked in front holding aloft a branch of rosemary wound with ribbons.

As she stood next to him Tom could feel the warmth emanating from her body. He looked into her eyes and smiled, trying to convey all the love he felt for her. Adoration that took him to heights he'd never imagined had existed. With all the danger Walsingham's spying may bring he would forever be thankful his journey had brought him to London. They both turned to the minister.

Whatever the man was saying was lost on Tom as he lifted his face to feel the cold breeze lifting his hair and disturbing Isabel's skirts. He could smell the lavender she carried and just faintly, the rosewater she'd washed in. Unfortunately, he could also smell the minister; a wholly unsavoury scent that he'd have preferred not to have noticed. He noticed every nuance except the one thing he wanted, to hear the man joining them in the eyes of God, was missing.

When the minister looked at him and gave him a little nod he knew his moment had come. With no words to confirm his vows he'd have to deliver his own in signs.

Stepping forward he wrapped her in his arms before moving back and taking her hand with his. Fishing in his pocket he produced a ring she'd given to him the previous day and placed it on her finger before laying his hand on his heart and holding it up towards heaven. Then to demonstrate that he would live with her until they died he put his forefingers on each of his eyelids and shut them. Finally, he pretended to dig a hole with his heel and to ring a bell as if tolling for a dead person, pulling on a rope that wasn't there.

He opened his eyes and looked down into hers which were now brimming with unshed tears. She reached up and clasped his face with her hands, the cold of the wedding band against his cheek as she stood on tip toe and kissed him. Then the minister turned to the church door and led them both in for prayers.

Chapter Thirty-Six

July 2021

Mathilde tried to explain to Rachel how she'd dreamed about the locket but she soon realised her sister wasn't fully paying attention to what she was saying.

'I've been awake most of the night with toothache,' she moaned, holding her hand to her face, 'it's like a pounding in my cheek. Honestly, it's agony. I've taken some paracetamol and it's done nothing.'

'I can make you a remedy,' Mathilde offered, 'a paste to put on your gum where it hurts. It works really well.'

'I'll try anything,' Rachel replied, pulling a morose face, 'I'm going to have to ring my dentist as soon as they open. If they're able to give me an appointment today could you look after Fleur please? It will mean driving over to Peterborough and back and she'll just whinge in the car; I don't think I can stand that today.'

'Of course, no problem. We will have fun together, yes?' She looked at Fleur who nodded slowly, her expression solemn.

'Can we go out with your camera?' she asked, and Mathilde confirmed that they could. Leaving the two of them at the table she went to her van to find the ingredients to make the tooth powder as her mother had taught her. It was an instant anaesthetic with thyme and cloves to numb the pain. She added some vanilla seeds to the paste to take away the bitter taste it left in the mouth.

'This works really well,' Rachel expressed her surprise as she walked through the house looking for Mathilde, her hand still holding on to the side of her face. 'I've got an appointment for mid-afternoon, so I won't be back until after tea time, is that okay? I can make something and leave it in the fridge if you like? I was going to pop home and see Andrew afterwards as well. I know it's cheeky of me while you're looking after Fleur but the dentist is only five minutes from home.'

'It's fine,' Mathilde reassured her, 'I can make us something for dinner.' She couldn't understand why Rachel repeatedly referred to the last meal of the day as the same word she used for the hot drink the English seemed to be addicted to, and so she continued to refer to it as 'dinner'.

They stood and waved Rachel off at one o'clock, Fleur holding tightly to Mathilde's hand. She hoped the little girl couldn't feel the thumping of her heart radiating through her body at the enormity of being responsible for her for several hours. She'd never been accountable for another human, ever. Even Shadow was more responsibility than she'd ever had before and already the kitten was very independent, wandering around the house and turning up in the kitchen for food or a fuss.

'Can we go out with your camera then?' Fleur asked.

'Later,' Mathilde agreed, 'I think as it is sunny today it should be clear tonight and there's a full moon. Let's go out then and take photos, hmm?' She'd had an idea when she'd been walking close to the marshes and she kept her fingers crossed it came to fruition.

'Okay,' the little girl agreed, before skipping back to the sitting room to continue her game with a space rocket and plastic pig. This babysitting might be easier than she envisaged, Mathilde thought as she followed her.

Fleur's patience, however, soon wore off and Mathilde found herself having to provide entertainment for several hours before it was dinner time. She wanted to tell Oliver about her dream and that she now realised the triptych and the locket were connected; both with each other and with the man she dreamed about. However, he'd told her he was going to meet up with a Tudor era historian to discuss the painting and the note she'd found and sure enough his phone was switched off. She left him a voicemail during which she stuttered and stumbled over her words and eventually gave up, ending the call with a muttered string of French expletives. He'd ring her back, she was sure.

After a dinner of omelette and potato waffles followed by yoghurt, Fleur was yawning and Mathilde wondered if she'd made the right decision deciding to keep the child up past her bedtime. But if she'd judged it correctly they could see a wonderful phenomenon not far from the house and she wanted to share it with this new niece with whom a connection continued to grow; a link between her and the past . . . and the future.

Outside, night was starting to fall. They rang Rachel and Fleur spoke to her and Andrew. Rachel promised she was about to leave to drive home whilst Mathilde reassured her that Fleur was about to go to bed, giving the girl a mock frown and holding her finger to her lips. The little girl pushed her hands against her mouth to stop herself giggling until Mathilde had ended the call.

'Do I really have to go to bed?' she asked, 'you said we could go out with your camera but now it's dark outside.' Her mouth began to wobble as her eyes welled up.

'Now is the best time to go out,' Mathilde explained, 'go and find your trainers and a jumper in case it's cold.' With a whoop of excitement Fleur ran away upstairs and Mathilde pulled on her own boots before setting her lens to accommodate the darkness outside.

'You stay here,' she told Shadow as he weaved his way around her legs, standing straight and arching his back, 'we'll be back soon.'

Outside the ground was damp with night dew but as she'd suspected the sky was clear and the moon bright: perfect conditions. They stopped at her van to retrieve a large torch and then set off across the overgrown front lawns, Fleur holding on to Mathilde's hand tightly as she pointed out moths that flew into the beam of the torch and watched the bats that darted about overhead. At one point, Mathilde drew her to a halt and showed her a pale, silent owl swooping low over the field to their left, its slow steady movement belying the constant watch with dark eyes on the ground below.

Eventually they reached their destination and Mathilde crouched down in the tall grasses. Fleur immediately followed suit, almost disappearing.

'We've come to see fairies,' Mathilde whispered, 'so we

must be very quiet.' Fleur's eyes grew round as she stared at her aunt and nodded silently. 'Watch the reeds in front of us,' Mathilde instructed, keeping her fingers crossed that something happened. Even with the conditions just right it was hit or miss.

They sat in silence for almost five minutes by which time Fleur's patience was wearing thin and she was shuffling about. Then, Mathilde saw it followed by another and then more.

'Look,' she pointed to the blue lights that bobbed about in the marshes in front of them. 'They're fairies. *Fées*. Can you see them?' She didn't need to ask, she knew the little girl could because she'd breathed out a long 'ooooh' as they began to appear. Adjusting her camera lens Mathilde fired off several shots of the marsh gases that danced before them, just like fairies. She preferred that name to the 'ghost candles' that she'd heard them called. Folklore was often morbid.

Slowly she swung the camera around to photograph the image she really wanted to capture. The little girl's look of wonder as she gazed at the spectacle, her features picked out in the pale blue moonlight that lit her profile. Shocked at her own emotions Mathilde felt her heart give an extra beat of love for this little girl. She'd lost so many years of being a part of this family and now she needed to grasp it with both hands. Her father had given her more than just a house, he'd given her a chance to live.

Eventually as they began to feel chilly from sitting on the damp ground, Mathilde suggested they went back to the house for hot chocolate.

'With cream and marshmallows?' Fleur's attention imme-diately skipped to the drink, the fairies forgotten as she walked with Mathilde back to the house, following the torch beam again. She looked down at the eager, trusting face upturned to hers. Could she ever walk away from this little girl? Another filament snaked out to wind its way around her heart and tie her to the hall, to her family.

'I don't know, if we can find some I suppose,' she agreed.

They were both wearing their pyjamas and drinking their hot chocolate with cream but unfortunately no marshmallows when they heard the sound of tyres on gravel followed by Rachel walking in through the back door.

'You're up a bit late young lady!' she exclaimed as soon as she walked in, giving Fleur a kiss on the head and glaring at Mathilde across the table. 'I thought you were about to go to bed when we spoke on the phone and that was about four hours ago.'

'We went to look for fairies in the dark! We found lots.' Fleur told her in an excited voice.

'Well, you need to go to bed now,' Rachel was firm as she ushered Fleur out of the room and upstairs, leaving Mathilde feeling as if she was about to get a telling off when her sister returned. She wondered if she ought to sneak up to her room as well before Rachel arrived back in the kitchen. There was no point she admitted to herself. If she wasn't told off tonight it would just be the following morning. She picked Shadow up from the floor and buried her nose in his soft black fur.

'Honestly, I thought you would be more sensible,' Rachel rolled her eyes as she walked back in the kitchen, 'what were you doing wandering around in the dark with my daughter? She'll be wanting to do it all the time now and I don't fancy going near the marshes, sucked into the mud and never found again.'

'It was an adventure with her auntie.' Even saying the word made her smile, acknowledging the relationship she thought she'd never have. 'And I always know exactly where the edge of the marsh is, we were never in danger. We went to watch the marsh gasses; they are called the *fée* in France. I told her they were fairies. I wanted to take some photos of her in the moonlight and I knew she'd enjoy seeing them and hoped for once she might stay still long enough for me to take some pictures.' She reached across the table to grab her camera and scrolled back through the photos she'd taken that evening, viewing them on the small screen on the back of the camera. She had to admit they were lovely shots; she was really pleased with them. Going over to Rachel she bent down to show her the photos.

'Wow,' Rachel gasped, 'they're stunning. The most beautiful pictures I've ever seen of her. You've captured the emotions on her face perfectly. She looks so innocent, such wonder in her eyes. They're incredible.'

'I'm pleased with them,' Mathilde agreed, going to the sink to rinse out her cup.

'You're still not forgiven for keeping her up so late,' Rachel told her. 'She'll be a nightmare tomorrow.' But she smiled and Mathilde shrugged and nodded.

Mathilde was halfway out of the door on her way to bed when she suddenly remembered the toothache and asked how it was. Rachel pulled a face.

'I had to have a filling and now the numbness has worn off it's sore again. Is there any more of that paste left?' she asked. Pleased to be able to offer her apothecary skills Mathilde passed her the plastic pot containing the rest of the tincture before wishing her goodnight and going to her room.

Before she lay down to sleep, she checked her phone and found a text from Oliver apologising for missing her call and promising to speak with her the following morning. With a smile on her face Mathilde was asleep within seconds, her head empty of any dreams weaving their way into her subconscious.

Chapter Thirty-Seven

January 1585

The week after their wedding was blissful. They hid away in Isabel's house and saw no one other than her maid Anne and the handful of servants she employed. None of the staff seemed impressed with their new master, barely hiding their disdain at his obviously humble beginnings. Tom had excused himself from work with Hugh, sending a messenger to say he was unwell and didn't wish to bring any sickness back with him. His boss was happy for him to stay away as any form of sickness meant extra work for him if it spread around the occupants of the palace.

They spent their days wandering in the garden where Tom planned his own physic garden to rival the one he used at Greenwich. After spending most of his life on the move he suddenly realised that finally he could put down roots, just like the plants he loved to nurture. He'd bring over his vanilla plants as well.

At night they lay in bed, a heavily carved four poster and

the most comfortable one Tom had ever slept in, and made love behind the drapes which concealed them. Tom might not have any words to whisper in her ears but he could show his love in the way he used his other senses, his touch and his taste as he enjoyed taking her to sensual places. Tom was determined that although he'd have to resume his work for the Queen he was going to return to their house as often as possible, if only to lie down in that bed. He felt a level of contentment he'd never enjoyed before. Even as a young child there was always a fear of losing people he loved, of not being safe: of not belonging.

He'd never been able to come to terms with the fact that the people he'd thought were family, weren't. That somewhere out there he had a real mother and father and possibly siblings as well; cousins, aunts and uncles. He didn't belong anywhere and after his father – well his adoptive father – was killed and they'd fled to France, he'd never felt safe again. Even though they'd settled in a comfortable farmhouse and his mother had made enough money growing her saffron for them to be able to enjoy a peaceful, contented life, he'd always been waiting for life to let him down.

At the age of fourteen he'd been apprenticed to the local apothecary but Tom had known everything there was to learn already from his mother who was extremely proficient in medicine making. She'd drawn him pictures to explain her own childhood and how she'd been taught by the monks near her home. He'd set off for Paris and from there Antwerp, always searching for somewhere to rest, somewhere that felt like home. Somewhere where he could be part of his own family. When he'd climbed aboard the boat from France he'd envisaged travelling to Norfolk to look for the family who'd lost him, or abandoned him all those years ago, and yet he'd found himself in London and now he had a wife and a happy life. He might not have found his roots but he was more than content with where he'd landed.

Neither Tom nor Isabel were expecting the response they received to their nuptials when they returned to the palace. She explained he wasn't to mention a word of their marriage to anyone until she'd told the Queen. She wasn't looking forward to the conversation, doubting that Her Majesty would have agreed with her choice of husband if she'd asked permission first. Although in theory as a widow she should be able to make her own choice – after all she'd married the man chosen for her the first time around – this didn't apply to anyone who was close to Her Majesty. For someone who didn't want to get married herself Queen Elizabeth certainly enjoyed interfering in everyone else's betrothals. It explained why Isabel was always careful to keep her locket hidden.

The first inkling Tom had something was very wrong was shortly before dinner time when a young page arrived in the stillroom, his face flushed from running as he panted and tried to explain what the matter was. Tom watched his mouth, trying to read it, but through the page's heaving chest and lost breath, Tom was confused as to what the boy was trying to say. He turned to Hugh, who had paused in his crushing of oak galls in the pestle and mortar, and waited for an explanation.

Hugh listened for a couple of minutes his head on one side and then turned to Tom, his eyebrows raised and his mouth fallen open.

'When you were away after New Year, did you get married?'

Tom felt his heart begin to race. He didn't like the feeling he was getting about what was unfolding and the hairs along his spine began to prickle with sweat as fear crawled up his back. He nodded slowly, watching Hugh's face carefully so he didn't miss any signs or nuances.

'There is mayhem in the state apartments and the Queen wants you up there now. I'd get changed if I were you, and quickly.' He indicated Tom's apron and hose which had splatters of ink on them and Tom pulled the apron from him, throwing it down on a stool before running to his room to change into his best pale hose and blue coat. He hurried back, smoothing his clothes, crumpled from where they'd been stored in a press, to find the page hopping from foot to foot in his eagerness to be back upstairs with Tom in tow. Hugh caught his arm as he walked through.

'Wait,' he said, 'who did you marry if the Queen now wants to see you?' Tom smiled, his eyes shining with pride despite his worry. Picking up his wax tablet he wrote Lady Isabel on it and showed Hugh.

'One of the Queen's ladies?' Hugh asked, 'are you a complete idiot? You'll be in gaol by suppertime, you mark my words.' Tom felt his stomach turn to liquid at the thought of being in dark and squalid conditions when being able to see was such an important part of his ability to communicate. But as long as Isabel was safe he'd gladly go. He turned and followed the page upstairs.

Just for once, Tom was relieved he couldn't hear the noise in the Privy Chamber. He could tell instantly it was chaos. People running about looking hot and flustered and in the middle of it all the Queen was stood, her usually pale face a most unbecoming shade of puce which clashed with the orange of her hair. She was waving her arms and her mouth seemed to be wedged open in a permanent screech as little globules of spit flew in all directions. He spotted Burghley discreetly wiping some from his doublet. Tom scanned the room for Isabel but there was no sign of her. The ladies were all cowering in a corner, their sewing and a lute laid abandoned on the floor as they rushed to get away from the Queen's rage. Across the floor other objects were scattered as if flung there in a fit of anger.

Tom bowed low and hoped she hadn't noticed him but he had no such luck. He kept his eyes firmly on his shoes which he noticed still had the remains of mud on from that morning's forage in the physic garden. How he wished he was out there with the plants now in that refuge of calm. Eventually someone gave him a push in the middle of his back and taking a step forward to stop himself pitching onto the floor he stood up again.

The Queen was once again sat on her throne and he watched as most of the servants and the ladies hurried from the room. Another shove from behind propelled him in front of the throne and he knelt down on one knee. He wasn't sure what was going on but he was certain it wasn't good and some extra subservience may help. He doubted it though. A movement to his left made him turn his head and he recognised the bottom of Isabel's dress; the one she'd been wearing that morning when they'd left Cordwainer Street together to return to the palace. Slowly he stood upright again until he could see her face. It was streaked with tears, her eyes red and swollen. He felt his blood begin to sing in his veins and he went to take a step towards her. It was at that point he realised they'd been joined by several of the

Queen's guards and an arm shot out to stop him moving. Now he was very confused. Isabel was keeping her eyes firmly on the Queen and he followed suit.

At first it was difficult to understand what was being said – or rather screamed – at them and seeing the blank look on his face she turned and spoke to Burghley, who translated her rant into words Tom could lip read. It didn't take long for him to realise exactly how much trouble they were in. Despite Isabel knowing that as a widow she had the right to wed whomever and whenever she wished, as she'd predicted the Queen didn't agree with her. She was furious Isabel had taken it upon herself to marry without permission, especially as it was he, Tom, the lowly assistant apothecary she'd chosen. He was a servant, despite the work he did for Walsingham.

The Queen turned her anger on Isabel and Tom found it easier to read what his wife was saying as she turned her face towards him and explained, tears running down her face, how they'd met up in secret in the gardens. She implored the Queen to forgive them, that they'd thought they were doing no wrong and how deeply they were in love, but her pleas were in vain. Two of the guards stepped forward and each grabbed one of Isabel's arms as they dragged her backwards out of the room. Instinctively Tom moved to stop them but was also immediately clamped by strong hands the size of shovels, ensuring he could not follow. He turned to Burghley again.

'Lady Isabel will be taken to the Tower,' he explained, 'she is lucky it isn't Newgate. She will remain there until the Queen decides she has been punished enough; if that ever happens. You are to be taken to Poultry Corner gaol.' His face had remained

253

impassive as he relayed the information and Tom looked towards the Queen, trying to think of a way to plead with her to release Isabel but with his hands kept immobile and Elizabeth now looking at a spot on the wall above his head, he too was hauled roughly from the room by the guards. Their fingers were digging hard into his arms and he recognised one of them who'd only that month been in the stillroom begging for some of his now famous toothache powder. How his loyalties had changed.

Once they were out in the corridor, they allowed Tom to stand up before they marched him downstairs to the jetty where a boat was already waiting. Tom looked up and down the river to see where Isabel was so he could send her a silent message of love and support but she was nowhere to be seen. A thick fog had descended, a heavy damp blanket kissing the pewter grey water and enveloping him in a deep embrace. It was as desolate as he felt. And he couldn't call to her. Not for the first time in his life he cursed his disability.

Bundled into the boat and accompanied by one of the guards – not toothache man he noticed – they pulled out into the middle of the river. Usually Tom enjoyed the journey; the feel of the wind on his face, dipping his fingers in the cold Thames and the smooth, regular movements of the oarsman as they moved through the water. Today though he sat with his silence, bolt upright, his heart pounding in fear. He could feel the vibration of the guard behind him speaking and watched as the boatman said *'neither would I'*. Neither would he what? Want to be going to gaol? Well, who would? Everyone knew what those places were like. He fervently hoped Isabel would be kept in decent quarters at the Tower.

Before long they pulled up at a set of slimy, rank smelling, green steps and Tom tried to scramble up them without losing his balance and slipping into the river. He was quite certain neither the boatman nor the guard would make any effort to fish him out again. Holding on to the cold wall beside him the stones rough and sharp beneath his hand, he carefully made his way to the top. The guard's breath hot on his neck with every step and once on the jetty he was dragged up dark city streets, the pitch-black night closing in on him, until they reached Poultry Corner. He was propelled across it and in through the gatehouse of a formidable brick building opposite. It looked dark and depressing and Tom felt a hundred melancholy ghosts gather around him, welcoming him to hell.

He was led straight down several flights of steps until he did indeed think he'd reached the depths of Hades. Except instead of being hot and fiery it was bitterly cold and damp, the stench of the Thames and rat urine mixing sharply in his nose. It was also dark; so black he couldn't see his hand in front of his face. There was no way that any natural light could penetrate so far underground and there wasn't a chance the guards would leave him a candle. Tom felt the floor vibrate with the force of a door being slammed shut behind him. He wondered if there was anyone else in there with him, given that he wouldn't hear them talking to him. Something moved beside him and then he felt it run across his feet. Just a rat; he expected there were plenty of those in the cell with him.

The only way he'd know what the room was like was to feel his way around as a blind person would and holding his arms out in front of him he shuffled forwards until they reached the slippery damp stone wall. It was so cold he momentarily took his hands off and rubbed them on his jerkin. The guard had been quick to take his blue coat away and he suspected he wouldn't ever see it again. Quite possibly he wouldn't need it anyway, he was doubtless destined for the gallows.

Putting his fingertips back on the wall he made his way around the room. It was tiny, he estimated about eight-foot square, with no furniture and no cell mate aside from the four-legged, long-tailed variety. Sliding down the wall until he was sitting on the floor, which had a few old pieces of straw on but otherwise was also freezing cold stone, he placed his head in his hands in despair. How had they ended up like this, in such trouble, when all they'd done was fall in love? He doubted he'd ever see Isabel again. All his hopes of coming to England and building a life for himself were likely to end up with him swinging on the end of a rope.

Chapter Thirty-Eight

July 2021

'So, what happens now about this letter, or whatever it is? What did Oliver call it again?' They were out in the garden and Rachel had found an old canvas deckchair. After several minutes fighting with it, she'd finally erected it and sat down with a cup of coffee. It creaked ominously as she lowered herself in until she was laid at a forty-five-degree angle. Mathilde waited for a moment to see if her sister fell through the threadbare seat and onto the ground but it seemed to be holding her.

'I don't remember, it's not a word I know in English. It begins with P,' Mathilde confessed, pausing in her digging. She was enjoying increasing the herb garden after finding some mint and sage overgrowing behind the old greenhouse. The solitude she'd sought working in this particular corner using her father's sturdy, well-loved tools – the ones where her fingers slipped perfectly into the shiny, worn dips and grooves his hands had created – was now being disturbed by Rachel bustling about and chatting. However, she was aware that she hadn't given her sister a lot of time recently and had managed to smile in what she hoped was a welcoming way when the deckchair and two cups of coffee made an appearance. As ever, Fleur was not far away chasing butterflies and squealing loudly flapping her arms every time a bee came within three metres of her.

'He's called another of his friends, I think,' Mathilde took a mouthful of her milky coffee and grimaced. Just as she would expect of an English person, Rachel was great at making tea but her instant coffee was appalling. Maybe it was time to go back to France, just to top up her caffeine levels properly. 'He certainly seems to know everyone if you have an art-based question,' she added with a smile.

'Well, I suspect it's a small world,' Rachel agreed, 'but useful for us. You. Otherwise, what would happen to these things? I wouldn't have even realised there was hidden writing on that letter. I must admit I can feel the triptych starting to draw me in too. It's so mysterious and the possible connection with our family is like a binding between us both and it.'

'I'm waiting for him to call me, I wouldn't be surprised if he starts dragging other people here to have a look. I can feel the bond as well; I told him I don't want it removed from here.' Mathilde put down her cup and turned back to her digging.

For someone who spent her life purposefully isolated the number of people now gathering around her like sudden clouds at the end of a hot day was disconcerting. She'd gradually been able to accept Rachel and Fleur but not Alice and Jack, who'd kept their distance. They were proof family wasn't always a good thing and if it weren't for Rachel she'd have caught the ferry home after the first sign of trouble and confrontation. And now Oliver. She couldn't help a small smile as she thought of his quirky grin and his blue eyes that were so open and friendly. His whole demeanour was one of acceptance and kindliness, so different to the people who'd shaped her life as she grew up. But she still had a lot of life to live.

Mathilde washed her hands in the kitchen sink after the transplanting of herbs and some additional weeding. She'd also unveiled some giant leaves that Rachel excitedly told her was rhubarb and was excellent in something called 'crumble', announcing she would cook it for dessert and take some home to Andrew at the weekend. Mathilde secretly thought it sounded stodgy and disgusting. Checking her phone she discovered a missed call from Oliver and instantly her mouth broadened into a wide grin. The muscles she hadn't used for so long she'd thought they'd atrophied permanently were now fully functioning. Pressing the return call button she held the phone to her ear. She'd left Rachel and Fleur chasing each other around the house in a big circle and hoped they didn't burst in while she was talking to him.

'Hi Matty,' his warm voice made her flush with pleasure. She would never allow anyone else to abbreviate her name but somehow him saying it was fine.

'Hey, I missed your call?' she said.

'It was just to let you know I've spoken to someone at the UEA – the university in Norwich – and he'd really like to take a look at the letter, especially given the context of where it was found. He got really excited.'

'Context?' she still had trouble with some English words.

'Where it was found. And that with the triptych being Elizabethan, or maybe even older given its vague similarity to Bosch, this strange document makes it historically very interesting. I promised we'd get it over to him next week; is that okay with you? If it's something of value historically he'll get a lot of kudos from announcing its discovery.'

Mathilde had no idea what 'kudos' meant, but she didn't like to keep drawing attention to her lack of English even after several weeks of dramatic improvement. She was so relieved they may be able to discover what the letter said and even more importantly why she could feel it joining her to the hall that she almost missed what Oliver said next.

'I'm away for a long weekend but I'll see if we can take it on Tuesday if you like?'

'Yes, that would be great, I'd like that. Thank you.' If she was disappointed that it was going to be several days before she saw him again she wasn't going to admit it. He was just a friend she told herself. In a month or so summer would be over and she'd be returning to her previous life. As if reminding herself she laid her phone on the table and walked outside to her van opening the doors and turning the engine over to charge the battery. She didn't want it getting musty or damp; it needed to be ready to go at a moment's notice. Always have an escape route: her mother had continuously repeated this as a mantra during her childhood. Not that it did her any good in the end.

Chapter Thirty-Nine

January 1585

Tom barely slept that night. In fact, he realised he had no idea if it were night or day in the sinister blackness of his cell. He couldn't stop worrying about Isabel and remembering the anguish on her face as she was dragged away. Neither of them had imagined their love would result in such a punishment. At some point he finally dozed off, his head on his chest, cold unwelcoming spirits packed in beside him. No wonder the room felt so sad, so despondent; the final resting place of numerous wretches before him.

Eventually, when he was so thirsty his throat was raw and all he wanted was one of his own warm saffron and honey drinks, a strong rush of a draught to one side of his face alerted him to the door opening. A faint light came from a candle carried by the same guard who'd locked him in and he crouched down and slid a chunk of bread across to Tom, together with a cup of small ale. Tom grabbed the platter and pulled it towards him before the light receded again and he was plunged back into the now familiar darkness.

He drained the cup in one go despite knowing it may be a long time before he got anything else to drink. Parched, he couldn't stop himself grimacing at the weak, stale taste. He'd bet a hundred gold angels the guards weren't drinking that. It tasted as if they had taken it straight from the Thames and not even introduced it to any hops, let alone brewed it with some.

The bread was dry and stale but he pulled small pieces off and chewed them until they dissolved in his mouth. At least it gave him something to do but it didn't stop the gnawing in his stomach. He hoped that meal was merely to break his fast and he hadn't somehow miscalculated how long he'd been locked up and the paltry offering was actually dinner.

Would anyone on the outside think to bring some food to him? Or to Isabel? He wished with all his heart that she was being treated well and that one of the ladies at court would arrange for some food and home comforts to be taken to her. He could only trust that someone – anyone – was persuading the Queen to release them, after she'd made an example of them both, and that he and Isabel could return to the peace of Cordwainer Street. Although he'd been poor and lived rough numerous times wandering around France and the Low Countries, always on his endless search for a home where he felt accepted, never had he been anywhere like this. He'd certainly fallen from on high he admitted to himself; from a luxurious home and a beautiful, comely wife, back to where he'd started from. Actually, worse than that.

When the door opened a second time, Tom jumped to his feet. It was less than an hour since his meal so he knew it couldn't be time for a second one. Was he going to get punished, tortured? In the gloomy half-light from the same candle stump as before the sick smell of burning tallow made Tom's stomach roll unpleasantly. The door opened wider and the guard beckoned him forwards. Hesitantly Tom inched forward, his body tense and his fists clenched waiting for the beating that might follow. Instead, however, the guard stepped to one side and pointed to the dark corridor in front of him and Tom began to walk, his legs shaky and his muscles cramped after a night constricted in a small damp space. He held on to the wall with one hand to guide him and to prevent himself from collapsing.

Finally, after a long, slow climb up the stairs where Tom stumbled twice and almost fell backwards, he reached the daylight which was so harsh and bright he immediately screwed his eyes up, squinting through his eyelashes. He looked around the guards' room from which lay the corridor and stairs that led down to the cells. Or *depths of hell*, Tom thought to himself.

The serjeant was scratching a quill on parchment in front of him and didn't look up but Tom barely noticed him as he spotted a guard in royal uniform standing in the corner, his face wearing a suitably grave countenance. Tom had no idea what a man like that would be doing in a place like this and it appeared that by the look of disgust on his face he was wondering the same thing. It seemed as though he was gaining Tom a pardon as the serjeant signed the parchment with a flourish and handed it to the young man, before almost throwing Tom's blue coat across the desk. The outer door swung open and Tom didn't need any encouragement to step through it and into the fresh outside air.

He drew in big gulps, filling his lungs as if trying to expel every trace of the rancid air he'd breathed for the previous twenty-four hours. Every smell he'd always taken for granted bombarded him. From the traders and market stalls nearby came the scent of warm pasties and hot peas, the earthy, country smell of vegetables and sweet apples. Even the aroma of horse dung – and a trace of the human variety – couldn't wipe the smile off his face.

The guard gave a jerk of his head and strode away and Tom, still having no idea what was going on, followed him, darting around the city goodwives and servants, their baskets full of warm bread which just made him salivate more. He wished that the man knew some of Tom's signing because he'd really like to ask if some food could be bought. He was so hungry he thought he might vomit. But they carried on walking, his legs like lumps of calves' foot jelly, until they reached a jetty where a boat bearing the Queen's pennant fluttered in the breeze blowing down the river. Surprised by the difference in the craft which had taken him downriver the day before Tom hopped aboard and sat down on a bench at the back, stroking the thick deep pile of the crimson velvet, pushing his fingers into its softness. It reminded him of the velvet gowns Isabel often wore. His heart beat faster at the thought she might be waiting for him when they reached the palace; he desperately wanted to smell the soft lavender of her hair, to press his lips against the smooth skin of her throat.

As soon as the boat docked the guard, who hadn't even looked at Tom during the journey downstream, jumped off and disappeared across the lawn and into the palace. Tom was unsure where to go and was about to return to the stillroom when he was stopped by a page. He recognised the young boy as the one who had taken him to the Queen for his punishment and when he was beckoned to follow once again, his euphoria at getting out of gaol began to increase. Surely he was being taken to reunite with his wife?

Instead of being led to the state apartments however, Tom was taken along a different corridor; one he instantly recognised. They weren't going to see the Queen, instead they were on their way to Walsingham's office. He'd been hoping to find Isabel back in her rightful place with the other ladies and his heart sank as he wondered when he would see her again. Then an insidious thought tried to push its way uninvited into his mind: supposing she was still in the Tower? Although he couldn't understand why he would have been freed and not her. He was the servant, she was the courtier.

He watched the page knock on the door and almost immediately it swung open, a guard stepping to one side to allow admittance. The page glanced at him and then began to trot away in the direction from which he'd come so Tom had no option than to enter the room and discover what was in store for him next. He imagined he wasn't going to like it.

Just like the serjeant earlier Walsingham was writing and although he must have been aware Tom was standing there, there was no indication of it. Tom was still feeling shaky and wished he could sit. Perhaps if he fell down, which was distinctly likely, someone might pay attention. Eventually Walsingham looked up, as if alerted by Tom's swaying from side to side, and nodded his head towards a chair. Tom noticed how he'd wrinkled his nose and shuddered a little and he couldn't help agreeing silently that he didn't smell very good. He kept his eyes on Walsingham's face knowing that the only way he was going to understand what was going on was by lip reading whenever the spymaster chose to speak to him.

'How was your night in gaol?' Walsingham's frigid smile did not reach his eyes and although Tom couldn't hear the tone in which he was being spoken to he could certainly make a good guess. He might not be behind bars anymore but he knew he wasn't forgiven. He tried to sign to ask the whereabouts of Isabel but Walsingham put a hand up to stop him.

'You are here because I have important work for you to do and I could not spare you to sit at your leisure doing nothing.' Tom's face remained passive, carved from stone. He hoped Walsingham would tell him where his wife was. Then a thought entered his head so dreadful he felt his blood run cold. Had they killed her? As if reading Tom's mind Walsingham continued. 'If you can do as I ask and bring me back favourable information Her Majesty will consider having Lady Isabel released from the Tower. Is that clear? You do as I decree and perhaps, she will be returned to you in one piece.'

Tom breathed out slowly. At least she wasn't dead. Yet. Whatever task Walsingham wanted Tom to undertake he'd do it. Anything to ensure his wife was safe. He nodded, his hands gripped together on his lap.

'I want you to follow someone for me. Find out what he is saying and who he meets with. It should not be difficult except you will need to be vigilant at all times. Do not let him realise you are there. Understand?'

Tom nodded. Walsingham's dark face deepened as if a shadow had passed in front of the sun. With his hair hidden beneath a black cap that came down to his face, he looked like the ravens at the Tower; the ones currently watching over Isabel.

'Do not let me down,' Walsingham enunciated and with a wave of his hand Tom was back outside the room on his own and unsure of what to do next. As he stood for a moment wondering a page appeared from somewhere inside the apartment and beckoning Tom to follow they began to walk for what felt like miles along dark corridors lit by occasional small windows with tiny panes of glass, throwing thin dull patches of light onto the floor which was covered with sweet smelling rushes, meadowsweet and lavender. Tom remembered the stench of his prison cell that morning and felt bile rising up in his throat. Would he ever get the smell of death out of his nostrils?

Chapter Forty

February 1585

Whilst relieved he was now free Tom was bereft that Isabel still languished in the Tower. He managed a single visit to her at dusk one evening, bribing the guards to allow him to see her for ten minutes. Even the sight of the twin towers of the Byward Tower gatehouse as he passed beneath them filled him with foreboding. He was starting to question his decision to marry Isabel. Despite his love for her, their union had placed her in grave danger. He followed a guard across the green to the brick-built Beauchamp Tower where he was shown into her chamber. Relieved to find her in relative comfort in the small room, despite the old and slightly rat-chewed tapestries, it was still cold. A small fire burned in the grate and Isabel together with the only maid she was allowed were both huddled close to it. After he'd finally released her from his arms, never wanting to let her free again, she managed to explain they only had a meagre allowance of logs a day and needed to eke them out. Tom immediately reassured her that somehow he would ensure they had more delivered. The room and the food were a far cry from what she'd been used to at court or in her own comfortable home. From the small windows she had a good view of the vicinity: the green below, the chapel and the huge dominating White Tower as well as the Queen's House where the Lieutenant of the Tower lived. She was allowed to walk along the ramparts to the adjacent Bell Tower when the weather permitted but he could see how being locked up was affecting her health. Her pale skin was now taut over her cheekbones, grey and sallow, and her eyes that always twinkled at him were dull and lifeless. Turning her back on her maid, she reached down into the neckline of her dress and pulled out her locket, pressing it into Tom's hand and folding his fingers over. He slipped it into his pocket.

After ten minutes, a banging on the door alerted Isabel and she signed to Tom that he needed to leave. He scooped her up, her slight body feeling like a Bartholomew Baby, the wooden dolls that were sold in large amounts at St Bartholomew Fair. Crushing her to him he was desperate to feel her heart, the movement of her lungs as she breathed against his chest, her lips against his. Eventually she wriggled a little bit and he put her back down. She ushered him towards the door.

'I will be fine,' she promised and not daring to look back and display the emotions cast across his face he followed the guards back downstairs and out onto the green. He knew from the location of her room she could look down and see him there but he deliberately didn't turn towards her. Someone may be watching him, he of all people now knew there were spies watching all the time, and he wanted to guarantee her life was as comfortable as possible. Turning to the guards he mimed wood chopping and twitched his head towards her room. One of them nodded and yet more groats changed hands.

Back in his stillroom Tom admitted to himself it was too dangerous to attempt another visit to his wife, even though every fibre of his being yearned to. By keeping his head down and doing as Walsingham had asked of him his conduct would surely bring about her release sooner than anything else. He had the name of his prey and all he needed to do was watch him and report back where he went and who he met with. He could certainly do that and pulling on his blue coat which had miraculously been returned to him when he left Poultry Corner, he went to find a wherry which would take him to The Cross Keys to see if he could find the man they called John Ballard.

Unconfined by buildings the bitter east wind whistled down the river bringing with it flecks of snow which stung Tom's face as he huddled in the bow of the small boat. His mind wouldn't stop churning over his misfortune; he'd been so close to all that he wanted, a safe home and someone who loved him, to have it all torn away within weeks. That moment of living as husband and wife had just brought home more cruelly that all he wanted and desired was forever destined to be out of his reach. Would he ever be able to live with his wife again? If he hadn't been taken on at the palace, if his vanilla and apothecary skills hadn't been noticed by the Queen . . . he could blame the chain of events that had brought him to this moment, he considered morosely, but without those things happening he wouldn't have met

Isabel and now she was his world. He would die for her. And he'd certainly go and spy for Walsingham if it would secure her release.

He found the inn quite easily and the two drunk men slumped on the floor face down outside gave him an idea of what type of establishment it was. Tom had expected a better class of tavern, Walsingham had intimated the plotters were minor nobility, but if the men were meeting to discuss dangerous conspiracies he supposed that maybe they'd meet up somewhere they were unlikely to be recognised. He wasn't about to question Walsingham's intelligence that he'd find his prey here.

Pushing open the door the room was hazy with smoke both from the fire, which appeared to belching out grey clouds with every swing of the door, and layers of drifting smoke from the numerous clay pipes. He hastily shut the door causing another plume to bellow into the room. An old grizzled man with matted, lank hair to his shoulders turned around on his stool and glared at Tom.

The room was small and as before Tom chose to stand at the side of the room where he'd have better sight of everyone than if he were sat at the only available table in the corner. Pointing to a jug of ale he was furnished with a cup and a jug and he handed over the coins gratefully before pouring the amber liquid and downing it in one. The air in the room not only made it difficult to see, it also made his throat hurt. He wondered how the others could sit in there for hours at a time with seemingly no ill effects. Perhaps it was practice. And, as another man staggered in and slammed the door shut, maybe the proprietor deliberately let the fire fill the room with smoke; it would certainly increase his sales as everyone, including him, doused their throats at regular intervals.

Tom looked around for his quarry as best he could. Walsingham had sketched a rough portrait of his face but one bearded fellow looked much like another and it was the man's physique he was searching for. Short and rotund and, he hoped, a little better dressed than the other clientele. Then his eyes alighted on two men deep in conversation at a table just to his right and he realised one of them was the man he was seeking. They were both wearing dull kersey cloaks and dun coloured breeches. Tom heaved a sigh of relief; despite the difficulty in seeing through the haze they were close enough for him to be able to see what they were saying. He wondered who Ballard's accomplice was.

Holding his cup of ale up as if to take a sip, he watched over the rim as the man he'd identified as Ballard said, *'They will be arriving by the end of this week. It has been arranged that they dock in Newcastle and will be taken to a safe house in Derbyshire and from there, to Oxford.'* He realised the other man was talking as his shoulder shifted slightly as he spoke and at one point his arms waved about. Tom cursed that he could only see one man at a time and decided to try and move to see who Ballard's co-conspirator was. Picking up his jug and cup he casually walked over to the fire and placed the items on the mantelpiece before pretending to warm his hands whilst trying not to cough from the smoke.

The other gentleman was taller and thin, almost gangly. He looked a similar age, possibly mid-twenties. Tom wondered why they weren't just out enjoying life but he'd seen the zealous fervour that Catholics had for their faith and anyone who would stand against the Pope. He watched as Ballard said something he couldn't catch but then there were a couple of words from his accomplice he instantly recognised: *Jesuit priests*. They were talking about bringing priests into the country; an operation that was treason and would end on the scaffold. He was certain Walsingham would be very interested in this information and he fervently hoped it would buy Isabel's release.

The two men stood up as if to leave and he saw the thin man pass Ballard a letter which was immediately secreted inside his coat. Tom turned to his ale and poured himself another cup. A sharp brush of cold air across his face indicated the two men had just walked out and he finished his drink while he waited to ensure they had left, before he followed them.

Outside the sky had cleared and already the cobbles were sparkling with a layer of frost under the moon which shone with an outer ring of white. A sign that a hard frost was on its way; he needed to get back before the Thames began to freeze and the boats stopped rowing. The moonlight threw sharp edged shadows across the street of the top-heavy buildings around him as if they would topple down on him at any moment. There was no sign of the two men and in the distance he could just see a night watchman, his lamp swinging, walking towards him. Tom hurried back to the wharf hoping a boatman would be waiting.

Back in his room, which was almost as cold as it was outside, Tom removed his coat and pulled his blanket around himself before going to the stillroom and making up the fire, sinking gratefully into Hugh's chair placed beside it.

Finding a piece of parchment and a quill he attempted to quickly note down everything he'd been able to read from the two men's lips. With the amount he needed to remember, again he used the small curlicues and marks to represent words, he covered half a page in a matter of minutes. From this he knew he'd be able to remember everything he needed to relay to Walsingham the following day, when without doubt he'd be expected to report back every nuance of the evening. There was no chance he'd forget something of importance.

Sure enough, the following morning he was summoned upstairs to Walsingham's apartment. Hugh had found him asleep in the chair in front of the fire and sent him to get washed and changed. As Tom stirred, the stench of stale smoke made his nose wrinkle up in disgust and heating some water over the fire, he took it in a pot back to his room where he used some lye soap and washed himself down before donning clean clothes.

Taking the memo note he'd written the night before he followed the page – a different one this time, older and more sedate – up to Walsingham's office where the usual rigmarole of the page knocking and another answering and ushering Tom in proceeded. This time he wasn't left waiting for quite so long and seeing the piece of parchment in Tom's hand Walsingham waved him forward, his palm outstretched for Tom to hand it over. Having done so, Tom was pleased to watch the spymaster's face as he realised it was impossible to read. Just for once, Tom felt as if he had the upper hand.

As before, Tom pointed to each mark he'd made and mimed what each meant. He'd added a separate sign for the name of Ballard. By the time Tom had relayed everything from the night before, Walsingham had gone from his usual austere, closed countenance to openly smiling and clapping Tom on the back.

'This is very good,' he complimented. 'I will make sure my men are watching the port at Newcastle for anyone who could be one of these priests. You have done well. And I must introduce you to Thomas Phelippes; he will be most interested in the code you write in. He also invents codes and I think you could work well together.' Tom had become confused during this speech but Walsingham wrote down Phelippes' name and then said 'come'. He beckoned and Tom followed him through a door set in the panelling at the back of the room then through several more Tom had never seen. Some of them were empty or just contained an occasional chest or press for hanging clothes in and they were cold with no fires in the grate. Tom watched his breath gathering into small white clouds as he hurried along behind Walsingham. It was no surprise the man always kept a good fire burning if this was how cold the rest of the apartment was. The troubled souls of past palace residents hovered in the corners; Tom felt he was being watched.

Eventually they arrived at a door and Walsingham walked into the room without a knock or pause; there was no argument about who was the boss around here. This room was more comfortably furnished with several thick tapestries to insulate the room, a fire blazing in a wide fireplace and a heavy bressummer beam mantelpiece stacked with pieces of parchment. The man behind the desk immediately got to his feet and they bowed to each other. A moment later Tom joined in. He could see Walsingham explaining about him as he put the paper with his shorthand on it onto the desk and pointed at Tom, along with much waving of his arms.

275

The other man, who Tom assumed was the aforementioned Phelippes, picked it up and scrutinised it before looking at Tom, his eyes half closed, assessing. Then he turned to Walsingham.

'*Yes, I can do that,*' he said, '*leave him here with me. I have an idea.*'

Walsingham patted Tom on the back as he left who turned to face the man across the table. He was short with broad shoulders and light sandy coloured hair and beard, a similar colour to Tom's own hair, his face pitted with pock marks. His jerkin was plain black grosgrain and fitted close, his white ruff matching the sleeves of his cambric shirt. When he smiled his eyes creased up until they had almost disappeared and Tom silently exhaled in relief. This man looked friendly and he was sure they were going to get on well. He was interested to see what Walsingham had meant about codes and ciphers and how he was to become involved with this additional layer of the spying machine Walsingham managed.

Chapter Forty-One

July 2021

Oliver arrived earlier than Mathilde expected on the Tuesday morning. She was sitting cross legged on a kitchen chair simultaneously eating toast and demonstrating to Fleur how to make a card tower. The little girl was too clumsy, pouting with frustration which just made Mathilde laugh. They heard his voice calling 'hello' as he walked around the corner of the house and Mathilde looked at Rachel for moment before leaping off her chair muttering '*merde*' and racing upstairs to brush her hair and teeth and throw some clothes on. As she took the stairs two at a time, below her she could hear Rachel greeting him.

Mathilde didn't even know why she cared if he saw her looking early morning dishevelled, but somehow it mattered and she pulled on some clean shorts and a T-shirt, brushed her hair and pushed her bare feet into a pair of Rachel's flipflops that had somehow become her own. Plaiting her hair she stared at her face in the dressing table mirror wondering whether or not to dig out her ancient mascara but decided that her sun burnished skin and brush of freckles across her nose and cheekbones were adornment enough. Outside the sun was already climbing across the Wedgwood blue sky, promising another warm day.

''ello, 'ello,' Mathilde greeted Oliver airily as she strolled into the kitchen where she'd been eating breakfast not ten minutes previously. Thankfully Fleur, now deprived of her entertainment, had disappeared into the living room so couldn't say something embarrassing about Mathilde disappearing the moment they'd heard Oliver's voice.

He was sitting on the chair she'd vacated minutes before and was nursing a cup of coffee, the steam making his skin flushed. His grin as he looked up warmed her whole body and she couldn't help smiling back, feeling shy and gauche like a fourteen-year-old, her stomach rolling with pleasure.

'Oliver has some good news,' Rachel said, pouring herself and Mathilde coffee and sitting down at the table, 'come and sit down and he can explain.' Mathilde slipped into the chair beside her sister.

'I received a call over the weekend. An eminent expert in cryptography is visiting the UEA this week to deliver a series of lectures to some of the postgrad students. It's a big coup for the department as he doesn't usually travel to the provinces; he mostly stays in London or sometimes Oxford. He's been to Yale and Harvard but never to East Anglia. Anyway, it's superb luck that we're going to be there today because hopefully he can examine your document after the lecture and maybe he'll be able to decipher it.'

Mathilde was pleased he was so happy but she had a knot of discomfort inside. Although she wanted to understand the

278

letter as much as he did she was afraid of what they may discover. The air around her grew colder. In the corners of the room shadows eddied and churned and she shivered.

'Mind you don't catch it on the door,' Oliver instructed as he and Mathilde slid the triptych wrapped in an old quilt into the back seat of the car. After seeing how small the boot was when they'd stowed the pet shop purchases she'd wondered how he intended transporting it to the university. She hadn't realised, until Oliver explained, how important it was for the experts to see the provenance of where the note had been discovered. It was now in its dark velvet pouch, nestled on top of the painting to prevent it moving about. Mathilde had suggested she lay it on her lap but Oliver had explained the heat from her legs could affect the integrity of the ancient document.

'The head of faculty has said we can wait in her office,' he explained, 'where the pieces will be safe.'

Mathilde nodded although her mind was elsewhere. Taking the items from the house was making her gut tense, acid bile clawing at the back of her throat. She looked back as they drove away, so unnerved that she was sure she would see a ghost watching from the window, but the blank panes of glass reflected the pale blue sky, streaked with the remains of herringbone clouds as they stared back reproachfully at her.

They had to drive around the university perimeter road three times before they found the badly signposted building they needed.

'Oh, for heaven's sake,' Oliver groaned as a notice

announced that there was no parking outside and they needed to park in the visitors' car park at the Sainsbury Centre. 'We can't carry the triptych all the way down from there,' he complained as he pulled up outside the office building, 'I'll stop here and help you carry it in, then I'll go and park while you wait with the pieces, okay?'

'You're the driver,' Mathilde shrugged. She rarely paid attention to any 'no parking' signs and abandoned her van wherever she liked. Any parking tickets were thrown in the nearest bin, knowing she'd be long gone before anyone came looking for her. She smiled at Oliver's law-abiding agitation as she helped him remove their precious cargo and place it on a conveniently empty table in the reception area before he headed back outside to park.

The office they needed was on the second floor and Mathilde breathed a sigh of relief when they were finally there and the triptych and letter were safely ensconced on the desk. A secretary had been told to expect them and brought through coffee and biscuits which they consumed on the other side of the room, well away from their precious cargo. Oliver kept looking at his watch and Mathilde couldn't bear to think of his disappointment if they were ignored.

Thankfully, at almost exactly midday they heard voices in the outer office and a group of people strode in. The older of the men who looked to Mathilde like a kindly old grand-father, his smiling face and twinkly eyes making her warm to him immediately, introduced himself as the Assistant Dean of the university, before he turned to another gentleman stood behind him.

'This is Professor Thornton,' he explained, 'I've told him all about your find and the chapel at your home, he's very interested to take a look.' The professor, to Mathilde's surprise a much younger man probably only in his early forties, managed a tight smile and a curt nod of his head as if he were conserving energy for the task ahead. Or perhaps for his lunch.

Oliver quickly unwrapped both items as if he'd been caught unawares. Mathilde could see how important this meeting was to him and that it may improve his career to be a part of it. He stepped to one side to let the expert take a closer look as he slipped his eye loupe out of his pocket and bent closer.

The room was silent other than the hushed noise of five people barely breathing. The professor nodded from time to time as he looked over the tiny scenes Mathilde now knew so well and then at the crest on top of the frame before moving on to the piece of parchment he was most interested in. He spent so long scrutinising it Mathilde wondered if he'd forgotten the rest of them were there. Eventually he stood back up, flexing his back, cramped after so long crouched over.

'And you say that you found this letter behind the work of art?' he asked, looking between Oliver and Mathilde. She was waiting for Oliver to speak but when he didn't she thought she'd better answer.

'Yes, I did,' she replied. 'There was a small gap at the top here,' she pointed, 'between the frame and the picture. I could just see something inside so I used some thin pliers to pull it out.' The professor visibly winced at the mention of her pliers and she wanted to giggle.

'Obviously I can't say for certain,' he began, 'but as you have already had the triptych dated and we know it's sixteenth century then it seems most likely this is authentic. It's an extremely exciting find; obviously in code which we can see, and quite possibly was written by Walsingham or one of his cohort. In the sixteenth century, at the height of the numerous Catholic plots to put Mary Queen of Scots on the throne, Walsingham used a network of spies to intercept the letters sent between the conspirators and the Spanish. Have you heard of the Babington plot?' He looked at Mathilde and she shook her head, making a mental note to add it to her growing list of English history to research. 'It resulted in Mary Stuart losing her head. Lord Burghley, who was the Queen's Chancellor, made sure his man raced between London and Fotheringay Castle where Mary was imprisoned, to ensure the warrant was carried out before the ink was dry.' He turned back to the letter in front of him. 'But what's even more interesting about this document is the hidden message written between the lines of code in some sort of crude invisible ink. We do know it was sometimes used by coders at that time. I need to have this properly studied by my colleagues in the laboratory here; this requires specialist chemicals to help expose the hidden words. Although you'll need further research done on the triptych in due course you don't need to leave that today.'

'Okaaay,' Mathilde wasn't sure about leaving the letter behind but on the other hand she really wanted to know what it said and whether it would help her to understand the disturbing dreams she was having and reveal more about the unhappy souls that hid in the shadows.

'When our investigations are complete we would ask that you give – or loan,' he added hastily, seeing her eyebrows begin to rise, 'the triptych and letter to a museum. They're national treasures.'

She hadn't even considered that anyone would expect her to hand the pieces over and she had no intention of doing so. They belonged at the hall . . . and maybe she did too? Making a non-committal noise and shrugging her shoulders she turned to help Oliver swathe the painting in its protective covers again.

Oliver collected the car and they drove home again. He chatted on about everything the professor had said as if Mathilde hadn't been in the room and she couldn't decide if he thought her English wasn't good enough to understand, which for part of the explanation was true, or if he was so excited he just wanted to tell himself all over again.

As they arrived home Mathilde let the breath she'd been holding all day slowly seep out of her. Getting out of the car she turned her face to the warm sun and closing her eyes, smiled for a moment. The triptych was back where it belonged and once the mystery of the document she'd found was unravelled she was certain that finally the weary ghosts who walked the corridors of Lutton Hall could be laid to rest.

Chapter Forty-Two

March 1585

Every night Tom lay down on his pallet bed beside the still-room, his heart hurting as thoughts of Isabel filled his head. His days were filled with assignments for Walsingham and he frequently found himself waiting in the dim shadows of taverns and playhouses, even the corridors of Westminster Palace, watching people's faces as they gave away their secrets. Three men were currently residing in the Tower because of information he'd passed on and he couldn't help making comparisons with his own wife in the same castle, albeit that her surroundings were more comfortable. Those men were being kept deep in the bowels of the bloody tower where the stinking cold stone walls absorbed the sounds of screaming. Despite the work he'd done for Walsingham the man didn't yet seem inclined to let her free. What more did he need to do?

Between his constant work and pining for Isabel Tom rarely had the time nor inclination to eat, just grabbing at anything he found in the kitchen when the cook looked the other way. His firm, muscular body was beginning to waste away, shadows where there had once been brawn, and his face looked aged beneath its tanned exterior. Dark bruises were smudged beneath his eyes, their deep grey now dull and opaque. Every waking moment was wretched.

He'd been sent by Thomas Phelippes to work with the Superintendent of St Bartholomew's hospital, Doctor Timothy Bright. As well as an eminent surgeon and a close friend of Sir Philip Sidney, who in turn was married to Walsingham's daughter Frances, Bright was fast becoming a cryptography expert; inventing shorthand to be used alongside the ciphers that were passed between Walsingham's spies and interpreting the frequent letters intercepted from France and destined for the papist plotters. Tom's ability to condense entire memos into one or two lines of shorthand was proving invaluable.

Eventually, one morning when the sun was offering a small promise of warmth and the trees in the grounds of St Bartholomew's were covered in tiny unfurling new leaves, Bright noticed Tom's slow decline.

'You look ill, my friend,' he mouthed slowly. After several weeks of working together every day, the doctor was now adept at speaking at a speed Tom could easily understand whilst still being able to keep a momentum so others barely noticed.

Tom just shrugged and shook his head, bending over the document he was translating into their new shorthand. The letter had already been coded but the additional process reduced it to a small piece of parchment which could be hidden anywhere on a person's body. Even in those parts where nobody would wish to look.

Bright tapped him on the arm to make him look up again knowing that unless Tom was actually facing him anything he was saying was instantly lost in the cool clean air drifting in from the open window and around them. Tom looked at him, frowning.

'If you are ill I can help you,' Bright said, *'but you need to tell me what ails you.'*

'Nothing that you can help with,' Tom wrote quickly on his wax tablet, 'my wife Isabel is still being held at the Tower and until the Queen releases her, I cannot see her. We are unable to live as man and wife.'

'Then we must do something to change this situation,' Bright replied, *'or you are of no use to anyone. Leave it with me.'* He returned to the work he was doing and Tom did the same. He had little faith that his friend would have enough influence.

Early the following morning the familiar page arrived in his room and passed him a note. Tom instantly recognised Walsingham's writing and wondered with a sinking heart who he was being asked to spy on next. The page was trying to mime an action. Eventually he stopped and looked at Tom, his face tilted expectantly. Tom had no idea what he wanted and used his universal sign of not understanding by shrugging his shoulders and holding his arms out to the side, palms upwards. Everyone now knew what that meant.

The page took Tom's hand and pulled him through to his bedroom and rummaged through the press in the corner until he pulled out Tom's blue coat. It was very grubby down one arm where Tom had needed to press himself into the corner of an alley to avoid being seen. He'd been watching a conversation between two Catholic agitators who Walsingham was very keen to know more about. The boy quickly rubbed at the marks with a corner of Tom's blanket until the coat looked slightly less dishevelled and then he handed it to Tom before doing a mime of someone bowing down on one knee.

Tom's heart began to pump hard in his chest and he felt his breath start to quicken. He was expected at an audience with the Queen which explained why the page was so agitated, trying to hurry him along and across the courtyard to the royal apartments. Why did she want to see him? Was Isabel unwell? Was he about to go and join her in the Tower? He'd be happy with that if it meant they were together but he absolutely didn't want to end up back in the stinking gaol he'd previously been in.

Following the page on his shaking legs, it took ten agonising minutes to reach the Privy Chamber. Immediately he fell to his knees, keeping his head bowed.

As usual he had no idea if he were being spoken to and so stayed there for a long while, just the occasional swish of a skirt out of the corner of his eye any indication there was still someone in the room with him. Eventually someone gave him a tap on the arm and he looked up to see the Queen, sitting upright on her throne, beckoning him forward. Tom was relieved to see Walsingham and Burghley with her, two men he trusted to give him a fair trial, if that was what this was about to be.

'I have told Her Majesty about your helpful work with Doctor Bright in the hunt for those who would depose or assassinate her. She has noted that you have worked hard on her behalf and as recompense has agreed to free your wife from the Tower.'

A sudden movement of pale green made Tom turn his

head and there before him was Isabel. She was wearing the dress she'd worn on the day they'd married only now it hung off her shoulders. The partlet at the top couldn't disguise her collar bone with deep shadows beneath. Her face was as beautiful as ever, despite her cheekbones and fine bone structure now sharp and angular, her skin as pale as the white linen he knew she'd be wearing beneath her gown. Tears slowly edged their way over her eyelashes and rolled down her face. Without waiting for permission Tom ran forward and scooped her up into his arms as if she were about to tumble to the floor. She looked so shaky he strongly suspected that she might. The hot wet of her tears trickled down his neck as he held her against him.

Eventually she moved away from him and he realised they were being spoken to. She had dropped down into a curtsey and he knelt on one knee, head bowed, waiting to see what she did. As she stood up again he followed suit, facing the Queen who was talking to Isabel; she nodded vigorously before taking Tom's hand and walking backwards out of the room.

Suddenly they were on the other side of the chamber door where the guards stood with their pikes, staring straight ahead. The door closed behind them and Isabel threw her arms around Tom before leading him to a nearby window seat where the sunlight from outside had warmed the embroidered cushion a little. He could see her face better here as she explained to him what had happened to her.

'The Queen has granted us a pardon because you have worked so hard for Walsingham and been able to assist in uncovering plots when nobody else could. She is very pleased with you and I am able to return to my home. I will no longer be expected to attend

288

Her Majesty. And I have another surprise for you.' She took his hand and pressed it against her belly. Beneath the solid form of her stomacher he felt a distinctive swelling. His eyes widened as they met hers and she smiled and nodded. *'We are to have a baby in the autumn,'* she mouthed, *'it must have been made in the days following our wedding before we were separated. I have seen a midwife, my maid insisted that one was brought to the Tower, and she says it will be born a little before Michaelmas.'*

Tom thought he would explode with happiness and his eyes brimmed with tears just as Isabel's had. He rubbed at them frantically with the back of his hands. He needed to be able to see clearly to be able to read what she was saying. Together they walked to the wharf and waited for a wherry to take them home.

Chapter Forty-Three

August 1585

Tom was loving his new life. Every morning he'd wake in their comfortable bed behind heavy drapes that made the interior around them murky, the muted light casting them into their own twilight world. The warmth from her body, her belly now much larger drew him to her and every morning he was reluctant to leave, returning to the palace or to St Bartholomew hospital to work with Doctor Bright. Walsingham seemed to have forgotten about him, at least for the present, and Tom felt the constant nag of fear wondering what the spymaster may ask him to do next. He knew the absence of assignments wouldn't last much longer. His heart thumped hard when he thought about the potential danger. He had a wife and soon a new baby to worry about.

He'd seen the way some of their neighbours looked at him when he left the house, the sideways glances and turned backs and he guessed that the servants had been gossiping. He could imagine their opinions of an apothecary suddenly married to a lady and living in the opulent house close to them. He was used to being looked down upon and ignored them.

Returning home one evening from the palace, Tom was informed by Anne, Isabel's lady's maid, that his wife had taken to her bed that morning and the midwife had been called. It was earlier than the baby was due to arrive, just eight months since their wedding and he spent a worried night walking around the parlour as the midwife and Catherine, a maid Isabel was particularly fond of, hurried back and forth to the kitchen for fresh boiled water on numerous occasions. Previously he'd prepared a tisane of pennyroyal to assist with birth and he pressed it into Catherine's hands as she passed by. He was thankful that, as had been pointed out to him, he couldn't hear the screams which apparently went with giving birth. All was as silent as ever in his world. But it also meant he wouldn't hear his own baby give its first cries, nor hear a giggle or its first words and he'd give anything to experience those things.

Eventually, as the first stirrings of light began to filter through the windows and the city skyline started to silhouette itself against the dawn clouds, he was dozing in a chair beside the fireplace, the embers now barely glowing, when the rush of air as the door was opened swept across his face. In one movement he was on his feet, his eyes trained on the candlelight in the doorway. The midwife was standing there, her face smiling as she stepped to one side and indicated he could finally go up to Isabel.

Taking the stairs two at a time he rushed into the bedroom, carefully averting his eyes from the pile of blood-soaked linens on the floor outside. The room was still in almost complete darkness, tapestries and carpets hung at the windows as tradition depicted, with low light coming from the fire blazing in the grate and the candles still lit in the sconces. Sitting up in bed, Isabel's face reflected the orange from the fire giving her a flushed look, her hair still stuck to her face in damp tendrils. She smiled at him gently, proffering the tiny swaddled blanket in her arms.

'Our son,' she said as she handed the tiny baby to him. Tom looked down at the sleeping child, the softest graze of hair across his head and his cheeks pink and soft. He couldn't stop the hectic beating of his heart and a wide, relieved smile spread across his face. He signed 'beautiful' then pointed to the baby and to her and she beamed. She looked exhausted and laying the baby in the wooden crib beside the bed he signed for Isabel to sleep as he tiptoed from the room. He knew he was leaving them both in safe hands, Catherine had come to them from a family of fourteen siblings and she'd helped in the birth of many of those babies. She loved Isabel as much as he did; he saw it in her actions and her care every day.

The sun was now starting to climb in the sky and Tom quickly pulled on his boots and jerkin, hurrying through the streets filling with the daily bustle of hawkers and trades people as he headed to the river. Hugh was always quick to complain about the time his assistant was missing from the stillroom and arriving late just because his wife had given birth wouldn't help soothe his irritation. He paused for a moment to buy a warm pie from a seller on the docks before climbing into a small boat and holding out the now tatty memo book with the list of his destinations. One of the pages of his book simply said 'The Tower' and he fervently hoped he never needed to show that to anyone again. He still shuddered as he flipped past the page looking for other places.

It only took a couple of seconds of Tom demonstrating himself rocking a baby for Hugh to realise why he was so late to work and after a quick congratulatory slap on the back he was despatched to the physic garden for comfrey. On his way he checked their vanilla plants; finally he could see tiny flower buds and he was hopeful they would grow seed pods and save him many hours trying to source them around the warehouses beside the Thames. He was now buying almost all of the sweet spice that arrived at Queenshithe docks and had even sent a message to the port at Norwich to send any that appeared in cargo there.

After dinner, where Tom realised how hungry he was, consuming several bowls of pottage followed by pie, cheese and apples, a note came from Walsingham's office ordering him to visit Doctor Bright. He showed it to Hugh and pulled his apologetic face but secretly he was delighted. The hospital was close to Cordwainer Street and he'd be able to get home quickly afterwards. He hoped this wasn't a day that the doctor wanted to work late into the night. His writing was so small it made Tom's eyes hurt to concentrate on it after a while and he already had a headache after so little sleep the night before. He was desperate to get home to see Isabel and their tiny son.

They didn't have a major breakthrough but he wanted to test out some shorthand he'd devised with Tom to ensure the Catholic plotters couldn't decipher it if they got hold of any letters. Together they worked on the passage they were coding for three hours until they were both pleased; they could easily condense three pages of writing into two short paragraphs whilst still being able to understand what it said. They'd done a good job between the pair of them and were sure Walsingham and Phelippes would be happy. Now they'd be able to relay the plotters' schemes on smaller, well-concealed scraps of paper.

Arriving home that evening the sun was hanging on the horizon and glowing deep orange; throwing long shadows across the streets as it danced against the sides of the houses, reflecting in the windows, which flashed as if they were on fire. Tom raced straight upstairs to see Isabel, not caring whether it was deemed suitable behaviour for a new father. He found both his wife and his son fast asleep, the room still dark and hot; he knew it would stay that way until Isabel had been churched when the baby was a month old. Until then she couldn't leave the room.

Perching on the bed he watched them both until Isabel stirred. He'd shifted his weight more than once hoping she'd wake up and he smiled to himself as his plan worked. She pushed herself up into a sitting position and peered into the cradle smiling sleepily. The baby's tiny perfect features were a replica of her own.

'So small,' Isabel mouthed, putting her hands close together to demonstrate. Tom nodded. He tried to think of a mime to ask her what she wanted to name the baby but eventually gave up in frustration and looking around the room found one of several wax tablets positioned around the house. 'Name' he wrote, passing it to Isabel.

'I thought Richard?' she replied, writing 'Richard' on the tablet in case he had misunderstood. This wasn't a question about dinner which occasionally got confused in translation, Tom expecting one thing and being served something else, this was the name of their son. He may never get the opportunity to call out to the little boy but they should agree on his name.

He nodded in agreement and made his sign for 'perfect'. Then in order to save time over the following years he invented a new sign for his new son's name, pointing to the word and then following it with his new sign: clasping the top of one arm with the other.

A movement beside his foot alerted Tom to the fact that Richard was waking and he bent to pick up the baby who was now red in the face, his eyes screwed up, his mouth wide open. Tom felt a pang of sadness he couldn't hear his son or croon words of comfort as he held the bundle of blankets in which Richard was swaddled tightly, against his shoulder. He could feel the tiny lungs expanding and the shuddering of angry breath but gradually they subsided into a gentler rhythm. Holding him out at arm's length, Tom and Richard gazed solemnly at each other. It was as if the baby understood the only comfort he would derive here came from the solid warmth of his father's touch.

The door opened and the wet nurse arrived, taking Richard and disappearing again. Isabel was looking tired once more and Tom kissed her gently before creeping out and back downstairs. He hoped that despite the new arrival cook hadn't forgotten his own dinner in amongst the caudles and custards being prepared for Isabel to regain her strength. Then, after so little sleep the previous night, he intended retiring to the bedroom which had been made up for him whilst Isabel was confined. He lay down, a wide smile stretched across his face. Everything he had ever wished for was finally his.

Chapter Forty-Four

'Come on, tell me what the experts said!' Rachel jumped up off the sofa as Mathilde walked in, leaving Fleur engrossed in a cartoon on the television as the two women went to sit at the kitchen table. Rachel was almost bouncing on her seat in anticipation. 'Is it some love letter written by Henry VIII and worth a fortune?'

Mathilde still had scant knowledge of the king Rachel kept referring to despite the research she'd done but she understood the second part of the sentence. 'No money for it,' she explained, 'they want me to give it to the university so it can be displayed in their museum.'

'Well, I can see why they'd ask,' Rachel replied, 'but you don't look very happy? This is a historical artefact of interest to people around the world. You can't hide it away; it should be enjoyed by everyone. Surely you can see that?'

Mathilde gave her now familiar non-committal shrug. How could she start to explain that she was certain the letter

296

needed to be in its home; this was where it belonged. Its soul was always destined to be here. At that moment, like a ray of light blazing through a gap in the clouds, she suddenly realised that was what she'd been starting to feel since she first arrived; her soul was fated to be at Lutton Hall. Rachel rolled her eyes and went to put the kettle on.

'Look, anything of historical significance should be displayed in a museum. There are many historians who devote their whole lives to studying the Tudors and now you've got a resource that's like gold dust to them. At least I assume it is as you haven't actually told me what it says.'

Mathilde began to explain further what had been said, disappointed her sister hadn't backed her up; after all they were family. Although she couldn't bring herself to explain the claim the hall now had on her as she worried Rachel wouldn't understand.

'The other bit in invisible ink is more exciting but it has to be deciphered really slowly so the parchment doesn't get damaged. It may take weeks until we know everything. Sorry I don't know any more today.'

'You don't need to apologise to me,' Rachel told her, 'this is your house now. It's your letter, your triptych. What you do is up to you. Whether you stay here after I leave or let it out. It's our ancestral home and we're all one family.'

'It's easy for you to casually mention our family as if it repairs the past,' she replied, tired after an early start to the day and not bothering to soften the edges of what she wanted to say, 'I cannot forget all that has happened to me and being here does not wipe,' she waved her arm about as she tried to think of the words she needed, 'everything from my life away. It's always here,' she banged her chest with her fist, 'in my heart. Always. Time does not heal this quickly. Maybe never.'

Rachel's face fell and ashamed of her outburst Mathilde walked from the room and out into the garden, tears stinging the backs of her eyes. She'd lived with her demons for so long, refusing to acknowledge her past and her insecurities. Everything Rachel had enjoyed as a child was all that Mathilde had missed out on and it hurt, even now. She'd never had the confidence others did, the self-assurance that could only come with family and a place to call home. And yet now it was here for the taking if only she could allow herself to.

Collecting her father's spade she walked over to the corner of the garden and pushed it into the earth. She could barely see where to dig as her tears ran down her face and fell onto the ground.

As ever, working in the garden slowly began to work its magic on her. The tranquil and soothing ambience. As if someone had their arms around her, telling her everything was going to be all right, helping to repair the huge hole in her life she'd thought would never be filled. Here in this cool dark space beside the small coppice, a voice was telling her that it was okay to let her guard down and relax. Nothing could harm her here, ever. No fires could burn their way through her soul and turn her life into a void.

'*Maman,*' she whispered as her tears dripped onto the earth.

'Hey Matty, I wondered where you'd got to.' Oliver's voice called across the vegetable patch. She'd forgotten he was still there and she quickly rubbed her cheeks on the sleeve of her jumper, the rough wool harsh against her face before turning around to face him.

'Just getting some more digging done,' she replied giving him a wobbly smile, knowing her cheery answer belied the state of her face. She sniffed loudly. 'I want to move some of the fruit bushes here.' She heard the snapping and squeezing of undergrowth as he crashed through the overgrown grasses, brambles and dried cow parsley until he was standing beside her. Taking her chin in his thumb and forefinger he tipped her head around until she was facing him. She paused, her foot still resting on the spade ready to thrust it again into the soft ground.

'Rachel said you were upset.' He looked into her eyes as if he wanted to search her soul but she deliberately shut him out, leaving her face blank.

'It was nothing,' she shrugged, 'it feels as if she thinks now I'm here with her – my family, in our home – then everything is wonderful in Mathilde-Land. As if the past, the first twenty-eight years of my life, have been swept away. How can she understand what it was like to grow up surrounded by mistrust, always running away? No father and no home.' She could feel her eyes welling up again and she tipped her head back to try and abate them. Always the past was there, waiting to reclaim her. 'Anyway, it doesn't matter.' She turned her head away and pushed the spade in again, pulling out a large sod and turning it over, the pale, dry mud the colour of milk chocolate falling back down onto the ground and scattering across her shoes.

'Of course it matters,' Oliver remonstrated, 'stop digging for a moment and sit down with me.' He took her elbow and gave it a little tug, gentle but insistent.

He led her to the greenhouse close by and they sat on the ground outside, the weeds there flattened by her daily to and fro to check on her plants.

'I think you're being unfair to your sister,' he put his arm around her shoulders, pulling her stiff body against him, 'how can she know how you feel unless you open up and tell her? She *does* understand about your childhood and she wants to help you, if only you'd let her in.'

'I'm trying,' she whispered, 'but as you English say "easier said than done".'

Oliver smiled. 'Your English has improved significantly,' he told her. 'Now, how are the vanilla plants?' She was grateful for him changing the subject. 'Did the germination work?'

'Of course,' Mathilde smiled, 'it always works. It took hundreds of years for someone in Europe to work out why vanilla could only grow in certain countries, that only particular types of bees can pollinate them. Which is why we have to do it ourselves. Nature assisted by man.'

'You're so good with all the plants and your herbs, why don't you do that full time? Instead of the photojournalism where you don't know when you'll get your next pay packet. And it must be dangerous, constantly driving around in that van and often in risky situations. It would be far safer.'

Mathilde was looking down at her shoes, picking at the rubber sole that was beginning to part company with the upper section. They wouldn't last the summer, that was for sure.

'Sometimes I imagine what it would be like. To be able to walk out of my home and tend my plants every day. They would always be here, waiting for me. Something permanent and unmoving.'

'Is that why you enjoy growing things? Because they put down roots?'

'No. I don't know. Maybe? I just like plants and gardens; they're calm, peaceful. And they stay in one place. But now I don't know if I've left it too late.'

As they'd been talking she was aware of the closeness of Oliver's body, the heat that was emanating from him. She turned from the patch of wild mint she'd been tugging leaves from to release its pungent smell and realised that his face, turned towards her, was only inches from her own. She let out a small sigh as he leant in further and kissed her, his lips firm and cool against hers. It felt the most natural thing in the world.

Chapter Forty-Five

February 1586

As Tom's home life slipped into a comfortable routine and a calm settled over him he began to worry more about the other side of his days, the secretive part. His reprieve from spying had been short lived. He'd only told Isabel the bare essentials, deciding it was better not to explain what he was having to do. He didn't want her to worry about a thing and he chose to leave large tracts of information out when he told her about his day. But more frequently he was being despatched to watch various individuals around London, in dark corners and furtive places, and to deliver coded letters for Phelippes. The sorts of environments he wouldn't choose to visit, places where a stranger could get their throat cut just for being exactly that, someone who didn't fit in, who wasn't a local.

He wasn't surprised when yet again he was summoned by Walsingham. This time however he was told to go down-river to his home at Mortlake, Barn Elms.

As the wherry slowly made its way downriver the weak winter sun was shining but it gave out no warmth, sharing the dusky blue sky with the pale moon hanging above him as if reluctant to leave, like the last guest at a party. The cold drifted off the Thames to curl its fingers through skin and slide into bones, an unwelcome visitor. The alehouses sitting along the banks of the river to attract the trade of the numerous ships moored there had tall columns of smoke climbing into the sky. When Tom breathed out he could see his breath condense into tiny clouds before clinging in damp droplets to his beard. He tucked himself into the bow of the craft to avoid any of the splashes from the oars and was pleased when they finally arrived at the jetty where he could alight.

Two guards were waiting as he arrived, barring his way until he showed them the letter demanding his presence. One of them said something to him but turned his face away as he spoke and Tom missed what was said. It must have been a question as they both stared at him waiting for a reply. Wearily and getting colder by the minute Tom went through his signing to indicate his lack of hearing and then watched as one of them said to the other *'what does the master want with a fool like him?'*

Standing as tall as he could and knowing his blue coat gave him the cloak of respect that his apothecary clothing did not – remembering what Marlowe had told him about his clothes making him more confident – he pointed towards the house and marched past them, leaving them to hurry in his wake. He could see their long shadows laid across the lawns still white with frost as they scurried behind him.

He couldn't turn around to see the guards' faces as he

was welcomed into the house but he hoped their snide expressions had been wiped off as they resumed their post standing in the freezing cold beside the river. To make a point he hurried over to the fire in the cavernous hall he'd stepped into and held his hands out to the warmth, rubbing them together as he did so. Now who was smirking?

He followed the steward through another large hall with a long table bordered by benches and wooden chairs, heraldic insignia and carvings of flowers and vine leaves decorating the top of the wainscotting, the ceiling covered in decorative plasterwork and into the next room where Walsingham sat at a desk even bigger than the one he used at the palace. Just for once he didn't continue what he was doing and waved Tom to one of two chairs in front of the desk. The other was already occupied by a young man dressed in a thick, deep green velvet doublet, a rim of ermine showing around the ruff at his neck. He smiled and nodded at Tom and mouthed 'hello' to him. Tom smiled and dipped his head, slipping into the chair beside him.

'Tom, this man is Nicholas Berden. He is an intelligencer for me but he is also a spy for Queen Mary. He is what we call a double spy. They think he is carrying letters from her to the ambassador in France but actually he brings them to me to be copied before they continue. And again, letters going to the Queen are copied and read by us before she gets them. Do you understand?'

Tom nodded slowly. He already knew letters written in code were intercepted, because he'd been working on those with both Phelippes and Bright, coding, shorthand, invisible ink. And it seemed this Berden was a messenger for both sides but only Walsingham knew it. He raised his eyebrows waiting to find out why he'd been summoned.

'*Berden is going to meet a gentleman I need you to watch carefully. He is called Anthony Babington. We believe he is involved in another of the treacherous plots to kill our Queen and put the papist Queen Mary on the throne. We need to stop these gentlemen, these heretics, and you are going to help. You are our secret weapon. Berden will introduce you as a friend and hopefully they will believe you cannot understand what they are saying. You are to go with him now to Babington's lodgings where he and some of his fellow conspirators are meeting this afternoon.*' He passed a purse across to Tom who weighed it in his hand. There were several heavy coins inside, this wasn't a few groats to pay the boatman or to buy ale. Whatever Walsingham was relying on him to learn was worth a lot to him. It also, Tom suspected, correlated directly with the amount of danger he was about to be placed in: blood money.

They arrived at the lodgings in Bishopsgate, where Babington's wife greeted them. It was a smart home; not what Tom had expected from Walsingham's unkind description of the household. The outside of the house had plaster pargetting, a decorative relief beneath the eaves, and the wooden framed oriel window was supported with carved horses. A young daughter peeped from behind her mother's skirts and Tom felt his heart give a lurch. If what Walsingham said was true then these two people would see the man they loved in mortal danger and they could end up homeless. He wanted to warn her but for once his inability to speak saved him from his morals.

In an inner chamber a group of seven men sat in a circle. They greeted their friend jovially with slaps on his back and passed him a cup of ale but they all looked warily at Tom and no greetings were proffered to him. Berden turned Tom around towards him so that he could see what was being said and introduced him, explaining they were close friends from France and that he was Catholic, whilst carefully making a big deal of Tom's lack of hearing and speech. Assuring them he didn't know about the conspiracy nor had any way of discovering it.

After this presentation the other men were happy to smile and nod in an exaggerated manner passing him a cup of ale and showing him to a chair, miming that he should sit down. Tom had trouble keeping his face straight with them behaving as if he were the village idiot. If only they knew.

The men immediately launched into a description of their plot. Tom was sitting in their circle but still missed parts as people all spoke at the same time and some faces were obscured. Nevertheless, he did gather they were getting letters from France and moving them onwards to Queen Mary by concealing them in the many barrels of beer delivered almost daily to Chartley Castle, where she was incarcerated. This was being arranged by one Thomas Morgan, orchestrated from where he was currently residing in a Paris gaol. The idea of the barrels was, the group considered, an inspiration and the brewer who'd only been referred to an 'an honest man' would surely have a place at Mary's court when she was finally on the throne; when the Catholic faith would reign once more and the country would be returned to Rome's loving arms.

Tom's thoughts on religion were cursory. He'd always found the experience of church tedious, unable to hear anything and the stone floor cold and hard beneath his knees. The stained-glass windows in France were a pleasant diversion, especially when the sun was shining through

306

them making a rainbow of patterns on the floor. He used to hold his arm out hoping the colours would filter through onto his skin. It was magical to a small boy, as if God were reaching out to him. But as he got older his fascination waned and now he had no interest in something he couldn't participate in.

As a child he'd followed the Catholic church because it was his mother's faith and they'd attended mass daily at the monastery in the village where they settled. When the former king, Henry VIII, had closed the monasteries in England his mother had secretly helped her friend the Prior leave for France and when she had later needed help in making her own escape, her friends were able to assist her. The irony that he was now supporting the Queen in keeping the Catholics out of the country wasn't lost on him.

Tom remembered Walsingham had explained the importance of committing each of the men's faces to memory so he could recognise them anywhere. Sitting in his own world and not required to contribute he looked around the group and studied each of them, their mannerisms and their physical shape. He was quite certain he'd be able to pick them out in a crowd instantly. Babington flicked the hair away from his face for about the hundredth time and Tom smiled to himself. People didn't realise all the small gestures they performed a dozen times an hour. Another of the men, who he'd seen Berden call Robert Pooley, held his arms out nervously, stretching his fingertips together with unfailing regularity. On their journey to the house Berden had explained that Pooley was also one of Walsingham's double spies, living on a knife edge of fear that he would be revealed.

Sitting in the stuffy warmth following an early start to

the day, Tom felt his eyes start to close, but eventually his comrade got to his feet and pointed to the door and he followed. The other gentlemen also got to their feet and bowed slightly while Tom was able to get one final good look at their faces in the firelight as they said their goodbyes. He kept his face blank in apparent non comprehension.

Once out on the street, his companion took his upper arm and walked him briskly away from the house as if he was about to turn tail and run. Berden's fingers were digging into his flesh as they dipped off the street and into an alley and he was finally set free, rubbing his painful arm. They carried on walking and Tom was only too pleased to keep moving, a stench of rotting vegetables and flesh rising up around them. The ground was slippery underfoot but he couldn't bear to look down and see what he was walking in as he tripped on a loose cobble and almost fell. He was relieved to reach the other end which opened onto the wider and brighter Threadneedle Street. In front of him stood the magnificent Merchant Taylors' Hall, the home of the Company of Merchant Taylors in all its majesty, the chapel for its members attached to one end. The two men turned to head down Cornhill towards Poultry Corner. Tom shuddered at the memory of that place.

'Sorry for dragging you away,' his accomplice apologised, *'I wanted to make sure those men were totally taken in with the idea that you have no idea of what is happening around you. We played it very well there; they think you're just a messenger who can be given an address and will have no idea of what you are carrying. The idiots. They won't realise their mistake until they are cut down from a rope to watch their own entrails being ripped out.'*

Tom smiled and nodded although he felt his stomach turn

over. Seeing Throckmorton hanged and later having to sit through Hugh explaining in pictures the horrific executions of other enemies of the Queen, cut from the hangman's rope before they were dead and eviscerated in front of the crowds, had convinced him he was not cut out for the blood and gore of a public execution. Walsingham was single minded in his quest to eradicate all of those who were not loyal to Her Majesty and he was intent on ensuring that those who displeased him realised the horror of the punishment.

The two men parted ways at Blackfriars. Tom had no idea where Berden was going next and he was thankful he couldn't ask him.

'Now you've met the key players,' he was reminded, *'and we believe the stage is almost set. You can expect to be asked to perform any number of tasks until the plotters are all rounded up and Queen Mary is where she belongs. In hell.'* Turning, Berden disappeared into the melee of people bustling about the quay, leaving Tom wondering if he'd misinterpreted the last part of what he'd been told. Whatever he was now caught up in was larger, much larger, than anything he'd been involved in so far.

Chapter Forty-Six

March 1586

Tom's stomach growled and he put his palm on it feeling the rumble against his hand. He'd never enjoyed Lent and its fasting, the monotonous meals of pottage or fish, and he ended up barely eating as he waited fervently for Easter. It was the one day when he didn't mind sitting in a cold church because the recompense was a huge dinner with dish after dish of delicious roasted meats dripping with grease, bowls of custards and marchpane cakes. He hadn't lost the sweet tooth of his childhood and if he hadn't devised an effective remedy for sleeplessness, he wouldn't have ended up where he was. It had started the chain of actions which now brought him to Temple Bar on the western fringe of the city, hovering outside the Plough Inn and waiting for another of Walsingham's men, Bernard Maude. He'd never met this man but apparently he would know who Tom was by looking out for a man in a blue coat whose eyes flitted around all the time, watching and taking in all that was happening.

He knew when Maude was approaching, even though he hadn't appeared in front of Tom. He could tell by the way that others moved out of the way of someone walking towards them, the shadows on the ground shifting and swirling and at the last minute he turned and plastered a wide smile on his face. If this accomplice thought he could outwit the deaf man he had a lot to learn.

Tom was rewarded with a surprised look on the tall man's face before he broke into a grin to match Tom's own and they bowed to each other in acknowledgement of an instant rapport. Maude took Tom's arm and pulled him to the entrance of a nearby alley where nobody was passing. The light was falling fast and Tom had to stand closer to see what was being relayed as he explained who they'd be watching that evening. Walsingham had previously explained that Maude was another 'double spy' so the men inside the inn were expecting him, thinking he was part of Babington's plot. Tom was to enter a few minutes after Maude and stand somewhere in the tavern where he could watch what was happening and read anything said between the group that may otherwise be missed. It would be noisy inside and it was easy to miss any undercurrents or suspicions but Tom could pick them all up.

Leaving him in the shadows Maude disappeared through the tavern doors and Tom did as he was bid and waited a few minutes before following him. Inside for him the room was as silent as everywhere else always was but he could see it was a normal evening, the abstinence of Lent didn't extend to meeting friends or drinking beer.

Tom scanned the heaving room before spotting his prey at a table close to the fire. He immediately recognised one of them, a man of limited height and a round stomach topped with a florid face, as the man he'd watched on his very first assignment when a package had been handed over in the back yard of The Magpie. Walsingham had previously explained to Tom that they now knew John Ballard was one of the key instigators of the conspiracy. A lynch pin, the sort of man who will slide away into the darkness if – nay when – they were brought to justice. While the lambs were brought to the slaughter, being taken to Tyburn in the back of a cart, the likes of Ballard would be on a small rowing boat half-way to the continent given half a chance.

The three men were eating bowls of oyster stew; Tom could smell the savoury aroma floating its way on the steam and his stomach rumbled again. It was hard to watch their mouths as they talked and ate at the same time, droplets of gravy dripping out and onto their beards. Together with the constant wiping of chins with cloths it didn't help Tom trying to read what was being said. However, at one point after several flagons of ale, Maude had no choice but to visit the garderobe and relieve himself, leaving the two collabor-ators on their own. Tom sipped his beer slowly as he watched them put their spoons down and dip their heads closer. He had to move his position slightly so he could still see Ballard but that meant he couldn't watch his accomplice at the same time. He had to make a choice of who to watch, but thank-fully it appeared he'd chosen well.

'I will be going to France within the next couple of weeks. I need you to deliver some letters to Chartley for me. Come to my house tomorrow and I will give them to you. Do not tell anyone of what you are doing. Maude and I will travel together to meet other sympathisers of the Catholic cause in Rouen and Paris, and *we are hoping to gain final agreement from the French and Spanish to raise armies, ready to strike at the same time that our plans come to fruition.'*

At that point Maude returned and sat down. Tom wasn't sure if he knew everything arranged for this visit to France, assuming he even knew it was happening, but at least he could inform his accomplice and Walsingham of the bigger picture. Whatever these men were planning it was going to be catastrophic unless it could be stopped. It slowly dawned on Tom that he was a key player in the machinery Walsingham was operating and his role was far from over yet. The quiet family life he so loved was going to be sporadic for several months if things continued as they were.

The three men got to their feet and said their goodbyes before leaving the inn. Immediately the table was occupied by two old men who looked as if they would fall if they didn't sit down and Tom slowly drained his beaker as he waited until he thought the others had dispersed outside. He'd been told on several occasions he must never be seen with any of Walsingham's men unless they specifically introduced him, or his cover would be blown. And despite the disruption to his life Tom couldn't deny how much he was enjoying being accepted as an equal for the first time in his life, on a par with an important group of men. Working at the palace had achieved all this and he'd always be thankful for everything he'd gained whilst working there: His wife, his son, and now finally, his self-assurance.

To Tom's delight, as Easter arrived and spring began to bloom into life, briefly his own life settled down. Being at home with his family at night was far more enjoyable than creeping around the dark streets of the city watching others. As he'd understood through Ballard's words, Maude, still secretly working for Walsingham, had disappeared to France. Babington also seemed to have slipped away and was rumoured to be at his Derbyshire estate with his wife and daughter. Tom thought if the man had any sense he would be attempting to hide his family far away from the approaching treason.

With more free time, Tom returned once more to his triptych which remained sitting on an easel in the small parlour beside the front door. He added the dark scene of the inside of the tavern trying to show on the surface the oppressive atmosphere, the heat and the smell, the jostling bodies. Then to lighten it he added a tiny portrait of Richard, now starting to sit up on his own and play with the simple wooden rattles placed in his cradle beside him. The little boy smiled at everyone and Tom loved watching Isabel singing to him. Although he couldn't hear the sounds he could see her face alight and smiling, her body swaying in time to the tune coming out of her mouth. And he loved picking his son up and blowing against his neck, tickling him, seeing him smile and inhaling the warm smell that settled in the folds of Richard's chubby neck. As the baby grew he watched Catherine talking to him and was relieved to see the way he turned his head to listen. It was obvious that his son could hear and speak perfectly normally. The wet nurse had now left and Richard was eating watered down pottage alongside his parents.

Tom was pleased when Isabel invited him back to their bed, and now Richard was thriving and growing he wondered when there may be the stirrings of a new life within his wife. He had a family of his own, a home, safety and security and he wanted to progress it further. The more babies in the nursery the more secure he'd feel. People who were part of him, who carried his blood in their bodies. His heirs would ensure his legacy would continue forever, a solid bloodline; roots in this land to which he had returned and would now never leave.

The warm spring drifted towards summer and the blossom on the fruit trees in the orchard which bordered the physic garden slowly glided to the ground. Tom was immersed in the idyllic tranquillity of married life and had no desire for anything to disrupt it. But on the twenty-second of May Tom found himself once again in front of Walsingham. After a quick bow as he entered the room, removing his coat and standing in just his shirt and leather jerkin he awaited his instructions. Because they would surely come; he was never summoned to this office unless Walsingham and his spies had use of his stealthy, silent ways.

'We have had news of Ballard who has now returned from France,' Walsingham didn't bother with any niceties, he was a busy man, 'and we believe the plot they are hatching will soon reach its culmination. I need you to watch Babington: where he goes and who he meets up with. All day, every day. He will in all certainty now begin to meet up with others who are involved in this plot to kill the Queen. We must observe his every move. You will find him at rooms in Hernes Rent, Holborn. Go now and report back to me everything you learn.' He dismissed Tom with a flick of his hand and Tom, bowing briefly and collecting his coat, left the room, his heart heavy. Whatever was going on he had the feeling Walsingham wasn't telling him all that he knew. His senses had always been more in tune with other people's body language. He could read what wasn't said as well as what was. This was becoming darker – much darker – and the air around him snapped and crackled with tension.

He was relieved to discover there was an inn directly opposite Hernes Rent where he could sit in the window and consume ale whilst watching the outside door to the building. It appeared to be home to several families, as old women, young women and small children all came and went. A beggar sat on the ground which had been transformed into a quagmire by a sudden downpour, whilst everyone stepped over him as they went on their way. He had started holding his hands out clasped together in a bowl shape but had slowly lowered them as they garnered no response. Now he sat with his head on his chest and Tom wondered if he was still alive.

His musings as he watched the world go by were interrupted by a suspicious looking character who scuttled down the street, looking over his shoulder occasionally between watching his feet. He couldn't look more dubious if he tried and Tom smiled to himself. If everyone looked as devious this assignment might be fairly easy.

Tom resumed his gaze up and down the street and he was rewarded a couple of minutes later spotting a face he now knew well. Ballard strolled along, stepping carefully across puddles and horse droppings covering the ground before he skirted around the beggar and glancing around, stole in through the doorway of the house opposite.

Tom nodded slowly to himself. The rats were starting to crawl on their bellies towards the trap. He had no idea where or when it would be sprung but he knew Walsingham and his men were starting to close in.

Chapter Forty-Seven

August 2021

This time the dream started less abruptly than before and Mathilde found herself in a dark room dimly lit by candles set into sconces on the walls. Sitting up in bed was the lady she recognised from other dreams and in her arms was a small baby, its face just visible from the tightly wrapped blankets. Mathilde stepped forwards and smiling she took the baby from the lady and stared down into its sleeping face. She ran her forefinger down its cheek and inhaled the soft milky newborn scent.

In her sleep Mathilde smiled at the happy scene but as she relaxed further the dream switched location and she was walking along a street, the icy air a sharp contrast to the warm bedroom, making her breath pool into tiny clouds in front of her. She stopped at a house that looked much the same as the others, its upper storeys leaning into the street almost touching the houses opposite making the street feel sinister. The man she was following knocked on the door and within seconds they were admitted to the dark interior.

Confused as to why she was there and finding herself in a room with several other men, the familiar blanket of silence enveloped her. They made little effort to acknowledge her and she was still sitting there, her eyes beginning to close in the warmth of the room when she woke up again.

She lay on her back staring up at the darkness that hung above her. She could still smell the sweet newborn scent of the baby, whoever it was. Had he lived here? She concentrated on how she'd felt in that dimly lit room looking down at the child. A feeling of fierce love and protection she'd never felt herself. She tried not to think about the second part of the dream in that crowded room where the tension was palpable. There was something menacing there, an undercurrent that scared her.

The next day Mathilde headed out to the garden. Kneeling on the ground, small sharp stones digging into her knees, Mathilde tried to pull up some weeds. She hadn't again seen anything strange in the coppice beside her since the evening after she'd arrived but she knew she hadn't imagined it. The uncomfortable feeling she'd had in the house when she first arrived had slowly transformed over the weeks from anxious to accepting, welcoming even, so perhaps that was why the spirit hadn't felt the need to visit her.

She wasn't getting very far with her task as Shadow, laid in the sunshine beside her, kept swiping his paw out at her hand, batting it softly. Mathilde laughed to herself.

'You're a happy puss now, aren't you?' She ran her fingers through his soft fur. 'You've made this place your home, eh?

That's a good thing, to have landed on your feet.' She paused for a moment as she realised her initial plan to take Shadow with her when she left felt like a distant memory. She couldn't uproot him from here now. So, if he had accepted a new place to live and was contented there, what was stopping her doing the same? She didn't have an answer to that question. Beside her the leaves fluttered and rustled despite the fact the day was still.

'Are you actually working out here or just hiding?' Oliver called across the garden, making Mathilde jump.

'Working, of course.' She leant forward and pulled some groundsel seedlings from the ground before turning and smiling at Oliver. 'Although Fleur was being very noisy this morning. I needed some peace.'

'It's such a lovely day, let's not waste it. Shall we go for a walk?'

'Don't *you* need to do some work?' she asked as she stepped across to where he was standing. He caught hold of her hand as if she'd walk away at any moment and gave it a squeeze. She looked into his sharp blue eyes for several seconds willing him to kiss her again, the attraction curling in her belly, a slumbering animal stretching as it started to wake. Her telepathic skills were obviously not working as he let go of her hand to walk back through to the weed-free brick-laid path which she'd slowly been clearing, now allowing them to access all areas of the vegetable patch.

'I'll have you know I've been up since five this morning working so I can come over here,' he told her. 'What do you say then? Do you fancy a stroll?'

'Okay,' Mathilde nodded and brushed her dirty hands

down her trousers. 'Let me wash my hands and grab my camera, I'll be five minutes.'

Running upstairs and creeping into her room, she collected her camera bag without making a sound so as not to alert her presence to Rachel and Fleur. She didn't want them to decide to accompany her and Oliver, disturbing the wildlife and the ambience.

'Which way shall we go?' Oliver asked as they set off down the drive, 'how many footpaths have you already investigated?'

'Most of them,' she admitted, 'except the one that leads off to the right near the end of the drive. Rachel said it runs behind the farmhouse where Alice and Jack live so I've always avoided going down there. I don't need any more animosity.'

'Unless they're hanging around at the end of their garden or looking out of the window I doubt they'll even see us. And don't forget this is all part of your estate now and it's a public footpath as well. Don't let them dictate how you live your life; you have as much right as they do to be there.'

She knew he was right, that she should ignore people when they were being antagonistic, but she'd seen what it could lead to. People whispering behind hands when she entered a shop and sometimes refusing to serve her. Shouting over their fences as she and her mother walked past, one time even throwing things at them. He was looking at her, waiting for her to agree with him.

'Yes, okay,' she could hear the reticence in her own voice but nevertheless as they reached the path she followed him, climbing over a gate locked with a chain and padlock.

'That's not allowed,' Oliver frowned as he held out the chain, 'this is a public footpath, look there's a signpost saying so.' He pointed towards a smart wooden sign. 'It's supposed to be kept open and maintained. That's something you'll need to sort out because it's your responsibility now. Or the long arm of the law will come down on you, hard.'

'Long arm?' Mathilde still got confused with some of the terms that he used.

'Sorry,' he apologised, 'the council or the police will pay you a visit because it's against the law to prevent people walking on footpaths, even if they go across your land.' Mathilde pulled a face. The last thing she wanted was to bring the authorities to her door, she'd experienced that often enough to know how it usually turned out and it wasn't well.

'I have big cutters,' she said, 'I'll come back and get rid of this chain.' Turning, she started to walk down the track.

It was soon obvious the path had been closed off for a long while as they battled through waist high foliage and brambles. To their left lay the now familiar reeds on the edge of the marsh close by. A deep green border to the flat lands beyond, stretching into the distance until they met the horizon and dissolved into sky, a blurred line between the world and the stratosphere. Lifting her camera to her face Mathilde crouched down until her eyeline was level with the tops of the grasses and she fired off several shots. Everything in her viewfinder was a straight line of colour; pale skies, dusky pink grass fronds and acid green vegetation, broad brushstrokes from a paint palette. Had the artist of her triptych stood here and looked out at the view, inspired by the evocative landscape?

Pushing their way through columbine and marsh marigolds whilst attempting to avoid the nettles, they came around a corner finding themselves at the end of the farmhouse garden. Surprised, Mathilde stopped abruptly and Oliver almost cannoned into her.

'I didn't think we'd be so close to the farmhouse,' she admitted. Over the waist high hedge the lawns sloped upwards to the back of the property where garden furniture was arranged outside on a patio. No old moth-eaten deckchairs here. Neat flower beds around the edges of the lawn were a mass of coloured summer flowers and in one corner the fruit trees that displayed their wares were starting to grow big and heavy as summer progressed. Mathilde could see that her love of gardening, which she'd recently realised was inherited from her father, ran in the family. She'd bet money this pristine, well-loved garden was the work of Aunt Alice.

As if thinking about her aunt made her materialise, she suddenly appeared on the patio and immediately began to stride down the garden towards them.

'Oh damn,' Oliver breathed. Beside him Mathilde wrapped her fingers around the bracken beside her and pulled hard, feeling them cutting into her skin. The muscles between her shoulders tightened into knots.

'Come to gloat, have you?' Alice's voice carried across the garden before she'd got to the back hedge. 'Just checking out what you own? How long before we're served with an eviction notice then? Or is that why you're here now, to throw it over the back garden out of sight? Are you too afraid to come to our front door? Oh sorry,' her voice switched from its high-pitched shriek to a sarcastic drawl, 'of course, it's *your* front door, isn't it?'

'I'm afraid we don't know what you're talking about,' Oliver spoke slowly and quietly and Mathilde guessed he was trying to defuse the situation before she opened her mouth and escalated it. 'We just thought we'd see where this footpath led.' He paused for a moment. Mathilde waited to see what response they would get about the gate being chained.

'Nobody has been down that path for years, what a surprise that you suddenly decided to walk along.'

Mathilde couldn't keep her mouth shut any longer. 'Of course nobody has been down here, there is a chain on the gate,' she pointed backwards from the way they had come. 'And that is against the police long arms,' she added. Beside her she heard Oliver snort with suppressed laughter but before she could ask him what she'd said wrong, Alice was running across the lawn towards the hedge just the other side of where they were standing. To Mathilde's horror her aunt now had tears coursing down her face. Mathilde could deal with angry – she was a master of fighting intolerance and prejudice – but she didn't know what to do with hurt and sorrow. Close up and with no make-up on she saw how old her aunt looked, deep lines etched into her face now awash with the tears that she made no attempt to wipe away.

'If you decide to sell the estate then we've nowhere to go, we'll be homeless. I wish you'd never been found!'

Before Mathilde could open her mouth to deliver the reply she was building up to, Alice had turned and was hurrying back towards the house, where Jack had appeared on the patio looking towards the shouting. Realising who was stood at the end of his garden he stuck two fingers up at her and Oliver, before helping Alice into the house. They heard the bang as the back door was slammed shut but not before Mathilde had slapped her upper right arm with her left hand and folded it up with a sudden jerk, a classic French response to Jack's gesture.

Mathilde looked across at Oliver, her eyebrows pulled down above her eyes. 'Did you understand that?' she asked slowly, 'I think I need you to translate.'

'Let's walk back along the path to the hall and we can talk there.' Oliver ushered her back and silently they began to follow the path they'd made through the undergrowth towards the locked gate.

They didn't speak again until they were walking back up the drive, Oliver holding her hand.

'She was really mad,' Mathilde blurted out, 'why was she crying and shouting at us like that? She was like . . .' she hesitated as she searched for the word, 'the devil. *Possédée*.'

'Possessed?' Oliver questioned and she nodded.

'Yes, she was a wild woman. I don't understand.'

'Actually, I think you do, more than you realise.' They had arrived at the turning circle in front of the hall and Oliver steered her round to the side until they reached the chapel and he sat down on the ground leaning back against the door. Mathilde joined him, the wood which had heated up with the morning sun warm and comforting. She turned her head towards Oliver. He was so close she could lean forward and kiss him but he had a frown creasing his forehead.

'What?' she asked.

'Your aunt. I know she's been an absolute cow since you arrived. She managed a few choice words just now. And your uncle's gesture.' Mathilde nodded; the two-fingered salute was the same in her own language. She hoped Oliver hadn't realised her response meant something similar.

'They're both miserable old people,' she muttered. 'I've done nothing wrong. I didn't ask for this house or their house.'

'But don't you see, that's the problem. You've appeared from nowhere after almost thirty years and now you own where they live. They're frightened. Two scared pensioners who think they're about to lose their home. Rachel told me they've lived there since they got married and now they face losing it they're quite naturally lashing out at you. Not because they hate you but because you have the means to take away their security. They can't jump into a converted ambulance and disappear over the horizon.' He got to his feet and after giving her shoulder a squeeze he started to walk back to the house leaving Mathilde where she was.

Of course she wasn't going to throw them out, she had no intention of doing so. She'd been so involved with her own emotions, the triptych and the dreams that she hadn't stopped to properly consider their feelings. She knew what she had to do.

Chapter Forty-Eight

July 1586

Tom could feel his clothes starting to tighten as he continued his surveillance over the next couple of weeks from the inn opposite Hernes Rent; the pies he consumed affecting his waistline. Isabel had laughed at him, grabbing at the excess flesh as they lay in bed together, their bodies slick with the perspiration of their lovemaking. He kissed quick butterfly kisses down the dip of her neckline, the taste of salt making his lips sting.

Increasingly Babington was being visited by different men and after one such meeting, Tom watched as a letter was handed over to a young boy who hurried away down a nearby alley. As soon as the door to the house was closed again Tom dashed after the boy, his long legs easily able to catch up with the child even though he was running. Leaning forward Tom reached out and grabbed the back of the boy's dirty shirt, lifting him completely off the ground. His feet in worn-out boots, the sole hanging off and his toes poking out, continued to wheel in the air for a few seconds. As soon as he realised he'd been apprehended he began to writhe in an attempt to shake himself free. Tom placed him back on the floor but held on to him firmly. The boy's face was red and Tom could tell he was shouting, his mouth wide and his eyebrows drawn down. Thankfully in the area they were now in nobody paid any attention to a child yelling and waving his arms around. Anyone watching would assume the lad had been dipping into Tom's pockets.

Gripping the boy's upper arm tightly he knew he couldn't haggle with him to hand over the letter, so instead he removed it from where it had been tucked away and taking a quarter angel from his pocket he placed it in the boy's hand. He knew it was probably more money than the lad had ever seen and instantly the boy's mouth closed as he stared down at it. Tom let go of his arm and put his finger to his mouth to indicate that there wasn't to be any talk of this transaction. The lad looked him in the eye and nodded several times and then he was gone, skipping around people on his bare feet as he disappeared into the underworld, the harsh city existence of the very poor. Tom slipped the letter inside his jerkin and after looking around to ensure he wasn't being watched he strolled away towards the busy Leadenhall Market and Phelippes' home.

The letter was immediately spread out on the desk as Tom helped to decode it. It was addressed to Queen Mary and explained in considerable detail how their plot was to be realised. Tom's eyes widened. This was the culmination of all the months he'd spent watching various people as they moved about London in the shadowed corners and the rough back street taverns. This was a threat to his Queen's life;

thank goodness he'd been watching and had managed to intercept this vital link in the plot.

Phelippes grabbed a scrap of parchment and started writing questions on it. He was scribbling as if he didn't have time to say the words slowly enough for Tom to read what he was saying. He asked who'd given the letter to the boy and who else was in the house at the time. There was only one answer to both questions: Anthony Babington. Although Tom silently considered that Babington was probably a pawn, instructed by men clever enough to stay hidden; not just Ballard but also the men who moved the pieces in France, fully committed to the plot to move their papist queen across the chess board and remove his own. Tom knew he himself was only a minor player in Walsingham's game but he considered he was a useful one. At least at present. The big players, the knights and the bishops would sacrifice him with no consideration if necessary and he must never forget that.

He was summoned to see Walsingham the following day where he received thanks for apprehending the letter; Phelippes was now on his way to Chartley with it. Now they understood the plan to overthrow Queen Elizabeth it was merely a matter of time before the conspirators were all caught. The spymaster had laid the trap and now he just needed to wait for the rats to run into it. As he handed over a heavy purse of gold as a thank you, Walsingham explained that he would doubtless need Tom's assistance again before the end of summer, when hopefully this particular plot would be laid to rest.

In the stillroom Hugh had barely been able to keep up with demand for the usual medications the court residents requested. Her Majesty may eat small portions but that didn't stop everyone else from gorging on rich fatty foods which later disagreed with them, and he was very pleased to have Tom back where he belonged.

As the long summer days wound on Tom managed to spend a few weeks helping replenish supplies during the quieter warmer weather; once it turned and became colder their services would be called upon more frequently. Now was the time to start stockpiling the ointments for chapped hands and chilblains. He realised how much he'd missed the quiet, serene work of the stillroom, the underlying scents of herbs being dried or crushed in the mortar bowl, and he hoped that now he could be left to do the work he was employed for. He was weary of watching.

But on the twenty-ninth of July he was despatched by Walsingham to deliver a letter to Babington. Shrugging on his blue coat he set off once again across the city. As he'd previously been introduced to the man there was no need to be furtive so he knocked on the door of the house Babington was currently occupying and handed the letter over. He knew how important and eagerly anticipated it was being the letter from Queen Mary agreeing in writing to the bloody plot to kill Elizabeth: an instruction for Babington to go ahead with the *assassinment* – the assassination. The letter that implicated Queen Mary in the conspiracy was what Walsingham had waited for. Tom was also well aware the letter had been doctored by Thomas Phelippes before being handed on.

Then, just when he thought his work was done, to his dismay within the week Tom was sent to follow Babington yet again. Walsingham had received word their prey was at his home and Tom spent an uncomfortable night in the doorway of a house opposite trying not to fall asleep, hoping the occupants wouldn't spot him there. At four o'clock as the sun started to push away the dark, filtering down through the tall buildings above his head, he got to his feet stretching his cramped limbs, and moved to lean in the entrance of a nearby alley, trying not to let his clothes brush against the sooty walls. The ground was beginning to steam as the sunshine warmed it, the stench it gave off making Tom's stomach turn.

Grimacing, Tom decided to take his chances and wait at the end of the lane, hoping that if anyone moved they'd come that way. The street was wider there and Tom was less conspicuous if he mingled with the early morning hawkers. The air was easier to breathe and was filled with the scent of fresh bread baking in the local communal ovens. What he wouldn't give to be at home with his wife and son in Cordwainer Street, eating cheese and fruit with the white manchet bread that cook baked. With that thought in mind he bought a loaf and waited until his surveillance was rewarded when the door to Babington's house opened and he slipped out, immediately blending in with the constant moving crowd of city people. Looking up and down the street for a moment Tom felt Babington's eyes fall on him and hesitate but Tom subtly bit into his bread and turned slightly, hiding his face and acting as though he was part of a conversation between two merchants stood beside him. He hoped it was just coincidence Babington had paused to look at him.

Thankfully as the others momentarily parted, Tom saw his prey disappearing down the end of the street and out into the wider thoroughfare of Cheapside. He hurried behind, keeping close to the buildings, ready to dart into a shop or behind a market stall at any moment. He needed to keep Babington in his sights or he'd lose him in the throng which continuously shifted and swayed like the flow of the Thames, the backbone of London.

Darting along beneath the cantilevered upper storeys and keeping to the shadows as he skipped around potholes, he was able to follow until eventually he realised they had reached the home of Robert Pooley. A quick knock at the door was immediately answered. Babington gave one final cursory look around him before slipping inside. This time Tom ensured he was standing inside a shop opposite, supposedly looking at a range of mousetraps. He ran his fingertips over the cold steel as he kept his eyes on the movements across the street.

There was no way of informing Walsingham about where he was. He'd been told not to let Babington out of his sight and who knew where he may go next. The man was emanating suspicion, Tom could almost smell it. And so once again, he resumed his waiting game.

Day turned to night. Tom was frustrated he couldn't leave his post for a minute to find a boy to take a message to Isabel, explaining his absence, and he hoped she wouldn't be angry about his disappearance. For all he knew, his quarry may have left via a back entrance but he needed to sit it out.

Finally, his surveillance was rewarded when late the following morning a city official and two royal guards arrived at the house and began thumping on the door with their fists. All around him the city folk stopped what they were doing to watch. Tom, his senses ever alert, saw the momentary flicker of a face at a window high up at the top of the house and was relieved to see that Babington was still inside. His wait hadn't been in vain.

Further along the wall from the house a small wooden gate opened slowly and to his surprise John Ballard's face peeped round. Tom hadn't realised he was also in the house. The guards also noticed him and gave chase across the garden behind the house, before he was caught. They dragged him between them as they marched away down the street, heading towards the river. Tom was confident they'd be entering the Tower through the dreaded Traitors' Gate.

He wandered further down the street, keeping the house in view while he wondered what to do next. His instructions were to follow Babington and he now knew the man was still in Pooley's house. How the guards had missed him Tom couldn't fathom but now he had no option except to continue watching and waiting. How long would this go on for?

By mid-afternoon Babington appeared to consider it safe to make his move. With Tom hot on his heels they traversed Carter Lane until they reached St Paul's Walk beside the great Cathedral. Here it was easy for Tom to hide himself amongst the jostling crowds trying to read the pamphlets nailed onto boards or stop to listen to the preachers who stood on boxes to levitate themselves, telling their stories to the public: they were wasted on Tom.

It was now some time since he'd eaten his breakfast and he dived into a tavern to buy a tankard of ale which he downed in one draught. He couldn't afford to take his eye off his target for a moment; he wouldn't like to face Walsingham if he lost Babington now.

Buying a loaf, cheese and plums he alternated mouthfuls of all three as he stood beside a print house and watched. Babington appeared to be waiting for someone as he paced up and down, bobbing his head about and looking through the throng of people. Tom was far enough away that although he could see what was going on he wouldn't be noticed if Babington turned his way. He couldn't risk that twice; he wasn't sure if he'd been recognised before but having been formally introduced by Berden that one time he needed to be extremely careful. He didn't want to uncover them both as not being who they pretended to be, not when they were so close to exposing the conspiracy.

Slowly Babington was joined by several friends, some of whom Tom recognised as visitors to his rooms. He had no idea how they'd arranged it but Babington must have got word to them somehow. Or this was a pre-arranged meeting. Tom crept closer until he could see what was being said.

'Ballard is caught,' Babington told them, twisting his hands as if washing them in non-existent soap, 'we are all betrayed. What should we do?'

'Nothing at present, in due course our plot will come to fruition,' came the reply. There then followed a heated argument of who would be able to present themselves to the Queen and be close enough to deliver the fatal shot. Tom could hardly believe his eyes. He was certain he now had enough evidence and decided to make his way back to Walsingham and tell all.

Chapter Forty-Nine

August 1586

AlthoughWalsingham was pleased with whatTom had discovered, he scowled and pushed the end of his quill right through the piece of parchment beneath it whenTom mimed the fact that Ballard had been arrested whilst Babington was upstairs in bed at the same house. Tom was thankful he wasn't one of those soldiers. After writing down the names and descriptions of other people he recognised outside St Paul's, Tom was finally able to make his way home.

Standing in the yard outside the stillroom he sluiced himself off with a bucket of cold water and put on a clean shirt. He smiled as he realised that the grimace on Walsingham's face earlier was probably due to the horrible smell emanating from him. Perhaps he'd be called up to the apartment less often in future.

Rubbing himself dry with a piece of sacking he put on the clean shirt, enjoying the feel of the clean linen against his skin and the smell of lavender where it had been stored.

The sun was now high in the sky, the heat pressing down on his head and drying his hair so it crinkled up into the soft curls which Isabel loved. He needed to visit the barber but not today. Right now, he just wanted his comfortable bed with his wife laid beside him and to sleep for a day and a night. Or several.

The worry was etched on Isabel's face as he walked into the parlour. His heart gave a thump of regret that he'd had to put her through the ordeal of him going missing for three days. She must have wondered if he was still alive and he cursed Walsingham as she flew across the room, the embroidery on her lap falling to the floor as she wrapped her arms around him, holding on so tightly he could barely breathe. Pulling his arms free from her clasp he hugged her to him. The room smelled of warm meadowsweet from the rushes underfoot and the rosewater she washed her hair in.

Eventually she let him go, stepping backwards and looking up at him. Now that her initial relief had left her he could see exactly how furious she was. Holding her arms out to the side, palms up, she raised her eyebrows before mouthing *'where have you been?'* In case he hadn't realised how angry she was she slapped his arm as well. He looked around the room for his wax tablet. This would take far too long to explain by mime and he was desperate to go to bed.

By the time he'd finished writing, erasing and writing more, Isabel looked confused with everything that had taken place. She shrugged, accepting there was nothing he could have done. Having been one of the Queen's ladies she well understood the chess game of the royal court. She followed Tom upstairs and sat on the top of the coverlet stroking his hair as he fell into a deep and dreamless sleep.

Tom had barely any respite in his spying assignments. The next day his heart dropped yet again as Walsingham's now familiar page arrived in the stillroom to summon him. He had hoped that his success in tailing and reporting back on Babington would have led to the appropriate arrests and finally earnt him a quiet, undisturbed life with Isabel and Richard. But it was not to be. These days he and the page needed neither notes nor signing and Tom didn't even bother with his blue coat which looked the worse for wear after sleeping in it for two nights.

In Walsingham's apartment the windows were open for a change and a soft breeze blew in. Tom wondered if this was due to the unpleasant smell which had accompanied him to their last meeting. It was different from the heat in the stillroom where the fire was constantly lit even in the height of summer. There was another man in the room who was introduced as a runner for Walsingham.

'My man is going to deliver a letter to Babington, informing him that the arrest of Ballard was nothing to do with the current conspiracy and the plotters should stay close beside him in order to be safe. I am hoping he will lead us to his accomplices so that they may all be arrested together. Then they can all be executed together. You are to keep watch to ensure nobody tries to slip away. Are you certain nobody saw or recognised you when you were watching last time?'

Tom nodded in reassurance that his cover was still intact, whilst hoping this wouldn't mean another three nights gone. He couldn't imagine Isabel being so accepting a second time, it had taken several days of his mute apologies before.

They were soon on a wherry and making their way to Babington's home where Berden had first introduced Tom to the plotters. Assuming his usual position, hiding in plain sight amongst the people milling about in the narrow street, Tom began his watch. He needed to ensure that if needed he could follow without being seen: one final time. He shuddered as his mind went back to watching Throckmorton's bloody execution. The information he was relaying to Walsingham would result in these men meeting a similar grisly end and he was uncomfortable with his part in the inevitable outcome.

Within seconds of Walsingham's man knocking on the door it was opened by their target. Tom could see lines etched across his face; he was a worried man. Standing on the doorstep and breaking the seal he didn't notice anyone watching him. His face fell as he scanned the coded words Walsingham had written. Without a word to anyone who may have been inside Babington let the letter fall to the ground as he pulled the door closed behind him and began to half walk, half run towards St Paul's. Tom paused just long enough to pick up the letter and push the pages into his pocket, before following behind, breaking into a jog to keep up. He hardly cared by that point if he was seen, these were the actions of a fleeing man and he doubted whether he'd look behind to see who was in pursuit. At St Paul's Babington stopped for a rest, speaking with a small scruffy boy who held his hand out for a payment before scurrying away. Surely the man wasn't thinking about eating at a time like this? He must know that the hangman's rope was tightening around his neck with every passing minute.

It wasn't food he was waiting for though, as within minutes he was joined by two of his accomplices. A short, heated conversation seemed to be going on with a lot of arm waving and shaking of heads before the three of them set off again. This time it seemed they couldn't sustain the same pace for long and as they slowed down, Tom was able to tail them more easily.

The journey was far longer than he'd anticipated and once again he found himself sleeping rough as they stopped for the night at an inn. He didn't dare enter in case he was seen. He fervently hoped they didn't hire horses the following day; he wouldn't be able to move at that speed and if he were riding his presence would be very obvious.

Thankfully though, after a night propped up under a mulberry tree, he spotted the three men now accompanied by two others he didn't recognise but who must have been waiting for the trio and they set off yet again.

It was another long day of walking and Tom was feeling very sorry for himself. He had no idea where he was going or what he could do to apprehend the traitors when he got there. He was on a wild goose chase. At one point the men paused under a walnut tree and Tom, who was in the nearby woods, ducked down and observed them through the leaves of a chestnut tree. The men seemed to be stamping on the soft walnuts before picking them up and rubbing the broken pieces over their faces. Tom had no idea what they were doing as his knees began to seize up while he continued to crouch down watching the group repeating their actions: stamp, pull apart and scrub.

Finally, they moved off and once they were far in the distance Tom stood up, stretching his limbs to get the blood moving around before he ran through the woods to the walnut tree. The shells were laid on the ground amongst the grass and picking one up he chafed it on the back of his hand, still confused as to what they had been doing.

As he scrubbed it hard over his knuckles, he started to realise. A deep brown stain was scored across his skin. It began to dawn on Tom the men would now look as if they'd spent many summers working out in the fields, the sun slowly turning their skin to the tanned leathery shine of a farmer's face. They were trying to disguise themselves, their soft white skin being a giveaway of their station in life. The fugitives were now tiny figures in the distance and Tom dashed through the woods to hurry after them. He had a suspicion that as the men had paused here to apply a disguise, they may soon be at their destination.

As he clambered over a fallen tree trunk, Tom could just see a large manor house partly concealed by trees around it. He was just wondering if this was where the men were headed when he felt the ground beneath his boots start to vibrate and, turning his head, he could see behind him a dust cloud created by a large group of guards on horseback. They could only be coming for one reason.

Stepping onto the side of the road he waited until they were close and then stepped out waving his arms to stop them. He wasn't sure if it was going to work and seeing the hooves thundering against the dry ground he was poised to dive out of the way at the final moment. Just as he was wavering the guard in front held his hand up and they all skidded to a stop, the cloud of dirt they created choking Tom. He took his flask of ale slung around his waist and swigged a large mouthful as he wondered how he was going to relay the information he had with no paper or wax tablet to hand. People he conversed with regularly could understand his signing but these men would have no idea what he was doing.

'This had better be good,' the leading guard said to him, *'why have you stopped us?'*

Tom started pointing up the road where Babington and his accomplices had now disappeared from sight before showing the brown staining on the back of his hand and demonstrating how the men had rubbed it on their faces.

'Wait, I know who you are,' he said, *'someone talked about a spy who could understand what people said even though he has no hearing or speech, is that you? Have you been following these men from London?'* Tom nodded again and was rewarded with smiles of acceptance around the group.

'Have they disguised themselves?' another asked and Tom nodded.

'Here, get up behind me.' The guard at the front leant down and grabbed Tom under his arm, swinging him up behind before kicking the horse into a gallop. Tom clung on to the bottom of the man's leather jerkin as grit blew into his eyes and ears. His feet had been aching from the constant walking and he was relieved to be off them but he wasn't entirely sure that it was any better slipping about on the back of a horse as they thundered along the road.

The arrests, when they came, were almost an anti-climax after so many months of watching and waiting. The group of men were hiding in the undergrowth of the grounds of Uxendon Hall, a place Tom had seen mentioned when Walsingham had been talking with Phelippes one day and apparently a known refuge for Catholics.

There was a scuffle as the men tried to evade the soldiers but they were vastly outnumbered. Wary of being seen and recognised by any of the men, especially Babington, Tom skirted around the commotion until he was hiding behind the guards' horses. They were huge, broad beasts, specifically bred to take the weight of soldiers in armour and chain mail, and he was thankful for the wall of hot flesh, steaming from the hard ride they'd just undertaken. He moved as they did, ensuring he was always secreted from view until the plotters were tied up with ropes to other mounts. As one of the guards lashed the rope around Babington's wrists to a horse Tom saw him gaze around bemused, as if incredulous that they'd been caught. With a signal from someone at the front, they moved off and the conspirators began their long journey back to London.

He waved away the offers of a ride as several of the guards pointed to the pillion space behind them on the saddle, proffering an arm to hoist him up. He'd hire a horse at the nearest inn and ride home alone. When all he could see was a cloud of dust in the distance, he began his long walk. His legs started to shake as the enormity of what he had achieved began to sink in.

Chapter Fifty

August 2021

Mathilde passed Oliver on the lane leading to Fakenham. She had the van radio on, the windows down and was singing along loudly to Abba. It was her mother's favourite song 'Dancing Queen' and it made her remember the happy times when her mother was more stable and would dance around the room in her faded cotton sundress whilst singing along. It was so long since she'd felt the urge to join in with the music and it was liberating, joyful. He flashed his lights at her in recognition and pulled into the side of the road. She was enjoying herself singing, however she was delighted to spot his car when she wasn't expecting to see him.

'Where are you off to?' he called as she stopped beside him, keeping her eye on her wing mirrors in case another car appeared behind her.

'Just into town, a few bits to buy,' she deliberately kept her answer vague. She'd made a decision and she didn't want one of his serious conversations about it. 'I didn't know you were coming over today. I'll see you when I get back, yes?'

'Probably not. I wanted to check a couple of things on the triptych and to let you know I may not be around for a few days as I'm leaving for a conference in Leeds this afternoon. I'm going to speak with some of my art historian associates there about your amazing find. Obviously please call me if you hear from Professor Thornton. Or just call me if you want to.' He was smiling as he explained but Mathilde felt a stab of disappointment she wasn't expecting, her heart dropping. She'd become used to seeing him frequently even if it was just a couple of hours; he always seemed to have a bona fide reason to visit. With a shock she realised she'd miss him.

'Okay see you soon,' she smiled airily to cover her disappointment as unexpected tears prickled the back of her eyes. She put the van into gear with a loud crunching noise and drove away. In her mirrors she could see that the black Mini remained where it was at the edge of the road.

Chapter Fifty-One

August 1586

Tom's part in defeating the plotters and the capture of Babington and his accomplices did not go unnoticed by Walsingham. He managed a rare smile as he patted Tom on the back, albeit at arm's length.

Walsingham warned him that now he'd shown what he was capable of doing and the help he could offer in the fight against those who'd depose the Queen, doubtless he'd be called upon again. He asked on more than one occasion whether Tom had been seen and he reassured the spymaster that he hadn't. For the time being he was allowed to resume his role as apothecary which Tom was thankful for. The smell of warm herbs and pungent medications which caught in his throat and made his eyes water were a balm to his soul. He hadn't realised before just how calm and soothing his work was and he and Hugh worked together in a silent partnership every day. Then each evening as the sun started to descend towards the horizon, its deep orange rays thrown out like fingers trying to clutch on to the final hours of the day, he'd run down to the river to find a boat which could take him home to where his love lay.

If he was enjoying his work with a new-found vigour it was nothing compared to the way his heart lifted as he walked through the London streets at twilight every evening. His feet could hardly walk as fast as he wanted them to and sometimes he'd break into a jog, so intensely did he want to see Isabel's smiling face and feel her arms wind their way around his neck as she laid her head on his chest. He'd tried to keep her from knowing about the danger he'd been in on that final task he'd undertaken for Walsingham but the pamphlets which littered the cobbled streets as they made their way hand to hand from the hawkers at St Paul's, told of the Babington plot and how the fugitives had been caught. His part was unknown apart from those closest to him and it hadn't taken long for his wife to realise.

Every evening in their contented family bubble, as soon as they'd eaten supper, they would spend their time playing with Richard who basked in the love and affection from his doting parents. There was no sign of a sibling for him but Tom didn't care; he couldn't imagine ever loving another child as much as he loved this one. He had everything he'd travelled to England for. Everything, and more. His heart hurt with his love for Isabel who was a finer wife than he'd ever imagined possible. His life was complete.

Chapter Fifty-Two

October 1586

When retribution came, Tom was completely unaware. Leaving the palace early that evening, he jumped off the boat at the quay and walked towards their home. The previous evening, they'd watched Richard crawl across the floor and attempt to pull himself up on the bench they were sitting on and he was keen to see if his son had managed it yet.

The Thames lay completely still as the boatsman's oars sliced through, flicking tiny drips of spray like jewels as they lifted out of the water, but as Tom walked through the city streets, he felt a slight wind whipping through the narrow streets. The orange of the setting sun was reflected in the windows of the shops and houses. At almost the same moment he smelt a whisper of smoke in the air. People around him were starting to walk faster in the same direction as he was going and dodging around them, he started to run. The orange reflection he could see wasn't the sun; something was on fire.

The heat of the flames seared his face before he got there but already he knew instinctively which house it was. The back of it was already ablaze, flames rearing up into the sky, licking at the clouds with fierce orange tongues. A long line of men threw leather buckets of water between them, before trying to douse the burning oak frame. Tom's heart beat in his chest as he looked wildly around for Isabel's familiar face. Never before had he been so desperate, his keen sight failing him when he needed it most. As his eyes swung across the crowds, they snagged on a face he recognised, one of the men he'd seen talking with Babington in The Cross Keys. Their eyes met and held just for a moment before the man slipped away and was gone.

Tom felt a tugging on his sleeve and turning he found Catherine, her face covered in smoke smuts, tears streaked down through the grey. In her arms was Richard, his head thrown back and his face red. Tom took him and rubbed his back whilst signing his wife's name. He was thankful he'd previously taught Catherine a few basic signs but his heart contracted in his chest as she started shaking her head and crying again.

Thrusting Richard back at her he ran round to the back of the house, trying to push his way through the men with their slopping buckets, the ground covered in puddles reflecting the flames which continued to burn out of control. He looked frantically, hopefully, for any signs of life within. Someone – he couldn't see who – had hold of his arms from behind, their fingers digging into his thick muscles to stop him running straight into the inferno. He struggled against the restraint but eventually gave in, taking a step back. The heat was singeing the hairs across his face and although the blaze was beginning to lessen slightly, he saw the back of the house was a shell, timbers blackened and fallen. If she'd been in their bedroom, she wouldn't have stood a chance.

One of the men paused in the dousing of the smouldering ruins to take Tom to one side, pointing to the ground. He was speaking without realising he was wasting his breath. Even without his deafness Tom was in another world; one where he was being enveloped in a blanket of darkness. The pain in his chest cut into him and he fell to his knees, barely noticing his companion who was showing him a pile of straw and kindling piled up against the corner of the house. This fire was no accident: it had been started on purpose.

The front of the house had not fared as badly as the rear but there was still smoke billowing out of the windows, the fragile glass in shards on the ground. The door swung open and for a moment he wondered if Isabel had run out and was somewhere wandering around, confused in all the smoke and people. He could feel in his heart though, in every strained sinew of his body as taut as the skin on a drum, she wasn't in the crowd. People were beginning to disperse, their buckets swinging desolately in their hands; they'd done their best and Tom knew he should be thanking them but even if he'd been able to, he was rooted to the spot, looking up at their house in disbelief. A hole had developed in his life as wide and dark as the gaping crevasse before him.

A tug on his shirt made him turn. Catherine was standing with Richard and she indicated behind her to where another woman, their neighbour, was waiting. She pointed to the woman and then to herself and Richard, and Tom nodded once, before turning back. At least he knew his son would be safe and well cared for. That was all that mattered now because how would he sleep ever again without Isabel by his side? His life was broken, torn apart forever.

He spent the rest of the night sitting on the ground close to the ruins of the house. With the front half including the nursery having escaped the worst of the flames, it explained how Catherine was able to escape with Richard, whilst Isabel was trapped at the back. How long had she screamed to be saved before the hot choking smoke and searing heat engulfed her? Had she called for him, even though she'd have known he couldn't hear? He was desperate to get inside the house to look for whatever remained of her but the stairs were now a pile of broken spindles and ash; there was no physical way of getting up to the first floor. Where he was sitting the thatch still dripped from the water thrown on it but the roof was totally absent at the back.

The first rays of sunlight glided through the layers of smoke hanging in the air, slim fingers of gold stroking the desolate scene. Tom got to his feet and walked slowly towards the door, the charred beams now more visible in the daylight. He pushed it back, feeling the creak through the palm of his hand. The smell of burning filled every part of his body, stinging his eyes and crawling into his soul like worms into a corpse.

Stepping inside, he lifted his feet over the beams and carcasses of furniture. A slight breeze was blowing through the house from the gaping opening at the back, disturbing the soft ash covering the floor, swirling around his feet. He sniffed the air for the acrid scent of burnt flesh but there was nothing. Every part of Isabel scattered to the shadows.

Turning to his right, he pulled the door to the parlour

open; the room Isabel had been most proud of. Perhaps because she always kept the door closed to stop Richard crawling in there it had fared better than the rest of the house, just a fine layer of soot displaying the terrible devastation that had torn through his home. The window however lay on the floor as all the others did around the house. Standing in the middle of the room still positioned on its easel, his triptych stared back at him as he slowly walked towards it. This together with his son, were the only legacies to his life.

Everything that had happened to him was immortalised there on the first two panels, the left one showing how his life had been as he wandered the continent in search of a family, a place to put down roots and call home. And then the larger centre panel depicted all he'd ever desired coming true. His work with Hugh at the palace, the stillroom and the physic garden where he put down roots of a different kind and his beautiful Isabel with her flashing violet eyes and her wide smile which lit up her face like the sun breaking through the clouds. Their wedding and their home were on there, the house in which he now stood just a shell of the comfortable life they'd shared. Baby Richard had his own portrait, tiny and swaddled, not the chunky laughing little boy he'd grown into. Would he ever smile again? Tom felt that he wouldn't. Couldn't.

And there dotted around between the scenes spelling out his happy life, were the dark times. The days and nights where he'd done as he was bid by Walsingham, the spymaster weaving a web of intrigue, stopping plots against the Crown with his extensive troupe of spies. A web which Tom had been drawn into, for once his disability seen as an advantage.

He'd been pleased at first, he admitted to himself even now that being useful to someone gave him a warm feeling, his deafness finally deemed to be a benefit. He'd been needed. But not as he had by Isabel. He'd seen that figure slip away into the crowds last night, a quick glimpse over a shoulder and the outline of a face depicted by the light of the fire destroying his home. A face that was familiar. He thought when he was spying he'd blended in with the background, a nobody. But somewhere he'd been recognised as a some-body and he'd paid the ultimate price for his loyalty to the Queen. Isabel had paid it. Removing his painting from the easel he turned to leave. There was nothing left for him here now.

Tom found Richard and Catherine in the house next door. Richard was full of toothless smiles for his father, unaware of how his life had changed forever. Catherine on the other hand had obviously been crying, her eyes red and swollen and seeing Tom they welled up again as the tears rolled down her face. Usually a compassionate man he simply didn't have the strength to comfort her and he kissed Richard on the top of his head, his silky hair still smelling of harsh smoke. Tainted with the scent of his mother's death. Signing that he would return later, Tom left the house and made his way to the palace. He had no idea where else to go. Yesterday he'd been so pleased with his part in the capture of the plotters and this morning he was filled with self-loathing. He had thought he was invincible; he was a fool.

The wind had increased and heavy, malevolent grey clouds rolled in across the rooftops, but he barely noticed as his clothes, the blue coat of which he'd been so proud now

351

stinking of the death of his wife, became sodden. It weighed on his shoulders as if trying to push him to the floor from where he'd never get up as the boat bobbed about in the choppy waters of the Thames. Eventually they moored up at the palace wharf and Tom stepped out of the boat wobbling slightly as the weight of the triptych threatened to unbalance him and tip him backwards into the greasy, unwelcoming water.

Tom hurried to the external door and from there to the stillroom, where, as ever, he found Hugh hard at work. If only he'd been left to do the same, his Isabel would still be alive. Hugh glanced up as Tom walked in and then did a double take at the sight of his friend, face and clothes both darkened with sooty smuts. Tom placed the triptych on the bench beside the still, before collapsing to the floor his head in his hands, clenching his hair as if to pull it physically from his scalp. He felt Hugh shaking him, trying to help him back to his feet, but Tom couldn't move. He was paralysed with grief as he knelt curled into a ball, rocking backwards and forwards. The strewings on the floor smelled of summer, of hay and balmy country days, and for a few seconds he was transported back to another time, his Norfolk childhood, running through golden fields with crops as tall as he was, catching the ears of the grain as he went, feeling it trickle through his fingers. The smell of summer and the beginning of life all around him. And now there would never be life again.

Eventually Hugh managed to help him to a chair and pass him some heated spiced hippocras. It slowly crawled down inside him, warm before it hit the chill of his heart. Hugh was signing to him to find out what was going on, the classic hands outstretched with palms upwards, used for any question. Tom waved towards where one of his wax tablets lay on the bench. Tom quickly sketched a house in flames and it was all that was needed for his friend to look at his appearance and understand. Tom couldn't explain why it had happened, even though he knew it. Hugh made a sign for Isabel, outlining the shape of a comely woman followed by rocking an invisible baby and raised his eyebrows.

Tom could hardly bear to tell him, once he'd admitted it to himself it would be out there for everyone to know; it would be real. Hugh shook him and raised his eyebrows and Tom knew he couldn't keep the awful truth to himself. He too rocked the invisible baby whilst nodding slowly, then made an outline of his darling Isabel and, his eyes filling once again, he slowly shook his head. Hugh threw his arms around his friend and held him close as Tom's body shuddered with the devastation that tore through him.

As his sobs subsided, Hugh took Tom through to his room behind the stillroom. It looked exactly the same as it had the last time he'd slept there, when he had Isabel and his life was complete. He leant the triptych against the wall facing away from him and lay down on his pallet. Her life had ended and so had his.

Chapter Fifty-Three

September 2021

Rachel threw her holdall into the back of her car. Her decision to start returning to her home at the weekends once more had been met with plenty of encouragement from Mathilde.

'I also need to start prepping for work again,' she'd admitted, 'the school holidays might be lovely and long but now I have to start some work ready for when we return to school, which is only two weeks away.' Her comments reminded Mathilde that she still needed to make some decisions about what she'd do in September. Her initial thoughts of selling up and returning to her previous existence now felt less certain than ever. How her life had changed.

She had just enough time to run upstairs and shower before she heard the sound of a Mini's tyres on gravel. Oliver's timing was impeccable and quickly brushing her hair and pulling it into a messy bun on top of her head, she smiled to herself giving a little skip of excitement, running down the stairs and into the kitchen, where he was putting a bottle of wine and some plastic delicatessen pots into the fridge.

'Morning.' He straightened up and grinned at her, his eyes lingering on hers for a second. Two seconds. Mathilde felt her heart begin to beat faster. She knew when he suggested they spend the day investigating the chapel properly followed by dinner in the village pub he potentially had more planned. She had dropped Rachel's new weekend routine into the conversation hoping he may get the hint, but it took another five days before he suggested the chapel and dinner. If Rachel was surprised Mathilde had disappeared with a dustpan and brush into her bedroom after displaying absolutely no domestic inclination since she arrived, she was sensible enough not to mention it.

'Hey,' her voice sounded gruff, she cleared her throat and started again. 'Are you all ready to make a start on the chapel? Do you have everything we might need?' She had no idea if any specialist equipment might be required. 'Oh, do you want coffee first?' she smiled a bit sheepishly, realising that as ever, her hosting skills left a lot to be desired. Luckily though, Oliver was now used to them.

'Not yet thanks,' he shook his head, 'let's go and have a look round first and then decide if we want anything?' She nodded and picking up the key and her camera she followed him to the chapel. Shadow was still too young to be outside but as usual he slipped out behind them, climbing a tree in the coppice to watch.

As ever the key required some wiggling up and down to make it turn but finally after Mathilde had begun to grind her teeth in frustration, it slowly turned, and they heard the sound of the lock clunk as it opened. Relieved, Mathilde gave the door an extra hard shove as if punishing it for being reticent to open.

Inside everything looked exactly the same as on their previous visit, the air still dancing with dust motes as they stood in the centre. A flapping above their heads made them both look up but there was nothing in the building with them.

'Must be on the roof outside,' Oliver said, 'probably spotted Shadow in amongst the trees.'

Mathilde walked slowly around the interior of the building until she reached the wall where the triptych had been hidden and the worn memorial plaque still remained. Oliver was on his hands and knees behind the table which they'd previously thought was an altar.

'What's there?' she called across, her voice echoing slightly as it bounced off the rafters above them. It felt wrong shouting in a church. 'What have you found?' she whispered instead.

'Nothing,' Oliver got to his feet and brushed the knees of his jeans, 'I wondered if there was a crypt under here, but I can't see any evidence of access in the floor. I looked outside when we came over here last time. It really is just a tiny building built for daily prayers. Not unusual for the era your house was built in.'

'This place *is* unusual,' Mathilde reminded him, 'we discovered an old painting behind a board, and I found a hidden document. It must have meant something to someone at one time.'

Oliver walked over to where she was looking up at the plaque on the wall. 'I know it's quite old, but I reckon we could dust the residual grit from that and read what it says.

Shall we try?' Mathilde nodded. She had no idea what residual meant but she did want to discover if this was someone's burial place. She waited impatiently for Oliver to return from the house with a step ladder he'd previously shown her in the boot room beside the back door. He'd suggested she could use it if she needed to replace lightbulbs and she'd smiled to herself, wondering if he really thought she'd bother to do that. She was used to the dark at night. Although, she had to admit to herself, night-time in the van wasn't as it was in the house, where she was never alone. Even if all the living people were out, she still had her ancestors to keep her company.

Mathilde stepped on to the ladder before Oliver could put one foot on it. He raised one eyebrow but said nothing, passing her the small brush he had brought with him.

'Brush it very gently,' he warned, 'we don't know how well it's attached to the wall.'

Mathilde gave it a little push with the heel of her hand, but it didn't move. She heard a sharp intake of breath from below her and she smiled to herself. Would he ever learn to keep his mouth shut when he didn't want her to do something?

Taking the brush, she began to sweep away the dust and grit collected in the grooves where it had been carved, so many years ago. The words became more pronounced but were still illegible. Frustrated, she climbed back down until she was stood next to Oliver. He'd caught her waist as she got to the bottom and left his hands there, she could feel the heat from them through her T-shirt. She didn't want to admit it to herself but human contact after so long without it felt good. Great, in fact. She'd wasted so many years.

'I still can't read it,' she admitted, 'do you want to have a try?'

'Of course, give me the brush,' Oliver held his hand out and stood on the ladder. The place where his hands had been felt cold now that he'd removed them. 'Don't forget I did a degree in ancient artefacts; I might be able to work it out.'

The chapel fell silent as he brushed away at exactly the same place that Mathilde had. She was certain he was doing it just to show her he was the professional as it looked no different, but she kept her mouth shut.

'Okay, I think I have something,' Oliver called down. 'Can you write some letters down if I read them out?' Mathilde quickly pulled her phone out and opened the notes, nodding her head.

'I S A B E L. Isabel. Well, that is straightforward then, have you got that?' The ladder rocked a little as he twisted round, and Mathilde almost dropped her phone as she leapt forward to grab it.

'Yes, I have it,' she confirmed, 'now can you please stop moving about? It isn't safe.'

'Wait, there's more. L U T . . . Lutton. It says Lutton. And it looks like *Requiescat in Pace* – Rest in Peace.' His voice tailed off and he slowly descended to the floor. Mathilde was looking at the plaque and Oliver took hold of her upper arms. 'It must be one of your ancestors,' he couldn't hide the excitement in his voice, 'what an incredible find for you. She isn't buried here, I'm sure of it, but we can look in the churchyard in the village if you like?'

'Not yet.' She shook her head. Before she went looking for another burial place, she wanted to consider this new connection between herself and these ancient family members. Perhaps later, when she'd got used to the knowledge her father was there. Although the thought that other members of her family may also be there gave her some comfort. 'Another time,' she suggested.

They both ate fish and chips at the pub, washed down with several pints of real ale which the pub brewed in an outhouse at the back. It was only nine o'clock when they got home but it was dark. As they walked up the drive the marshes lay to their right, the gloomy depths disturbed occasionally by the flapping and squawking of a duck. The small blue phosphorous lights danced about reminding Mathilde of the time she'd taken Fleur on their night-time adventure. It was only two months ago but felt like a lifetime.

'Will-o'-the-wisp,' Oliver said, 'that's what they're called round here.'

'In France, we call them *les feux follets*,' Mathilde replied, whispering so as not to disturb the nightlife that was starting to come alive in the bushes and trees around them. She tilted her head on one side as the soft call of an owl somewhere in the distance was answered from a tree close by. She looked up but could see nothing in the deep shadows.

Back at the hall, Mathilde offered coffee, tinkering about in the kitchen. She wasn't sure of the etiquette of taking a man to her bedroom even if they were alone in the house. As she continued to shuffle cups and the cafetiere on the kitchen side, she felt his arms slide round her waist from behind and he kissed the space below her left ear. She shuddered with a longing she hadn't even known it was possible to feel.

'Shall we forget the coffee?' he whispered. Mathilde nodded and as he took her hand, she followed him willingly upstairs to her bedroom.

They lay together in bed, naked skin pressed close. Mathilde had never felt safer than at that moment, laid in his arms. Nothing would hurt her again; she was sure of it now and the thought of it made her eyes well up until a tear dripped down onto Oliver's chest.

'Hey, what's up?' He moved himself away a little so he could tilt her face up to his. 'Why are you crying?'

'Happy tears,' she explained, 'I've realised that finally I've found my home. A life that's safe. And I have my ancestors to thank for that. And you,' she added.

'I've done nothing,' he admonished as he pulled her in again, 'you're just where you always belonged.'

They were soon both asleep but as her clutch on wakefulness began to loosen, Mathilde felt the familiar jolt as she fell into a dark dream. The dream of the triptych. But this wasn't like before, this was real life. Her life. The heat in front of her whipping up a wind that threw sparks up into the sky dancing like the gases in the marshes, skittering across the starry background. The orange and yellow of fierce flames that had engulfed the building, the tiny cottage they were living in. She tried to push forward but strong arms held her back and her mouth was open in a scream she couldn't utter as the burning roof beams crashed into the rooms below and another billow of heat burst out. Someone dragged her backwards as she held her arms out towards the inferno, trying to get closer.

Suddenly the scenery changed. It was daylight, the sun heavy on her back warming the skin and instead of the bitter smoke she could smell warm hay and the citrus tang of lemon thyme crushed underfoot. In front of her lay a landscape she recognised in some way, planes of smooth, even fields stretching into the distance where they merged with the horizon in a shimmer of gold. Her heart felt at peace.

Then as before, abruptly she was back in her bed, staring up in the cool dark air. She leant out of the bed and switched on her light, waking Oliver in the process.

'Are you okay?' he asked, shielding his eyes from the glare of the lamp.

'Yes, sorry. I didn't mean to wake you. I had another dream, it was the fire,' she whispered, 'just like before. It was where my mother died. But it wasn't. The house was much bigger in the dream. Not here though. The same villagers trying to pour water on and extinguish it and the same crowds of faces lit up by the flames. Caught in hell. It was as awful as I remember, the heat, the hopelessness. Nobody could get near to rescue her. The fire department discovered afterwards that one of her candles had caught the kitchen curtain, a simple, avoidable accident. I was back there watching it all over again. It was the third panel of the triptych: the end of the journey. And then, I was here, in the garden. I could smell the herbs and I felt a sense of calm and happiness. Maybe not happiness,' she amended, 'but a release, like I've finally been set free from my past; relief that I was home. Does that sound mad?'

'It sounds to me as if in some ways, your life has emulated the life of the artist of the painting.' There was a pause while he tried to think of a simpler word than 'emulate'. 'Follow. Your life has followed his, in a rough way. Your journey from France, your artistic skills; you may not paint but you earn your living with your camera. A fire that at some point seems to have ended all hope for you both. Until you arrived here at this house which has somehow restored it again.'

Mathilde nodded, understanding what he was saying. She had certainly felt safe and at home here. She lay back down again, staring up at the ceiling above her. Had he wondered where life would take him next? Or whether finally he could stop searching for all that he'd lost?

Chapter Fifty-Four

November 1586

During the following week, Tom's physical body moved about but his spirit lay on his bed unresponsive. Or perhaps it still stood in the hallway of the charred remains of his home where the scent of death would linger forever. He'd laid on his bed for a day without stirring until Hugh had gently coaxed him into the stillroom and although it was discouraged for food to be consumed in there he made Tom eat soft jellies and custards and a rich mutton and barley stew that was almost vomited back afterwards.

Once he'd eaten something, Tom dragged himself back to Cordwainer Street to find Catherine and Richard. Thankfully they'd been taken in by their neighbours and Catherine signed to him that everyone was happy for the three of them to stay until Tom could organise a new home for them all. Tom thanked them but declined a bed, explaining with a few hand signs that he'd sleep at the palace. He had no idea how he'd finance a new home for them. Isabel had money left to her by her first husband along with her home, but Tom didn't know how she had accessed it or where it was held. And unless he could find out he had barely any means to support his son; only what he earned as a lowly assistant apothecary and that which Walsingham had previously given him.

At the thought of the spymaster, Tom was nearly sick again. If he hadn't been so caught up in his secretive work none of this would have happened. He'd have been producing medications at the palace during the day and returning to his home with Isabel at night. They'd have grown old together with a nursery full of robust, healthy sons and daughters. Now he only had Richard to remind him forever of the woman he loved. He'd had everything that he'd ever wanted and now once again he had nothing. It had been given, and it had been taken away.

Taking his paints out he selected the orange and yellow hues and began to daub vicious flames across the third panel in wild strokes, filling it with anger and fire. When he held his hand over the image, he could feel the scorching heat rising up, licking at his fingers.

On the eighth day of this desolate new life, Tom spotted the shadow of the page boy from upstairs approaching down the corridor to the stillroom. He knew the way the boy moved, quick and light on his feet as if he was used to darting out of the way of blows. Immediately Tom looked around him, ready to make his escape. Never again would he stand in Walsingham's office to be given instructions. Whatever the punishment, he would refuse.

Before he could disappear, the young lad was in the room, pointing at Tom and then beckoning, before turning to speak to Hugh. His face was in profile so Tom couldn't see what was being said, although he'd already got his palms up in front of him and was shaking his head in refusal.

'*The Queen has summoned you,*' Hugh spoke slowly, '*you don't have any choice my friend.*'

Tom wasn't expecting this. What did she want? He supposed it had been brought to her attention that Isabel had died, his wife had had several friends amongst the other ladies.

He looked down at what he was wearing. He'd been sleeping in his clothes for the past week and had nothing clean to change into. Everything other than what he was wearing, had been destroyed in the fire. Brushing a couple of pieces of straw from his hose, he rubbed his hands across the ends of his dirty boots. They came away black with soot that still clung to him even now, days later. Out at the pump he quickly splashed his hands and face, before following the page once again.

The first time he'd been to the Privy Chamber he'd been in awe of the riches and opulence of the palace furnishings as he approached the Queen's private rooms, the strewings and rush mats on the floors replaced by thick carpet, portraits on wood-panelled walls shining with polish. But this time he walked with his shoulders slumped and noticed nothing. The smell of pomander in his nostrils couldn't rid him of the eternal smell of smoke which followed him everywhere, a floating cloud of wraiths.

As they approached the doors the two guards who stood with pikes crossed stood to one side and the page knocked before opening the door and displaying his usual reverence, immediately going down on one knee, his head bowed.

Behind him Tom did the same. He kept his head down looking at the floor until he felt a gentle tug on his sleeve and turning his head slightly he could see the upside-down face of the page boy, his dark hair as soft and sweet as Richard's as he smiled and waved his hand to indicate Tom should now stand.

Tom wobbled a little as he stood up, his inability to eat over the past week making him shaky and weak, especially after a long walk from his quarters to the centre of the palace. He raised his eyes slowly towards the Queen sat amongst her ladies. The space where Isabel had once been a gaping wound in the tableau. There was no sign of Walsingham or Burghley and Tom allowed himself to breathe a little easier.

The page remained beside him and Tom realised that in lieu of anyone else he was supposed to sign anything he couldn't lip read. Given that they'd barely communicated more than a dozen times over the past three years Tom couldn't imagine this was going to go well. He watched the Queen speak with his eyes squinting as he tried not to miss a word.

'We have heard of the awful fire in which our lady Isabel perished.' The Queen spoke slowly enunciating each word. Tom could understand every terrible part of what she was saying. He nodded before looking down quickly so nobody could see the tears that sprang up. After rubbing his eyes with the back of his sleeve he watched again as the Queen continued.

'We offer you our condolences. Did your son survive?' Tom nodded.

'I will miss your late wife very much; she was always so cheerful

and a joy to us all. I understand that you are now homeless and feel this tragedy is partly the fault of this court. And also, Walsingham, who has used you to great effect in his strategy to stop the plot which would have seen me dead and my cousin on the throne. Therefore, I propose to grant to you a new home and a stipend to support you and your son for all the work you have done on my behalf. And also, in memory of your wife. I've been told that you were originally from Norfolk so I shall give you one of the empty manor houses seized from the Earl of Arundel. My Lord Burghley will give you the deeds and you are relieved of all duties to this court.'

Tom was not sure what to make of this turn of events, until he glanced at the page who was miming the words *'thank you'* and putting his hands together and bowing as Tom himself did when thanking someone. Tom quickly turned to the Queen and thanked her as she inclined her head to dismiss him. He backed away towards the door, however he was stopped as the Queen beckoned him forward once more as if something had suddenly occurred to her.

'I've been informed that as well as an exemplary apothecary you are also a fine artist and have painted a triptych, is this true?'

Tom wasn't sure of some of her words but he could lip read 'triptych', so he nodded again.

'I will have it framed for you as a gift from me. Please give it to my page when you return to your rooms.'

Tom tried not to let his surprise show on his face as he nodded and thanked her, twice, before scuttling backwards out of the room. The page had accompanied him and they had to wait while Tom leant against the wall for a moment, trying to grasp everything that had just happened. He was to be given a new home with Richard in the place where his journey had first started. It could never begin to mend his heart but it was the beginning of a new life.

Back downstairs he left the page to relay everything to Hugh while he went to collect the painting, now dry after the savage addition he'd made to the final panel. He folded the two outer panels to the middle and handed it over, wrapped in a blanket to ensure it didn't get damaged or dropped on its journey.

That evening Tom went back to find Catherine and explain what had occurred that day. He had to do a number of pictures for her, his signing and her understanding lacking a connection as he tried to describe it all. Eventually she understood and agreed to go to Norfolk with him and Richard before bursting into tears, thrusting his son towards him and hurrying away. Tom felt his own tears running yet again down his face and drip onto the baby's soft dark hair. Richard looked up at him, disturbed in his banging of a rattle against Tom's chest and smiled his familiar grin, the image of his mother. Whatever happened next, despite his heartache, Tom reasoned he would always have a part of her with him. He and Richard would be a family forever more.

Chapter Fifty-Five

December 1586

The cart containing their belongings rolled along the track until it stopped outside the hall. Catherine and Richard were both dozing in the back and Tom dismounted from the gelding he'd bought when they were ready to leave London. There were few items salvageable from his home, but what he could find he'd collected together. As promised his triptych was now mounted in a heavy, ornate frame decorated in gold leaf and bearing the crest of Queen Elizabeth. A local seamstress had managed to sew some clothes for both Catherine and Richard before they left and he'd sourced some bed covers even though they no longer possessed any beds to lay them on.

Burghley had presented him with a rusty metal hoop containing a collection of old keys, together with the deeds to a manor house situated in the wild Norfolk countryside, and now Tom pulled them from his pocket as he looked up at the building in front of him. It was solid and square, criss-crossed with pale oak beams, the panels between washed a soft worn cream. The thatch looked patchy and would need immediate attention or they'd feel the full brunt of the winter weather as it leaked through to the rooms below. He felt the air shift from movement behind him and he knew the drovers from whom he'd hired the cart would want to get unloaded. They needed to be on their way to King's Lynn where they were picking up goods to take back to London. Selecting the biggest key on the ring he pushed it in the lock, wincing a little as it ground slowly round.

The door swung open revealing a large, open hall. At the far end stood a wide stone fireplace, still covered in soot and ashes as if the previous occupants of the house had been evicted with their belongings in the middle of their everyday lives, their existence halted. Tom gave a shudder, wondering what happened to the family. He knew that once the Duke of Norfolk had been executed his family and tenants were immediately ejected and he couldn't imagine the guards had been very sympathetic. He was reminded of the stories he was told as a child, of how his mother had fled Norfolk with him and his siblings before the same thing happened to them. Thankfully the ancestral home had been returned to his brother Henry when he became an adult and appealed to the Queen, and now Tom was living in the same county. Here he was, finally back where he belonged, but without the person he most wanted there with him. His life had turned full circle and should now be complete but instead all he had was a half-life.

Catherine appeared behind him, her hair across her face where it had escaped the linen coif as she slept. She put Richard on the floor and on shaky legs he tottered across the flagstone floor, enjoying the space, his arms out sideways to steady himself. Looking around the room as Tom had done, she nodded approvingly. It could have been a lot worse.

Tom didn't have time to explore any further as he helped the drovers lift their scant belongings from the cart and into the house. Within an hour all was inside and looking through the sacks Catherine found a pan in which to boil some water before going outside to search for a woodstore and some kindling. Tom picked up his axe and followed her.

By the time night fell they had organised everything as best they could, having made lumpy temporary mattresses from hay in the barn. It appeared to have been there several years but following the summer heat it wasn't damp and would have to do until they could find some fleece to make something more permanent.

Although the sturdy oak stairs at one side of the hall led to four bedrooms, as Tom had feared the thatch had already let in water, the floorboards warped with the damp; he would need to repair it before they could use upstairs. They settled down to sleep in the main hall for the night but Tom lay awake for hours staring into the darkness, the space beside him as empty as his heart.

It took several weeks for them to settle in. Tom undertook the repairs that needed doing, built rudimentary furniture and ensured there was a good supply of split logs ready for the fire in the great hall which constantly burned. The grounds were extensive and included a decent sized wood with a small thicket closer to the house. He also discovered, almost hidden by the trees that had tried to reclaim it for themselves, a small private chapel.

Tom shuffled through his keys until he found one that

unlocked it, but it took a hard shove with his shoulder to push open the door which had swelled with damp and age. Inside light flooded in from the tall windows, the tops of which were decorated with stained glass in a host of rich colours depicting the Norfolk coat of arms. Despite the dirt and dust and cobwebs the light filtered through, dancing across the floor as if welcoming him to this holy place. Other than two rows of wooden pews, covered in a layer of dust so thick it barely moved in the draught he made, there was a simple altar at the end of the nave. No crucifix there of course, anything of any value had been taken. But as he looked around the bare stone walls, Tom knew exactly what he was going to put in there. A fitting home for it.

Planting the many herb cuttings, still in small pots he'd brought with him, took a little while to do. He wanted just the right place and he fought his way through the tall grasses and saplings around the gardens close to the house until he found it. A corner that overlooked the meadow beyond where his chickens wandered amongst the half dozen sheep and cow he'd purchased days after arriving. It was peaceful here in the lee of a thicket of trees. For the first time in a very long time he felt a fragile, gossamer thin mantle of peace slowly descend about his shoulders. Here – maybe – he could find a trace of the solace he'd been searching for.

In amongst his belongings squashed at the bottom of a sack, Tom found the screwed-up tatty blue coat. He pulled it out, once more transported back to the day Walsingham had handed it over and the pride he'd felt when first wearing it. All those memories spun across the room, dancing in front of him. Kit Marlowe explaining how he stood up straighter in it, how it had given him confidence when facing the guards at Barn Elms. His face darkened as he recalled the serjeant at Poultry Corner who'd wrenched it from his back, not expecting Tom to need it again. And his sulking face when twenty-four hours later he'd returned it. Wearing it on his wedding day when his heart had soared to the heavens as Isabel vowed to be with him forever. Turning it around he looked at the stains across the back and arms from where he'd followed and watched, hiding in alleys and doorways and sleeping in the woods. And it smelled, tragically of the last time he wore it. It reeked of smoke and there amongst the images that danced before his eyes of his London life flickered the flames that had taken it all from him. He swung his arm around in an arc, banishing the hallucinations before him as they spun away and were absorbed by the fabric of the walls.

He tucked it over his arm, intent on throwing it on the fire he had smouldering outside. As he did so, something fluttered to the floor and bending he picked it up. Turning it over he looked at the piece of parchment for a moment wondering what it was, before the memory seeped back into his consciousness of Babington dropping it as he hurried away on his final journey. Written on it was the now familiar coded shorthand he'd worked on so many times with Doctor Bright. Looking out of the window at the landscape that surrounded him and the ancient oak trees that sat on his land he remembered how Phelippes had shown him how he made invisible ink. He had one last task to undertake before he could close the door on what had happened.

Slowly but surely Tom built up his physic garden in the corner of what became the kitchen garden, spending every day when the weather allowed digging, weeding, or sometimes just gazing across the fields as if his mind were in another place. He still nurtured his vanilla plants but they wouldn't give forth the pods which had initially drawn him into the web of intrigue and terror of the court. They'd done their work and there was nothing left for them to do.

Other times he could be found sitting in the chapel. He'd had a memorial stone erected for Isabel but he could never give her a grave. This was the closest place he could come to be with her. He couldn't sign to her now. The triptych had been put on the wall beside the stone but the third panel with its fiery depths of hell distressed him so much that in a fit of sorrow he had boarded it over so he could no longer see it. A final image of her locket was added to the board, the chain snaking its way across to point towards her memorial plaque. He'd told his story in the only way he knew how: using his artistic skills.

Before he mounted the triptych on the wall, he slipped the sheets of parchment into the back between the painting and the frame. An explanation forever more of the terrible part he played in the death of his wife. Thanks to his work with Doctor Bright nobody would ever find it or be able to read his story.

Chapter Fifty-Six

September 2021

Finally, the day came when Professor Thornton emailed to inform Mathilde the document had been deciphered and he'd like to come to the hall to reveal all. He was keen to see where the triptych and subsequent document had been found and she agreed immediately.

'At last, we get to find out,' Rachel said when the day arrived, humming under her breath as she plumped the cushions in the drawing room. In the hall both her and Fleur's packed bags lay ready to go in the car. School term started in two days; summer was over.

'Do you think it'll explain why the triptych was hidden in the first place? Maybe it's a confession about stealing it from Elizabeth I. Or spying for her. I hope we get to discover what it was all about. Will Oliver be here in time?' Rachel asked. Mathilde knew he was already on his way because he'd sent her a text when he left but she didn't want her sister knowing about their relationship. Not yet.

'I expect so,' she replied, trying to sound non-committal.

'I hope he is in case we need him to explain anything historical and technical. And he's as desperate as us to find out what it all means,' Rachel said smiling, 'if he isn't here, he'll have to ask the professor for a full report. We'll only need the layman's details.'

Mathilde frowned. Just when she thought she had a grip of the language someone used a word that meant nothing. 'Layman?' she repeated.

'Sorry. We're not the experts,' Rachel explained, 'so what he explains to us doesn't need all the detail Oliver will expect. We only need a simplified version.'

Professor Thornton and Oliver arrived outside the hall at the same time, followed closely by the postman, who passed a bundle of letters through his van window before driving off again.

'I'm being Postman Pat today,' Oliver laughed as he put them down. He gave both women a brief kiss on the cheek before taking the professor across to the chapel, as promised.

Rachel shuffled through the envelopes. 'Still getting post for Dad,' she said in a small voice, 'just when I think I've told everyone. Oh, this big envelope is for you, were you expecting something?' Mathilde took it, wrapping her arms around it protectively.

'I'm sure it's nothing important,' she shrugged, 'shall we go and wait for the others?'

In the drawing room she perched on the arm of a chair and pushed her index finger under the flap of the envelope, removing the sheaf of paperwork.

'What's in your secret envelope then?' She hadn't realised

her sister was right behind her, trying to peer over her shoulder. Quickly she shoved everything back in. 'Bill of sale?' Rachel's voice began to rise. 'A sale document? And from Mr Murray, I saw the letterhead. I thought you were waiting until the end of summer before you decided what to do. And no discussion with me, your sister? I know the hall is yours now but it's still our family home!' By this point her voice had risen and as Oliver and Professor Thornton walked into the room they both looked decidedly uncomfortable, moving to the table and gazing at the paperwork spread out before them with intense interest.

'It *is* the end of summer,' Mathilde hissed through clenched teeth flapping her hand, 'I'll tell you later. I want to listen.' She was embarrassed it had taken her so long to arrange something she should have done weeks before and wasn't looking forward to admitting her thoughtlessness to her sister.

'Yes, we'll talk later,' Rachel agreed in a low voice as she looked away. Mathilde could feel the disappointment and dismay emanating from her as tears prickled at the back of her eyes.

Professor Thornton cleared his throat loudly and the gathered ensemble turned to face him.

'So, I can now confirm this document is as we first suspected, one of a series of letters that travelled in 1586 between Mary Queen of Scots and those involved in the Babington plot. Except,' his voice rose a little, his excitement at the events of history almost palpable, 'it was intercepted at some point by a man called Thomas Phelippes who compiled codes to try and thwart the plotters. The letters from Mary, who was a prisoner at the time, were taken by double agents and subsequently copied out with additional assignations suggested, to draw the conspirators into the web that Queen Elizabeth's spymaster Sir Francis Walsingham was weaving. This is an important piece of the puzzle and absolutely fascinating. Especially because as well as being in code it was also written in shorthand, an extra layer of intelligence. We have very few examples of this work although we do know it was originally devised by a Doctor Bright, the Superintendent at St Bartholomew's hospital. Over four hundred years ago, isn't that incredible?' By this point the professor's enthusiasm was overflowing and everyone in the room was smiling with him.

'What about the palimpsest, the words written in invisible ink between the lines of the letter?' Oliver asked.

'Ah, now that is a private document. It explains to us why it was hidden but it should be read by the family, it's not for me to disclose.' He placed a typed sheet in its document folder onto the table. 'It's all here,' he said, 'the original is still in our temperature controlled safe at the university, until we can come to an agreement as to where it is going to live on a more permanent basis. I'd like to talk to you at a later date,' he turned to Oliver, 'to discuss what you have discovered about the triptych in order to see how it reflects what we now know about the owner of both the painting and this house.'

Oliver nodded and with a shake of everyone's hand Professor Thornton was gone, the sound of his car fading into the distance as the three adults stood in silence on the front step. Everything Mathilde had been waiting for, the explanation as to why the triptych was hidden in the chapel and the story of her ancestor, was there in that document on the table. Everything that the ghosts who'd followed her since she arrived couldn't tell her.

Deep in thought, she hadn't heard the sound of a car approaching along the drive until it pulled across the turning circle with a loud series of the horn beeping. Behind the wheel was Alice and beside her, Jack. He was clutching on to the dashboard, the scared look on his face demonstrating the speed and recklessness of his wife's driving.

'Just the person I wanted to see.' Alice jumped out, and for the first time since Mathilde had met her she had a big smile on her face.

'Aunt Alice, what on earth is the matter?' Rachel stepped off the front step as if ready to intervene.

'Matter? Nothing's the matter,' came the reply. 'We've come straight over to thank our niece.' At this point her bonhomie dissolved as did her face and it folded up like a sinking suet pudding as she burst into tears. Rachel hurried over but Alice put her hand up to stop her. Mathilde had taken a step backwards.

'No, let me finish,' Alice continued, 'I can't deny that I was bitterly disappointed when this girl turned up out of the blue after so many years. None of us expected her and I especially didn't want her here. She threatened our lives, our home, and I was shocked and frightened. But that doesn't excuse how I behaved, I was unkind and I was wrong. What would Peter have said? I can only apologise from the bottom of my heart for my dreadful actions.' She advanced towards Mathilde who instinctively took another step away from her. 'But today in the post we received a letter from Mr Murray informing us that she's transferred the deeds of the old farmhouse to us. So, we don't have to worry anymore about the roof over our heads. How can I ever thank you?'

This time Mathilde wasn't quick enough to avoid her aunt who enveloped her in a perfumed hug which threatened to squeeze the breath out of her.

'It was nothing. I should have done it earlier. I'm sorry that I didn't.' Her voice was gruff by the time she was eventually released. Over her aunt's shoulder she could see both Oliver and her sister looking at each other, eyebrows raised.

Rachel gathered Alice and Jack up and took them into the kitchen to make a cup of tea; *the panacea of all English problems*, Mathilde thought. Oliver was still standing where he'd been during the spectacle that had just occurred.

'Why didn't you tell us that was what the documentation was?' he asked, 'we presumed you were selling the hall.'

'I was ashamed,' she confessed, 'I should have done it when I first arrived. I, more than anyone, know how it feels to be worried about the roof over my head, but it took you and Rachel to point out what was right in front of me. I should have realised why Alice behaved as she did. I was stupid.'

'No, you weren't,' he put his arm around her shoulder and held her to him, 'why would you immediately think of that when you faced such a cold welcome when you first arrived? You've come such a long way since then even though it's only been three months. Let's go and join the rest of your family for a cup of tea, eh? Then you can read the letter your ancestor left for you.'

In the kitchen, Mathilde allowed Rachel to give her a big hug and whisper 'sorry' in her ear. She could feel the warm damp on her sister's face where she'd been crying and she returned the hug.

'Me too,' she said quietly pulling her sister closer, before sitting down to join in the impromptu party around the table as Rachel produced glasses and a dusty bottle of cognac alongside the ubiquitous pot of tea.

'Dad could always think of a reason to get out the brandy,' she gave a watery smile and sniffed, 'and I think now is a good time to continue his tradition.'

'To family,' Alice said, holding up her cup as they all clinked their various cups and glasses together, echoing the sentiment. Never had anything sounded sweeter, Mathilde thought to herself. Excusing herself she ran up to her bedroom to collect something she'd been waiting to give to Rachel, now feeling it was the right moment.

'This is for you,' she said gruffly as she handed it over. She didn't tell her sister that originally she had thought to give it when she left. Now she knew in her heart that would never happen.

Pulling off the tissue wrapped around it, Rachel uncovered a framed photograph of Fleur, one of the images from the night Mathilde had taken her out to the marshes.

'Oh, it's perfect, thank you,' Rachel breathed.

'The final piece of my family jigsaw,' Mathilde said, looking across to where Fleur was sitting with a glass of milk. She winked at the little girl who grinned back.

'Shall we go and look at the secret letter then?' Oliver asked, looking at Mathilde and Rachel who both nodded. Alice and Jack looked at the others questioningly but followed as the ensemble walked back through to the drawing room again. They waited silently as, her hand shaking slightly, Mathilda picked it up. The room felt calmer now, the confrontation from before dissipating in the air. Picking up the clear plastic folder containing the translation Mathilde began to read.

'This is my story. Tom Lutton. I travelled across the seas in search of a home and safety. Not once, but twice. I served my Queen as apothecary, as spy, and through that I lost she who held my heart and my love. This triptych will in all eternity tell my story. I found all that I did seek and now I live out my days with our son in the flat lands from whence I started my journey.'

She lay it back down on the table, and turned to look at the triptych, still open beside her. Telling his story and telling her story. They were two sides of the same coin. The fabric of the house exhaled slowly, the spirits of centuries past slipping away, finally at ease.

Without a word she stepped around the others, walking back out through the front door and around the side of the house, collecting her spade as she went past. A robin perched on it followed her, hopping from branch to branch until they arrived in her corner of the garden. She needed to be in the place where she had always felt closest to him, the man that she now knew was Tom Lutton: her ancestor.

He'd loved this spot too, she was certain. No wonder she felt the draw to here, the calm and peace it gave her. Pushing her spade into the soil she began digging, methodical clump after clump of earth which quickly grew into a mound as she dug the ground where he'd found solace too.

The ring of her spade hitting something and stopping her going any deeper made her frown and pushing it into the ground beside where she was digging, she tried again. There were plenty of flints which had already caused difficulties.

The same thing happened. Carefully she knelt down and began to lift out a clod of dirt, followed by another, and then another. Something was under the ground here close to where she'd made her herb bed and scrabbling with her hands, she continued to clear it away. Shadow lay on a patch of thyme watching her whilst basking in the warm sun.

It took almost two hours of hard work to finally unearth it. Rachel had come out at one point and placed a mug of tea on the ground but it grew cold, untouched. Eventually Mathilde stood up, her hands on her hips, legs balanced apart on the pile of mud she'd cleared. Before her lay a long stone slab, barely weathered after all the years of being buried. She brushed off the last of the dirt with her hands. Carved in the top it simply said *'Tom Lutton, died 4 August 1607. A traveller, but now he is home.'*

It was his gravestone, so close to where she'd been working for weeks. Her ancestor, and her father's ancestor. Perhaps his child, the baby she'd dreamed of, had laid him here in the corner of the garden which he'd loved, as did she. It explained the peace and tranquillity enveloping that special space. Running her fingertips through the tall grass beside her, she let it slide softly against her skin. She had been a traveller too, but now, she was home.

Acknowledgements

So here it is – I wasn't sure I could write this notoriously difficult second book, but then the words started to flow and Tom and Mathilde began to tell their stories.

I certainly couldn't have reached this point without a lot of help, collaboration and handholding from some amazing people. Firstly, a huge thank you to my brilliant editor Molly Walker-Sharp who knocked this book into shape and is so encouraging which I really appreciate – you are a star! Also thank you to the marketing department and the entire team at Avon who do such a sterling job – I am incredibly grateful to you all.

My heartfelt thanks also go to my lovely agent Ella Kahn at Diamond Kahn and Woods. Your perception and suggestions are always so helpful and spot on, and I am extremely grateful that you're at the other end of an email and you never mind how daft my questions are. Thank you for your continual support and enthusiasm and for always being on my team.

A very special mention must go to my virtual office

colleague and beta reader Jenni Keer, who makes every day at the desk so much better. Thank you for living in my phone for the past year and for your constant cheerleading. Thanks must also go to my fellow members and very good friends at the Suffolk and Norfolk chapter of the RNA, especially Heidi Swain, Rosie Hendry, Claire Wade, Ian Wilfred and Kate Hardy, who are always ready and willing to wave pom-poms and are endlessly supportive. You guys rock!

I couldn't have written this without some specialist help from certain quarters. First of all, thank you David Hollingworth for your assistance in checking my schoolgirl French; I shall be over to visit and test it out further at some point! Also thank you to Sarah Voysey for your inspirational camper van conversion which certainly helped when planning out Mathilde's ambulance. And a very special mention for a fantastic bunch of people (you know who you are!), who are always ready to answer absolutely any question I can think of – what a mine of expertise you are. An extra special thanks to Sara, Lisa, Fiona, Catherine, Eleanor, Mary, Rhian and Rebecca for helping me out of a hole.

Of course, I wouldn't have been able to sit down and write *The Queen's Spy* without all the support and assistance I get at home so I owe a massive debt of gratitude to my husband Des, who very kindly plays golf at every opportunity to leave me in peace. Honestly, Des, words cannot express how thankful I am to have you! No, really. And also thank you as ever to my lovely children, your support is much appreciated and this book is for you cherubs.

And my final thanks must go to the wonderful readers who've been so incredibly supportive over the past year. I cannot begin to thank you enough for your enthusiasm; it's been truly heart-warming. To hear how much people enjoy reading about my characters and then sharing those thoughts in their reviews is simply the very best accolade I could ask for – you all brighten my day, and I am hugely grateful. If anyone hasn't yet found me on social media please come and say hello!

Twitter: @claremarchant1
Instagram: claremarchant1
Facebook: /ClareMarchantAuthor

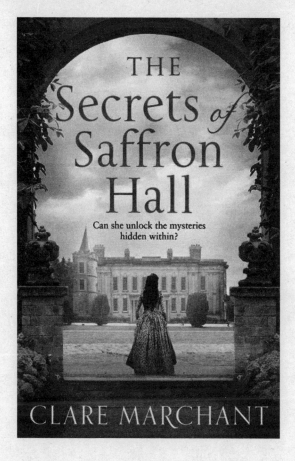